All the Beautiful People
We Once Knew

All the Beautiful People We Once Knew

a novel

Edward Carlson

Skyhorse Publishing

FIRST EDITION

This is a work of fiction. Names, places, characters, and incidents are either the products of the author's imagination or are used fictitiously. Any resemblance to actual persons, living or dead, events, or locales is entirely coincidental.

Skyhorse Publishing books may be purchased in bulk at special discounts for sales promotion, corporate gifts, fund-raising, or educational purposes. Special editions can also be created to specifications. For details, contact the Special Sales Department, Skyhorse Publishing, 307 West 36th Street, 11th Floor, New York, NY 10018 or info@skyhorsepublishing.com.

Skyhorse® and Skyhorse Publishing® are registered trademarks of Skyhorse Publishing, Inc.®, a Delaware corporation.

Visit our website at www.skyhorsepublishing.com.

10 9 8 7 6 5 4 3 2 1

Library of Congress Cataloging-in-Publication Data is available on file.

Cover design by Erin Seaward-Hiatt

Print ISBN: 978-1-5107-1631-5
Ebook ISBN: 978-1-5107-1632-2

Printed in the United States of America

For Natalie Jasmin and Zachary John

"[W]hat has been done is nothing, start again."
—Derek Wolcott obituary, *The Economist*, April 1–7, 2017

1

I FELT HIM COMING. Surfing through the hallway atop his big kahuna personality. Joshing his secretary he needed the dictation typed like yesterday. Whenever she was done playing Bejeweled. Now slapping the back of his fellow partner. The baby boomer he nicknamed Whitey, despite the fact his name was Goldman.

"Jesus, Robert. Not so hard."

Fleeger hyenaed with delight.

"Yes, it's true, Whitey, I'm a real gorilla."

But more important than Whitey's low threshold for physical pain, Fleeger explained, there was a whopping new case in from WorldScore. Not from the top top, but almost. And the relationship, he continued, with WorldScore, he gloated, was still working out very well.

"Very well?" Whitey asked.

"Very well."

And WorldScore remained very satisfied with Kilgore's work product.

"Very satisfied?"

"Very satisfied."

"Good," Whitey said.

"Better than good," Fleeger replied, faux chuffed. "It's fucking great."

Now Fleeger this way cometh. I shut down the newswires and lefty blogs. Ensured no evidence of my distraction remained in the window behind me. As if the gigabytes of news I consumed online would eventually etch the glass. Like shadows fixed to walls by a nuclear blast. Pen in hand, I crouched behind the flat screen, fingering papers as Fleeger entered my office pocket-balling loose change. Behold the firm's youngest partner: advancing hairline, teeth like dice, fistful of jaw, Hoboken Republican. He smelled like classic Right Guard, the stuff sprayed from a golden can.

"Harker, my man," he said, unclipping his phone. The miasma reappeared, which happened sometimes, especially in late afternoons. Some mysterious plasma that prevented me from seeing him in full contrast. What the partners and clients mistook for stamina and conviction was in fact his terrific refusal to engage in the complexity of being human. It forced me to squint at him. To protect my eyes from his bigness.

"There she is," he said, flicking his screen with his hammerhead thumb, now spreading open her picture. "Lucky number twenty-three."

He shook the girl before me atop the palm of his dashboard. Soon to be sport fuck number twenty-three since separating from Kath O'Shaughnessy. Another Brazilianed millennial Snapchatter with whom he had nothing in common. I accepted the girl with both hands. She was young, tan, ethnic. High-end retail sauce. Ready to be stacked between his collection of chutneys and cans of La Morena and allspice, possessed by the cheerful sexuality of a Southern California girl in estrus. Hatha yoga and kegel exercises. *Sarda chiliensis lineolata*. Gripping her tight, careful not to drop her, I touched her face to access her caption:

'20's PARTY IN LOS ANGELES. <u>FUN!</u>

"Very impressive," I said.

"I know."

"I'm referring to the properly inverted apostrophe. Acknowledging the missing but implied nineteenth century."

"You're a douche."

He snatched for his phone. I dodged him. He grabbed me and snatched again. I conceded defeat, handed him his cherished appendage.

"I'm proud of you," I added. "This one at least knows some grammar. But as a rule I'm skeptical of women who use exclamation marks."

"Her name's Tara," he said, redocking his device to his thin belt and hoisting his pants around his thick hips. "And she says the photo fails to do her justice."

He hissed the word justice. Like a black pastor at an affordable housing rally. He wanted to play. I raised his Reverend Wright one Etonian backbencher.

"You must therefore advise Miss Tara that as a member of the New York bar you are professionally licensed to make all determinations regarding justice."

"Shouldn't I also mention in good standing?"

"You'd be a fool not to."

"I'll be sure to let her know."

Fleeger bent over. All oarsman haunches and shoulders, like a beast that ambulated on its knuckles. From the Kilgore tote he launched a new case file, his Chinese yo-yo of an index finger commanding me to look. It was the new assignment from WorldScore, first-class premium AAA underwriter of pharmaceuticals, private armies, war risks, infrastructure loans, mortgage-backed securities, climate change, terrorist attacks, aviation disasters. Risk in profit™. A fresh new claim by Major Mike "Bud" Thomas for wartime employment workers' compensation; past, present, and future lost wages; physical and psychological injury; permanent and total disability. Age: forty-six. Residence: White Haven, Pennsylvania. Fleeger placed a walnut oxford wingtip atop a bankers' box housing my one pro bono case involving a Chinese stowaway, now Chinese amputee due to a vessel's faulty hatch cover. The case dormant and unbillable as the man fetal-positioned in a Louisiana immigration prison sans one left leg below the knee. Fleeger tucked his pants into pink leopard-print socks, removed a portable shoe polisher from his Kilgore tote, and buffed sheens to his extra wide Allen Edmonds.

"I need you to write up a report on this bastard this afternoon. So you can stop all you're pretending to do and focus on this," he said, still buffing. "We have a preliminary conference before Judge McKenzie *primero cosa en la mañana* so do it now. And then let's get the ninja on him. I want to surveil this hairy asshole."

He loved the way he spoke, the way he said "ninja" and "surveil" and "hairy asshole." But for me it meant clean and easy tenths of an hour on the timesheets. In re *Thomas v. FQ/WS*, 444-15 RF/SH: telecon with investigator re surveil re hairy asshole: .3 hrs.; email exchange with investigator re surveil re hairy asshole: .4 hrs. We had now entered the billing segment of today's interaction. Fleeger couldn't resist.

"Should finally give you something to do."

"I have plenty to do."

Fleeger exhaled and looked over my desk and placed his hands beneath his suit jacket.

"This case could be good for you, Stephen," he explained. "It's interesting, so you won't feel it's beneath you. It's an important case for WorldScore, and if it's an important case for WorldScore, it's an important case for me, and if it's an important case for me, then it's an important case for you. Should also enable you to finally put some points on the board. What are we here for if not to put points on the board? Right?"

Fleeger shot an invisible three-pointer.

"So?" he asked.

"So?" I replied.

"Carpe diem, motherfucker."

I told him OK. Would give it my all. Make it my top priority. He picked up his tote but, not quite ready to leave, he pointed at the shellacked wooden plaque tacked to my office wall. A gift from the editorial board of my slightly-below-average third tier Midwestern law review.

GREAT MINDS DISCUSS IDEAS.
AVERAGE MINDS DISCUSS EVENTS.
SMALL MINDS DISCUSS PEOPLE.

"This, just so you know, always kills me."

The miasma reappeared. It was thicker now.

"Just make sure you write up that memo today so we know what we're talking about tomorrow before the good judge. And remember, whatever you do, be first class."

I reciprocated the thumbs-up as he exited my office, discovering right then and there why Iraqi Arabs considered the gesture obscene.

Here I was. Neck deep in insurance defense litigation with no instinct for extraction, let alone self-preservation. Insurance against risk in exchange for billions collected in premium. The premium in turn deposited in interest-bearing accounts, money market accounts, then invested in portfolios, hedge funds, deep pools of capital for fees plus interest, that in turn irrigated the financial markets for a point or two as it cascaded down the flues. Now it was Kilgore's turn to dip in the pewter ladle and take a drink, allotted in six-minute tenth-of-an-hour increments scribbled on the timesheet. Points on Fleeger's board.

I studied the new file and jotted illegible notes on a yellow legal pad about Thomas's past and present. Former Air Force airman then Special Forces pilot then Afghan military instructor employed by FreedomQuest, a private military contractor based in North Carolina. Now alleging that an aeron struck him in the neck and caused a cervical spine injury. Permanent back pain resulting from long-haul flights in and out of Bagram (degenerative disease to the lumbar spine). Traumatic trip and fall while fleeing incoming mortar fire (herniated discs, Achilles tear, torn rotator cuff). Followed by emails to FreedomQuest's human resources department demanding compensation for hidden psych injuries caused by a car crash while working in Kabul. Thomas's multiple requests for worker's compensation denied by FreedomQuest's in-house counsel due to lack of causation, lack of objective proof of injuries, injuries sustained outside the scope of his employment. Triggering Thomas's almost daily email accusations to his former employer re FreedomQuest's failure to respect his service to country, failure to provide him maintenance and cure,

5

alleging corporate treason, abandonment of a wounded warrior, that they treated him like a dog, that he was now a shadow of his former self, unable to provide for his family, make love to his wife, exiled from the pleasures of hearth and home.

"Sir, I am not a litigious person but I have no choice," he proclaimed again and again, "but to turn to the courts and assert my rights." Seeking an award for total and permanent disability benefits at seven-eighths his average weekly wage for life plus lifelong treatment for multiple herniated discs, post-traumatic stress disorder, limited ranges of motion to the upper and lower planes, hip arthritis, sleep apnea, erectile dysfunction. Emails from FreedomQuest's in-house counsel offloading the matter to their worker's compensation underwriter, WorldScore. WorldScore in turn dumping the case onto Fleeger. Here it was. The identity and contact information of the WorldScorer overseeing this manmade catastrophe: Celeste Powers. Senior Executive Vice President, Global Head of Claims, New York, New York. Thewy Englishwoman of confidence, we met once before, at an industry conference: Litigating Against Disability Insurance Claims, Sheraton Miami, 2012.

It was the beginning of the end of the day. My professional focus possessing a half-life of barely two hours, I reopened the newswires. To be Reutered. Politicoed. Huffposted. Dzohkar Obama Trump Lindhed. Some kernel of escape from Kilgore LLP in compulsively gorging myself with online media. Ice flakes the size of Texas breaking free from the Arctic mass. Fresh alerts from NASA about a brewing geomagnetic solar storm; a potential coronal mass ejection of solar winds that threatened satellites, airplanes, vessels, power grids, data servers, GPS units, cell phones, ATMs, the entire global financial system.

Once I could shoulder through the work for hours. Longer than anyone, including Fleeger. But not anymore. I was morphing into a new species. Soon my eyes would almond and blacken. I would become half alien. Hands branching tapering fingers to access increasing amounts of data. The way a Dutch woman raised in Bangkok will eventually pretend she is Thai. Almost. Something had shifted and this lack of focus, this addiction to distraction, now permeated everything. My ability to lawyer had disintegrated into zeros and ones. Atoms and quarks. Here, behind this desk, in this law firm called Kilgore on the twenty-fifth floor above Lower Manhattan. Launching air balls at Fleeger's scoreboard.

With massive effort I reopened the Thomas file to keep the clock running. I studied the medical reports and employment records and again combed through his emails from Kabul station to Freedom-Quest. Communicating concerns that the unsecured two-story house the company provided him in Kabul was a target. ("Sir, I am very concerned for my safety.") That the supervisors who managed the station were both incompetent and drunk all the time on contraband whiskey smuggled in Listerine bottles. ("Sir, in my twenty-plus years in the armed forces I have never witnessed such low morale.") That the supervisors retaliated against him for voicing his concerns to HQ by assigning him menial tasks. ("Sir, I find it demeaning to be assigned routine office work.") That his instructing Afghan military officers in an enclosed classroom environment was unsafe. ("Sir, I am getting real concerned about my exposure to Afghan personnel who I do not believe were properly vetted for Islamic terrorist sympathies.") Pleading for authorization to carry a pistol while driving his work truck, which in turn went unanswered.

With that elusive urgency crucial to decent lawyering I typed up a strategy for tomorrow's court conference, constructing ramparts of arguments from the federal regulations. Yes, of course we respect his service. But it remained Thomas's burden to prove his alleged injuries arose within the scope of his employment with FreedomQuest and not during his previous military service. It remained Thomas's burden to provide objective evidence that supported his allegations. And it remained Thomas's burden to provide objective reports from licensed, board-certified physicians that he suffered the injuries he alleged to have suffered, that the injuries would not fully heal, and that he had in fact reached maximum medical improvement. At which point the regulations mandated Thomas undergo further medical evaluations for statutorily apportioned loss of use of his bones and ligaments. Only after which Thomas would be entitled to some percentage of weekly compensation. Tomorrow's strategy: question the veracity of Thomas's allegations and calendar discovery production. Then kick the can down the road with talk of settlement. Because this is what we do. In the meantime, appoint WorldScore's preferred private investigator, Honda Tadakatsu, to film Thomas doing anything that impeached his credibility and disproved the extent of his alleged injuries. I added up my points: 3.8 hours of solid billable legal work carved from a weekday afternoon despite failing to escape the constant temptation to sulk.

Outside, big high-pressure systems blew out late winter gales and the office building lurched, swinging elevator cables behind gypsum drywall. If you dropped capsules of dye into the gusts they would smother the city with clouds of impenetrable color. I forced myself to lean against the window and peer below. Steeled myself against mentally simulating the building's collapse into a silo of molten steel and pulverized plaster. From the bookshelf I retrieved the cordovan case that housed my father's heavy German-manufactured binoculars, gripped the worn leather strap, and glassed a petroleum barge anchored in the olive chop between Manhattan and Governor's Island. One hundred and ten thousand barrels of Number 2 fuel oil bolted against the hydraulic force of two converging Manhattan rivers.

My computer pinged. I hurried to it.

"The hits keep coming," Fleeger announced via email. Heralding the federal court's dismissal of a direct class action lawsuit filed against WorldScore for insuring Wuxi Hexia, a Chinese company accused of marketing antifreeze-laced cough syrup to Panamanian infants. The federal judge mandating suit be filed in Panama, where the damage occurred, or China, location of Wuxi's corporate headquarters. Thus saving WorldScore millions, probably more.

"Props to Harker and Attika for their hard work on the briefs!"

He and Tara already had something in common.

"Drinks in an hour to celebrate!"

I typed Fleeger a reply. A direct quote from Wuxi's Chinglish website.

Pursue the most lofty service.

His response was immediate.

     Regard heart as the origin.

I trumped him one last Wuxi command.

     Take customer as the reveres.

Until he bounced it back.

     With the own duty of the understanding.

I was overdue for a good drink and Fleeger knew it.

"Do not bail tonight," he emailed.

"Or what?"

"Or I will kill you."

2

SLEET PECKED AT MY office window, with a sound akin to plastic pellets. Building blocks of toilet brushes, duck decoys, PVC pipe. The red diodes atop the skyscrapers raced ahead, fell behind, pulled even with one another.

I continued the professional hustle, jotting more entries on the timesheet. There should be stars next to the entries, I thought. Value for Money™, that's what WorldScore called it, their antichurn campaign. Directly at odds with Kilgore's 2,100-hour annual billing quota, divided by the annual salary of a midlevel associate at a medium-tiered law firm, equaling about $64 per hour. Sitting in her cubicle, probably watching *Law & Order* online, Fleeger's secretary cleared her throat before answering the ringing telephone.

"I'll tell her."

She hung up the phone.

"Attika. Robert wants the watermelon."

Attika's bodyless head appeared in the door across the hall. Milk chocolate Bobby Brown foundation and a hint of thick-jawed Indian about the cheekbones and chin.

"With tapioca balls?" Attika asked.

"He likes to spit them."

"Really? I always thought of Robert as much more of a swallower."

They laughed. I rose from my desk to join the exchange, signaling to the ladies that I too could play. Because we were almost friends

Attika fake smiled at me and stuck out her tongue in a naughty way, then walked to the elevators. The tightening girth of her pencil skirt directly proportional to the number of hours she billed while sitting in a chair. Fleeger's secretary reinserted her earphones and I could hear the music. Either Frampton or Guns N' Roses. The former reminding her of her first husband, the latter reminding her of her third.

I let her be. We had nothing in common. Some people were incapable of offending me and she was one of them. Blood pleasurably coursed through my legs as I walked the law firm carpet splotched with Keurig coffee stains, through the file room of closed cases, past the shelves of leather-bound hornbooks, around the cubicles protected by mass cards of saints and angels and jumbo pumps of hand sanitizer. For the chemical annihilation of rotavirus, herpes simplex, common flu.

The footfalls, the pen clickers, the wedding band against the banister tappers. Like listening equipment positioned in the Negev, I heard all of what was said. Heard all of what they didn't want anyone else to hear. About their constipation. Potential malignancies. Non-elective laparoscopies. Just the thought of a downtown mosque. Decimated 401(k)s and flex-spending plans and the dirty protestors bivouacked along Broadway and the river and shitting in the alleys and the immigrant janitors who pilfered Hershey Kisses and Jolly Ranchers from the glass scallop candy dishes. One of whom now headed straight for me, the least threatening soul on the planet: limping, eyes cast downward, dumping office trash into his vinyl-sided cart with a Virgin Mary hood ornament, probably on statins or insulin. We passed port to port. That ubiquitous nightshade synthetic lavender scent Kilgore's management committee voted to infuse into the janitors' papery tunics—to uniformly (de) odorize them.

I entered Fleeger's office and approached him hunched behind his desk in a leather chair broken down by years of bad posture. The office beaten-in, molded around him, like a baseball glove. A thick groove etched into the drywall behind his desk, the plastic floor-mat worn thin by heavy brass casters. He pointed at his middle flat screen while someone bickered in the Bluetooth device blinking in his ear.

"Peach?" he mouthed. He wanted my advice about which color to assign Tara on the spreadsheet of women he fucked, was fucking, would fuck since separating from Kath O'Shaugnessy.

"Wise choice," I replied.

He placed his hands on Tara's imaginary hips and mimed reverse-cowgirling her behind his desk. Scowled while doing so.

After twenty-two women post-Kath, Tara was Fleeger's first peach. By the simple act of texting him, she had demoted herself from any girl on the street, riding the subway, chatting at a bar, sitting in class, striving at work, trying to make art, to a row on Fleeger's cherished spreadsheet. There were now too many of them, to the extent he needed to employ the MS Office suite to keep straight the details. Alma maters. Professions. Hopes and Aspirations. Food allergies. STDs. Potential of anal. I liked that. A special touch. The potential of anal equals the potential of you, dear. A foolproof timeline from text messages to compromised selfies to intercourse. Provided Fleeger didn't botch the details and commit the technical foul of mistaking Tara for someone else. Lime-green Sonia: Bryn Mawr College. Women's studies. PricewaterhouseCoopers. Spanking. Cherry-red Jazz: Touro College. Half-Haitian. City planning commission. Pegging. No dice.

"Listen. Lazlis. Shut up and listen."

Fleeger adjusted his ear device, hunched over, gave Lazlis the finger. I circled his corner office. Laminated *Super Lawyers* covers. Dusty golf trophies and acid-etched crystal Manhattan skylines and Tiffany's apples in recognition of Fleeger's steadfast contributions to the insurance defense bar. A framed photograph of Fleeger and his fellow Princeton oarsmen in tiger-stripe singlets—dicks like doorknobs—launching a coxswain into Lake Quinsigamond after winning Eastern Sprints. Which he once boasted John Glenn had proclaimed a thrill greater than orbiting Earth. But that was a lie. I looked it up. John Glenn attended Muskingum College in New Concord, Ohio. And the Fighting Muskies, largest member of the pike family, don't race Eastern Sprints.

"But I want you to ask yourself something, Lazlis. What can you prove? What. Can. You. Prove? The good Major has no provable work-related injuries, Jimmy. No contemporaneous medical records. No internal reports that corroborate his version of events. No immediate hospital visits or, or anything. And if he wasn't injured while working for FreedomQuest in Afghanistan then it's not covered by the WorldScore policy. It's just not. You know that. It's just not.

"Why aren't we going to pay him something to make this go away? Let me count the ways. Because there's no coverage, Jim. Because we're not a charity, Jim. Because we're not the VA, Jim. And if it's not covered by the worker's comp policy the WorldScore underwriters wrote for FreedomQuest then we're not going to pay for it. So put on your glasses and read the fucking policy."

He pretended to kick the man as Attika entered Fleeger's office holding two massive Styrofoam cups. Fleeger closed the spreadsheet and gave Attika a thumbs-up, mouthed "First class." Her complexion richened, foundation creamed around the eyes. Neither her Tory Burch flats, nor her avocado-relaxed bob, nor her pencil skirt comported with the massive cursive *Jamal* tattooed to her left bicep. I didn't possess enough of whatever it took to ask her about it. Not for lack of interest but rather my aversion to sounding like an asshole.

"Lazlis, I leave you with this. If you want comp for Mr. AfPak, and you think he's entitled to seven-eighths of his maximum earning capacity—for life—and you really think that's a justified position based on the medicals and his employment history—and that none of it, not one shred of it, predates his employment with WorldScore— then bring it up tomorrow before the judge. Bring it up before the judge. I beseech you. You know why? Because we both know this guy is a fucking bullshit artist and we ain't going to pay one dime homey until we see some objective evidence that his injuries—which we don't accept for a second are actually valid—arose in and during the scope of his employment with FreedomQuest. This is a VA matter at best. At best. And Jim? Jim? Jim? Remember this: Hogs get fed, and pigs get slaughtered. Tell the Major that for me."

He tapped the earpiece. Blew up his hands as if they were a tiny mushroom cloud.

"Jesus, I hate that guy," he said.

Attika handed Fleeger the Styrofoam cup and he grunted while taking long sips. Black tapioca balls transiting the transparent straw.

"What does that even mean?" I asked.

"What does what mean, Harker?" he replied.

"'Hogs get fed and pigs get slaughtered.' I don't get it."

"What's there not to get?"

"Can you explain it to me?"

"It sounds good. That's all that matters."

I let it lie. Would bill it to the file, 444/15 RF/SH: office conference re hogs vs. pigs; debating jargon: .2 hrs.

"What did Lazlis say?" I asked.

"He said Thomas is loopy. That's he's loopy and he's seriously injured, which is what Lazlis always says. And that Thomas is armed to the teeth. They're all armed to the teeth. Half the country is armed to the teeth. As if that will somehow coerce us to drop our pants and pay him comp? And then it's he can't work and he can't pay his mortgage and he can't buy food for his family and he's essentially living off the fat of the land. Which supports my suspicion that he is not nearly as injured as he pretends to be. And then it's fuck you, Fleeger, pay me. Well I'm not bending over. WorldScore doesn't pay us to bend over. So tomorrow we'll be in court before Judge McKenzie arguing discovery deadlines and disclosures and HIPAA-compliant production of medical records and I imagine at some point Lazlis will pack up and walk out of the conference with a chip on his shoulder. Which is fine."

He launched a battery of tapioca balls into his trash can.

"Why do I eat these?" he asked Attika.

"Because they're delicious," she replied.

"They're too high in gluten."

"Since when did you stop eating gluten?" she asked him.

14

He ignored her, back to his roll.

"Well you know what, Harker? I too would like to collect a check for a couple thousand dollars twice a month while staying home and oiling my fucking rifle but comp doesn't work that way. So we're going to litigate it. This is all you, baby. What's up with that memo? Come on. Chop chop."

I handed Fleeger the preconference memo and he leaned back in his chair and nodded with approval. The satisfaction of one's clone deftly completing an important task while your noncloned self bullshitted with pretty associates and flirted with potential clients and racked-up Taras and jostlebagged on the telephone. Fleeger handed the memo to Attika.

"Attika, read this. This job ain't about who's smartest or went to the best law school. Lord knows Harker didn't. It's about energy. About fusing knowledge with conviction. Not for the sake of the client, but for the firm, as a profit-making enterprise. Now if I can just train Harker here to do this every day, even when it sucks, instead of whenever something happens to catch his interest."

"Don't be a dick."

"Look. He's fighting back. Good boy, Stephen."

Usually there was no reason to argue with Fleeger when the facts worked against you. Facts were like arrows he launched from atop his plinth at those who dared to challenge his assertions. But the day's work, the quality of the day's work, the heavy lifting of law and facts, had burned off the passive malaise, and in doing so stiffened my spine, erected my posture. I felt tall. Which I was. I just often forgot. It was a rare feeling, would disappear in no more than a couple minutes.

"You get the ninja on this?" he asked.

"Working on it."

"Attaboy, Stephen. Honda Tadakatsu. Always gets his man."

Fleeger pantomimed a samurai bow.

"No smoothie for me?" I asked.

"None for you my man," Fleeger said.

"Why not?"

"Because you're a hater."

The miasma reappeared. It was faint but present, tinged red. Fleeger stepped from behind his desk and around a Venn diagram mounted on poster board propped on a tripod, prepared in anticipation of litigation.

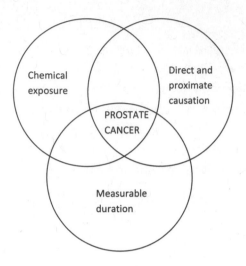

"Why do you hate, Stephen?" Attika asked.

"What does that even mean?" I asked. "Doesn't hate need an object?"

"You're still hating," Fleeger said. "And don't hate on Attika. If you do we're going to have a problem. Right sister?"

"Right brother," she said.

She did this thing where she was the cool black female enabler of Fleeger's untoward white man behavior. Laughed at his jokes. Figleafed his crassness. Goosed his entitlement. Like Robin to Howard. But it wouldn't last forever. At some point she would have to get in line with the rest of us. They gave each other a fist pound and Fleeger collapsed into his leather chair and strapped on a new pair of orange Vibram FiveFingers.

"Hey Attika, think I can draw with these?"

"Is there a warning on the box?" she asked.

"Let's put a pen between my toes and see if there should be. Otherwise we'll sue them."

Fleeger gripped a ballpoint pen with his strange gloved foot, concentrated and chewed his lip.

"What do you think?" he asked her, holding up his sloppy stick-drawing of a smiley face.

"Very impressive," Attika said.

"Here." He autographed the drawing, now with his hand. "It's for you. I want you to have it."

She clutched it to her chest.

"Robert. I'm so honored."

Fleeger approached me in his fingertoe shoes and pulled me tight, our polar vectors opposite, somewhere between antimatter and kryptonite.

"I love you," he said. "You know that?"

I said nothing.

"Everyone ready for some cocktails with the WorldScore gang?"

"You know we have a court conference tomorrow morning in re Major Ash-hole."

I sounded fake. Even to myself.

"Nice. I like it. Very childish of you, Harker. Good work. Now come on, let's go."

One final slurp of the plastic straw and Fleeger tossed the smoothie into the trash can. He stared at me.

"It's a conference, Harker," he said. "Lazlis will say 'blah blah blah' and we'll say 'blah blah blah' and then the judge will kick the can. And as long as we don't say anything stupid we'll be fine. Besides, I'll be there holding your hand in case you have another panic attack in court."

Nothing was sacred with Robert Fleeger. The bonds of professional camaraderie didn't preclude him from exploiting confidences to his advantage. There was a warning deep inside this disclosure before Attika—Stephen, don't ever be so foolish as to confide in me that which you fear I may one day use against you. You had a panic attack arguing in court, you fled the scene, you told me about it, that's your fault. Because you incriminated yourself with failure. Because weakness is vulnerability and vulnerability undermines the client's case, which in turn undermines him, and in turn undermines the firm. I stewed, knowing I couldn't stew for long because Fleeger would smell it on me and salvo me with facts, cross-examine my indignation with the truth. It's true, right? Am I wrong? Tell me I'm wrong, Harker. Attika watched what I would do next, a kernel of empathy there, because she had been on the receiving end as well. Some part of us remained helpless in his presence. But only because we chose to be here.

Fleeger inserted his massive shoulders into a black wool overcoat and wrapped his neck with an orange silk scarf. I remembered a former word of the day, one of those rare nouns you remember without memorizing. Because some words are like that. Filature. The process of reeling raw silk from cocoons. Thousands of silkworms impaled on mechanical looms having their insides spooled via an industrial process that resulted in Fleeger wrapping a proud Princeton Tiger scarf around his neck at this very moment.

"Come on, man." He rubbed my shoulder, his act of penance. "Let's have some drinks. Nelson will be there. You can make fun of him. He'll make you feel better about yourself."

There was a release in this. The toxicity evaporated as we resumed our roles. I had asserted myself and he reciprocated with a shove. Some golden balm now as our moment of conflict receded.

"The endomorph?"

"Attika likes Nelson."

"I think he's funny," she added. Right on cue.

I thought otherwise. Nelson was no lure for me. I was incapable of embracing him as a brother in consideration for him sending me WorldScore cases. I demurred, told myself I shouldn't go, knew the protest was futile. Because after spending the workday behind a computer screen typing digital words into a digital document billing clients at tenth-of-an-hour increments, Anthropocene man finds the pull of the Irish bar inescapable. And he repeats the pattern. Over and over again.

"Come on," Fleeger said. "Let's go. Be a man."

I looked at Attika.

"Yeah, Stephen." She was talking to me a lot today. "Don't be such a pussy."

Fleeger reverted into his wingtips and we exited the office and entered the elevator. He removed a ChapStick from his pocket and moisturized his fleshy lips. The lobby's overhead lights burned brighter and the floor tiles shined shinier after a solid day of legal work. Floor tiles like fly eyes, identical hexagonal facets. We exited the building through the carousel doors and entered the wind and diagonal sleet and stepped over plastic bits and straws and packets cascading down storm drains, as the whistles and beats of the Occupy protestors rounded the corner. Their daily vigil outside the New York Fed drawn to an end. Wet scarves and soggy sweaters marching behind an American flag hanging upside-down from a bent pole once used to clean swimming pools. Cops in midnight blue, belts of hogties, trailed them atop white mopeds with blinking blue lights.

"Whose streets? Our streets," a black man with a face scar like a Bob Evans sausage hollered through an old bullhorn as he approached me, waving a pamphlet with pink and black hands. "Read this, brother," he commanded, but with warmth, still through the bullhorn, now walking away, Doppler effecting "no justice, no peace." *The Arc of the Universe Bends Toward Justice* the pamphlet's title.

Fleeger looked at me as if I just committed treason and I tucked the pamphlet inside my suit jacket pocket. A crusty girl with a shaved head and two asymmetrical dreadlocks pointed at Fleeger, then at her crotch, told him to suck it.

"Lovely," Fleeger replied, thereby demarcating the nether boundaries of his post-Kath promiscuity. I took a shot.

"You don't want to hit that?"

He looked at me with disgust.

"No, Harker. I don't want to hit that."

The blinking mopeds followed the protestors down the mild slope toward the East River and we turned west on Maiden Lane. Fleeger worked his phone, his professional success contingent upon responding to a maximum number of emails within the requisite amount of time. Both Attika and Fleeger now texting and stepping over the curb and up the stairs and into the bar in tandem, still working their phones. I rolled and lit my daily cigarette and smoked standing beneath the pub's circus tent awning and watched the sleet spiral-doodle puddles in the neon-lit gutters, debating whether I deserved a Lorazepam. I told myself I did. I removed the amber bottle from my swish messenger bag fashioned from recycled plastic bits with a seat-belt buckle for a strap and decapped it. One left, the last one. In need of a prescription refill, I would have to call it in soon. I shook free the pill stuck to the inside of the amber bottle. For work-related anxiety. I didn't need it now. I told myself I deserved it. To turbo-charge the booze. I swallowed the bitter white pill and commanded myself to keep it under control. I would be fine. Just another tiny stain about to melt into my liver.

Furtive, across the street, a brown kid descended a fire escape and jumped to the ground clinging a bucket of pitch. Five stories above he had graffitied the building's facade with runic-like markings followed by big block letters that read: IXXI THE PEOPLE OF 4EVER ARE NOT AFRAID IXXI. The kid tossed the bucket into a Dumpster and hurried into the subway station of Chase Manhattan Sapphires and round red 2s and 3s.

3

FLEEGER NO-LOOK BACKHANDED ME a pint of Guinness and waded shoulder-deep into happy hour. Apotheosis of the profession, he possessed a Rolodex of inside jokes and because of this people adored him. They discarded their conversations midexchange to pump his hand and hear what he had to say. About punitive damages awarded for pain and suffering. Venal lawyers. Corpulent plaintiffs. Incontinent judges. Laughing about a case. Yeah that case. Where plaintiff so-and-so alleging such-and-such had the audacity to sue their client.

"Get a job."

"Yeah, get a fucking job."

"Get a fucking job."

Now amassed here at O'Grady's, like some hidden panel of that Hieronymus Bosch triptych. Downtown law firm insurance broking financial services short-selling day-trading to scrape a halfpenny off a penny happy hour bar. The Garden of Earthy delights. Chunky fake jewels and clunky titanium wristwatches. Melting foundation and glittery powdered eye sockets and nosegays of deodorant. Gargoyle andirons and designer Pogs to the tips of every pump. A plague of Pogs shall go up upon thee, Pharaoh. I slipped inside the crowd and rested my elbows against the oak plank bar and watched Attika raise the lid from a wrinkled aluminum tray and tong buffalo wings onto a red plastic plate. As the crowd rubbed up against me, my psychosexual radar failed to detect a blip.

"Hey man, be first class and order my friend here another scotch on the rocks," Fleeger commanded someone.

Money Man on high-def flat screens above the bar, in the corners, nodding with financial wizardry. A septuagenarian futures trader ringing his brass bells and chyrons blinking—WUXI HEXIA FIRST CLASS—WUXI HEXIA FIRST CLASS—WUXI HEXIA FIRST CLASS. On account of the Federal District Court's dismissal of Plaintiffs' massive class action lawsuit against Wuxi and their insurer WorldScore. Thus saving investors a bazillion. Money Man now giving Wuxi the thumbs up.

"First class."

"Hey man, that's you," someone told Fleeger.

Fleeger thanked him. Thanked a few others. Acknowledged it was a big win indeed. But that he couldn't do it without . . . himself.

The crowd's hydrostatic forces shifted, revealing Honda Tadakatsu sitting alone at the bar, two symmetrical clumps of gray white hair like Beats by Dre, fidgeting with a camera lens and donning a tactical vest. Another lens hanging from a neck lanyard and a few more tucked inside his mesh pockets. The bartender poured Honda a scotch and soda and he drank from the tall glass and returned to the lens.

"Mr. Tadakatsu," I said. He looked up at me. His eyes were a series of graphite and carbon dials. He smiled. He couldn't recall my name.

"Stephen Harker," I said. We shook hands.

"Of course. From Kilgore." The Australian accent afforded him a humorous gravitas, thus humanizing his geeky obsession with camera lenses. "I'm sorry but after a while you guys all kind of look the same."

"I'll try not to be offended," I replied.

He handed me his business card. Honda Investigations. *Always gets your man.*

"So I got your email today, Stephen. Regarding the new assignment for this Thomas fellow. But you're too late."

He shared Fleeger's practice of referring to plaintiffs by their last names, to render them less than themselves. Before you sued the client you may have been Major Mike "Bud" Thomas. But now we'll just refer to you as Thomas, because now you're a cocksucking Plaintiff.

"WorldScore put me on this guy a few months ago. Out in White Haven, Pennsylvania. Very apropos, I might add. Less than three hours by car but man I had no idea it was so fucking depressing."

I pointed at the barman. An Irish featherweight with two bushy clumps of nose hair that accessorized his eyebrows. I instructed him to put Honda's drink on the Kilgore tab.

"OK, horse," he replied, unsure whether horse was what he called me.

Honda removed a soft pack of Mild Sevens from one of his mesh pockets and extracted the last cigarette and placed the empty, crushed soft pack atop the bar. The barman swept it away. I lit Honda's cigarette and rolled another for myself.

"They're getting a lot of these guys, WorldScore is. Forcing them to fight bogus compensation claims by guys returning home from the wars. This could be your bread and butter, Stephen. No shortage of work indeed and kind of interesting as well. They're not some corpulent Dominicana in the Bronx suing Geico in New York Supreme for back pain to make a couple grand and spend it on gladiator sandals and an Xbox for the baby daddy. These guys think they have some God-given right to tear it all down. Even if it means we'll be walking around in loincloths and beating each other with clubs."

I asked him what he had thus far.

"No home runs yet. But we'll get him. We're gonna surveil the guy."

He winked. Told me he learned a couple of interesting things about the man thus far.

"And?"

"He's got a deer stand mounted in a massive buttonwood tree in his front yard. Three stories above the ground. With floodlights and motion sensors. And these plastic deer arranged in his bushes: big bucks, does, Bambi, which I assume he uses for target practice. That would be a good shot for us, don't you think? Thomas launching arrows at plastic deer positioned in his rhododendrons. Kind of refutes all those ortho claims. I also ran his name through the Pennsylvania game commission website. To see if he has any hunting licenses."

"Does he?"

"Nothing."

"*Ninja!*" Fleeger yelled, crushing Honda atop his barstool. "Always gets the man."

"Always gets *your* man, Robert."

"Whatever. Who invited you?" Fleeger asked with faux disdain.

"Celeste asked me to come."

"Dude what's up with the Australian accent? I thought you were Japanese."

Honda stared at him.

"Whoa man, just kidding. It's so sexy."

"You always act like an ass, Robert?"

"Only when we win a big case," he replied. "Gives me carte blanche to be a dick. Not an ass. A dick. Big difference, Hondo. Get it straight."

The happy hour crowd cheered the arrival of Tucker Nelson, his coat collar flipped, as if to protect his neck from an approaching lance. "Rabbi." Fleeger greeted Nelson with more kisses as Nelson struggled with his zipper. The WorldScore claims handler who laid the first flagstone on Fleeger's path to partnership in exchange for taproom fealty and Kilgore tickets to the Jets, Devils, Boss. Nelson finally managed to remove his expensive purple coat, a patchwork of octagons, and rolled up his sleeves to commence the hard work of drinking.

"Well if you're good friends with Fleeger then I should be good friends with you too," Nelson crooned as someone handed him a Beam and Diet Coke. He stirred his drink with a red straw while behind him a sinewy woman with worsted black locks took careful steps atop high heels to avoid stepping in anything gooey. She was Celeste Powers, WorldScore's global head of claims, eyelashes battered with mascara, eyebrows plucked into skeptical commas. Fleeger placed a big mitt on her lower back.

"Aren't unwanted sexual advances a violation of the rules of professional responsibility?" she asked him.

I sipped my pint.

"Yes, but first you need to put me on notice."

"Notice of what?"

"That it's unwanted."

He vised Celeste with his arm.

"Trust me, Robert. It's unwanted."

She remained unfazed, immune to taking offense, as Fleeger ghost-sprayed cologne and offered his neck for her to take a sniff.

"Must be the Wuxi," he said. "Come on. Smell it. It smells like victory."

She abstained from smelling him but played along.

"Precluding over a thousand Panamanian infants from obtaining compensation for allegedly ingesting contaminated cough syrup insured by WorldScore's sloppy, bonus-happy underwriters?"

"Warrants a Nobel prize," I said, then finished my pint. Celeste sized me up, entered me on the agenda, and returned to Robert. A thrum dangled from the hem of her tight black wool dress. I ordered another Guinness from the featherweight bartender. He half-poured the stout and set it aside to cascade on a perforated metal tray. I would have to wait a minute before drinking.

"Now Robert, we have some important matters to discuss tonight." She sounded half serious. "This is no time for fun and games."

"There's always time for fun and games," he replied.

A delicate dance commenced just beneath the surface. It was like watching a tiger shark contemplate mating with a killer whale. Except I couldn't tell which was which—who was who—whale or shark. She was a different species than him. Wouldn't fit on his spreadsheet, because she required a specialized source code. At the minimum greater abstraction, a faculty that he lacked. I took a stab.

Celeste Powers (Mrs.) (classic black-and-white).

Apologized:	Taste:	Accessories:	Assets:	Vehicle:
Never	Simple. Elegant. Black. Handspun. Hand-tooled.	Platinum quatrefoil spinning at left wrist. Leather-bound book with mottled edges tucked inside classic Louis Vuitton purse large enough to hold a Redweld. Byzantine Christ bookmarker probably from the Met gift store. Stainless steel points at the heels of lavender-soled Anthony Bacigalupos.	Options. Commodity futures. Collateralized debt obligations. Real estate— both in the city and on the island. Wealthy and older husband. Probably very expensive furniture. Tapestries. Rugs. Impressionist paintings.	Helicopter. In the event things fell apart. Again. For good.

"Wuxi is now in the past, Robert," she said. "And besides, I've complimented you enough. And compensated you plenty. It's not like you did the work pro bono."

"I like the way you say pro bono," Fleeger interrupted. "You really own it."

She ignored him.

"There is a synergy at work here, Robert, and I want to see where we can take this. You've generated some goodwill and at the same time we're staring down the barrel of a new gun. So yes, sure I'm here to congratulate you about Wuxi—good work, smart chap, and all that—but more importantly to discuss Kilgore's internal capacity."

Celeste slapped the Redweld portaged inside her Louis Vuitton and Honda appeared at her side and Nelson fell in line behind them. Wonder Twins activate. This gathering tonight now about Fleeger's capacity to handle more defense work. She had the orders and the strategy, she explained, but she needed a team to execute the plan and accomplish the objective. Each worker's comp claim WorldScore successfully refuted constituted another boon against the surge of unemployed, underemployed, broken, addicted, and/or mentally crippled men returning home from Afghanistan and Iraq with no jobs and no option but to sue their former war zone employers for benefits. To keep their manhood intact. Private welfare via spurious litigation. The system was ripe for abuse. For every legitimately injured military contractor who returned from Iraq with one-and-a-half arms there were scores of dudes filing dubious insurance claims for impossible-to-refute PTSD and subjective back pain. All to obtain twice-monthly payouts that almost always went toward purchasing the sundry tools associated with irrefutable American manliness: hunting bows, rifle scopes, 3D camouflage golf carts for tooling around in the woods while hopped up on beneficent prescriptions for opioids to cure phantom ailments. An entire ghost economy built up around insurance claims, Cabela's, and drive-through pharmacies.

Fleeger backhanded me Celeste's Sol and it slipped. I caught the bottle mid-descent. Scar along her left patella, morning dabs of bergamot, her steel-tipped heels punched dimples into the burgundy carpet. The tiny advanced footwear of professional women who'd never borne children. She ignored me while accepting the beer bottle I offered her and the barman handed me my third or fourth Guinness.

"You've been defending WorldScore for some time now," she said to Fleeger. "What has it been? Nine years? You're quite the loyal foot soldier."

"Nelson sends me work and all I have to do is buy him drinks," Fleeger said.

"How convenient," she replied.

"For Nelson it is," Nelson said. A purple shadow covered his left eyelid. I couldn't tell if it was a sty or if he'd been hit. The color matched his coat.

"Hello, Stephen," he said.

"Hello, Nelson," I replied.

Nelson upticked his head. Said it was always good to see me too brother and shuffled off to speak with Attika, who instructed Nelson to order another drink on Kilgore's tab.

"And you are?" Celeste asked.

"Stephen Harker. Pleasure to meet you."

We shook hands.

"I love a lawyer with a sweaty palm," she said, wiping her hand against her outer thigh. "It means he has something on his mind. Robert tells me you are the top associate on his team. What makes you his top man, Stephen?"

"I'll have a Blue Moon," Nelson told the barman.

"Sorry, horse. Keg is kicked."

"Stephen's already working up the Thomas file," Fleeger informed Celeste.

"Why do you keep calling me a horse?" Nelson protested.

"Ok, horse. If you want a Blue Moon I'll have to check downstairs, but you'll have to wait."

"Stephen tell Celeste how qualified you are."

"Robert's prone to exaggeration," I said.

"God I hope not. Are you prone to exaggeration Robert?" Mocking my use of the word prone. I couldn't do anything right with this woman. "Let me try with him. So what makes you so qualified, Mr. Harker? Years toiling at Robert's beck and call?"

The main problem with this evening was that everyone was trying to sound clever. And I couldn't walk away and I didn't want to be here. The moment hung there like the moment before you suspect something momentous will happen. Because you think you've been here before, and that maybe if you focus you can foresee the momentous event about to occur, right there on the other side of the following seconds. And that in thinking you can predict what

28

will happen next you confirm your own omniscience. But then you can't. And it doesn't happen. Because it's a ruse. A small skip of the machine that tricks you into thinking you are on the cusp of significance. Because you are not Nostradamus. And you were a fool to think you are.

"Who needs another drink?" Fleeger asked.

"I'll switch to a chardonnay," Celeste said, now checking her phone.

Fleeger dispensed the alcohol, leading us around the bend. Nelson grabbed an orange slice from behind the bar and the barman launched a rag at him. I wanted space to breathe and recalibrate, succumb to the temptation of my vibrating phone. Hoping to read it wasn't a coronal mass ejection potentially menacing satellite communications but instead a Betelgeuse-sized ball of plasma careening toward Earth, broken free from the belt of Orion. Ladies and gentlemen, our mistake. My hopes for astronomical Armageddon dashed by a Bloomberg tile announcing a steep rise in India GDP. Nelson lit a long, thin cigarette and Fleeger waved away the smoke. "There you go horsebox," the barman said as he positioned another Guinness before me on a napkin.

The alcohol had supercharged the benzodiazepine, the mixture now soaking into my marrow. No longer producing T cells and white blood cells but something mean and reckless. I rolled and lit another cigarette. The tobacco did something too. No mere inert substance, it stirred the pot, summoned the stench of things I promised myself not to think about while drinking.

"Stephen, I ordered us some food," Attika said. I looked at her. "You look like you need to eat." I wanted to tell her those were the kindest words I had heard all day. Nelson tapped his fork against his bottle to announce a toast.

"For what?" Fleeger asked.

"For your Wuxi victory, man," Nelson explained. "It's huge."

We raised our glasses to Fleeger. My black suit reflected in the platinum quatrefoil spinning at Celeste's wrist.

"To Wuxi," I said, tipping my beer toward Attika.

"To Wuxi," she replied.

Celeste removed her cashmere cardigan, revealing a trilobite ribcage and a body of constant vigilance. Fleeger, chin down, took her in, looked at me, motioned with his head, and reentered the screen of his mobile phone.

"Now, Stephen, you can no longer ignore me," she said. "This is no time to be shy. After all, it sounds as if we'll be working together quite closely. So let's try to get to know each other a bit, shall we? To build up my confidence in your capabilities. And unfortunately I must say I still need a bit of convincing. So now you must tell me something about you. Something personal, perhaps."

Her teeth matched her pearl necklace.

"Don't you prefer these personal details to reveal themselves more naturally?" I asked. "Without all the questioning? Isn't that more English?"

"No, Mr. Harker. You're wrong. You're thinking of the French. They're the ones who don't ask any questions of one another. So. Impress me. I'm here to be impressed. Surely you can engage me in some form of stimulating, intellectual conversation. After all, I'm the client. I'm here for you to charm me. Then you do the work and I like what I see and I send you more work. And before long you're sitting in Fleeger's seat. But it takes a little initiative, Mr. Harker. It takes a bit of ass kissing. So come on. Pucker up, young man."

"Tell her about the time you raced horses drunk with the Quiché Indians in the Peace Corps," Fleeger said.

"Hmm quiche," Nelson purred. Like it was a dirty word.

She ignored them both.

"Let's start with the present. You've been at Kilgore eight years?"

"Just about."

"That's almost as long as Robert."

"A few less," I replied.

"And yet he's a partner."

The gaps between her words disclosing that maybe perhaps she shouldn't but she was going to anyway. To test the voltage of the third rail.

"That's true," I said.

"Is there a story you don't want to share with me, Mr. Harker?"

"I don't want to bore you, Celeste."

"Are you suggesting I have the capacity to be bored?"

A wrinkle appeared across Fleeger's forehead that only I could interpret. Stephen, this is all you. I took a long draught from the pint glass and gestured for another as the barman set down rounds of whiskey, chardonnay, pilsner, stout, along with steak tip sandwiches, nachos, jalapeño poppers, bacon potato skins for Nelson, and a plate of fried calamari. Celeste surveyed the food with horror, mortal enemy of all that yoga, and I seized the distraction, excused myself, glanced at Fleeger's lap phone on my way to the bathroom. His big thumb scrolling through selfies of Tara: bending over, peach crotch thong, in the mirror, wearing only a towel, kohl-tipped eyes, beckoning him. I entered the bathroom and stumbled to the urinal and pissed on a mound of ice cubes. "I fucking hate this," I said aloud, hoping no one heard me and leaning my forehead against the cool bathroom tile wall. Do you reject Satan? And all his works? And all his pomps? The motion dispenser failed to squirt foamy soap into my moving hand. I worried I was disappearing. I stumbled back to my drink like it was a life raft.

Outside the bar's picture window, beyond the script of the saloon's standard, the sky was now oily black. Green bankers lamps hanging from the coffered ceiling reflected in the big window, like in cocaine bathrooms where the mirrored walls reflect themselves reflecting themselves into infinity. I watched a number of my hands raise a number of glasses to my number of faces, piercing Maiden Lane and extending into space.

"Tough spot for a rookie," someone yelled at the bar.

I took stock of the scene. Nelson and Attika now throwing darts in a nook, hands on each other's hips and shoulders. Honda long ago disappeared. The crowd dispersing for the Metro North and Long Island Rail Road and PATH trains to New Jersey Transit. Celeste and Fleeger gestured for me to join them as the barman shifted what remained of the picked-over food to a small square table, where Celeste's Redweld was positioned like a centerpiece. Still-life with litigation. Fleeger clipped his phone to his belt and refocused and I took a seat.

"Look, gentlemen. The reason I came here tonight, the real reason, is that I desperately need you to give this Thomas case your maximum attention."

"You got it," Robert said, sipping a fresh beer.

"Do I, Robert? Do I really? Just so you totally understand the situation, there is only one person I answer to in top management and he only answers to the one person at the very top. I'm one tier from executive throne level. And to stay there I need to deliver results, but to deliver results I need to delegate the litigation. That's what you guys are. My delegatees. And in exchange for you being my humble legal servants I shall pay whatever invoices you send me. Within reason, of course. You want to bill me for reviewing documents, studying surveillance footage, 'file review,' I don't care. I won't sweat the details. You're still cheaper than most of the big midtown firms, and besides, in my opinion they lack the grit to get this done. So I'll pay your bills. But you two." Celeste pointed at the Redweld. "The higher-ups want to send a clear message with this one. Which is that Thomas isn't getting anything more than nuisance value for his alleged physical injuries and certainly without a doubt absolutely nothing for the bogus PTSD claim. Wuxi made them nervous. You handled Wuxi with aplomb. Major Thomas makes them nervous. Now WorldScore wants you to handle Thomas with aplomb too."

"We're on it," Robert said.

"Really?"

"Really. Stephen's on it. I'm on it. We're on it." He flipped his wrist back and forth between us. "Right Harker?"

I nodded.

"Good," she said.

Fleeger paid the tab with his Kilgore platinum card and Nelson approached the table with heavy feet, sweat blistering his pink forehead. He sat next to me. He was drunk.

"I think she likes me," he whispered, nodding toward Attika, who now held a fresh glass of rosé. She draped an arm across Nelson's slouched shoulders, rounded him, and sat on his lap, dangling long legs, one of her flats now Tory Burch pogless.

"Don't be such a gossip, Mr. Nelson," she said.

It was time to go. I said my goodbyes but refrained from shaking Celeste's hand, lest she comment again on its moisture. Fleeger escorted Celeste outside to a black town car steaming exhaust as Nelson played with Attika's hair, tucking it behind her ear. Bold move for a white man. I located my swish messenger bag fashioned from recycled plastic bits, slung it over my shoulder, and exited the bar as Fleeger closed the car door behind Celeste.

"We don't need a fucking glorified claims handler telling us how to handle the litigation." He almost spat. "I don't care where she thinks she is on the executive pyramid. We're the frontline attorneys and we'll handle Thomas the same way we handle every fucking case."

"Which is how?" I asked.

"Fucking flawlessly, dude."

Fleeger stretched his long arm around me. Told me good work tonight. With the drinking. With engaging Celeste. With not being too mean to Nelson. I thanked him and he told me to go home, get some sleep, conference in the a.m., J. McKenzie, look sharp, courthouse, first thing, see you there. He ascended the stairs to O'Grady's and I commenced the walk home, toward the stacked halogen lights of WorldScore One, the cranes atop the Manhattan high-rises almost victorious in their reach.

4

THE TEMPERATURE HAD DROPPED and black ice sheened the streets, absorbing the colors of the city at night. Orange, amber, yellow, red. A message buzzed my phone and I patted myself for the dopamine fix. A fresh alert from NASA advising that a radio telescope constructed inside the caldera of a dormant Hawaiian volcano had recorded the sun releasing a burst of intensely magnetic plasma. I walked north on Water Street listening to the sun. It sounded like white noise.

A bulk carrier steamed south atop the East River, giant oyster shells of halogen lights floating on a river of insoluble antibiotics and synthetic estrogen. She rode in ballast, with a high freeboard, unladed with cargo, rumbling beneath the Brooklyn Bridge to where the slope of the city exposed its inhabitants to the rising sea. Staunch and watertight, chamfered, bulbous bow, slanted stern. The M/V *Golden Dolphin*, Nassau, Bahamas. Not the largest of her class but still massive and bearing the weight of state-sponsored industry. Probably China. Possibly Japan. On her way out now, through New York Harbor, the Verrazano Narrows, the Lower Bay, and then to sea.

The day's fifth or sixth cigarette rolled with ease in the cold riparian air and I continued walking north. Now toward the protest camp, with its increasing magnitudes of pitch-black graffiti, both runic and Cyrillic.

DONKEE JOTEE
WHEN YOU PAY WRONG YOU PAY TWICE

The protestors were making a mess of the place, occupying the open spaces, beating paths of mud through the landscaping, pitching tents in the raised flower beds, sleeping on flattened cardboard boxes anchored with rocks and chewed-up heads of winter cabbage, demarcating the boundaries of their pro-democracy camp with torn strips of yellow police tape. Shouldering bundles of paper pulled from the downtown Dumpsters to fuel the fires that warmed this squatters' colony of no justice, no peace. Garlands of clear lightbulbs with filaments like incandescent moths. Silver packets torn to access condoms or shampoo. For fucking or washing. Light & Easy. Fair & Mild. I walked home beneath the trellises of the elevated highway.

A girl approached me. Curvy and busty inside a zipped-up Puffa jacket, almost dwarfish, which accentuated her curves.

"Hey, don't I know you from high school?" she asked, taking me by the hand, walking us backward. I let her. She leaned against an iron truss and unzipped her jacket, revealing cleavage clawed with stretch marks.

"Not a chance," I replied.

I stepped to her, knowing I shouldn't. The drinks plus the pill had distorted my judgment with false invincibility. Now that I was talking the first step had been taken and then a second step taken and I would put up a small fight but the juice of the exchange would drown whatever qualms still wimpled inside me. I accepted the tariff of dread, knowing it would possess a half-life of no more than an hour.

"You sassing me?" she asked. "You gonna sass me some more?" She smiled. One sharp canine peeked from behind her cracked and pink upper lip. Like a calcium stalactite, useful for peeling citrus rinds and opening cans of beans. She tightened my tie knot and I gripped my swish shoulder bag. I remembered an article I read years ago in *Science Thursday*. About an entomology study in which sexually rejected male fruit flies turned to booze to cope. I was at the apogee of need. Where the arc of the universe bent not toward justice but hookers. Easily susceptible to the charms being hocked by this cheap purveyor. I would keep it manual. Maintain a safe distance. Thereby limiting the exchange of fluids and cells.

"Where you from?" I asked her.

"Is that your conscience panging away? Thinking you need to get to know me first?" She placed my hand inside her jacket. Her body was warm and softened by nursing. The clot needed clearing. She gripped my lapels as I maintained one hand inside her jacket. I felt nervous and needy and wanted it over with.

"Is it me or is everyone talking too much today?" I asked.

"Must have something to do with all that solar magnetism they say is coming our way," she said. "Supposed to make us act real wild."

She danced wild with her hands and then took hold of both of mine. No good reason for me to follow her now as she led me into an alley illuminated by ultraviolet neon lights, down chipped concrete steps, around a cheap Asian screen and into a parlor of stalls. She pulled back the curtain and I climbed onto the massage table and, now supine, she unbuckled my pants. Shadows beneath the curtains an inch above the floor, of other men here with other girls, fishers of men, high heels tapping against linoleum flooring. The girls should wear coveralls, I thought. Like at Jiffy Lube.

"Wash your hands," I said.

A porcelain sink glowed beneath the neon ultraviolet light and an attendant handed her a soap cake and towels and the girl dropped a coin onto the attendant's plate and I could smell the carbolic soap emanating from the steamy basin. Like the soap with which I once cleaned dirt and paint from my cracked hands after a day of manual labor. The girl and the woman discussed the exchange. The room was cold and I could see their breath. She returned, smiling with that one long tooth, blue and purple and now I was blue and purple and her hands were blue and purple and my stomach was blue and purple. I remembered another word of the day. Daguerreotype. Here it was, burning images onto purple trays.

"Now we can talk," she said, buckling my belt. "We can pretend we are on a date. So you won't feel so guilty."

I pressed twenty bucks into her other hand.

"You don't want to be my boyfriend?"

She pouted. I handed her an extra twenty.

"Take it."

She gripped the bills.

"I've seen you down here before," she said. "Walking along the river and through the protest camp."

"It's possible."

I refrained from telling her it was on my way home.

"You down here looking for something? You looking to join up with Jupiter?"

"Who?"

"There's this guy down here at the protest camp named Jupiter and everyone thinks he's a prophet. He's even got a bunch of disciples who follow him around, writing crazy words and figures all over everything. They say they're developing a new language. Jupiter says we're all slaves and that slaves must learn to speak a new language that only the slaves can speak. That is incomprehensible to the master. Are you a slave? Hablas español?"

I refrained from making any obnoxious comments. The strap on my swish messenger bag reminded me of tomorrow's court conference. I had to leave.

"I don't think I like you anymore," she said. "I think I'm done with you."

"That's fine."

Outside, the mounted patrol approached the alley, cantering atop cobblestones and hard asphalt. Despite the fact these parlors existed, with bricks and mortar and cash registers and neon lights, they felt illicit, subject to a raid. I didn't need to be seen with her. There was a system and an order and I spun inside that order and she spun outside it. With no way in other than through a man's zipper. She twisted her hair around her finger while standing in a puddle of purple light. I placed our encounter in a black lacquered box and kicked it overboard and walked away. She watched me, but with different eyes, like those painted on the side of a Bedouin's van to ward off evil.

The cold rain resumed and the protestors pulled tarps over the entrances to their plastic tents. I followed home the trail of amber lights, through the campus and citadels of municipal authority, beneath crumbling gargoyles, cracked concrete, dripping verdigris, turned west at Confucius Circle, crossed Bowery, more graffiti to the ancient facades, entered Chinatown, and walked through cold, new rain toward the giant crying neon baby who wants

scallions and

beef and

chopsticks full of golden noodles.

Mei runs to the window above the walk-up's front door. "I want to kiss you," she says, covering her red lace bra with my white cotton dress shirt. This moment made for cotton. Together we once formed the first person plural. Us. Me and you. She spoke Chinese between bouts of breath that sounded like tiny orgasms. A marriage based on orgasms. Nothing more. *When you pay wrong you pay twice.* I shouldered the building's heavy glass door and climbed one narrow flight of stairs. The apartment's metal door sprung shut behind me and the bang echoed throughout the walk-up. Piles of clothes and papers and books and magazines. I dropped the Jacob's Ladder on the floor and lay on the couch, face burrowed between two stain-resistant pillows.

5

VOMIT BURPS AND GRAPEFRUIT juice and Fleeger emails. Reminding me of this morning's court conference in re Major Bud Asshole. Commanding that we cut off ze head of ze snake. Confirming my attendance at the annual Risk Rewards dinner. More exclamation marks. He was under Tara's influence already. This year honoring . . . him! COMMAND PERFORMANCE! Another email from Fleeger's secretary warning about the toxicity of air fresheners—proven cause of bone cancer and endocrine disease. For a woman whose boss built a career defending Air Wick and Johnson Wax against specious toxic exposure claims she was especially attuned to fake news stories promulgating myths about the links between artificial scents, household aerosols, and terminal illnesses. I lit the gas stove beneath the wedding gift Le Creuset teapot, sat down at the faux vintage dinette Mei left behind, and peeled and chewed a mealy clementine.

When Mei was here I wanted her gone and now that she was gone it was not what I expected. Or what I expected but also not, perhaps much like the marriage itself. We had performed as expected, and by doing so assumed we were destined to reap the rewards: golden Manhattan honeymoon of double income no kid (Dink!), a move to Greenpoint (for the extra room), followed by a child (our first), Kilgore partnership (strong probability), another child (so blessed), real property in Pelham or Rye, perhaps Montclair (financial security assured), above-average biracial children enrolled in above-average multiethnic public schools destined for above-average private universities and above-average careers (medicine and/or finance). But we never made it past the honeymoon. Instead, something foul and slothful moved into the apartment before the first anniversary. Some spirit animal that subsisted on unfulfilled expectations took residence on the couch. Nested behind the walls and under our bed. Scratching the box spring and drywall at night. Gnawing on brick. Consuming the scraps left behind in the kitchen sink. Bringing with it depression and insomnia, flabby triceps, hours in front of the mirror trying on dresses, shouting matches, a permanent sink full of dishes and food, pizza boxes too big for the trash can and thus piled on the floor, plastic containers of old saag paneer stacked in the refrigerator, anxiety pills in the medicine closet (of which I'm out), vitamins to lose weight effortlessly by boosting one's metabolism, unused sex toys, lingerie of ingrown hairs, Lululemon pants, juice cleanses, more Lululemon pants, moments of intimacy fraught with insecurity and fear, Chinese calligraphies harking happy home that failed to fend off the spirit beast gnawing at the edges of our mutual matrimonial benefits package.

Living via genitalia and emotion, we had denied ourselves the sedate pleasure of a tranquil home. Not legally bankrupt but bankrupt nonetheless. In spite of, because of, the electronics, and the brunches, and the mimosas, and the tender eateries, and the tender boutiques, and the pop-up galleries, and the designer weed delivered via skateboarders, and the artisan cocktails poured by mustached, suspendered bartenders who could three-count a perfect 1.5 ounces of Tito's without a jigger. As if this was a skill. Mei telling me so. Me refuting her. Her calling me condescending. Me rupturing. A failure of the entire marital financial psychological operating system. To the point when you couldn't even cross the street together, let alone make significant decisions, let alone decide which entrée to order from the David Chang restaurant or bottle to select from the pinewood shelves of le boutique sommelier. Until the last quark of attachment stops moving and dies. Behind bolted vault doors. Double helixes of secrets stored in sealed pneumatic tubes. To protect each other from each other's smallpox. Pending one final act of mercy.

Let me mansplain something to you dear, now that you're gone. You see, there was a formula we needed to follow: I work, you work, we work. Not I work, you whine. Not I work, the subway is too crowded. Not I work, the winter is too cold. Not I work, I return home to you crying in a robe, rivulets of mascara, saying you couldn't leave the apartment. Indicting me for all the pain, it's my fault, I'm certain to give you cancer. Talk to Fleeger's secretary about that. She'll educate you. It's the Blade Plug-ins you love, not me. And then it stops, it comes to an end, not because of kindness or empathy. But because we lacked the necessary reciprocal respect for resolution. And still the sloth remains, lying on the couch, scratching itself, popping cheese puffs, complaining about the WiFi. And there it stays until you're gone. And all that's left is the vintage dinette. Which the spirit beast couldn't care about less. And then he too finally leaves, out the door and down the street, with his funny, furry little body, in search of another marriage to gnaw.

Downstairs in the building's courtyard, Gregg the Super's bare arms rose above the coppice of faux Christmas firs worshipping the sun, and then down. He crawled inside the tiny fake forest and knitted his legs into a full-lotus position as his mushy cat stretched and yawned atop a beam of rotted fencing. I entered the shower of brown tiles. Attempted to think up a poem. About cirrhosis of the spiritual gall-bladder. About an almost empty bottle of dandruff shampoo, bobbing in the shoals of mildew. I exited the shower and stood naked before the mirror, afraid to examine my mouth, lest I spot some white dot of incontrovertible oral cancer. From all that going down on women, as reported by the *New York Times*. I wiped the bathroom mirror and examined my receding hairline. Mei appeared, looking back at me, the woman on the other side of the fog.

"Stephen."

"Mei."

"I'm sick."

"I know."

41

"I'll stab you."

"Then back you go."

"To where?"

"To the planet of malfunctioning women."

I stepped on the lever, tossed a clump of my hair into the trash can, and commenced struggling with the wrapper of a high-protein, high-fiber breakfast bar. I got dressed, felt hot, dizzy, a bit drunk still, opened the window and breathed in damp cold air as the pan-Asian flute of Gregg's morning meditation coursed through the courtyard and now up through my window, as if transported by a clear plastic tube.

"Stephen," Gregg said. His torso swept left, his torso swept right, as if holding a medicine ball, now preparing to launch a javelin. His bald ponytail swished in the opposite direction of his kinetic body. "Would you like to savasana?"

I told him no thank you.

"I think it would be good for you."

Instead, I lit the tawny butt of a hand-rolled cigarette and blew smoke out the window. *Habemus Papam.* Opened the swish messenger bag and removed the Thomas file and scanned the memo I wrote in preparation for today's conference. I couldn't read it. Either because I knew it or I could fake it. Besides, Fleeger would do the talking. All I had to do was sit there and not fall into a black hole while pretending to take notes. Which was always possible, especially after drinking.

"Stephen?" Gregg asked. He climbed the fire escape and stood outside my window, his bushy black armpits emitting an effluvium of sage. "I haven't seen you around. Busy at work?"

I told him I was.

"Come practice with me?"

"I don't downward dog."

He peered into my apartment.

"You know you're impeding your mindfulness with all this clutter."

"The garden looks good," I said.

"You know God was a positive thinker."

He was always telling me what I knew. I blew more smoke out the window. We said goodbye and I closed the window with too much vigor and he paused before descending the fire escape. My shoes still soaking wet from yesterday's night walk home, I rummaged through the bottom of the closet for another option and uncovered a box of footwear with a padded logo. Euro shoes designed for both office and gym. A gift from Mei. I wore them once to brunch, maybe to a party. Having no choice, I laced them to my feet, grabbed my swish messenger bag, took one final shot of Tropicana grapefruit juice, and extricated myself from the glue trap of the apartment, feeling podiatrically reborn.

6

PUMPING ELBOWS AND HIPS, I speedwalked to the courthouse, glands activated with sweat and anxiety to guarantee my arrival on time. The city's grid now part of my endocrine system; from point X to point Y in exactly Z minutes. A flawless space-time machine fueled by high-protein, high-fiber breakfast bars. Tiger in my tank, I cruised through Chinatown. Past wooden shelves of glass pharmacy jars filled with roots and powders. Cartons of dried duck parts. Schools of salt-water fish half-buried in chipped ice. Five-gallon buckets of crab. Dragon fruit. Durian fruit. Jackfruit. Red sauce jars with green lids. Frozen stiff cardboard boxes. Mexicans in yellow boots bearing garden hoses. Bubble tea. Eyeglasses. Hello Kitty. Lucky Cat. Chinese men fist-smoking Shuangxis and Chinese grandmothers smacking their thighs and doing jumping jacks. Try Falun Gong for better circulation. Midstride the proboscis of a lost European tourist poked me in the chest.

"Wall Street?" he asked.

I bounced in place in my Euro sneakers. He was me. He looked just like me, but for his whiteout slacks and white shoes. He recognized this too, began bouncing as well. Must be the magic shoes, I thought. We bounced, synchronized. I stopped bouncing and he reverted to himself, someone other than me. I told him to keep walking that way, gestured with my hand, down Water Street. In that vicinity. Fifteen minutes tops. Follow the cops and the blockades.

And watch out for the protestors. They'll target those pants of yours with their rotten projectiles.

My hustle resumed, I again checked the phone. No word yet from Fleeger. A tincture of tartar-fighting mint and bile bubbled and arose from the other side of my epiglottis at the thought of him stranding me in court to handle the conference alone. This dreaded incessant phobia of falling apart, now sans benzo life preserver, last one popped for extra buzz. Self-sabotage via panic attacks and shot nerves hours before the main event commenced, the consequences of failure augmented by age. Jesus, man up. This would be nothing. Is nothing. There would be a court conference with Fleeger before a judge involving other people's money and Lazlis. Lazlis being the lowest shade on the threat spectrum, ultrapurple, myself being the highest, Kilauea red. My involvement would entail little more than jotting notes on a legal pad while Fleeger bickered with Lazlis about what WorldScore would refuse to pay Thomas.

Value for money.™

I cleared invisible hurdles through the canyons of old Gotham. Past jailhouse guards crowding young black men, some dressed as women, into a prison bus with grated windows. One of them blew me a kiss and I felt a slight tickle. Because he hit the bull's-eye. I pinged the tickle against every preconceived notion of myself and came up straight, but also wondering if and when the line would veer off into another dimension. I entered the courthouse's stiff copper doors and heaved the tickle down a black hole, where it smashed atop last night's lacquer box. A US marshal watched me as I struggled with myself, which likely did something suspicious to my face.

"I only eat the sausage," he said to his colleague, still watching me, chewing something. "The rest are too damn sweet."

The conveyor belt took away my bag. I emptied my pockets into a small gray hand bucket and passed through the hulking metal detector and the guard pointed at my shoes.

"What do you call those?" he asked.

"I don't think they have a name," I lied.

"I don't think I've ever seen quite a pair. How much you get them for?"

"They were a gift."

"They look comfortable. Think I'm going to get some."

I refrained from telling him what they probably cost—get out of here—and bounced across the foyer restuffing my pockets, past Lady Justice bandaged blind and two stories tall, as though salvaged from the prow of a decommissioned aircraft carrier.

"Fuck." I exhaled and entered the elevator, exited the elevator, rounded sharp marble corners, and pressed open the courtroom's heavy wooden doors. I took a seat near the back and watched from the shadows.

Up front, before the bench, huddled the commercial lawyers of the Anthropocene era, combing through their accordion files and litigation bags. Commercial plaintiff to the left—pink parboiled cranium. Commercial defendant to the right—resembling a frilled lizard. While throughout the courtroom sat members of the New York Bar awaiting their turns before the court. Proud. Shifting. Clearing their throats, separate but synchronized, like brass-bottom dolls tolling Carol of the Bells. They nodded to one another at about the same time.

"Hey buddy," Lazlis said, standing above me. I stood and shook his hand. He was short, with a spherical protruding belly. Blackheads dusted his nose. "Don't you work at Kilgore with Robert?"

I told him I did, and that we met before, at last year's Risk Rewards dinner. He wore a copper bangle around his left wrist to cleanse his blood of impurities.

"Well, like I told Robert yesterday, I'm sorry to do this to you."

"Do what to me?"

"But then again you didn't really give me a choice."

I asked him again.

"Robert didn't tell you?"

"Tell me what?"

"That we filed an emergency motion yesterday afternoon to compel WorldScore's immediate payment of uncontroverted benefits to my client?"

A yawning chasm cracked open behind me and I pitched back-ward and disappeared into the void.

"It went up on the electronic docket yesterday afternoon. Aren't you attorney of record for this case?"

"Robert is."

"You guys don't communicate?"

There was nothing I could say.

"Well, here's my daily act of grace. Ave Maria."

He reached in his bag and handed me the papers.

"I got an extra copy of the motion. Good thing my client's still downstairs, otherwise he'd skin me alive for helping you."

"He's here?"

"Yup. Drove up last night from White Haven. Said he wouldn't miss this for the world given that his life depends on it. Now he's arguing with the marshals about letting him carry his tactical folder into the courtroom."

"His what?"

"It's a pocket knife of some kind. He keeps it clipped inside his pants pocket. Some kind of chic redneck thing. Says he won't go any-where without it, even more so because he's not permitted to carry a concealed firearm in New York. Hey, don't worry, young man, he won't be armed by the time he gets up here. There's no way the judge will allow it."

"Unbelievable."

"Look, I'm telling you what I told Robert yesterday. This guy is a fucking lunatic. You'll see it in the report attached to the motion. Which is why I really, really want to settle this one, OK? He's lit-erally calling my office every day asking when he's going to get his money. Telling me not to mess with the ice bear."

"The what?"

"The ice bear."

"What does that mean?"

"I have no idea. But it's starting to freak me out and my secre-tary doesn't want to answer the phone when he calls. He's picked up on that too and now he's calling from unlisted numbers. Because he knows I don't want to speak with him five times a day. But he keeps calling, as if harassing me will get him paid quicker. He might be right, which is why I'm whining to you about it. First, I could manage him by explaining there was a process and that we had to follow the process and blah blah blah but eventually he would get paid. But I'm running out of scraps to toss him. And, truthfully, you guys aren't helping. It's been fourteen months since WorldScore cut him a disability check. Which is why I had to file this motion. And which is why Judge McKenzie now has to hear this motion. You think I like writing motions? I hate writing motions. So how about you guys do me a solid and give him something now, OK? It doesn't have to be a lot. Just what he's entitled to under the regulations. That way he won't come after me."

He winked.

"Let's settle this one today. Settle this one and I'll throw my next shitty client who sues WorldScore under the bus and you'll look like a hero and I can move on and keep my secretary from leaving me."

I lacked the authority for this. Any agreement to settle now would constitute high treason against Queen Celeste.

"I'll do my best," I said.

"Don't give me that, young man. Robert knows me. We've done hundreds of these cases together. He knows I'm not too greedy. Just get WorldScore to authorize some kind of modest income stream soon so we can keep this whole thing moving forward without me having to file any more motions and before my client blows up a kindergarten."

I told him I would get back to him on the settlement despite knowing it was a nonstarter and thanked him for the copy of the motion. He pawed my shoulder and took a seat near the front of the courtroom and propped a stack of papers against his ample belly, which he proceeded to study.

The motion possessed heft. What remained of the blood in my veins that had not yet turned to vinegar and sweated through my armpits returned as newer, richer blood. I texted Fleeger—"Did you know there's a motion?"—and jotted billing notes to the top right corner of Lazlis's memorandum of law. 444/15 RF/SH: in re court appearance; in re study/review plaintiff's memorandum of law; in re prepare for oral argument against motion to compel payment re comp benefits. Time spent preparing for oral argument while studying the file in court double-billable. Like rolling double sixes. A trick Fleeger taught me. Incapable of processing Lazlis's sloppy boilerplate syntax, I flipped to Exhibit A, Thomas's neuropsych evaluation performed by Dr. Henry Spectrum, chief military psychiatrist at the Philadelphia VA.

Here was Thomas in print. Pack of Marlboros and four-plus beers per day. Wild boar and deer hunts. Refurbishing straight-sixes. A contentious custody dispute over his thirteen-year-old daughter. This I underlined to investigate further. A cuckolding ex-wife and his second wife pilfering his pain meds. Sundays with the Baptist band. From 2001 to 2007: Piloting C-130s in and out of Bagram and Baghdad with the Air Force. Two medals for valor and three commendations for marksmanship. Special dispensation upon honorable discharge. From 2007 to 2013: Kabul District Assistant Manager for tactical operations at FreedomQuest. Thomas increasingly agitated by FreedomQuest's failure to protect him and his men, until the home office just didn't want to deal with him anymore. Same as Lazlis.

Upon Thomas's termination the disability claims start rolling in, which FreedomQuest referred to their workers' compensation carrier, WorldScore, who in turn controverted Thomas's claims for failure to provide timely notice of injury to his employer; failure to file the proper forms with the Department of Labor; failure to establish the requisite nexus between the alleged ailments and his former employment; requisite nexus between job responsibilities and alleged ailments presented with insufficient particularity. Dr. Spectrum noting that WorldScore's refusal to compensate Thomas could be a factor in his expanding profile of mental and physical ailments, for which the VA doctors had prescribed Thomas a daily cocktail of oxycodone, Klonopin, lithium, trazadone, Ambien, methadone, and morphine.

Still, the doctor's diagnosis under the PTSD criteria set forth in the DSM-IV as propounded by the American College of Psychiatrists: Thomas's presentation as a severely disabled former military contractor employed by FreedomQuest was bona fide.

The ice bear cometh.

Fleeger was late. I checked my phone. Still no Fleeger. I texted him a ? Then, motion?

The little blue bar on the phone signaled the messages' delivery. I scanned through the memo I typed yesterday. The words had grown fuzz. I resumed sweating at the thought of Fleeger not showing up, of me toe-to-toe against Lazlis. A maroon speck of light zipped around the courtroom's cherry oak paneling, sunlight refracting through Lazlis's class ring. Fordham. Boston College. Now at rest on the courtroom's crown molding. Now moving across the ceiling. Now circling as Lazlis noted the pages propped against his belly.

A concussion of sudden knocks against the court's hardwood door announced Judge McKenzie's arrival. The commercial lawyers stood as the judge ascended his bench and flopped into what looked like a dentist's chair. With a looping hand he scribbled notes, motioned for counsel to sit, and leaned into a Nerf-ball microphone.

"Ah yes," the judge said. "A bona fide commercial matter. Ships. Money. Indemnity. Steel. None of it arbitrary and capricious. You're both reasonable commercial men. No reason to go wasting the court's time when we can quickly dispose of this matter. Keep my docket moving. So, counselors, where shall we begin? How about plaintiffs? Mr. Lomax, I presume?"

"You're the boss, applesauce," Lomax replied.

"What do you mean?" the judge asked, amused by the unorthodoxy.

"It's an expression," Lomax said, his spiking blood pressure crimsoning his already-pink cranium.

"Which means what?" the judge wanted to know.

Lomax was stumped.

"Don't tell me you're asserting something in this courtroom that you don't understand, counselor. That would be foolish. I'll ask my clerk. It's queer, isn't it?"

"Yes, judge," the clerk said, fresh from law school with the serious demeanor of a privileged and intelligent young man who never smoked grass.

"I thought so."

The lawyers in the courtroom mumbled, shifted under the weight of their massive pubic mounds, as the judge swatted at a plump, black fly circling his bench in erratic figure eights.

"Well let's get on with it," the judge said. "Plaintiffs? You first."

Lomax thanked the judge for providing plaintiffs an opportunity to address the court. Defense counsel tapped his teeth with temples fashioned from the horn of an oryx, his Rolex requiring constant reclasping. Lomax handed the clerk a thin stack of documents and commenced spooning his case to the judge.

"The plaintiff, our client, American Pipe, Your Honor, is a Wyoming limited liability company. And now, Your Honor, when you buy steel pipe, especially steel pipe imported from the Orient, well, you need to survey that pipe before the pipe is loaded onto the ship. At which point you take possession of the pipe. FOB ship's rails."

"FOB. Got it."

"FOB. That's correct, Your Honor. Because at that point, what you need to do is, you want to ensure that the pipe's shaft isn't bent. You need to ensure you have a straight shaft."

"I take it you don't want a bent shaft, counselor?"

"That's correct, Your Honor. And to make sure you don't have a bent shaft, what you need to do is, you need to slide a pig through that pipe prior to delivery. To ensure that the pig doesn't drift."

"So you don't want a drifting pig either, Mr. Lomax?" the judge said.

"No, Your Honor, you do not want a drifting pig."

"No bent shaft and no drifting pig. OK, I get it."

"Because if you have a pig that drifts, well, that pipe is not suitable for its end use."

"Which is what, Mr. Lomax?"

"Fracking."

Lomax continued.

"Your Honor, now, if that pig does not drift, and that shaft is bent, then the pipe lacks the requisite tolerances for the energy industry. And the energy industry, as you are aware, Your Honor, is all about tolerances."

"Thank you, Mr. Beasley," the judge said.

"Lomax, Your Honor."

"Of course."

The judge resumed scribbling with his looping hand.

"I'm Beasley," defense counsel informed the judge.

"Of course you are too," the judge said, still focused on his scribbling.

There was another long pause as the judge pondered next steps. He slapped his bench.

"Now counsel, I'm not going to allow this matter to go to trial. No reason to. If we put our minds to it, I think we can settle this case today. What do you say?"

"Your Honor, the Oriental defendants will sit on any settlement recommendation you make," Lomax insisted.

The judge rubbed his beard and Lomax and Beasley tapped themselves, the latter his Rolex, the former his skull. Or was it the other way around? I couldn't tell anymore. Bomax and Leasley. The Lorax and Mr. Bigglesworth. Their lower torsos stretched beneath the tables and fused. Soon they would exit the courtroom atop one pair of legs, arguing with the court and themselves and talking to clients on individual mobile phones, walking as one but facing and snapping in opposite directions.

Outside, ten stories below, a Chinese man hoisted a red Chinese flag up a length of pole atop a Chinatown tenement. I checked my phone. Nothing from Fleeger. I remembered to panic.

"Collectively, counselors, you are going to spend two hundred grand to try this case," the judge said. I half-expected him to lean back in that chair and for his clerk to insert a saliva ejector into his mouth. "And then there will be appeals, and then this painfully simple matter will drag on for years. So, I'm going to put this pipe case out of its misery today. The parties will settle this matter for $450,000. Given the reports, and the clear damage to the pipe, and the cost of litigation, I think that's a fair sum. What do you say?"

The judge knitted his hands behind his head. His eyelids fluttered.

"Mr. Beasley, will your client agree to settle for that amount?"

"I will communicate your recommendation to my client, Your Honor."

"And what if they don't accept your recommendation, Your Honor?" Lomax asked the judge. "Then what? What then?"

"Then I want you to fuck him, Mr. Lomax," the judge replied. "Any way you can."

The judge knocked his gavel against the bench and resumed writing with his looping hand as the counselors rose from their tables, packed their litigation bags, and stretched their lower backs. Celeste entered the courtroom, palm against the big wooden door to keep it quiet. I didn't know she would be here. Did Robert tell me she would be here? Did she tell me she would be here? My volcano resumed spewing muddy lava as I recalled last night. Potato skins. Horse. Merlot. I capped the dread with a cone. Unsure of what I knew or what I forgot. Because there was no time for it. I checked my phone again. Still no message from Robert. I texted him again. "Celeste is here." If the response was not immediate then the response was not forthcoming.

Celeste gave the judge a little wave and he sat up and smiled at her and then she rolled her eyes at me either because of last night's festivities or today's hangover and looked around and mouthed: "Where's Robert?"

She wore a different black dress than yesterday but the same quatrefoil. I motioned there was space next to me for her to sit. She ignored my gesture and took a seat two pews ahead. This was a power play, I thought, somewhat juvenile under the circumstances. Now she and I were playing a game as well. She removed a file from her bag and reviewed its contents while crisscrossing her legs, considerably thicker in today's shorter dress. A plump drop of sweat detached from my left armpit and splattered against my ribs. The judge exited the courtroom and his clerk descended the bench, spoke to Celeste. The two looked in my direction, Celeste pointed, and the clerk approached, now standing above me.

"Are you from Kilgore?" he asked.

I told him yes.

"We're beginning."

"OK."

"The judge wants to discuss this matter in chambers."

I hoisted my swish bag over my shoulder and followed the clerk up a small flight of stairs. My insides buzzed with fear at the thought of falling apart in McKenzie's chambers. Celeste preceded me up the stairs. I wanted to bite the back of her thighs.

"Stephen, where is Robert?"

"We got it covered."

"Oh dear, this is a catastrophe. Stephen, should I call him? Or did you call him? Do you think we should proceed? What do you think, Stephen? Can you handle this alone?"

"I think I got it."

"You think you got it?"

We passed behind the judge's bench and I surveyed his looping notes. A massive, intricate doodle of squares and circles stretching almost from wall to wall.

"Yup."

7

PLUSH AND WAINSCOTED, THE judge's chambers reinforced the popular perception that the law was noble and dignified. Clerks and secretaries engaged in focused, diligent effort assembling rulings and proposed orders from Redwelds, the Redwelds stocked with tidy folders, the tidy folders flagged with 3M color tabs. It's not what the words say, they taught us in law school, it's what they do. Single roses, framed photographs of bald eagles in flight, Vaseline Intensive Care, tiny firkins of mint-green Listerine. Skin care and oral hygiene the basis for a CVS or Duane Reade on every corner of the city. Metropolis of halitosis and dry skin. We followed the clerk across the embossed emerald carpet: Lazlis, followed by Celeste, then me. Add a platter of tuna fish sandwiches and small bottles of Canada Dry and old men in white towels watching golf on a flat screen and you'd have a country club clubhouse. Whatever you do, be first class.

I followed the clerk and Celeste into the jury room, where Thomas sat alone behind the large wooden conference table, picking at a callous on his hands. My slop tanks churned and bubbled but the contents remained under pressure beneath an innocuous blanket of inert gas, staunch and firm against self-sabotage. A task made more difficult, but not impossible, by the residue of last night's alcohol still percolating through my system.

I studied Thomas. Platinum-blue eyes and a round face, like that new moon emoji, but the gay biker version with a walrussy handlebar mustache. Bolero-cut Carhartt, work jeans, strong hands webbed with capillaries. I couldn't discern how he had entered McKenzie's chambers without me spotting him in the courtroom.

"Still no Robert?" Lazlis asked.

"Food poisoning," I lied, shaking the phone.

Thomas pointed his thumbnail at Lazlis. It was blackened.

"Hazards of the honey-do list," he said. He rolled his head backward, looked up at the ceiling, and returned to the horizontal cervical plane. Up and down. He did this again and again. Soft pack of Marlboros stuffed inside the workman jacket's breast pocket. Haboobs and rotating helicopter blades had embedded his skin with sand and dust, giving him a grainy, orange complexion.

"I see," Lazlis replied.

"But she said she'd leave if I didn't start acting like a man. Taking care of my husbandly responsibilities."

"I understand," Lazlis added. Failing to endeavor interest in what his client had to say as he unpacked his litigation bag.

"She said there was no point living with a man if she didn't get anything out of it. So then I did this."

He pointed at his blackened thumbnail, at rest on the table, as if it was an inanimate object. Something found in the woods. A rural Pennsylvania scarab.

"Did what?" Lazlis asked.

"Smacked it with a hammer."

"Ouch," Lazlis replied. "On purpose?"

"Why else?"

Thomas did it again, this neck roll, as if to crack his cervical spine and relieve some internal pressure where his head fastened to his body. I remembered another former word of the day: withers. The highest part of a horse's back, behind the neck.

"Of course," his lawyer replied.

"But she wanted the photos hung on the wall and it just had to be done yesterday. I tried to tell her."

"Tell her what?" Lazlis asked.

"That I can't hit a nail straight anymore. Not with these shaky hands."

He raised his hands for Lazlis to observe their instability. The frequency of the shakiness was too high; it seemed like an act. Lazlis nodded that he understood and Thomas resumed rolling his head, like an insatiable birdie, rocking back and forth. Celeste indicated that she wanted to talk and I followed her to an opposite corner of the room.

"Why does he keep doing that thing with his head?"

"Looks like some kind of tic," I replied.

"It's bloody distracting."

"Maybe that's the point."

"Maybe."

She huffed her annoyance and we took our seats across the broad wooden table from Lazlis and Thomas and I removed my notes and memoranda from the bag at my feet. I didn't know what I would say. Yet I was uncommonly calm. As if the anticipation of the event was more fraught with peril than the event itself and now that I was at the point of commencement I could feel it, this event but also myself: competent but also present, almost monolithic. Through the nylon of Celeste's dusky stockings the veins in her left thigh outlined a constellation. Of Paul Bunyan, with an axe over his shoulder and his loyal Ox at his side.

"Ah yes," the judge said again upon entering the room, robe now unbuttoned down the front to reveal a yellow dress shirt and red tie, his dutiful clerk in tow. "Another disability claim by another wounded American hero. Clearly outside the scope of my original jurisdiction per Article 3 of the US Constitution. But I digress. Celeste, it is so good to see you."

He patted the table where he could almost reach her hand.

"Good to see you too, Judge," she said.

"How's that rich husband of yours? Still flying around the world making gobs of money?"

My instincts were correct, my mental chart from the night before accurate.

"He's good. Thank you."

The judge growled. A meow growl. Like a tiger cub. We all looked at one another, to confirm that we correctly heard that, except for Thomas, who was again looking at the ceiling.

"Now guys," the judge said. "Talk to me on a first-name basis. Mr. Thomas?"

"Yes, sir."

"Pleasure to meet you."

"Pleasure to meet you too, sir."

"I understand you were involved in an incident downstairs with the marshals."

"I wouldn't call it an incident, Your Honor," Lazlis added. "It was more of a misunderstanding."

"Well, counselor, it was enough of a misunderstanding that the marshals felt compelled to escort your client up here through the prisoners' elevator. That doesn't happen every day. Not in civil matters. Criminal matters, of course, they use the elevator all the time. It's a fact. But another fact is that I just want you and your client to know that the marshals are right on the other side of that door." The judge pointed at the door and looked at Thomas. "Do you understand?"

"Yes, sir," Thomas replied.

"Good. And now I'm sure you also understand why I can't allow you to carry your knife into my chambers. Not that I have anything against you. Or your knife, for that matter. After all, you're an American hero. But I've got people here I'm responsible for. Good people. And it's protocol. And if there is one thing we enforce around here these days it's protocol. I'm sure you understand protocol, correct?"

"Yes, sir," Thomas said. His tic, for the moment, had ceased. Celeste sipped from her to-go cup, the little mantra dangling from the string of her yogi teabag imploring us to live for one another. The judge surveyed the room.

"Where's Mr. Fleeger? Isn't he counsel of record for WorldScore?"

Everyone looked at me.

"He's ill," I said.

"And you are?"

"Stephen Harker, Your Honor."

"Also from Killmore?"

The judge winked.

"Kilgore, Your Honor. And yes."

"Just fucking with you, buddy," the judge said.

Lazlis laughed out loud. For a moment I thought he would give the judge a high five. Celeste studied me, lips pinched in pensive observation.

"And you, Mr. Lazlis, any objection to proceeding without counsel of record present?"

"No, Your Honor. I have no objection to proceeding without counsel of record present." Lazlis said, shaking his head, struggling to contain another laugh.

Thomas leaned in his chair toward Lazlis and whispered.

"Your Honor, my client has a request."

"Which is?"

"The jalousies, Your Honor."

"What about them?"

"The sunlight is bothering my client's eyes." The sky outside was slate gray, all direct light absorbed and softened by late-winter cloud cover. On the other side of which the sun now revved its internal juices to launch a galactic wad of radiation at planet Earth. "Mr. Thomas would like the jalousies adjusted."

"Adjust the jalousies?" the judge asked.

"If possible, Your Honor," Lazlis replied.

"Well, OK."

The judge motioned for the clerk to adjust the jalousies, thereby darkening the room with shadow. Thomas was doing this on purpose, I thought, to plumb the depths of our accommodation while exerting influence within the group.

"Let's get started," the judge said. "Mr. Lazlis, how about you first?"

"Your Honor, I represent Major Mike Thomas, the individual sitting here to my right."

"Air Force service number six seven six eight three four four. Now WorldScore claim number fifteen slash one two two seven eight six nine."

"Thank you, Mr. Thomas," the judge said. "Very helpful. Did you get that down?" the judge asked the clerk.

The clerk nodded and Lazlis continued.

"Now as you will have seen in my submission, Your Honor, Mr. Thomas has served this country faithfully, first in the Air Force and then after 9/11 as a military pilot in and out of Iraq and Afghanistan. After faithfully serving this country, my client accepted an offer of employment from a private company called FreedomQuest, which company entered contracts with the US Department of Defense, pursuant to which Mr. Thomas provided the US government with vital military support functions in and around Kabul. I don't want to get too involved in the details right now, Your Honor, but essentially we're here today to move the court to order FreedomQuest's workers' compensation carrier, WorldScore, to pay Thomas the statutorily prescribed compensation benefits to which he is entitled on account of the injuries he suffered in Kabul. Now as you are likely aware, Your Honor, federal law mandates WorldScore to maintain Mr. Thomas's living standards and to treat his injuries while we litigate their permanence and loss of use. However, WorldScore has not made a benefits payment to my client, nor authorized a doctor's visit, as required under federal law, for over a year. To be frank, he's in a tough spot, and the tougher that spot gets, the more I feel he's being pushed into a corner to accept less than he is entitled to under federal law."

"What are we talking about here?" the judge asked me. "Maintenance and cure? Is that what your client allegedly owes this man?"

"Similar, Your Honor," I said. "Though those are maritime law terms that apply to seafarers. Thomas, under the law, is more akin to an injured longshoreman."

Lazlis tapped his fingers on the table. Thomas resumed his tic. Celeste cooled her tea with a tiny glistening mouth. I continued.

"This is essentially a federal workers' compensation matter that should be resolved administratively by the Department of Labor under federal statutes. Which shield companies such as FreedomQuest from facing tort litigation in federal and state court for injuries that their employees allegedly suffer working overseas in war zones."

"But he's a soldier," the judge said.

"He was. But then he became an employee with a private company."

"Didn't you hear the man?" The judge pointed at Lazlis.

"Your Honor, he may have been a soldier," I replied.

"Once a soldier always a soldier."

"Yes, Your Honor, that is true, perhaps. But the capacity in which he is suing FreedomQuest and their insurer WorldScore is as a private employee claiming certain benefits pursuant to a private employment contract."

"Well, then he's an employee and a soldier." The judge looked at Thomas. "Did you carry a firearm, sir, while deployed to Afghanistan?"

"Affirmative."

"Did you discharge that firearm at the enemy?"

"Affirmative."

"Did you take incoming fire from the enemy?"

"Affirmative."

"And what are you doing now for work?"

"I can't do much because of all the pain. But I occasionally pick up odd jobs."

"What kind of odd jobs?" I asked.

"What do you mean?" Lazlis interjected.

I continued. Feeling in stride.

"Mr. Thomas. Do you pick up odd jobs like construction, or landscaping? Odd jobs that require physical labor? Or do you pick up odd jobs like working in a store or an office?"

"Just odd jobs."

"Yes, but what kind of odd jobs?"

Thomas stared at me while resuming his tic, conveying a silent threat.

"That's enough, Mr. Harker," the judge said. "You're badgering him, and badgering this man is not something I'll permit in my chambers. He was deployed overseas. Now he's doing odd jobs to stay afloat."

"Your Honor, respectfully, I disagree with the use of the word 'deployed.' He was not 'deployed.' He was 'employed.' And there are a great number of individuals who carry firearms as part of their employment who are not soldiers. Just as there are private security guards who carry firearms who are not police officers."

"You have a point there," the judge said. "Mr. Lazlis, anything to add?"

"Your Honor, respectfully, these are the types of details I cautioned in my motion against paying too close attention to today, as the details surrounding Mr. Thomas's multiple injuries are too voluminous to resolve at one hearing. We are simply here today to move the court to order WorldScore to pay Mr. Thomas two-thirds of his salary now and to authorize treatment of his injuries as we litigate the permanence of those injuries and the scope of loss of use of his extremities."

"Your Honor," I interjected. "Just as the law arguably mandates WorldScore to perform certain functions with respect to payment and benefits, it also requires Mr. Thomas to comply with various administrative processes. There is a system, Your Honor, designed to prevent chaos and protect WorldScore from being forced to ladle out cash to every individual who alleges injuries from working overseas as a US military contractor. There are forms and there is procedure. There is reporting and there is substantiation. And from what I have seen Mr. Thomas, and Mr. Lazlis, have simply discarded this process while essentially threatening . . ." I caught myself from falling backward into the burning cauldron of magma at the center of the earth. "Pay up or something bad will happen. It's blackmail."

"Sounds like blackmail to me," the judge said. "Anything to add Mr. Lazlis?"

Thomas stared at me. Burning with rage or impotence, hard to know which, gelding or bull. That tic had stopped, we'd put an end to that for now, his small platinum-blue eyes expressionless but observant as the gears in his head that prevented him from striking the nail to hang that which just had to be hung began to turn. I could hear them. Big Mike will strike at twelve. Lazlis spun his college ring. The soft bits of Thomas's labor-thickened hands crimsoned, soon to start popping off fingers.

"Your Honor, my client was Special Forces. He fought for this country and he fought for our freedom. And now WorldScore would rather see him starve, lose his home, and not treat his injuries than provide him the benefits to which he is entitled. So that WorldScore can pocket the premium they collected from FreedomQuest and keep it rolling in the money markets."

I could see where we were going. All of us now crammed together inside the whiskey barrel, Lazlis leading us over the falls, plunging into patriotism.

"Nothing about Mr. Harker or Ms. Powers even remotely compares to what my client has sacrificed for this country. And I will not permit them to make him suffer anymore."

Splash.

Thomas resumed his psyops tic. I felt hollow, quick, like a corked bat. Ready to whack them both. The judge's magnified eyes tracked the volley.

"Federal law shifts the burden from employee to employer in these cases," Lazlis replied.

"You haven't proved a prima facie case," I replied.

"You're forcing my client to carry all the burden."

"You haven't proved a prima facie anything."

"I beseech Mr. Harker to rebut the presumption that my client's injuries resulted from anything other than his employment in Afghanistan with FreedomQuest."

"Enough, Mr. Lazlis," the judge said. "We get it."

"And for that FreedomQuest needs to establish an intervening cause. Which it can't do."

"Enough, Jim," the judge bellowed.

Thomas stopped midtic. Outside, fingers ceased striking keyboards and someone closed a window. The claylike mask of concern that sealed Celeste's face the moment she spotted me today alone in the courthouse without Fleeger had softened. She seemed almost pleased.

"Your Honor, please excuse my zealous advocacy on behalf of my client but I have hundreds of these cases and this is the first time WorldScore has simply refused to pay anything at all while we litigated the scope of injuries. It's very frustrating. Very frustrating. And I have good reason to suspect there may be some conspiracy to make an example of Mr. Thomas."

"Come on now, Jim," Celeste said. "There's no conspiracy. It's all in your head."

"Excuse me, Celeste, are you an officer of the court? Are you? I didn't think so. So then why are you talking?"

I stepped in.

"File the proper forms, follow correct administrative protocol, provide us with proof that your client can't work—something other than Dr. Spectrum's VA report—and we'll contemplate making modest payments to Mr. Thomas while we litigate the permanence and scope of your client's alleged injuries."

"Sounds reasonable to me, Mr. Harker," the judge said. "Sound reasonable to you, Mr. Lazlis?"

"I need a solid guarantee that Mr. Thomas will receive bimonthly compensation payments now to keep him and his family afloat while the litigation proceeds."

"What do you say?" the judge asked me.

"Agreed. But in exchange we want to depose Mr. Thomas as soon as possible."

"Deal?" the judge asked Lazlis.

"Deal," Lazlis replied.

The judge shot up from his chair, almost free to do something else.

"You two are big boys. Work it out. Exchange your discovery now. Start producing documents. Mr. Harker, I'm sure you'll want to see some medical records. Then you can depose Mr. Thomas. And then I want you to settle this case and get it off my goddamn docket. It's a waste of fucking time. Make it go away. So both Mr. Thomas and I can get back to living. Sound good to you?"

"Yes, sir," Thomas replied.

The judge winked at Thomas, kissed Celeste on the cheek, and departed with a flurry of black robes and irascible impatience, his dutiful clerk holding the door for him.

"Please keep your word," Lazlis said to both me and Celeste. He sounded earnest.

"We always keep our word, Jim," she said. We packed our bags and slung them over our shoulders. "You don't need to worry about that."

I passed behind Thomas, half expecting to discover his spine protruding from the base of his skull. He leaned forward, as if submitting himself to his executioner. There it was, the source of his discomfort. The knob of a flaming red furuncle pinpricked with pus and irritated by the stiff denim collar of his bolero-cut Carhartt.

Hand-rolled cigarette number one. I deserved it, the way most lawyers think they deserve a jolt of vice after appearing in court. Federal police officers in midnight-blue uniforms foot-patrolled the courthouse grounds, hips weighed down by tactical gear, and I inserted my face inside the hand cave to light the cigarette. The sky, the hardscaping, and the courthouse facade formed an arena of granite. Celeste descended the stairs behind me, moving like a spider atop black heels with red soles. After mating, the female eats the male.

"Not bad, counselor. I'm almost impressed. Not that there's any excuse for Robert standing me up, but it wasn't the catastrophe I feared it would be."

I nodded in feigned agreement, releasing twice the smoke I inhaled.

"You know what the play is now, right?" she asked.

"Pay him nothing?"

"No, not pay him nothing." I thought she would play slap me. "We just won't authorize payment anytime soon. Or at least not until Lazlis starts producing documents responsive to our discovery demands. Make Lazlis start digging through Thomas's military and personnel files and soon he'll realize what he's up against. He probably has this case on contingency, so the more we make him work now on culling, studying, redacting, and producing discovery, the more we incentivize him to settle later for a fraction of the initial claim. WorldScore indefinitely delaying settlement while Kilgore works up the file is, for now, the same thing almost as not paying Thomas anything. Lazlis gets agitated, Lazlis fatigues, Lazlis communicates to Thomas what Thomas comes to understand is attainable. Which will be quite less than he thinks he deserves. Maybe a bit for the ankle and the back. Eventually. But absolutely nothing for the PTSD. We have to let it marinate for a while in Thomas's disappointment. Meanwhile, I'll send you some of the surveillance footage Honda recently shot of Thomas at home. There's no home run, but it's a start. Some stuff in there we can work with. But congratulations, Mr. Harker. You did a lot better in there today than I thought you would."

"Is that a compliment?" I asked.

"Yes, it's a compliment. And I almost never give compliments so you should be very pleased with yourself."

She shivered and adjusted her scarf.

"Can I ask you a question about Robert?"

I told her yes she could ask me a question about Robert.

"Is he divorced yet?"

"Separated."

"So he's not not here today because of some female drama, right?"

"I doubt it."

"Good."

"Why?"

"Because I need him to be unfettered."

"Trust me. He's unfettered."

"I don't believe you. And trust me, Stephen, I can tell when a man places a bit too much emphasis on attaining the brass ring he thinks he'll find between an attractive young woman's legs. He was practically a horny teenager on that phone of his last night."

I refrained from repeating the transparent lie that he was sick and she handed me her luxurious handbag adorned with leather swirls and tassels as she inserted her hands into black leather gloves that stretched beyond her wrists, covering her tiny, expensive quatrefoil. Man-child Christ of Byzantium with his gilded halo gazed up at me from the marked pages of the leather-bound book she carried in the bottom of her bag.

"Last night he told me you're his best friend."

66

I feigned disbelief.

"He did. He said you were like a brother to him."

I felt embarrassed. Couldn't hide it. She looked at my feet.

"Bold footwear Mr. Harker. I didn't peg you for such a fashionista."

I hated that word. Refrained from telling her so. Between her Birkin bag and my Hogans we probably appeared to Thomas like domestic enemies. To be punished by summary execution.

"You don't like speaking with me, do you Stephen?"

"I have a deep-seated fear of professionally competent English women."

She laughed.

"You don't find me irresistibly charming?" She displayed herself with her black leather hands. Now more comfortable with me, almost candid, and I, in turn, reciprocated. I eased up. Felt the pleasure of doing so.

"Look, Stephen. I really need Robert dialed in here on this case. I'm not saying you didn't do a good job in there. You did. But I need Robert to step up his game."

I reminded my ego that my existence on this planet did not depend on successfully litigating federal workers' compensation claims against former military contractors on behalf of WorldScore.

"There are cases that no one above me in the food chain cares about. Which is almost all of them. But then there is the occasional case that becomes very important to some very important people, individuals who usually don't bother to care much about the day-to-day doings of the lilliputian handling the litigations."

"Until they do."

"Correct. And now they do. And now I've been tasked with fighting this one. And in doing so I've gone way out on a limb to recommend Robert take the lead. But now it's my judgment on the line as well. In addition to his."

I told her I understood.

"Do you really, Stephen? Because I have a hard time believing you can understand what I'm about to tell you because I haven't really discussed it with anyone outside of WorldScore."

"They're worried about opening the floodgates."

"Yes, they're worried about opening the proverbial floodgates. They're always worried about opening the proverbial floodgates. But the thing with insurance is there is always going to be some loss anyway. Claims will arise that eventually you have to pay, despite how distasteful it may be to do so. But the debate now is: How does WorldScore allocate that risk. Risk being loss. And you guys need to understand that there is a system-wide refactoring in the works. We are refactoring here, Stephen. We are thinking outside the box. And we want to own this space. We want to insure with the same élan as, say, Google. Or Microsoft."

I restrained myself from mocking her use of the words élan and insurance in the same sentence.

"Refactoring triggers a whole bunch of things at the same time. Creativity. Innovation. Disruption. But this is the type of case that throws off all our plans and corporate strategies in which WorldScore has invested millions. Because the problem with insuring people is that you're insuring people. It's not just about these private soldiers returning home claiming injuries we can't disprove. It's also about costs. And let's just say there are gathering forces who strongly believe we should axiomatically pay these claims on most advantageous terms to the company. Let Thomas submit his claims online and then promptly send him his payment, but on the condition he waives his rights to litigate and accepts less than what he's owed. And thus the company would save on both ends. By paying Thomas less."

"And by not paying lawyers."

"Precisely. Automation is coming, Stephen, even for the lawyers. Algorithms designed by code writers in the basement who lack the same appetites for scotch and soda as you and Robert."

"And you would rather fight?"

"Yes I would rather fight. Which is why you are here and Robert is supposed to be here as well. Because I've sided with fighting for what is right so as not to reward bad behavior as opposed to mitigating what is wrong in exchange for a profit. Jesus, not everything can be automated on this planet. Which means I've sided with the humans over the botnets, or whatever the fuck they're called, being designed to do your job."

Behind Celeste, at the base of the federal prison across from the courthouse, a mother and daughter, virile women, Redstaters, stood clutching strings of helium-inflated Mylar balloons rotating Happy Birthday. Four stories above the street a figure appeared in the thick plastic slit of an opaque, chicken-wired prison window. The mother and daughter released the balloons and the balloons floated upward, twisting silver and ribbon, lighter than air and reflective, away, now toward, now closer, now before the figure in the window, the shadow of a head watching them float upward and beyond, toward the court-house, now across the prison roof, still bolted with cables to prevent another brazen escape attempt via helicopter.

"Stephen?" Celeste asked.

"Yes."

"Where did you go?"

"What do you mean?"

"You just disappeared for a second. What did I just say?"

"Let's pinch Thomas a bit. To see if he pops."

"I don't know why but this one so rubs me the wrong way."

"And you don't like that?"

"I don't like being rubbed the wrong way at all."

The daughter collapsed to the hard, cold ground and the mother struggled to pick her up. Celeste dialed her town car.

"Oh dear," Celeste said, watching the women try to regain their composure, phone held to her ear. "The heart is such a delicate mus-cle."

"How so?"

"Because it's capable of being shattered by other people's poor decisions."

A black Lincoln town car braked behind her. She kissed my cheek and the driver opened the car door and closed it behind her and I walked south toward the office. My pocket buzzed with the impa-tience of a breaking story. Multicolored Snowfall in Siberia after Downed Satellite Ignites Drought-Stricken Boreal Forest. Twelve words unlikely to have ever before been assembled in a sentence, let alone a Reuters headline digitally pushed to an iPhone.

Way up ahead, across the expanse of the granite arena, Thomas and Lazlis walked toward lower Broadway, Lazlis lugging a beaten burgundy litigation bag and Thomas relying on a four-pointed cane, an orthopedic brace fastened around his lumbar sacrum. As if one misstep could cause his entire musculoskeletal system to crumble. A beetle on its back. Behind them crept Honda, between shrubbery and streetlights, hidden by statue, geometry, poles, clicking his long telephoto lens, symmetrical patches of gray-white hair, checking the shot on the screen, switching in lenses from the pockets of his tactical vest, getting his man. Thomas turned and stared in Honda's direction, all intuition and reflex, and pointed at Honda for Lazlis to see, who pivoted his client again toward Broadway by the forearm. Lazlis didn't want to hear it. As they continued walking Thomas strapped a respiratory mask to his face and over the top of his large white and brown head, small white filters, pupalike, now pulsing with his every inhalation of the city's hostile air. A cold light rain commenced, tessellating the sidewalks and releasing the scent of spent petroleum imbedded in the macadam.

8

WHEEZING A BIT LIKE old klezmer on vinyl, I entered the office building, told myself I needed to stop smoking, take up jogging, good for replenishing cells and reversing permanent lung damage. Pharmaceutical sales reps in matching purple golf shirts—Team Paxil—shouted at one another as they exited the elevator bank, one of them now making a suck dick motion to the former NYPD security guard with busted knees who told them to keep it down.

"Hurry up, G."

"Yeah, G. Come on, hurry up."

They brushed past me on their way outside, disappearing into upturned collars, millennial anthropophagi safe from drizzle and doing little dances on the sidewalk. The elevator doors closed. Money Man on the building's internal miniscreen recommending diversification into gold, silver, pla-ti-num, mag-knee-ze-um. Also doing a little dance. Yesterday everyone was clever. Today everyone was doing a little dance.

"The key to sexcess," Money Man proselytized, clanging a bronze bell knotted around the neck of a golden calf. "Is a high-return approach to private equity secondaries."

I entered my office knowing where everything belonged. On the floor. Draped over the back of a chair. Chucked on the windowsill. My computer inbox pinged with fresh emails. A selection of photos of celebrity wardrobe malfunctions. NSFW, yes, but this is Kilgore, so here we have it. Brown and pink areolas in sheer dresses atop red carpets. Miley Cyrus. Halle Berry. Mila Kunis. I flipped papers stacked on my desk, searching for the hatchway to focus, my attention snagged by shocking discoveries for joint relief, how the brain is hardwired to learn a language in ten days, knowing that if I didn't start at it early, knowing that if I expended too much adrenalin in court, it wouldn't happen for the rest of the day. The back of my mouth thirsted for beer.

Papers fell to the floor beyond my reach. I reaccessed the Internet. Kilgorellp.com. No one looks like this anymore, except for maybe Fleeger. Attika with a spazzy, enthusiastic telephone-chord weave. Me with a cheeky smile and fuller hair. Professional portrait photos taken when the lawyers were younger, ambitious, full of promise. Before they metamorphosed with age into exceptional billers by the hour. Steeped in alcohol, mayonnaise, ham, nondairy creamer, tuna fish, spray tan, rugelach, from young and taut, high cheek boned and lean into fermented and soft or gristled and mean, with indelible circles around the eyes, thirty-plus pounds, a few extra chins, and a couple hundred thousand dollars deposited into the annuities of contentment. I commenced typing a memo to file 444-15 RF/SH: In re court conference in re Thomas. Scribbled on the timesheet 3.1 hours: attend conference before J. McKenzie; preparation re same. Debated whether 3.1 was too much. Celeste was there. She would know. I dropped it to a 2.4. Fuck it. Bumped it up to a 3.5. I returned to the empty screen of a Word document and filled it with words spelling out where we went from here, recommending a modicum of payment to Thomas now to keep him from shooting up a kindergarten.

Lawyering, good lawyering, demanded a specific hubris borne of energy and focus. It required you to take yourself seriously. It required you to take your arguments and your invoices and your memoranda of law as seriously as you took yourself. And it required you to take yourself as a lawyer lawyering seriously. That was the difference between good lawyers and the rest of them. And because you took it seriously you pumped it with urgency and vitality, with a depthless self-respect for the profession because the profession is, was, you. Countless hours contemplating, arguing, strategizing, and writing—writing above all else—facts and arguments that shall be, at their very core, relevant.

I, instead, focused on what was irrelevant. The geography of the claim. The progeny of the pharmaceuticals. Google Earth images of where the incident occurred. The etymology of strange new nouns contained in new files. I didn't care about duty and breach of duty and causation and damages and severing same from false allegations in an effort to successfully refute the client's liability. I didn't care about the end goal. I cared about what was interesting. Pustules and military helicopters and the Mahdi Army. As a lawyer I was addicted to distraction. If there was something to distract me from lawyering I embraced it. And then faked the rest.

"We now write to advise you of today's developments before Judge McKenzie and to provide our thoughts and analysis re future handling."

My will crumbled. I relogged on to the Internet. Anthropocene man scratching his digital itch with digital clicks. I needed more eyes. A ring of eyes and two more arms to keep up with the breaking news. Vishnu of digititus. I peeled myself from the computer screen. My corneas felt sticky. I stared into the nothingness of the popcorn ceiling. Outside my office porcelain fingernails—Tic Tac orange, Tic Tac cherry—clicked against the secretary's plastic keyboard.

"Hi, Stephen," Attika said, standing in my office door. Silver pencil skirt and black heels and that conspicuous Jamal.

"You OK?"

I told her I was fine.

"I saw a TED lecture by this gastroenterologist who explained what acid reflux does to your esophagus. Totally gross. I'll send you the link."

"You're too kind."

"Oh, do you feel bad again today?" She smiled. "Don't be a jerk, Stephen."

"Why not?"

"Because it doesn't suit you."

I shoehorned myself into productivity and spent the next three hours typing discovery demands for Fleeger's review and comment prior to transmittal to Lazlis, demanding a complete copy of Thomas's medical and military records. HIPAA authorizations. The names and addresses of all doctors seen and a list of all medications prescribed in the past ten years. Any and all court orders regarding custody, mortgage, marriage, liens, debt. Any and all documents and communications pertaining to Thomas's employment with and discharge from FreedomQuest. Any and all documents, information, records, notes, etc. etc. etc. relevant to impeach the man's credibility and tarnish his brass.

The briny urinals and mouthwash-stained sinks of a law firm bathroom. I splashed cold water on my face and finger-combed my thinning hair in the wall-length mirror.

"Harker. Don't flip out. I recognize you by your gay Euro shoes."

I faced the stalls. Fleeger's eye watched me through the crack of the metal doorframe.

"Where were you this morning?" I asked.

"Throw me a paper towel will you? So I don't have to waddle out of here like a duck with my pants around my ankles. I don't want to give Whitey any more nightmares."

I lobbed one over the stall door, incredulous that I had just done so. It landed in his hands with a little wet smack.

"Fire in the hole," he shouted as he exited the stall in sync with the rushing toilet. Because all that Ivy League rowing made him a whore when it came to scat as well. He watched himself in the long bathroom mirror unclasp mother of pearl cufflinks.

"How'd it go before the judge?"

He knew it went fine. Had it not he would have already let me know he knew it hadn't.

"OK," I said.

"That weird smell happen when you get nervous?"

"What weird smell?"

"You emit this odor when you're stressed. You're like a skunk."

I told him he was an asshole.

"What did you learn about Thomas?"

"That he's sensitive to light."

"Handy."

"He's got a boil on his neck."

"So he's stressed. Also handy."

"He calls himself the Ice Bear."

"What does that mean?"

"No idea. But according to Lazlis, the Ice Bear cometh."

"Just never let Lazlis get you on the ropes. Otherwise he'll pummel you." He jabbed me inside and his knuckles nicked my ribs. I grimaced, struggled to push him back. His shoulders were twice the size of my palms. He still hadn't washed his hands. "Best to avoid him with quick movements."

Again I struggled to shove him.

"Jesus, Robert," I said.

"Jesus Cristo, Roberto," he repeated, like a gay *Boriqua*, swinging his palms. "Jew listen here you *maricón*." He unclasped the second cufflink in the mirror.

"Where were you this morning?" I asked.

"Don't worry about where I was."

"Celeste was there."

"I know Celeste was there." He feigned a frown of concern. "World-Score's naming me to their Risk Rewards panel this year. And I'm chief presenter at their annual Litigating Disability Insurance Claims conference. Again. This time in Atlanta. Which turns me on just thinking about it. So you really think they're going to punish me because I sent a seventh-year associate to handle a court conference with Lazlis?"

"Did you know he filed a motion to compel us to pay?"

"Yup. You would have too if you filed a notice of appearance."

"You never told me to."

"Jesus, Harker, can you do anything on your own?"

75

I stared at him in the mirror. He pivoted and faced me. We were now in Fleeger world. A universe wherein he was incapable of comprehending the legitimacy of another person's concerns. It was coming on.

"Look, Stephen. Kilgore doesn't suffer pussies. *Repetamente.*"

I looked away.

"No no no, Stephen. You need to understand this. And I'm not letting you leave here until you say it."

He blocked the bathroom door.

"Say it."

That miasma reappeared, rendering his face opaque, almost melted. I could no longer see his face. To escape, I capitulated.

"Kilgore doesn't suffer pussies."

"Good boy. Now, if I had told you I wouldn't be in court this morning and that you would need to handle Thomas alone you would have curled up in a ball all night worrying and it would have been fucking terrible for you. Because you have a very special habit of making yourself miserable by tricking yourself into thinking you're having a nervous breakdown when in fact you are just fine. But by doing this thing to yourself you sabotage your ability to get the job done. Which, my man, by the way, you are fully capable of but for this nasty habit of convincing yourself you're about to have a panic attack whenever you're stressed, until it reaches a fevered pitch and then it pops and you move on and perform just as well as anyone else in your position. You also wouldn't have gone drinking last night, and that, *mi amigo*, was much more important for your professional development than anything that transpired today in court. But by not telling you about the motion, I guaranteed your ability to handle it. I took yourself out of the equation. I risked catastrophe to do that for you. Now, stop expecting apologies about things that don't warrant them. It was a fucking motion. Don't guilt me about it. Besides, from what I heard you knocked it out of the park. Give yourself some fucking credit, man. God knows I do so all the time. You should try it too."

He reverted to himself, face no longer melted, but for his lips, which resembled two pieces of sashimi.

"You know WorldScore wants to start automating the claims?" I said.

"I do."

"And you're not concerned?"

"Look . . . Harker. Probably nine times out of ten, probably ninety-nine times out of a hundred, if you think you know something I don't, there is an incredibly strong possibility that you're wrong. Remember when the overpriced consultants WorldScore hired recommended scrapping the billable hour? That was five years ago and, well, here we are, still billing time. Which, by the way, you are wholly deficient on again this year. I looked at your time in accounting and you, my brother, are way behind all the other associates. You're already like three hundred hours behind Attika and we're not even halfway through the second quarter."

He handed me his phone and lathered his hands.

"I don't want this."

"Watch," he said. I tapped the screen. A video commenced of Tara bounce-dancing upside-down in black heels wearing only a peach thong, like the plump end of a balloon puppet. Fleeger hoisted his pants around his broad hips, tightened his belt, and re-docked the phone to his waist.

"One of life's greatest pleasures," Fleeger said.

"What's that?"

"Fucking younger women."

He rubbed his hands through his badger-brush hair.

"Who loves you?" he asked.

I didn't answer.

"Who loves you, man?"

"You do," I replied.

He placed his hands on the back of my head and pulled me forward and kissed my temple. This time I didn't feel repulsed. This time he felt like my brother.

"Celeste told me you handled yourself well today," he said, patting, squeezing, rubbing my shoulder. "That you were clear and organized and convincing and that you didn't give up anything you didn't need to and that we're moving forward according to the plan. That's how you make it happen, Stephen. All you have to do is make her think you share her concerns. Soothe her worried soul. Besides. We know what will happen. It's the same thing that always happens. We work up the file, bill the shit out of it, put the screws to Thomas, and settle south of WorldScore's pain threshold. It's fucking cake. So start typing up the discovery demands."

I told him I already did.

"Good boy. Just send them to Lazlis." No need for him to double-check them, he said. He was certain they were sufficient.

"We also got Thomas's deposition in a couple weeks."

"Have at it, *amigo*."

He opened the bathroom door.

"What are you doing after work?"

I hedged. Told him I had no plans. That maybe I would exercise. That I could use a quiet night.

"Bullshit. You popped a cherry and you didn't get creamed. Let's go to one of those trendy spots in the Village you like. Some hipster foodjouise place where the curry always destroys my intestines. We'll talk about Thomas over beers and bill it to WorldScore. In re office conference Major Bud Asshole."

Like a pre-regatta ritual, he slapped the metal doorframe as he exited the bathroom.

I dropped the discovery demands addressed to Lazlis in the mailroom's outbox, returned to my office, and watched the river traffic through the heavy German binoculars. The image was crisp and round. No ships. No seafarers. Only the ubiquitous Staten Island ferries, like bath toys for giant toddlers, a flotilla of anchored barges laden with fuel oil, and a yacht named *Sudden Impulse* motoring south atop the Hudson, flying the red and Union Jack ensign of Bermuda. I wanted to tell her owner this was redundant. That you can't possess a delayed impulse. Or a planned impulse. That an impulse was by its very nature sudden. Tightening my grip on the binoculars' leather strap, I surveyed the unlit windows of the prewar apartment building across the street, chipped facade and rusty fire escapes. Hoping to spot someone on a couch, having sex.

A clerk entered my office walking backward and pulling a silver cart. She was Spanish and smiled and wore a navy-blue Kilgore mailroom smock and said thank you and have a nice day all the time to everyone. I signed the delivery slip and she handed me a yellow interoffice folder stamped confidential. Unspooled its red string and extracted a cover note from Honda, also stamped confidential. A quarter-inch of surveillance reports and a compact disc. This would do for the day, I thought, spying on Thomas, legal voyeurism. The disc downloaded its digital contents to the server, safe and protected by the attorney/client privilege behind the Kilgore firewall.

"Keep it moving," Fleeger said as he hurried past my door, clutching a rolled paper baton and barking orders to other associates about other cases that needed attention. Attika behind him writing notes on a legal pad while taking long strides. The surveillance disc completed its download and I clicked play.

Mid-April. Midmorning. Thomas's home: split-level, rural-exurban, constructed of yellow bricks and white aluminum siding. Neon and black NO TRESPASSING signs stapled to the trunks of budding trees and an American flag javelined to a wrought-iron porch painted white to match the siding. Deer stand constructed two stories aboveground in a buttonwood tree that towers over the property. Honda swings the camera to a side window, setting Thomas fully in frame on the edge of a king-sized bed and bare chested, moisturizing a serrated scar across his right shoulder and scratching his shoulders, his hairy chest, his scalp with vigor until he stands in frustration and huffs from the window. Honda switches off the camera.

Late June. Midafternoon. Thomas in sunlight atop a Craftsman tractor mowing whorls of dirt and new grass the length of his multi-acre property. He pulls down tight a digital camouflage cap to shield his eyes from the dust. His chubby daughter, pink twelve-ounce cans for arms and a de-collared Misfits T-shirt, chases the tractor, out of control, swinging in pursuit of her smiling father. She stumbles in the tractor's wake, strikes the shabby yard hard, now a heap of hair, and Thomas dismounts the machine. Runs to comfort her like it's an emergency. It's no use. She turns from him and almost composes herself and stomps into the house, rigid, arms stiff at her side, no longer swinging at play. Opting to hide in her room and salve her pride with Glenn Danzig's mellifluous vocals.

A tallow-skinned methadone harridan steps onto the pressure-treated deck holding a cocktail glass, gin and tonic, vodka soda, with a lime, and closes the sliding screen door behind her with a finger. She lights a long white cigarette. There is no sound. She points and yells at Thomas. The camera bounces. The camera switches off.

Mid-September. Late afternoon. Thomas plants a four-pointed cane and stumbles from the door of a burnt sienna GMC Avalanche, picks himself up off the ground and hoists a thirty-pack of Budweiser cans from the truck bed, bumper festooned with American gun-owner defiance. DON'T TREAD ON ME. ΜΟΛΩΝ ΛΑΒΕ. TERRORIST HUNTING LICENSE DOI SEPTEMBER 11, 2001. Constantly hyped for war. Thomas enters the house via the open garage door, past the open hood of a vintage Ford, stumbling and swinging his cane and lugging his beer. Moments later, with heavy feet, he exits the rear of the house and descends from the pressure-treated deck onto his property without cane and gripping a Bud. At twilight the sky and the wooded horizon fuse. Red and black, shadows and blue. Thomas lowers himself onto a beach chair, inches above the ground, shakes free and lights a Marlboro, and watches the woods while smoking. The camera switches off.

Early December. Late afternoon. Brown and yellow leaves scatter beneath Honda as he walks through a forest of deciduous trees and approaches what at first appears to be an abandoned space colony. Heavy-duty tents connected by a corridor of plastic sheeting. White appliances stripped of their parts. Mounds of plastic tubes and rubber pipe jacketed with clasps. Fifty-five-gallon drums. A rusted COSCO shipping container with shiny padlock. Soggy fiberglass insulation. Fresh lumber. The fuselage of a single-prop airplane. Two cylindrical transformers that appeared stripped from utility poles and dangling heavy wires, deposited here at the end of heavy tire tracks. And a tarpaulin, beneath which Honda uncovers a gasoline-powered generator while filming. On the edge of all this there is a hillock of black soil, freshly dug, which Honda approaches, climbs, and from atop of which he films an empty open pit with no discernable purpose other than an illegal dump or mass grave.

I stood behind my desk staring at the computer screen, recognizing the failure-induced paranoia with which I was too familiar, from before my migration east to the city in search of more and finding less, but escaping the toxicity of blame and fear and the debilitating toll they exacted: lack of vigor, lack of affect, lack of effect. "Maintenance is preservation." Those were the words my father tacked above his workbench, where with persistent energy and focus he would spend his weekends and evenings refinishing and repairing the possessions of his home: household appliances, wooden bookshelves, automobile transmissions, rifles, especially rifles—"because there's God in a rifle"—handguns, remote control cars, power tools, coating them with paint or grease or lacquer or oil or WD-40, ball-peen hammering the dents, planing the splinters, tightening the bolts and screws, preserving that which must be maintained. Until the personal and financial losses set in around him, losses like white-tipped mountains that he couldn't pass, not even him, and then the stagnation, with its buildup of bile and decay and righteousness, from the inside out, followed by an all-consuming fear: of phantom enemies foreign and domestic, scapegoats, barcodes, black helicopters, the IRS, commodity markets, race wars, the future itself. "Bunch of niggers or Muslims shoot up someplace and *you* want to take *my* guns. I don't think so." As that which was unknown became that which was not to be trusted. And so the future belonged to the fearful and armed.

This case was different, I told myself, staring at Honda's menu of surveillance, and this was just the first course. Embers of empathy and disgust rose and glowed, brightening the higher they floated. As if the embers were liberated from the laws of physics to waft higher and higher into a starless black night. Swirling empathy and disgust for Thomas. For who he once was and what he allowed himself to become, white and sniveling. So quintessentially un-American. With my finger pistol, I took a shot at WorldScore One. At the gilded cherub atop the prewar high-rise of municipal government. At the computer screen. At the skyscrapers capped with industrial cubes of translucent light. Cubic zirconia of finance, their electric, rectangle moons illuminating the solitary tango of a tiny janitor twenty-five stories below, positioning his yellow teepee signs of *piso mojado* and pushing his four-wheeled bucket through the hardscaping of 1 Chase Plaza like a mop.

"It's as simple as this," Fleeger said, standing in my doorway, a hand on Whitey's shoulder. "Some of the partners are going to get what they want and be fine with it. And some partners are going to be upset and get over it. That's all there is to it."

"You're right, Robert," Whitey replied. "You're right."

Whitey entered Attika's office and closed the door behind him and Fleeger gestured for me to follow him to the conference room, held open the door for me to walk through, and took a seat at the conference table. I sat next to him. On the table before us a glossy photograph of Thomas dressed in Mossy Oak 3D camouflage and hunter-orange cap, platinum-blue eyes and a steady hand dialing the brass tang sight atop the barrel of a Kentucky rifle. I knew the gun. My father had one.

"Celeste, Stephen is here with me," Fleeger said, leaning into the three-pronged conference phone splayed on the large wooden table.

We exchanged hellos.

"So Celeste, what do you make of this surveillance footage Honda sent us today?" Fleeger asked. He looked at me. "Go," he mouthed.

"That we got him good?" Celeste asked.

"Almost," I said. "But not quite. I think we need to see more."

"Yes, but what about that thirty-pack of beer?" Celeste asked.

"That's what she said."

"Seriously, Robert."

"There's no wincing, no visible pain as he carries it, no limping," I said. "It partially refutes some of his allegations about his back and shoulder pain.

"But at the end of the day it's only a case of beer."

"Exactly," Robert said. "I'd like something more physical."

"I totally agree with you both. I'll have Honda keep at it."

"Celeste, don't give Lazlis anything for now," Robert added. "Let it ride for a bit. No reason to make any hasty decisions."

"I love it when you're engaged, Robert."

"I can't lie, Celeste. I am personally offended—personally chuffed—by this hairy asshole."

Fleeger held the photograph of Thomas the hunter.

"Yes, but what about today's agreement in court that we start paying Thomas some modicum of compensation now as we litigate the case?" Celeste asked.

"I haven't seen any order on the docket signed by the judge commanding payment. Have you seen a formal order, Stephen?"

"Nope."

"Me neither," Fleeger added. "We'll pay when we're ordered to, and right now there's no order. Maybe we'll get lucky and it will fall through McKenzie's giant crack. What are you doing tonight, Celeste?"

"Why?"

"I'm taking Stephen out for dinner. Want to join us?"

"Robert I don't think I can handle another one of your dinners anytime soon. But I appreciate the invitation. Next time, I promise. Anything else? Stephen?"

"I think we should undertake a fact-finding mission to Pennsylvania," I said.

"Why?" Robert asked. This confused him. He looked at me, displeased that I hadn't vetted this with him before making the suggestion.

"Lazlis today produced a mental health evaluation by a VA psychiatrist named Dr. Spectrum. In the report Dr. Spectrum notes that Thomas is subject to a family court order in Pennsylvania banning him from being alone with his daughter. We should get a copy of that order."

"I still don't see how that's relevant, Stephen," Fleeger said, punishing me for springing the surprise suggestion. "What do the family court records have to do with his alleged injuries?"

"They attest to his present state of mind and to his motivation. He needs the money because of his daughter."

"He needs the money to survive," Fleeger added.

"Yes, but it's more than that with this guy. There's something else. More primal. And the more facts we have about him, and what's really motivating him, the more forcefully we can impeach him at his deposition."

"Pennsylvania approved," Celeste said.

Robert concurred, so long as Celeste was onboard. We said our goodbyes and ended the call.

"Dude, I don't like surprises."

"I know. I meant to bring it up earlier. Didn't have a chance."

"Even still, you're doing a great job on this case. Celeste is very pleased with your work product so far."

"I haven't done anything."

"Sure you have. She's following your recommendations. You handled yourself well in court today. But most importantly, she likes you. And that's a very good thing. Probably the most important thing to keeping the client. So keep it up."

He stuck out his tongue and made a ghoulish sound and shook me by the shoulder.

"You're becoming a real bastard, Stephen. Good work."

I didn't know how to respond and let the comment pass. We agreed to leave in fifteen minutes. Fleeger squinted his eyes, pulling them into tight slits, and commenced speaking pure Wuxi.

"Love is the inspiration," he said.

"Progress most divine."

He slapped my back.

"Attaboy."

9

THE HYBRID TAXI TRAVELLED north beneath an elevated highway, past fifty-five-gallon drum fires ablaze inside the protesters' camp and African peddlers arranging silver jewelry and DVDs beneath blue plastic tarps and food vendors roasting chestnuts and kabobs beneath red-and-yellow umbrellas in the glow of spinning rainbow-bright LED.

HALAL.

FRESH.

DELICIOUS.

Robert whisper-spoke into his phone with Tara or another potential slay and a song came on the radio.

"You like this band?" the driver asked me in the rearview mirror, dangling Muslim worry beads tapping against the windshield.

"They're famous," I replied.

"This song is called 'We Are the Champions.'"

"Come on, dude. Do we know this song?" Fleeger asked, now off the phone. "They play it at every Ranger game."

"Yes. Big everywhere," the driver said. "The band is called Queens."

"Queen," I replied.

"Yes, Queens," he said.

"You're both wrong. The band is called Kings."

"No, Queens," the driver said.

"I know, buddy." Fleeger smirked. "Just fucking with you."

The taxi climbed onto the highway, switching from battery propulsion to internal combustion. Now above the East River and traversing between the three bridges and around the city of halogen lights, reflecting long and conical across the blackened river, playground of kraken and leviathan. We exited at Houston Street and the taxi stopped at a red light. With a sharpened pinky nail, the driver dug inside his ear. He spotted me watching him and continued digging while staring back at me in the mirror. Fleeger thumbed his phone, through more images of more women, mainlining dopamine.

Now past jewelry shops flaming with gemstones beneath jade chandeliers. Red-enameled casino shuttles. The vulcanized tires rolled north on Bowery, flushing away precipitation, echoing the shapes of the buildings and cars we passed. Yellow black red black yellow black red. Tangerines stacked inside infrared pagodas to please the ancestors and pitch-black runics scorched to the brick face above the fire escapes. IXXI IXXI IXXI IXXI IXXI. By the people of forever who are not afraid.

Fleeger paid the driver and we exited the taxi and entered the restaurant, passing beneath a sign of neon-blue kanji, both of us bathed in aqua-blue light as Robert confirmed our reservation and we followed the Asian hostess into the loud, dark dining room. A thousand points of candlelight. The hostess wore a sleeveless dress, each arm tattooed with an AK-47. Thomas's kind of girl, I thought. She pulled back curtains as we entered deeper into the restaurant with no discernible name in English. "*Domo arigato gozaimasu,*" the chefs yelled in unison while focused on the careful work of plating food.

I spotted her first, watching from a dark corner as Robert pushed through the crowded dining room, occasionally knocking into chairs. She saw me and bit her lip, coated in hot magenta, and said something to a man I didn't know who turned around and so too did Soncha, Kath's old, dear friend. Whom Fleeger once nicknamed Hezbollah. The three of them conspired while watching us follow the hostess.

Kath's hair was darker than the last time I saw her. More burgundy, less Fanta. She had dusted the space around her eyes with
silver and cobalt particulate. Before she was confectionary, like one of
those swirly lollipops you buy as a kid at the boardwalk and display
on a shelf and never lick. Now, watching us and tearing at a licorice
fingernail, she looked like a Givenchy model in a Penthouse ad. Separating from Robert had revealed something unctuous and black. The
hostess motioned for us to sit. Robert looked at me.

"What?"

I nodded in Kath's direction.

"Fuck."

"You have to say hi to her."

It was only right, it was the adult thing to do, I said. Fleeger
approached Kath's table and kissed her cheek while she remained sitting and he told his almost-ex-wife it was good to see her.

"Jesus, Robert, I'd never expect to see you here."

Kath waved her arm around the dining room, making circles
above her head.

"Why's that?" he asked.

"Because you hate these types of places. All of this. He even hates
chopsticks," she said, addressing Soncha and pointing at Fleeger.

I leaned in and kissed Kath's cheek. I wanted to tell her to behave.

"It's my fault," I said. "I dragged him here."

"Stephen. Are you still defending Robert all the time? He's a big
boy. He can handle me. Is it just you two?"

Robert told her it was.

"Good. Then come sit with us. We'll make room. Stephen, come
sit next to me. We'll get cozy."

Fleeger hesitated.

"What are we going to do, Robert? Sit here in the same restaurant
and pretend we don't know each other?" Kath walked to our reserved
table, burgundy heels and a black poufy skirt that deemphasized the
flatness of her hips, and lifted a chair not quite above her head as the
diners and the waitstaff watched her. She was half-drunk.

"I hope you'll have enough room, Robert," she said. "I know how proud you are of your big thighs."

Fleeger took his seat, palms down on the table, looking over his shoulder as Kath rubbed the booth dictating me to sit next to her. This was a bad idea. Her green and gold hoop earrings rested on the shoulders of her black cashmere sweater. I kissed Soncha on the cheek. The girl with forty braids, penciled in tonight behind eyes of Ra. She belonged on a palanquin, in jesses and bells, with dinars threaded through her hair. And she loathed Robert.

"Good to see you too, Stephen," she said.

The new man and I shook hands. His neck possessed extra degrees of rotation, an attribute that became more manifest as he struggled to comprehend the new dining arrangement.

"OK, so now we are five," he said. He was French and perturbed, because he no longer had the two women to himself. Because the Americans had arrived.

Fleeger placed his elbows on the table and folded his hands in front of his mouth while Kath rearranged napkins, wine glasses, and cutlery in a futile effort to make us comfortable. I asked her how she was doing.

"Really very good, Stephen," she said. She touched my arm and looked at me. "Very busy. And very good."

"And you, Soncha?" I asked.

"I'm good," she said. Answering me sideways. "The same."

"Soncha and I were just discussing our upcoming trip to India," Kath said.

"Cool," I replied, bobbing my head. Still bobbing my head. Bobbing my head too many times.

"And I've been shooting a lot of film and photography of the protestors and the protest camp," Kath said. She exuded the confidence of a woman utterly finished with the man she had married and ecstatic about the new life she created for herself, free of burden. The way women almost always can be and the way men almost never are, except for maybe Robert. "I've been much more productive since leaving Robert."

"Maybe I should try the same," I said.

Kath punched my arm and smiled and Robert grunted and hailed the waitress to get over here. He and I ordered bottles of Okinawa pilsner and the Frenchman ordered a pomegranate juice and seltzer and the girls ordered refills of shiraz. Kath opened a small tin of moisturizer and placed it under my nose.

"Do you smell it?"

"Smells like weed."

She sniffed the tin. There was a fresh tattoo on her forearm, 灭度, beneath the symbol for Black Cat Fireworks.

"I love the smell of marijuana," Kath said. A bit too much already. "And the THC bonds with the lipids to replenish the dermis."

"You can't bring that in here," Fleeger protested.

"And why's that?" Kath asked.

"Because we'll get arrested."

"Jesus, Robert. It's moisturizer, not a joint," Soncha said. "And besides, no one even cares anymore. It's practically legal. Everyone knows that."

"So," Kath said, flipping her hand to indicate her and Soncha. "I have an announcement to make. We're planning on going to the Kumbh Mela in a couple weeks."

I looked at Robert. He didn't know what Kath was talking about and he didn't want to be here.

"You have visas?" I asked.

"We need visas?" Kath asked.

"Yes."

"Then we'll get visas."

"You'll need to act quickly."

"How do you know this, Stephen?" Soncha asked. "Why do we need to act quickly?"

"I just read it takes a couple weeks to get Indian visas. And that a lot of people assume it can be done in a day or two when it takes weeks. It's like the world's biggest bureaucracy."

"What is?" Soncha asked.

"The Indian Foreign Ministry."

I felt foolish saying this. Now I was involved and I didn't want to be involved in their plans. I needed to pivot.

"But that doesn't apply to me, Stephen," Kath said. "I'm American. Then again, I know I'll get sick. So I guess there's a bright side too. We can just focus our creative energies here instead of India. Oh, I don't know what to do. Stephen, what should I do?"

I shrugged my shoulders.

"Stephen." She punched my arm. "I need more than that."

"You must drink charcoal," the Frenchman said. "The carbon will coat your intestines and protect them from harmful bacteria." He dropped a line with his hand down his thorax.

"So what Kath? We get sick," Soncha said. "It's the experience that matters."

"I want to film the pilgrims wading into the Ganges," Kath added, excited again about the journey ahead. "And then juxtapose the footage of the Sadhus with the images of the protestors downtown living in the camps and fighting the cops. One side religion. The other side protest. Which is kind of like a religion, right?"

"How so?" the Frenchman asked.

"Well they're both anti-capitalism," she replied. "Or supra-capitalism. That's one way they're similar."

"Did anyone hear what Stephen just said?" Fleeger interjected. "That there's not enough time to get visas?"

"So what, Robert?" Kath asked, dismissive.

"So if you can't get visas then the entire discussion of your upcoming trip to India is fucking moot."

"Moot?" the Frenchman asked.

"Robert don't be such a naysayer," Kath said. "We'll find a way."

"We are going," Soncha confirmed.

"Yes we are. But what about our camera equipment?"

"What about it?" Soncha asked.

"I don't want to carry all that camera equipment around Hindustan," Kath said.

"We'll just pay someone to carry it, Kath."

Fleeger gulped down his beer and ordered another. He wanted all this having nothing real to talk about to cease and Kath and Soncha knew this and conspired to keep it going.

"I'm pretty sure the sadhus will charge you a fee to film them," I said. "They're known to be stingy with their souls."

Fleeger stared at me, his flash jury again convicting me of conspiracy and treason.

"Who?" Soncha asked.

"The sadhus. The holy men you want to film."

"Why are you so negative, Stephen?" Kath said. "Jesus, you're becoming like Robert. Is anything possible?"

The server placed on the table pewter bowls of curries and sauces and plates of origami-cut vegetables for dipping: a swan, a crane, a cat, a horse, lotuses, and tulips.

"But I thought money was against the principles of the sadhus," said Kath.

"Enough with the fucking sadhus," Fleeger retorted.

I spooned curry into a small volcano of basmati rice as Soncha and Kath gave each other an invisible high five.

"And how about you, Jacques?" Fleeger said. "What do you do?"

"Who is Jacques?" the Frenchman asked as Fleeger fumbled his spoon into the sauce. "I am a businessman."

"All right," Fleeger said. "Finally someone at this table who does something useful. Can I get a fork for this please?" he asked a passing busgirl. She handed him a fork and he stared at her tattooed face. "I feel like I'm at fucking Coney Island."

The stick of bamboo that had taken root at the base of Fleeger's ass the moment we entered the restaurant now shot upward through the chamber of his spine. Sitting taller than the rest of us and from across the table, he attempted a hostile takeover of the dinner conversation.

"So what's your business?" Fleeger asked the Frenchman.

"I import furniture. Now from Italy. But sometimes from Brazil and sometimes from Indonesia."

"Is that lucrative?" Fleeger asked.

"Not at all," the Frenchman replied.

"I want to go to Indonesia," Kath said, truncating Fleeger's efforts.

"It's a shithole," the Frenchman replied.

"It's the land of ten thousand islands," she insisted.

"That's Minnesota," I said.

"Trust me. It's a shithole," the Frenchman said. I liked the way he said "hole." Accentuating the o with his small mouth. "And they always rip me off."

"Of course they do," Soncha said. "That's the price of doing business there. Otherwise the deal is too sweet. They can't make the deal too sweet otherwise you won't go back."

"I don't know what you're talking about, Soncha. Who doesn't like a sweet deal?" the Frenchman said. "Kath, go to Hawaii. Much nicer. Less corruption. Less Muslim."

"I'm Muslim," Soncha said.

"You're different," he replied. He put his hand on Soncha's lap and she held it. She accepted this for now, conscious that her position wasn't advanced by arguing with the Frenchman in public.

"So then you appreciate, Pierre, that there is a system," Robert continued.

Pierre agreed but didn't understand what Fleeger was talking about and I was certain his name wasn't Pierre either.

"What's your point, Robert?" Kath asked.

"That's my point, Kath. Indonesia and India and wherever else you want to go and shoot your photos and make your films and fantasize about even though you don't have a clue. They're outside the system."

Kath stared at him as Soncha texted and Fleeger told us all to forget it. Explaining was pointless, he said. The Beijing piglet arrived atop a stainless steel cart, surrounded by bowls of epoxy-thick dipping sauce and chopped green onions and a plate of steaming tortillas.

"The specialty," Jacques Pierre said. "I ordered it ahead of time."

"Can I get another beer?" Fleeger asked the busgirl, almost hostile, while she fileted the pig and forked it onto small plates. As he attacked the food, deep beneath the tablecloth Kath's stocking toes fondled and stroked the soft space above my ankle. She found it above the Euro shoes, unsheathed my sock to expose my ankle, and as she did so I filled with a substance similar to warm water, infused with glistening electrolytes. She placed her hand on my thigh and made small finger eights and looked at me.

"What do you think of the pig?" she asked.

Soncha took a bite of her pork taco, dripping sauce onto her plate.

"Looks good," I said.

We had played this before. Once in the Dominican Republic and another time at O'Grady's the night Fleeger became partner. It was a little game she liked to play, a little expression of her little independent affection, a little protest against little conventions. I was too thirsty for contact to worry about Fleeger across the table. It was all biology and need; no room for morality let alone the ethics of friendship in the vacuum of my current state.

"How long have you two been together?" Fleeger asked Soncha. I could barely hear him. I felt like I was underwater.

"We're not really together," Soncha replied.

"You're not?" Fleeger asked.

"We make love. Sometimes we fuck but mostly we make love."

"Amen, Soncha," Fleeger said, tipping his beer at her. "Finally something we agree upon."

Kath released her grip from my thigh.

"Don't go getting superior Robert. Their approach is holistic and internal and at the same time expansive." She stretched her arms to dramatize the universal application of her beliefs. "But Robert, come on, let's face it. You're incapable of making the necessary sacrifices to really touch someone."

"What does that even mean?" he asked.

"I don't know Robert but I can't keep explaining everything to you. When I do I sound false and annoying and pretentious. You make me annoy myself. It's like we speak different versions of English. You're too bold. Maybe it's because you've dedicated your existence to representing insurance companies."

"Like the little green geckos on your television?" the Frenchman asked. He chuckled.

"They're actually very big green geckos," I replied.

The Frenchman whispered something into Soncha's ear and he rubbed his hands through his feathered part while leaning backward. Fleeger looked exposed, stranded on the dark side of his legal apotheosis, as Kath prepared to again bullwhip his pride. She resumed stroking my thigh beneath the table and the server set down a plate of drizzled plums. Soncha lit a cigarette and blew smoke in Kath's face, as if she was a shaman preparing Kath for spiritual battle. The Frenchman draped his arm over the back of the chair and looked out the restaurant's tinted windows.

The soft, easy side of Fleeger that led us here tonight had long ago disappeared. Tiny lights now flashed behind his dark eyes, red green yellow, red green yellow, as he computed his next move. The computation repeating itself until the code was cracked and the decision made. Kath, in turn, closed her eyes, breathing in through her nose and out through her mouth. The moment hung there. She took more breaths. She opened her eyes. She was clear and calm.

"Soncha."

"Yes Kath?"

"Remember the time I invited you and some of the girls over for brunch? Right after Robert and I returned from our honeymoon?"

"I'm not sure, Kath. Which time was that?"

"Remember there was the Bluetooth speaker on the kitchen table?"

"I do remember. We called it 'the incident.'"

"Yes, and we laughed about it at the time. Robert had just gotten home from the gym and was taking a shower while I was pouring mimosas and the girls were all sitting around the table. And then suddenly there was this sound of people fucking emanating from the speaker."

"I do remember that."

"It was really loud, wasn't it? And the woman was yelling I think in Spanish as she took it. Was it in Spanish?"

"I think so."

"And remember how it kept getting louder and louder as we sat there at the kitchen table. With our flutes of mimosas and our eggs Benedict. Not quite sure what to do or say. Because Robert and I had just gotten back from our honeymoon and it was obvious to all my friends who had just been at our wedding that my new husband was masturbating in the shower at that very moment. Turning up the volume on his phone in frustration to hear the pornographic pounding except he didn't realize that the sound was playing on the speaker in the kitchen."

"So embarrassing."

"You know I never told him about that?"

"You didn't? Why not?"

"Maybe because I respected him at the time?"

"You two are fucking cunts," Fleeger said.

He clicked his teeth. The Frenchman looked away and Soncha smoked, both in slow motion, as Kath flung a full glass of shiraz against Fleeger's chest and chin, soaking an expanse of cotton and silk indelible red. Fleeger pushed back from the table and shoved his chair back into place with both hands.

"Stephen," he said.

If I stood now he would discover the full extent of my treason.

"Who are you? Batman?" Kath asked him. She looked at me. "Does that mean you're Robin, Stephen?"

Rage blocked Fleeger from forming words. His big jaw clenched so tight his square teeth were about to crack. The waitress stepped out of his way and the chefs lauded his departure from the restaurant with an incongruous chorus of Japanese salutations.

I watched him through the tinted windows. Lurking on the sidewalk. Needing something to ram, to gore, to release the toxicity coursing through his veins. Kath slid into Fleeger's chair and gave him the finger. I wanted back her hand and foot and I wanted to step outside.

"Such a child," she said. "What's he going to do? Fight me?"

"I can't believe Robert was just here," Soncha said.

"Marriage," the Frenchman said. *"Est merde."*

Now I could stand and I exited the restaurant to check on him. *Domo arigato gozaimasu. He's your best friend. I told you so.* The night smelled of snow. Of cold metallic humidity. At the street corner Fleeger rummaged through the bottom of a municipal trash bin, reached in with one long arm, and extracted a broken hockey stick. He banged it against the ground to test the integrity of its thwack, looking it up and down. He possessed his faculties. He would listen to reason. I pressed my hands against his chest. His pectoral muscles felt like catcher's mitts.

"Robert," I said, pushing against him. He pressed through me. The machine that had computed his response also demanded execution. He smashed the hockey stick into the neon-blue sign above the restaurant door. Smashed it again. Smashed it once more. Inert particles of blue neon gas spinning into shards of broken glass. He tossed the stick into the gutter and stepped into a taxi. I reentered the restaurant and as I walked across the dining room the patrons and the waitstaff watched me.

"I need to go," I said.

"My God, such a dramatic response. That was so much fun," Kath replied. "I never would have thought it possible to get such a reaction from him. He's really changed. We should do this again sometime."

The Frenchman made a noise as if to ask for what, for this?

"How were you married to him?" Soncha asked.

"I guess I was into beastiality."

"Has its place," Soncha said.

"Yes but eventually it gets old."

"We should go now," I said.

"Nonsense," Kath replied.

She attempted to order another round of drinks and the waitress looked at the manager and the manager cut us off while speaking on the phone. I suspected he was calling the cops. The Frenchman paid the bill and I thanked him and remembered Fleeger's offer to treat me to dinner on WorldScore's tab. The previous good humor of it all. The Frenchman waved me away. It was nothing, he said. The chefs abstained from lauding our departure with Japanese exhortations of good fortune.

Outside, the restaurant staff swept up the broken glass and surveyed the damage and watched us as we congregated on the sidewalk and prepared to leave. Soncha lit another cigarette. All of us now exhausted with one another. I shook the Frenchman's hand good night, kissed Kath on the cheek, attempted to hug Soncha, who blocked me. We shook hands instead.

"Come out with us, Stephen," Kath said.

"I have to go."

"Come anyway," Kath said.

"I can't," I said. "I have a thing."

"OK," she said, and kissed me. Her two front teeth scraped my cheek. It wasn't an accident.

We walked in opposite directions. I turned around and returned to the restaurant. The staff still sweeping the glass and the manager still talking on the phone. I interrupted him.

"How much was the sign?"

He covered the receiver.

"I've already called the cops."

"Yes, but how much to replace the sign?"

He thought for a minute. He would charge a tax. On top of the premium.

"Fifteen hundred."

"I'll give you eleven. But I have to pay by card."

"Twelve fifty."

"Twelve fifty and this is over?"

He nodded yes. I handed him a credit card and signed the receipt and stuffed a copy in my wallet and walked home. Not quite steeped in booze as usual but halfway there.

10

I AWOKE IN THE dark apartment surrounded by blinking lights. Green stereo receiver. Red high-speed Internet modem. Gregg's perennially white Christmas lights reflecting in mason jars stacked on the stainless steel Ikea drying rack. I rose from the couch and navigated the dark apartment, like one of those deep-sea creatures with a small organic bulb attached to the front of its skull, highly evolved to the point of overspecialization, viability limited to thirty thousand feet beneath sea level. A ghost shark. Fleeger had sent me a dozen text messages while I slept. A new message every two sips from a pint. Imploring that I meet him for a drink. Asking where I was. About his behavior and the property damage and whether the cops were looking for him and even a question about Kath's reaction. Until the momentary guilt and self-awareness devolved into what the eff protestations and how come you're not responding and I guess I'll have to handle this myself thanks a lot buddy fuck you. I refrained from texting him he owed me $1,250 for the broken sign. Because I wanted him to sit in it for a while. Outside the snow fell heavy and rich.

Someone knocked on my door, shaking the deadbolt. For a second I thought it was the cops. I unclasped the chain, turned the knob, and there stood Gregg and Kath. He wore a gray Gore-Tex snowsuit, holding a plastic red snow shovel, and she sparkled in a black shearling tunic flecked with fallen snow. The toe cleavage bunched in her long pointy heels looked pink and raw.

"Stephen, this woman informs me she's your friend."

They looked like a red-state artist's rendering of New York City as American Gothic. I confirmed she was indeed my friend.

"She's crazy. She was riding her bicycle in this blizzard. She just hopped the curb with no hands and fell in a pile of snow. She could have ruined her beautiful face."

They were perfect for each other. Gregg reached up to touch her cheek and Kath blocked him with a quick side hug.

"Don't say such terrible things about me, Gregg," Kath said, impatient and drunk. "I thought we were friends now too. After you rescued me from that wretched snow pile."

She pushed past me and entered my apartment, burgundy heels hammering the pumpkin pine floor, and dropped her bag on the stain-resistant couch.

"Oh, but we are friends," Gregg confirmed. "How could we not be? After I practically saved your life?"

Kath leaned back across the threshold of the apartment and kissed Gregg's cheek. A telepathic thank you darling from her to him but she would stay here with me now yes. She wanted to be here. I thanked him as well, wished him good night, and closed the door. Too much time passed before I heard him walk away, tapping his shovel down the staircase.

"I was in the neighborhood."

She collapsed against me. Nuzzled her cold, wet face against my neck. She smelled of shatterproof vodka and wet wool and cigarettes and squeezed me now with her arms wrapped around my waist. The snow melted atop her thick hair, forming patterns of clear beads, like something glued to a South Asian bride on her wedding night. There was a mass to it. I gripped its chords and density and kissed her mouth and her flesh released a wave of something warm from inside her clothes. She didn't wear antiperspirant that smelled like flowers or baby powder or cucumbers. Instead she wore some musky perfume, rare and European, chopped and distilled from the hairy pouch of a diminutive Eurasian deer.

"I'm cold," she said.

I forced myself on her. Laid her on the couch. Gripped her cold wet calf and squeezed the ball of her muscle. She caught my lip between her teeth. I pulled back and examined her almost translucent shin, mottled with faint brown spots and wispy red hairs.

"Stephen, I'm so cold and wet."

"Do you want to take a shower?" I asked.

She nodded, turned away, and stared at the floor.

"I'll get you a towel and start the water."

She asked if I had anything warm she could wear and I told her yes I did I would look. I wanted to clean the bathroom, remove my hair from the sink and shower drain, de-mold the grout, replace the shower curtain. But there was no time for any of this. We were onto something. The bathroom filled with steam and I led her to the tub. Or rather she let me do so. She pushed me out the door and locked it behind me. The spatter against the bottom of the tub changed its rhythm as she stepped in and out beneath the showerhead. I pulled the blue flannel duvet over my unmade bed and pretended to sleep on the couch, discerned the orange light of the opening bathroom door. I wanted her hands on me without me having to move or ask, my nerve endings broadcasting the message that I needed her to act voluntarily. Because she wasn't mine to take. She showed up here; she was hers to offer.

"I take it you don't have a hair dryer?"

"Why's that?" I asked with eyes closed.

"Because you're balding."

She stood over me, pushing her fingers through my thinning hair, cozied next to me on the couch, sat on her hands. Full of small disappointment, I stood and placed my hands on her wide, warm hips. She didn't say no and she wouldn't say no. She would let me take it. I pressed forward. She opened the towel. The space between her pointed breasts expansive and freckled with her true color, not this black deep red thing she co-opted from Soncha. I moved alongside her. Her long bellybutton juiced extra pink by the hot shower.

"Stephen?"

"Yes."

"You sure this is what you want?"

I mumbled.

"Promise me."

I promised and proceeded to persist. She puckered. She was a puckerer. I pushed my way in. She turned her head and closed her eyes and there it was. There we were. I needed this. Inside she was warm and ribbed like corrugated tin. The roof of her soft pink corrugated shed. It was rare for me when it was like this. I didn't think. I put my hands around her neck. Between her neck and shoulders.

"Stephen?"

"Yes."

"Nothing."

I dug for it across the arm of the stain-resistant Raymore & Flannigan couch. The connection that apparently makes one feel the earth again beneath one's feet. Something cracked. Now gulped for air. One, two, three, four last times. The swollen gills of a pink fish hoisted from the sea. More desperate with age. Infecting the host. She detached from me and I moved south along her white length. My nose between the capital Y of her now closed legs. She sat up.

"I want this instead."

She lit an all-white American Spirit with a wooden match. That one for her, this one for me.

"You feel better now?" she asked, as if she had just lanced an abscess.

I told her yes.

"And don't worry. I have an IUD. I won't make that mistake again."

I hadn't thought of this, because I had placed the burden on her. She reentered the bathroom, locked the door, sprayed a small jet inside the toilet bowl, and doused herself clean with the porcelain cup atop the sink. I wanted to ask her what mistake but I knew what she meant. In the past I would have probed and dug until I uncovered the hidden thing, with a righteous fervor, as if I was taking confession. But there was no reason to do so now. Let a woman have her secrets. There's a reason for it. Because it's better that way. Outside the snow fell heavy and quiet. I felt off but didn't know whether to talk or ignore it. The problem with talking in these situations is that it results in more talking, and when a woman asks you questions looking for answers about what it is you want to discuss and you can't reply with any kind of clarity or honesty a woman will turn on you. Better to let it dissolve on its own accord.

Gregg's lights blinked inside the heavy snow, amassed atop the plastic boughs, admonishing me to quit myself. Kath exited the bathroom wearing the towel and looked around the apartment. I feared she wanted to leave.

"It's like a tomb in here, Stephen," she said. "Did you find my warm clothes?"

I wrapped myself in an itchy wool blanket and pointed at the closet. Kath reached for the pair of sweatpants and thermal shirt I set aside for her and knocked over a cardboard box that tumbled Christmas ornaments to the floor. Little silver balls with handwritten-note filling, from Mei to me and me to Mei, for opening once a year, to cherish how far we'd traveled the road of life together. Another ornament lay chipped on the floor, of cartoon deer in love. "Mei" the doe in heels with long black eyelashes and "Stephen" the antlered buck wrapped in a red scarf. Embarrassed and goofy in love.

"Jesus this is depressing, Stephen. Why do you keep this stuff?"

The deer ornament landed in the trash can. She cracked open a little Christmas ball, scooped out the note, like the bloody red center of a cherry jubilee. I almost protested but didn't.

"I love the way you tie your tie."

Kath faux-barfed.

"Evil temptress, perform thy act of mercy," I said, and all of it landed in the trash can. She dressed inside the towel and sat half-lotus on the couch, and from her oversize handbag removed a purple clutch with saffron stitching and a row of tiny mirrors. The small flame of her disposable Bic heated a chunk of hash and it crumbled and flaked in her licorice-manicured fingers. Like an English girl she rolled a spliff with two papers glued together to form a capital L. It was quarter to one.

"Stephen?"

"Yes?"

"You need to reach that point where you don't care about Mei anymore. And only when you reach that point can you let go."

"OK."

I didn't bother to tell her she had it all wrong.

"I think we need to perform open-heart surgery on you. It's bleeding all over the place. I can help you. But you have to trust me."

I didn't know what she meant. I feared she was going to recommend bondage, submission, prescribe pain for me to feel again, walk on me wearing heels. That this was why men entered realms they avoided or feared or thought they abhorred, in order to feel again.

"Is that what you want?" she asked.

"I don't know."

She handed me the spliff like it was an exclamation mark.

"I don't think so," she said. "I don't feel it."

The taste of the smoke opened neurons and paths to people and places I hadn't thought of in years. Relegated to the past. On the other side of the Atlantic Ocean. Rooted deep in northern Michigan. Abandoned in Detroit, lost in Chicago, escaped to San Francisco, failing in Los Angeles, miscarrying in Westchester. No longer recognizable. Just a series of adjectives. Successful. Failure. Wealthy. Broke. Talented. Family. Ill. Divorced. Married. Infertile. Dreadlocked. Scandinavian. Londoner. Gone. Kath relit the spliff and walked around the apartment smoking. A hash ember fell from the tip and scorched the varnish of the pumpkin pine floor. She filled the kettle with water and the gas burner ignited with small clicks and she set the kettle on the blue flame. "Want to come with me to Philadelphia in a few weeks for my brother Benjamin's fortieth birthday party?"

"OK," I said, though I harbored doubts we would execute the plan, because she liked to announce grand plans, like going to India without a visa, despite the fact Philadelphia was only an hour by train. She pulled on the spliff and handed it to me. I took another drag and felt liquor hash dizzy and the need for a cigarette. We circled the coffee table holding lighters.

"Does your brother still have that goofy Om tattoo on his lower back?" I asked, aware I was taking a shot.

"Stephen." She pulled me on the couch and took my hand and placed it in hers. "Be especially wary of dismissing everyone who's not you, OK? Stop judging. It's a bad habit."

"OK."

"You promise?"

"I promise."

"And you'll go to Philadelphia with me for Benjamin's birthday party?"

"OK."

"And we'll have a good time?"

"OK."

"You won't be like all those other men who are always breaking their promises to me?"

I had nothing to say, looked at my hands.

"Hey Stephen," she said.

I looked at her.

"I like you."

"Really?"

"I've always liked you. And I think you're super hot. And smart. And funny. And . . ."

The water boiled inside the green teapot. She felt warmer now and I couldn't release her. The steam whistled as my Sputnik reentered her atmosphere. This was more like it. I hurried to pour and steep the tea but in doing so singed my thumb, for the briefest of moments stuck to the teapot, and I fumbled with the kitchen spigot, submerged it in running water. Kath looked confused. Now she got it. She inserted my thumb in her mouth and we looked at the blister. White and pellucid and the shape of Greenland.

"I want chicken tikka marsala," Kath said. "And garlic naan."

"OK," I said, despite the fact it was now quarter after one.

"And I want goat biryani," she said.

"I thought you were a vegetarian."

"And that's why I ate pork tacos earlier tonight?"

She intuited my sensitivity. Her intuition was half-accurate but didn't warrant mentioning.

"I was. I used to be a vegetarian, Stephen. Thank you for being so considerate. But I am no longer. Is that what you want me to say?"

I told her to fuck off. She smacked my ass. My phone continued to buzz. Three more messages from Fleeger. Saying we needed to talk. That we needed to talk two hours ago. Come on man write him back—it was important. Ten cigarette butts jammed the ashtray. The intercom buzzed and Kath handed me my robe while scrolling through Apple TV.

The Bengali who both managed the Indian restaurant and delivered its food walked toward me, oiled sable part, gripping plastic bags.

"Your food, sir," he said.

He made me feel like a colonial master. That was his shtick and he worked it. Guaranteeing that his red velvet Indian restaurant in the West Village withstood the forces of commerce and fashion. Chicken tikka masala with a side of atavistic colonialism. But for the fact he was Bengali, and thus more inclined to be a poet than a sadhu, for the proper fee he would agree to play along: lungi, wooden beads, bindi, chillum, for Kath and Soncha to film.

"Sacred beads of Vishnu?" he offers her.

"Thank you," Kath replies.

"Chillum to connect with Ram?"

"May we film your sadhuism from this angle?"

"You may film me from any angle you wish. Master has already paid."

I paid him cash and Kath tickled me behind the door. He cocked his head to inquire just what the devil was going on here. The ten-dollar tip—on account of the snow—made him shy. I handed the plastic bags of food to Kath. She knotted the blanket at her chest like a sarong, positioned the plastic containers on the coffee table, and dumped the ashtray.

105

"I want wine," she said.

I poured her a glass of merlot. She pouted.

"They forgot the raita."

"It's OK," I said.

"But I want it."

I bit my tongue and called the restaurant.

"No problem, sir."

We began making love again. Another knock at the door. This time Gregg stood next to the Bengali, still holding his snow shovel.

"Stephen?" Gregg asked. "He said he has your raita?"

The Bengali handed me two plastic ramekins of raita. I thanked him and we nodded and he exited the building.

"Hi, Gregg," I said.

He looked at my robe. The spring slammed the door shut and Gregg stood on the other side of the door tapping his plastic shovel against the ceramic floor tiles. Kath's curved breasts swung inside the blanket sarong as she descended on the food. I handed her the raita and she held my hand while eating from the plate on her lap and then I handed her a torn piece of warm garlic naan.

"You're such a good man, Stephen," she said.

Small movements beneath the duvet, a kit of alighting pigeons, another chunk of spent hash scorched the floor. We lay naked beneath the blankets. Stroking and sleeping, waking to stroke again. I walked naked to the window. The snow had stopped and Gregg's courtyard was dark and electric and white, the snow illuminated from within, like an incandescent South Pacific lagoon where the coral glows when you insert your toes into the sea. I wanted to move to Norway, live on a lake, build stone walls, raise mountain dogs in the European countryside with Kath.

My phone buzzed the nightstand. Another message from Fleeger. Telling me I let him down bro.

"Who was that?" Kath asked.

She didn't have the right to ask that yet.

"Work."

"Work or Robert?"

"Both," I said. She snuggled into the pillow. "Can I ask you a question?"

"Yes."

"Why did you marry him?"

She rolled onto her back. We should have remained under the blankets not asking each other questions.

"I told you I don't want to talk about him."

"No you didn't."

"Well you should know that. You're not an idiot but you're also an idiot. A real man would know that a woman doesn't want to discuss her ex-husband while lying in bed with another man."

She curled into a ball and pulled the blanket over her head and turned armadillo on me. I told her I was sorry. She didn't reply. We lay in silence. How did this happen? Again I told her I was sorry, and again, forcing my arm around her shuttered waist. I wanted to tell her to fuck off, get out, but worried what would happen if I did. There were too many perils: snow, bicycle, ice, Fleeger. Against my better instincts I focused on appeasing her disappointment.

"Hey," I said. "I'm sorry."

"You should be," she replied. Still hiding beneath the covers.

I never should have opened the door for her tonight. Should have questioned the motive and the genuineness of what she said and did from the first moment beneath the table. I had been weak. Failed to ask myself and answer whether this was what I wanted and needed. A net positive. Potentially constructive and supportive and good. She hadn't chosen me. She showed up here drunk—for a screw and some naan. I left her in bed sulking, replenished my glands with a cold bottle of beer, sat in the gray miasma of smog that still hovered above the couch, and crawled back in bed. She curled up next to me and put her hand on my chest and in that moment the trap was sprung. The small, injured mammal released.

"I'm sorry," she said.

I kissed her forehead and we fell asleep.

I awoke in Kath's mouth. She worked me harder. Sorrel gray roots parted black. I grabbed her skull with both hands and she gagged me deeper and then exited the bed with her mouth closed and turned the squeaky faucets and entered the shower. This time the door remained open. I told her I was going to the store to buy breakfast.

"Get me an avocado," she said behind the shower curtain with a face full of water.

I typed a reply to Fleeger. Thought about it and thought about it. One of those rare moments when you convince yourself that exhaustion equals a sick day and you act upon it. I informed him I would be in tomorrow. That I was sick, snowed in, snowed under with a stomach thing, fucking curry. His hammerhead thumbs were no use to him now on this post-blizzard morning of pseudo-cuckoldry. As I exited the apartment building I confirmed for myself that he knew nothing about me and Kath. Gritty sodium kernels crunched beneath my feet. Kath's bicycle buried beneath a mound of Gregg's diligent snow removal, an empty bottle of Georgi vodka deposited in her metal basket.

My phone buzzed the newswire and I scrolled it with my blister. The coronal mass ejection still wreaking havoc. A container ship grounding off Sicily due to a malfunctioning navigational system. The successful launch of a Chinese rocket carrying a satellite to monitor shifts in solar magnetism. Standing applause by the PRC standing committee. Black suits and brilliantined hair. While waiting for the light to change I broke through a puddle of ice with my heel. Wooden crates and frozen cardboard boxes piled on the Manhattan sidewalk. I overpowered the broken pneumatic door and entered the deep-fried-smelling Gristedes, where a giant sluggish Haitian watched me as he fastened price tags to the bottom of tin cans. The butcher, crisp in delicatessen whites, also watched me while dolloping mayonnaise salads Iwo Jimaed with neon-orange prices. I grabbed a dozen eggs and an avocado and a twelve-pack of Budweiser and queued, pondering the deeper meaning of the Shop Rite brand personal lubricant display next to the cash register.

"Get the fuck off me, man," a brown woman yelled near the mechanical exit, swinging a skinny arm at the Korean store manager as the pneumatic door opened and closed, detecting movement, unsure what to do, the woman now kneeling. A jailhouse arrow tattooed to the manager's forearm exercising his merchant's right to detain her. From deep within her coat pockets he extracted a box of condoms, a spool of wound tape, and a tube of Vaseline intensive care. She sobbed at his feet. I dropped the beer and the groceries on the conveyor belt.

"How much for her stuff?" I asked the girl behind the register. She looked at the manager.

"Eighteen dollars," he said.

I nodded that I would pay. Handed the girl a hundred-dollar bill to ring up the sale. The manager rolled his upper lip inside his lower lip and raised his hand from the woman. She sprung from his grasp without the gauze, the Vaseline, the condoms, all of it abandoned on the floor, now running past the store windows: ***SEDETSIRG*** !!!woN ELAS NO, 94.6$ MAH DELIOB, 99.3$ YRD ADANAC. Like some distraught alien trapped in the city with no chance to return home, accursed by the angry god she had offended.

"They're yours now," the manager said, double-bagging her items and handing them to me, in a bag separate from the avocado, beer, and eggs, which I appreciated.

Kath would be gone, I thought, as I opened the apartment door. She stood in the middle of my living room wearing a padded black bra and her poufy skirt, picking lint from her sweater. A fresh spliff smoking in the ashtray and coffee brewing in the press.

"Want an omelet?" I asked.

"Just the avocado."

She sat in the chair by the cracked-open window and smoked, chewed on a fingernail between drags, checked her phone. She had something on her mind and she wanted to leave.

"Tell me a new word, Stephen."

"*Loup garou.*"

"What does that mean?"

"It's French for werewolf."

"That's so fucking sexy."

I guzzled a Budweiser and sliced in half her avocado, cut the halves into strips, peeled off their almost reptilian skins, and arranged the exposed green fruit on a plate. Drizzled the skinless strips with juice from a plastic lime.

"Planning on something new for us?" Kath asked as she surveyed the items in the bag. "Every girl likes the cheap stuff."

"It was an act of charity."

"Really? What's up with the surgical tape?"

I grabbed for her. She dodged me, ate with forefinger and thumb, asked for a toothpick. I handed her a small box.

"What are you doing today?" she asked.

"Lying on the couch and drinking beer."

The avocado made her dance on her seat like a happy little girl.

"Soncha just texted me. There are like a hundred dirty protestors near the World Trade Center fighting with the cops and this guy Jupiter who's like their spirit guru has them all punching back. And apparently some image of the Virgin Mary appeared in the windows of the Mercantile Exchange overnight and the Mexicans are saying it's a miracle and the protestors are saying it's a sign that the universe is on their side. It's a total shit show. Let's go shoot some pictures with my new camera."

"Maybe," I said, refraining from disclosing to Kath that an entrepreneurial masseuse had already informed me about Jupiter, independent of her and Soncha, as if that meant anything at all or anything at all anymore. The same way I no longer cared about bands or DJs or art the way I used to; my ear no longer to the ground; that portion of my spiritual spleen atrophied and shriveled.

She poured herself coffee.

"Maybe is weak, Stephen. I need stronger than maybe."

Maybe I should have been interested but at that moment I wasn't and I wasn't about to pretend I was.

"Stop," she said, breaking my grip, as I pulled her from the kitchen chair. I lit one of her all-white American Spirits. "You'll wish you did."

I sensed the impending arrival of zombie decisions. The capitulating revenant charged with manning the woman. I half-attempted to commit myself to trekking with her in the snow and wrapped myself in a blanket on the couch, struggling to disavow the post-sex half-drunk exhaustion that resulted from less than a half-night of sleep.

"OK," she said. "Got to go. I'll text you later."

She kissed my forehead and the door slammed shut behind her. Spliff still smoldering in the ashtray as a shadow of smoke curled and rose in the square of sunlight reflected on the wooden floor. Kath's breakfast avocado, pierced with toothpicks and suspended inside a rocks glass, perched atop the windowsill. I fell asleep on the couch, facedown in a puddle of her scent, like a pig hunting truffles, snowed under by another storm of the century.

11

THE IPHONE VIBRATED ON the coffee table. It was an ominous blocked number. I debated whether to answer. It was almost noon. The vibration ceased. If it was important they would leave a message. The blocked number called again.

"Stephen?" Celeste asked, frissoned with urgency. "Are you on the road? Have you gone to Pennsylvania? What did you find?"

I willed myself to sound awake. Told her I was leaving shortly and poured myself a cup of cold coffee.

"Why haven't you left yet?"

"I was waiting for the roads to clear."

"What did you take—a snow day? I need you on top of this, Stephen. Fleeger told me you were already on the road. Let me know what you find at the Pennsylvania courthouse ASAP. The higher-ups are very curious to learn what you discover. Teach them, Stephen. This could be very good for our position versus Thomas. They're growing keener on you, Stephen. They see real potential. You're the tip of the spear here so don't let us down. We're all counting on you."

I surveyed the three empty beer bottles on the coffee table I drank since breakfast. I had no choice. I was on the move.

"I know I can always count on you guys."

She hung up the phone before I could utter another word. I admonished myself for succumbing to her fabricated urgency, located the swish messenger bag with the seatbelt strap beneath the pile of yesterday's clothes, walked to the parking garage, and rented a car from Hertz. On the corporate account. A midsized Detroit sedan with giant plastic nobs and a digital dashboard and soft wide seats. None of the pieces quite fitting together.

The temperature had dropped and I rubbed my hands together as the engine heated the car. I typed the address for the White Haven courthouse into the satellite system. Almost three hours each way, provided the sun didn't zap the GPS. A day's worth of billable hours clocked while driving from New York to upstate Pennsylvania and back. I sipped a cup of coffee purchased from the Korean bodega. Law Coffee™. Blue Mountain and organic and Folgers Crystals and La Colombe and even coffee brewed from beans egested by Indonesian palm civets—those brands I could grasp. As brands. But not Law Coffee. I exited Manhattan though the drop and dip of the soot-covered Holland Tunnel, vertigo under control but barely, the sedan's bouncy suspension tugging the car to the right.

"And the Knicks drop another and so too do the Rangers. Must have something to do with all that solar radiation they say is still coming at us." "No that would be if they both won, Chuck." "Up next: traffic on the twos." Debt relief. Credit repair. Joint relief. Pain repair. The car bounced across the Kill van Cull, too much play in the steering wheel as I summited the outer crossings, skyways spanning black water, past the abandoned coal-fired cathedrals, through a latticework of cast-iron drawbridges raised for the passage of cherry-red tugs and coal-black barges navigating narrow channels laden with combustible commodities.

Now past the port. Brackish and greasy and stacked with containers. I didn't want Kath. I didn't want Celeste. I didn't want Kilgore or WorldScore or cocktails with the client. I wanted this. Bunkers and vessels and strategic commodities. For discharge at Byway. Linden. Bayonne. Where the New Jersey landscape absorbed the drippings from the standpipes and the manifolds. Feedstocks stored in giant gasometers for baking at various heights and temperatures until the molecules separated and reconnected into petrochemicals that smelled like tuna fish and maple syrup. A skyline of smokestacks cracking open raw Nigerian and Arabian petroleum stripped from the holds of the giant maroon-hulled tankers berthed in the black tributaries of the Hudson and Raritan Rivers. The smell of diesel and salt water, sometimes tar. Cargo tanks parceled for loading in New Jersey destined for Yokohama, Pusan, Antwerp. Styrene. Sulfuric acid. Benzene. Toluene. "Rare, exotic stuff," my father would say when warning us to keep away from the chemicals stored in the basement. Crystal clear building blocks of plastic, insulation, fiberglass, PVC pipes, bacteria-resistant automobile and boat parts, food containers, and carpet backing. Yes, carpet backing. Clean in and out, free on board, cost insurance and freight. The physical reality of geopolitical infrastructure. In sync with the rhythms of the Anthropocene era, the manmade planet. With its alkaline seas and halogen cities and heavy-metal extractions and chaos. The city's computer chips pining to be plugged into the motherboard. Ready for docking with something larger. Leaving the planet behind. Scrambling into the new. No more apiaries. No more tartar thistles. No more old man and the sea. Just the thrust and hum of the time.

"National Transportation Safety Board issuing warnings today that any increases in solar radiation could result in flight delays."

The lumbering rise of an airplane in flight as the pilot pulled back on the throttle, spewing contrails and data. Radar Cavalries. Triangle billboards: for Coke, Parx Casino, the NBA on TNT. Cars circling closer and closer, like pilgrims around the Kaaba, water down a drain.

"Traffic on the twos."

Honk

    Honk Honk

        Honk Honk.

"Brought to you by the Dominican Republic. Golf, swimming, sun, and sand. Five star resorts and Michelin fine dining. You can have it all in the DR."

The airplane engines have obliterated space and time. We exit the plane in Santo Domingo and enter a different world, of sweet-smelling disinfectants and burning trash. I queue to buy pesos and Kath enters the bathroom to strap into her bikini top and Robert retrieves the rental car from some guy he found online. "Cheaper than Budget and doesn't give a fuck." Kath now in bikini top and me clutching pesos as we bypass the gold shirts and black collars of the lounging Dominican taxi drivers.

"Maybe we should have just called an Uber," she says. I refrain from advising her she's an idiot.

Now working our way north on the road to the Samaná Peninsula, older gentlemen walk the shoulders in collared shirts and straw hats, with big arms and strong shoulders, beneath streetlights festooned with portraits of a young president assuming the prime of his power. Robert removes wayfarers from his pocket and presses them to his face as he navigates the elevated highways. I lean out the window and gulp the humid, sweaty air. Miles of rows of defoliated palms. The thin brown trunks of the slashed and burned bush. A black snake smashed into flakes by a procession of automobiles traveling the toll road north from the city to the playa.

"Do you think we need to worry about cholera?" Kath asks.

"Of course we need to worry about cholera," Robert replies.

We descend from the plateau into a lush valley. Robert guns the gas to overtake a truckload of black soldiers holding rifles across their laps, sweating in uniform, expressionless beneath camouflage caps. Kath covers her bare, pink freckled chest with a thin yellow scarf. We climb steep mountains that shield the plains from the sea, switchbacks and ruts, and Robert watches me in the mirror as I bounce across the back seat. We pass terraced hills, painted shacks fashioned from rebar and cinderblocks.

"It's all the same," Fleeger says.

"What is?" Kath asked.

"Every time we go to an island on vacation it's always the same."

"Tell that to him," Kath says, pointing at an old man draying sacks of cement on a wooden cart.

Up ahead there is a wall of fire. Kath ceases her search for phone service. We round a curve and come upon a car in flames. Consuming the cabin and devouring the upholstery and blistering the paint. A boy wearing jean shorts wants to smash the driver's window with a stick but it is no use. The car is too hot and the smoke too toxic. His thin forearm shields his face. I feel the heat on my cheeks as we drive past the burning car. There is a man buckled into the driver's seat, still gripping the steering wheel and wearing sunglasses as his face tightens into a smile.

"Oh God," Kath says, and Fleeger parks. He and I run to the car but there is nothing we can do, just like this boy in jean shorts standing next to us. People step forward from their cinderblock homes and watch, standing on small verandas atop concrete staircases. An old woman crosses herself and Robert and I stand watching the burning car. It is sublime to watch fire destroy something. Growing before you as it feeds its destructive appetite. We retreat as *bomberos* descend the hill hanging from the sides of a small firetruck. They pull the man's body from the car, carbonized in the driving position, and douse his corpse with white foam.

Robert drives slower now as we descend the mountain. We hypothesize about the fire and Kath tells Robert he shouldn't have stopped because he could have been killed and he insists he was never in any danger and she says it was all very disturbing and we agree that it was all very disturbing. And then it disappears as the ocean presents itself before us, an expanse of blue so open and clear you could see the curve of the earth. As if we inhabited a blue quartz planet.

Kath implores Robert to drive slower because there are no guard-rails here. We enter the beach town and merge with scooters and fish-mongers and mango sellers and I realize that I feel no different than when I boarded the plane. Fleeger turns into the resort driveway and a fat man with a large gold-plated belt buckle stops us, flanked by skinny security guards gripping shotguns with both hands. I look inside the weapons' chambers. The guns are unloaded.

"Are they supposed to make us feel safe?" Kath asks as the fat guard waves us through.

I drop my bags on my room's tile floor and pop a lorazepam and walk to the beach and lay on a chair. A young man in blue-and-white

116

striped livery takes my order. I grip the Cuba Libre as the sun warms my stomach. There are more Americans at the bar, husbands and wives, Delaware blondes. Strong jaws and missing chunks of skin and fake breasts and FitFlops. Louis Vuitton luggage and tennis rackets and golf clubs. It would be best if we all avoid one another. I order my third drink and fall asleep as hummingbirds vibrate in the tree above me.

Fleeger and Kath sit at a nearby table drinking with lipless Americans and light-skinned Dominicans wearing Carrera sunglasses. Kath looks bored. The waiters place sandwiches and cocktails on their wobbly table and the Dominicans smoke Marlboros and someone offers one to Robert. He declines and leans forward with his elbows on the table rubbing his palms together and Kath runs toward me with a giggle, now wearing a rhinestone bikini, her new black cat tattoo wrapped in a red bandanna to protect the ink from UV rays. She grabs my arm, giggles, "Come on, Stephen," and pulls me from my chair and I follow her into the sea, across the sand, proud of my dive as she leans backward into the small waves. She swims deeper, slickening the sea with SPF 75, and Fleeger turns his back on us. A massive back in a gold golf shirt pointing a finger in conversation. Kath's breasts and shoulders are sunburnt. She leans against me. She is wet and taut.

"Why is he so boring?" Kath asks.

She slips her hands into my shorts and tickles me and I watch the men playing cards and someone lights Fleeger's cigar. Nothing feels wrong about this at all as she rubs me inside my shorts, like she is washing clothes in a lake, and when she and I are done she swims ashore and lies on a towel on her stomach and lights a white cigarette. I surf a small wave into the sand. Enter my hotel room, shower, pull on jeans, feel the tan against the denim, and sit on the concrete veranda, watching Fleeger throw money on the table and Kath standing at the bar on one leg, sipping from a straw.

Something small and aviary darts past me. A hummingbird, metallic and green and red. It bangs into the bungalow window and falls to the ground. It flaps a wing and rolls on its side and flips and rolls again, discomfited by the cement. I watch its constant repositioning, moving in circles to hide beneath a solar-powered garden light. I return to my chair and light a cigarette. The bird shutters like a cicada, its beak jammed in a crack as it pants beneath my shadow.

I pick up a large stone and drop it on the bird. It is smashed but still pants. I drop the stone three more times. Now it is destroyed. Two open gashes to its tiny ribcage reveal strange, gray contents. The bird no longer metallic and green but gray. I dig a small hole in the mulch and place the bird in a shallow grave, entomb it beneath a rock to protect its corpse from scavengers.

12

I CROSSED THE ANCIENT cement canyon of the Delaware Water Gap and entered Pennsylvania. Floodlights hoisted above the interstate where the traffic narrowed through a harrowing construction zone. Exits to Perkins Family Restaurant, Cracker Barrel, Ramada Inn, Lackawanna College.

Atop the still Susquehanna River, a square-bowed tug pressed a flotilla of barges laden with gravel, sand, and road salt as a freight train rounded the anthracite buckles of the Appalachian ridge hauling tanker cars plugged with Bakken Crude east to the refineries. Somehow evocative of World War II. A landscape disclosed by winter: bridges fashioned from stone, a disturbing number of fallen trees, a pipeline sluiced a track of dirt the length of a low cleared mountain, where it crested and continued north.

The traffic slowed and dispersed as I exited the interstate. Long truck beds laden with more steel pipes, little pink flags spinnakering at their mouths, forged in China, barged up the Mississippi and Ohio Rivers from New Orleans, for fracking Pennsylvania gas country. Adverts along the roadway for endocrine surgery, discounted laparoscopic procedures, Cancer Centers of America, drug and alcohol rehab. The afternoon sky darkened above a snow-piled Walmart, half-boarded-up strip mall, and a facility that specialized in genetic testing and screening for cancer and paternity. Are you my daddy? A small quarry, a cement depot, the steep triangle roof steeple of a

Methodist church with a roadside marquee exhorting passersby to keep Christ in Christmas. A wood-paneled minivan braked in front of me, Confederate flag and Hillary for Prison bumper stickers, someone's joy machine, words across the tinted rear window fashioned from white shoe polish that read:

MY FRIEND DIED FROM DRINKING

I'M DYING FROM SMOKING

DON'T QUIT . . . JOIN US.

I drove into open space and descended collapsing hills covered with late-winter snow and wisps of winter wheat, verges pinkened by road salt, and remembered why I was here, the work purpose of this drive. Destination on the left in one-quarter mile. The modern courthouse constructed on open land, surrounded by ample parking, empty on all sides, a limp American flag at half-mast. I turned the steering wheel and parked.

No security at the courthouse. No hot pastrami on rye. No hustle. A telephone rang unanswered. The clerk's counter empty as well. I pressed a soft, illuminated doorbell for service, spurring movement behind the shelves of folders where a short woman in a floral blouse hoisted herself from her chair and approached the counter. She was built like a lantern battery, with a gold cross imbedded above her red cabbage breasts and a haircut not too different from Fleeger's, but with perhaps a bit more gel.

"May I help you?"

Her battery was low on juice and I had no idea what it would take to charge it. I informed her I would like to review a case file but that I couldn't recall the docket number, had left it in the office. She provided me a small rectangular piece of paper to inscribe pertinent information: name of parties, name of counsel. I had little to go on but Thomas's full name and for counsel I listed myself. With the same low energy she searched the computer for the file, disappeared into the stacks, and returned a few minutes later with an accordion file marked Commonwealth of Pennsylvania, containing long green manila folders bolted with tiny brass fasteners.

"I can't let you leave with these but you can review them over there," she said, pointing at a counter. I asked if there was a copier. She said there was but it was broken. And besides I wouldn't want to spend the fifty cents it charged per copy, which was what it cost now and probably soon would cost a dollar if they ever fixed the machine. I refrained from telling her it was on the WorldScore tab. It was fine, she said, if I wanted to photograph the contents of the file with my phone.

Heavy paper weighed down the file and I felt that Hondaesque, voyeuristic excitement of uncovering more salient facts for impeaching Thomas's credibility. One folder for administrative matters, setting forth the names and addresses of the parties. Another folder containing filing receipts and administrative cover sheets. A verified complaint by Regina Thomas née McAdoo against her husband Mike "Bud" Thomas seeking divorce due to irreconcilable differences. A stipulation of divorce signed by the parties agreeing to joint custody of the minor child Caitlyn Josephine Thomas and the equitable division of marital property. Mr. Thomas to retain sole possession of the real property at 143 Mill House Road in exchange for the payment of certain sums due and owing to Ms. McAdoo. Boilerplate lawyer language reciting the Pennsylvania statutes governing the divorce followed by facts of the marriage—when, where, how long—to establish the court's jurisdiction followed by numbered paragraphs concluding with a signed court order dissolving the marriage. Affidavits signed by the parties attesting they did not enter the joint stipulation of marital dissolution under duress. I photographed the entire divorce file despite the fact it appeared to lack anything incriminating other than the reality of another busted marriage.

Toward the back of the file there was another folder, lime green and stamped and new, containing a verified complaint by Pennsylvania's Department of Human Services—Child Welfare Services (DHS/CWS) against Mike "Bud" Thomas. Ms. Regina Thomas née McAdoo—unfathomably keeping his name—now alleging that her former husband had sexually and psychologically abused their minor daughter Caitlyn Josephine McAdoo. That Ms. McAdoo had provided sufficient evidence for DHS/CWS to move the Court to rescind its previous order for joint custody and abolish Thomas's rights to unsupervised parenting. A report from a school psychologist corroborating Ms. McAdoo's concerns. Another letter from Thomas's previous lawyer advising the Pennsylvania court his representation of Mr. Thomas was limited to the marital dissolution and did not entail the new matter regarding custody. A letter from Thomas to the Court explaining that the allegations his former wife lodged against him were 100 percent false, that he was an injured Operation Enduring Freedom veteran, that his ex-wife was addicted to painkillers, that she had done this to him because he refused to subsidize her addiction, and that he was waiting for disability payments to rehire a lawyer but preferably one who wasn't such a bastard. The judge granting Thomas 120 days to retain counsel to challenge the protective order that would remain in effect pending adjudication. So ordering that the minor Caitlyn Josephine Thomas shall be relegated to the sole custody of her mother Regina McAdoo. So ordering that Mr. Thomas shall have no unsupervised contact with his daughter absent the continuous presence of the following individuals, including Thomas's second wife, Joan Thomas née McFarland. So ordering that in the event neither parent proved capable of fulfilling their parental responsibilities to the Court's satisfaction, the child to be placed under the protective custody of DHS/CWS.

"It's a shame what they've done to this man," the clerk said, Thomas's file now bridging the gap between us.

"I see that."

"He plays bass guitar every Sunday in our church band. He's a good man. Feeds half the church with all that venison sausage and jerky he makes. You should ask him for some."

"I will."

"It's that drug addict he was married to. She's the problem. And to think he had to come home to her after going over there to defend our freedom." I peered around the corner of the file shelves. On the wall above her desk was a framed photograph of the old, black, parallel World Trade Center towers and exhortations to Never Forget and reminders that Freedom Isn't Free. "So you're his new lawyer?"

She possessed solid clerical instincts. Suspicion began to gnaw at her.

"I'm an attorney," I said.

"Yes, but you must be Mr. Thomas's attorney. Correct?"

My quasi-misrepresentation had gone on long enough. I told her I was not.

"But you represented you were."

"No I didn't. I said I was an attorney. I didn't say I was his attorney."

"Then why on God's green earth would you want to review that file?"

It was time to go. Her position was compromised; I feared soon she would start blowing a whistle. The folders wouldn't fit inside the Redweld. I handed the bulky mass to her as she lectured me.

"Sir, the information in that file is strictly confidential and should only be viewed by officers of the court, the parties themselves, and their attorneys."

"You never said that."

She pointed at a sign on the wall written in all caps: PER PA. CODE XYZ 123 ALL FAMILY COURT RECORDS SHALL ONLY BE REVIEWED BY THE PARTIES AND/OR THEIR AUTHORIZED REPRESENTATIVES. Ignorance of the law was no defense. Her lantern battery now fully charged, there was no reason to argue.

"Won't happen again," I said, and hurried from the clerk's counter, refrained from triple-checking the photos I took of the files' contents. Outside, the car was cold but the engine ignition immediate and blowing heat. I half-expected the clerk to follow me from the courthouse, standing on the low steps, shaking a fist and chewing Thomas's jerky. I drove a mile toward the rock-hard hills, turned right, toward a cluster of quasi-suburban houses, drove some more, pulled over to the black-and-pink verge, and confirmed that I digitally possessed the photos, the legibility of their contents, their relevance in establishing Thomas's underlying motivation to jack-up his claims for injuries that didn't exist. Anxiety set in, congealed and then firmed; I had violated the law, evidenced by the slip of paper. More a dishonest mistake, but certainly the clerk would inform Thomas of this event after playing bass with the Baptist band, evidence of my civil espionage forwarded to Thomas and then to Lazlis and then to Judge McKenzie followed by potential sanctions and Rule 11 violations and then a citation for unethical conduct but certainly nothing as significant as disbarment let alone jail time. I was already litigating against the allegations. It was an honest mistake. The clerk was complicit. The engine clicked and the upholstery settled and I could hear myself move in the driver's seat as I struggled again to be comfortable with myself and debated whether to call Celeste and Fleeger and tell them what I had found.

I exited the car and my hands shook from adrenaline or cold or both as I rolled a cigarette, bits of tobacco bouncing from the paper as I struggled to lick the gum. The case against WorldScore had consequences for this man. I got it. Consequences and expectations that the consequences be resolved in his favor.

I looked up from the tip of the crooked, barely lit cigarette at the small green road sign ahead: MILL HOUSE ROAD. I again checked the photos on my phone. I was correct. This was Thomas's street. The distant sound of the far-off wind. A sound I hadn't heard in years, the cold wind of the country in winter. The temperature dropped by the half-minute and flurries now circled and fell, silently landing in the winter wheat. I shifted the car into drive and turned left onto Mill House Road. My phone buzzed with messages from Fleeger. Three of them sent in the span of my cigarette, each relaying the same question:

Dude, where's the report?

Thomas's house appeared smaller in person than it did in Honda's surveillance video. As if set down by giant hands on acreage surrounded by woods. The deer stand and the steps of a makeshift ladder bolted to the large trunk of a bone-white buttonwood, bleached by winter. I exited the car and entered the woods, crunching dry leaves. Someone had stapled neon-orange NO TRESPASSING signs to almost every other birch or maple tree. The woods surrounding the house thickened with shadows as the low clouds progressed across the remains of the day.

I watched the house from the woods. No lights in the windows of the home. No soft yellow bulbs. No blue television screens. No Avalanche parked in the driveway. A half-cord of circulars piled by the front door. The wind shook the American flag pegged to the wrought-iron porch, scattering cracked rhododendron leaves across Thomas's long front yard. I looked around me. There was no one there. I returned to the warm American sedan, engine still settling, and prepared to leave.

A school bus braked in front of the house and the door opened. Not quite a teenager—a tween—descended the bus's stairs and jumped to the ground. She was dressed all in black: sacklike black dress, black tights, bat wings of eyeliner, swinging a spiky rubber bookbag that looked like a naval mine, capable of blasting a hole through the hull of a destroyer. The house's front storm door banged shut behind her. I watched in the rearview mirror as Thomas's Avalanche accelerated around the corner, GOTTA GO decaled across the windshield. Fear of a confrontation hummed and buzzed and deep down inside my intestines percolated their contents and I ducked behind the dashboard as Thomas turned into his driveway riding the brakes and gunning the engine at the same time. Grapefruit-sized red rubber testicles swung from beneath the rear bumper, festooned with messages of vindictive patriotism. The horn blared on repeat until Thomas's daughter exited the storm door. She sauntered down the porch steps and climbed into the cabin of her father's truck. He hugged and kissed her. They looked at something she held in her hands and he backed the truck from the driveway, his one free arm around his daughter's shoulders as he pulled her close and again kissed the top of her head. They were on a mission, I thought. And he was in violation of a court order. And I probably would have done the same, though I possessed no context to know this for certain.

I followed the Avalanche's long, red brake lights. Snowfall broke up the traffic, denying me frames of reference, like driving inside a cloud. I peered forward to locate the truck, the little lights atop the high cabin angry and red, and followed Thomas onto Interstate 80, hidden inside a vortex of snow. I imagined his fellow Baptists reacting positively to the truck testicles at Sunday church, as Thomas lifted his bass guitar case from the truck bed of his burnt-sienna Avalanche. Nice balls, Bud. Thank you, Pastor. He exited the highway and I let up a bit, putting some distance between us. The Avalanche entered a shopping mall parking lot. I exited the car behind a bank of snow-dusted SUVs and watched Thomas descend from the cab. Swinging no four-pointed cane. No thick, plastic orthopedic brace fastened around his thorax. No cervical tic where his neck met his shoulders. Same bolero-cut Carhartt and easy movements of his arm again across his daughter's shoulders and he snugged her close as she tapped away text messages. He stopped walking and scratched his head, scratched it hard, chiseling grooves into his skull to satisfy this itch of the damned that couldn't be sated. His daughter spoke to him and he stopped scratching and together they entered the shopping mall's clear, bright automatic doors.

The car doors locked behind me with a press of the fob and I entered the mall, wary of Thomas's platinum-blue eyes greeting me behind the tritium sights of a .45 millimeter Glock. I felt exposed in the brightness of the mall, multitudes of me reflecting in the premature teardrop Easter Sale ornaments hanging from the mall's window ceiling. Conspicuous among the too much noise, too many counters and stands hocking crap, too many Starbucks cups and Bluetooth gadgets, too much butter and perfume, too many people staring at their phones. Through the narrow slits of the crowd I glimpsed multiple Thomases: stocky, denimed, proud, Spydercoed. With distended centers of gravity and jackknife mustaches and close-set eyes. I rode the escalator to the mall's mezzanine and leaned over the brass railing and watched the American crowd below. Swinging shopping bags and sniffing their wrists and yanking their kids and scrolling through Facebook as they walked and waddled. Fat and fungible and proud and smeared with makeup. I disdained them.

Thomas and his daughter entered a store constructed to look like a Polynesian hut, outfitted with images of highly-defined abdominal muscles stretched over male pubic bones. I ordered a mango smoothie from an Asian American girl crusted with tanning foundation and returned to the brass bannister. I thought of Kath and smelled my fingers. Her bouquet of metal and musk and some hand-cut tobacco. This was good, I thought, because it was under control. Ten minutes later, Thomas and his daughter exited the hut, she swinging bags of hairless twelve-packs. Again he scratched his scalp, attacking it, the shopping crowd moving past him now, a boulder in the stream. His daughter reached up and took both his hands and told him to stop. Not for her sake but for his. For a moment I thought he would crumble. She draped her father's arm across her shoulders and they exited the mall through the automatic doors.

I hurried down the escalator. Knocking into people, swimming through the crowd. I wanted to tell him that I was sorry. That I didn't know about the custody battle. That I empathized with him. That he was special. That I'm sorry for what we were doing to him. But that he needed to get over this, whatever it was. That we were not so different. But that he still possessed agency. That he could still control his fate. That this victim thing wasn't working for him and because it wasn't working for him we had to work against it. You see, that's my job. The same way you flew airplanes, I have to do this. But you have to move on. You have a good kid and you're not old and she will need you but you have to move on. You have to get over it and you have to move on. There is no other choice. The sedan door handle cracked and I started the engine and the heat resumed and again I pursued Thomas. Move on, man. His angry red lights once again visible atop the traffic. I will tell him this. I will do what I can to get this case settled but you have to move on. I will do this for him so long as he moves on. I let up. Knew he was heading home and the direction from here to there.

Thomas parked the Avalanche in the driveway. Soft bulbs illuminated the wood-paneled living room behind white curtains. I stooped across the crunchy yard, around the side of the split-level house, thinking

I could be disbarred for this, not really caring anymore but possessing no faith in my judgment. I crouched between the air conditioning units and listened for a sound, any sound. Nothing. Orion's belt blinked clear and bright, unclouded by the city's halogen smog. I circled the house, around the black ash pile of a spent bonfire. Standing now in the middle of the backyard, surrounded by blackness, the wind in the woods behind me, I felt nothing.

I closed in again, upright, bold, undetected. Filled with the clarity of spent adrenaline, I ducked into the shadows and studied the kitchen from beneath the pressure-treated deck. A box of Stove Top Stuffing on the counter. A half-drank two-liter bottle of Diet Pepsi. Wonder Bread. A carton of Marlboros. A small skyline of amber pharmaceutical bottles of varying girth and height. Crouching beneath the deck, I approached small windows and peered into the basement. The house smelled fusty. Of creosote and dust. Files of papers lined shelves or lay piled on the floor, spilling into smaller piles and leading paths to larger ones. There was an order to it. As if arranged by a strange insect, one that ate pulp for spinning into a web of paper, no doubt Thomas's responses to my discovery demands. I pressed in for a deeper look. There was a workbench surrounded by pegboard for hanging tools by hooks. Hand drills. Planes. Chisels. Screwdrivers and pliers arranged by size. Canisters of mineral oil and metal bits stored in glass baby food jars, readily accessible for projects such as maintaining Thomas's long Kentucky rifle, its walnut stock wrapped in protective rags and snugly vised beneath the neon tube light above Thomas's scored workbench.

Upstairs the daughter whined. She didn't want to do it anymore, she said. It was Joan's job. Thomas explained under his breath that Joan was no longer here and she knew why and it was for the better and now he needed her to do this for him so come on get over here and do it. After all, he bought her those clothes. Now it's her turn to show a little appreciation.

Stomach churning, I rose from beneath the pressure-treated deck and stooped around the side of the house, eyes level with the beige carpeted bedroom floor.

"No, dad. It's gross," the girl protested as Thomas unbuttoned his flannel shirt sitting on the bed. He pulled his undershirt over his head, revealing a body of black hair and deep, thick scars. He pressed a bottle of moisturizer into her hand and she capitulated and squeezed its gooey white contents across the length of his shoulders and down the sides of his back. Over the rotator cuff and shrapnel wounds. As she rubbed in the cream, he smoked a cigarette, watching them both in the mirror above the dresser. He closed his eyes. She rubbed in more cream, now into his back, along the sides of his spine. He tamped out the cigarette, lay down on the bed, and turned off the light. I stood there in the dark. The empathy was gone. I felt repulsed. The girl pulled a blanket over his half-naked torso and exited his room.

I circled the house. The girl now curled into the crook of a La-Z-Boy, texting. My footprints were visible in the snow. Certain the falling snow would cover them, I texted Fleeger that I had a productive trip to Pennsylvania. Good news to report. Getting on the road. We'll talk in the morning. His replies were immediate.

Risk Rewards tomorrow

Don't forget

Need report for Celeste pronto

13

I LACED ON A suit and stiff dress shoes for tonight's Risk Rewards dinner and walked to work, the swish bag's seatbelt buckle tightened fast against my chest. Global warming had begun to feel like nuclear winter. The snow continued to fall, silent and large, breaking up the movements of the city, as if someone had edited frames from the footage. I fought the urge to check the phone, admonishing myself to be still, to take in the moment, that these moments were rare. Once again I caved to digital temptation, downloaded a fresh email from Fleeger cracking the whip and copied to Celeste. Saying that whenever I was finished playing with myself he needed the report re Pennsylvania court findings, future handling, deposition strategy, etc. etc., like yesterday. He did this for show. Because he was an asshole.

Protesters stirred about the camp sipping steaming beverages from Styrofoam cups. In the wet, slow snow they mustered, a mass of bedraggled individuals in an almost silent vigil. I followed them as they marched south along the East River and beneath the elevated highway toward Wall Street. A crusty, tattooed protestor—her skin infused with permanent muck—extracted a Sharpie from the pocket of her tattered, hooded sweatshirt and vandalized the capstans as she passed them. IXXI IXXI IXXI IXXI. Once for mooring ships at Fulton Street, now for graffiti and security against truck bombs targeting tourists and Halal guys and steel-hulled windjammers. I detached from the crowd and entered the office building.

During my brief absence from the office Lazlis had answered my discovery demands. I counted the boxes piled on my floor. Twelve boxes of Thomas's medical and military records, most likely extracted from Thomas's basement and rolled in here by dolly. Redacted military records. Operation Nifty Package. Nerve maps of where it all hurts. Numbness to the extremities. Colonoscopy reports. Polyp scans. Kidney soundings. Inflamed glands. Concerned I would contract Thomas Syndrome by handling his records, I set to work, steeling myself against the pull of online media.

Now was no time for distraction, not when the trip to Pennsylvania was still fresh. I printed the photographs of the Pennsylvania court records and unboxed my steel ribbon of productivity and commenced the hum and click of billing law and time to World-Score. Digging between my teeth with the shards of a toothpick while my mental machine extracted salient facts from the documents and converted them into a report. Thomas's military commendations, combat reports, discharge evaluations, custody battle, at home alone with his daughter, his motivation to sue, to exaggerate his injuries. "Thomas's presentation as a disabled former military contractor with an expanding litany of mental and physical ailments likely motivated by the need to fund custody proceedings in Pennsylvania." I processed salient facts into clauses, clauses into lines of attack during his deposition, about prior warzone deployment with the US military. About postdeployment employment with FreedomQuest. About his relationship with his ex-wife and his daughter and the allegations his ex-wife made against him to Child Welfare Services. About his inability to lift his arms above the shoulder plane. About his financial predicament. About the incoming gun and mortar fire he allegedly experienced in Afghanistan and its lack of evidentiary support in any of the military or employment records. Postulating, why is that? Why doesn't it mesh with your previous statements? Why doesn't your version of events, your lawyer's version of events, mesh with anything contained in the twelve boxes of records we received? Explain that for me Bud. Make us, me, WorldScore, understand.

I wanted to crush him. My arguments snapped together and fused into strategies for future handling. I continued writing, immune to the temptation of electronic distraction while atomizing Thomas into facts. Into multiple one-tenths of an hour, points for Fleeger's board. With each posited question, each flagged inconsistency, the veracity of his allegations vanished bit by bit, eclipsed by our version of events. I was erasing Thomas with lawyering, erecting in his place our version of events. Solid legal work akin to drafting blueprints with words, constructing an alternative reality of chosen facts applied to the Code of Federal Regulations to support the predetermined conclusion that Thomas deserved nothing.

Fleeger stood in my doorway gripping his Kilgore tote and a paper towel, yellow schmutz smeared on the shoulder of his black pinstriped suit. I played offense.

"You owe me thirteen hundred bucks," I said.

"For what?"

"I paid for that blue neon sign you smashed. To keep the restaurant from calling the cops."

He looked tired and irritated.

"Good man," he replied.

Except for the fact I made love to his almost ex-wife. My treachery had now almost vanished, receded behind the curve of the Appalachian Mountains.

"He's suing WorldScore to fund his custody battle," I said.

"Who is?"

"Thomas."

"So what?"

He had no time for this now. There was a stain on his shoulder that demanded bitching.

"It goes to his motivation," I continued.

"Who cares about his fucking motivation? We just need to know whether he can return to work so WorldScore's not paying this asshole comp for the rest of his life."

He shifted gears.

"Look at this, man." He pointed at the stain. "These protestors are like fucking rats. Pissing on the sidewalk. Living in the subways. Throwing shit at people for having a job."

He scrubbed the stain on his shoulder with a white rage. Whitey entered stage left, like some stand-up act in the Catskills, ready to juice Fleeger on cue.

"I don't know. Some bitch troll. I think it's Boston cream," Fleeger explained to Whitey. "I hope it's Boston cream."

Whitey feigned concern.

"That's nice fabric, Robert."

"Yes, well, Whitey, I'm fine, thanks for asking."

"It's just a stain, Robert. I'm sure it will come out."

"Only because we have Risk Rewards tonight did this happen."

"It's the gods, Robert," Whitey said. "They test us all."

He patted Fleeger's lower back and exited stage right and Fleeger stepped into Attika's office. His finger-toe pedigraph still taped to her office door.

"He was asleep," Fleeger scolded her. "Why did you wake the dog? I told you not to wake the sleeping dog."

She mumbled a reply.

"Well then you call Nelson and tell him that. Let's see how many cases he sends you now that your settlement recommendation destroys his reserve limits. How many times do I have to tell you, Attika?" He struck the palm of his hand again and again against a bookshelf of published federal decisions. "You don't litigate the case you want. You litigate the case you have."

Fleeger exited Attika's office and removed the stained suit coat, cufflinks like clementine lozenges, and handed the coat to his secretary. He needed it dry cleaned like yesterday, he said. Dark blotches of sweat bloomed in his French-blue armpits. He smelled like barbecue. Attika brushed past him, exiting her office holding something beneath her eye with a finger.

"You're not going to cry are you?" he asked her.

"Technical foul," I said, making the motion.

"Technical foul," he replied. As if he had Down syndrome. He breathed through his nose. I granted him time and space to compose his partnerhood. He inquired about Thomas. I told him I was writing it up. Writing what up, he wanted to know. All of it, I said. You find something we can use in PA? I told him I did. Nothing that's going to get us into trouble? Worth the risk, I replied. He told me to be careful. I told him he could bail me out. That the case was proceeding according to plan. He wanted to know whose plan. My plan. Our plan. The plan. He wanted the report re future handling and deposition strategy by the end of the day. In order to review and forward to Celeste. I confirmed it would happen.

"And we have this thing tonight," he added.

"Whatever you do, be first class."

He gave me the finger. The receptionist breathed into the intercom.

"Mr. Fleeger, you have a telephone call on line three. She says it's urgent."

"Lucky number twenty-three," I said, but he was already on the move, his middle finger still floating in the doorway.

I reentered Thomas's medical and military records for six good billable hours. Up through his intestines. Into his lungs. Across the surface of his spine, observing the calcifying anchor hitches. Now steaming through his veins, on the lookout for Thomas's attack vehicle, Hamid Karzai at his side, pointing straight ahead in his purple-and-green robe.

"Be careful, Major. Taliban."

"I'll blast him, Hamid."

"Allahu akbar."

The day was ending. Fleeger emailed me, demanding the report, admonishing me for spending enough time on it already. Send it to him now and he would get it across the finish line. He wanted to read it. I closed and transmitted the Word document. Outside, the snowfall resumed, now in opposite directions, like effervescent lorazepams, Alka-Seltzers, lottery balls. I picked up the binoculars and glassed the apartment windows across the street. Orange with light, purple with screensavers, empty of people.

"Stephen, stop staring out the window," Attika said as she stood in my office door.

"I think I'll jump," I replied.

She laughed. Back in good spirits. Kilgore's Atta-girl.

Fleeger sat hunched over his desk, report in hand, slashed and rewritten in the margins with a red felt-tip pen. Armpits still blotched with sweat, he looked up from the document.

"Dude. This isn't a litigation report. It's a fucking epic poem."

I couldn't determine whether this was unacceptable.

"Nothing about the report resembles an epic poem."

My reply was weak. Yet still I was right. The report was eleven pages long, double-spaced, almost 4,500 words, focused and diligent. Fleeger leaned back in his swivel chair and propped eggplant-black wingtips atop his crowded desk.

"You spent the day travelling to and from Pennsylvania—which you, not me, recommended to Celeste—and all you come back with is the fact that Thomas has a custody battle with his wife? Which is his main motivation for suing WorldScore? That's your big insight?"

"How is it not?"

"What does that have to do with separating his alleged injuries from exposure to WorldScore?"

"It establishes his motivation."

"His motivation is to get paid. That's it. Since when did his motivation become an issue?"

"It's always been an issue. He says one thing, we say another, he has a financial motivation to not tell the truth in order to collect a bigger payout."

"That's your insight?"

"It is."

"You're missing the point again."

"The point is that he's a bullshitter."

"If that's an offense then me and you and everyone in this place is guilty of being a bullshitter. Then we're all fucking frauds. Our only objective is to sever his alleged ailments from his employment with FreedomQuest. Fuck, you have got to pin this to the ground, brother."

"I do pin it to the ground."

"No, you don't."

"Then what do I do?"

"I don't know what it is. It's hard to describe," he said. "You poke at it. You kick it over and study it for meaning. You're too distracted by what you find interesting and so you keep missing the point."

He gestured as if this was something dirty.

"You're a personal injury insurance defense lawyer, Stephen. I know you may not like it but that's what you are. For now at least. So stop trying to make this guy so fucking interesting. Don't try to make anything about this case interesting. No one's even going to read your report except for me. Celeste maybe but what she really wants is tangible confirmation that she can feel with her hands that we're on top of things."

"You sure about that?"

"Yes, I'm sure about that. Just as I'm sure this report won't do it for her. Because all you're giving her are more questions than answers."

He leaned over in his chair and attacked something beneath his desk.

"For example, you're obsessed with the deer stand in Thomas's front yard. You mention it like five times in your report. So he has a deer stand. The point is not whether there is a deer stand built atop a buttonwood tree in his front yard, but whether he built the deer stand himself. If so, what tools and materials did he use to build the deer stand? How heavy were those tools? How heavy was the lumber? When did he build the deer stand? Before or after Iraq?"

"Afghanistan."

He resurfaced from beneath his desk.

136

"Whatever. And then the point is, are, whether he still uses the deer stand. And if so, whether he hunts with a compound bow or with a rifle. It it's a rifle, how heavy is the rifle. How much recoil? What caliber? Can his shoulders and back withstand the recoil? If it's a compound bow, then how much weight does it take to pull the string? And if it's fifty pounds or thirty-five pounds or whatever then how does he have the strength and the orthopedic dexterity to climb up a tree and launch an arrow with enough torque to kill a deer, when he's alleging torn rotator cuffs and slipped discs and maybe even the PTSD comes into play too. He says he can't concentrate? Then what's he doing while sitting in the deer stand? Whittling dicks? And if he testifies during the deposition that he can't hunt from the deer stand anymore, then we have Honda video him doing so. If he says he can then we run it past our orthopedic specialist and ask for a professional opinion as to whether Thomas's alleged injuries permit him to return to work now, someday, or in the future in some capacity and if they do and he says he can't . . ."

Fleeger lost his train of thought.

"This is your case, Stephen, not mine. Why is it that after almost seven years of practicing law you continue to lack real impact? It must be my fault. Have I not taught you correctly? You don't know how to advocate, Stephen. You marvel. Ponder. Expostulate. You have this counterproductive habit of trying to sound profound all the time. It prevents you from being aggressive."

He returned under the desk again looking for something, and resurfaced. Whatever it was he couldn't find it.

"There is something inherently unaggressive about you, Stephen. You need to be a shark. You just do it."

"Just do it."

There was a pause.

"How are we going to beat this guy if you're in love with him?"

Hot anger coursed through my shoulders. Along my cheeks. Flushed through my capillaries. I wanted on the offensive. To tell him about Kath. About my dick in her mouth. That he was incapable of operating outside his comfort zone. That his dimensions were limited. That he was limited to this and this was his all.

"I'm not in love with him."

"Bullshit. And if not, then what is this report? Rhyme of the Ancient Mariner? Kubla Khan? Stormed Tora Bora on horseback. Self-sufficient survivalist. Collection of woodworking tools. Single dad under duress. Black powder boar hunts."

"Bear hunts."

"Who fucking cares? The problem is this guy's your hero. We're barely out of the gates with this case and we're under McKenzie's microscope and I put this whole thing in your hands and this guy is your fucking hero."

"No he's not."

"Yes. He. Is. But you know how we defeat your hero, buddy? By not denying the fucking truth. And the truth is that this guy is faking his injuries to obtain a payout he doesn't deserve represented by that sack of shit Lazlis. Looking to take something from our client that isn't his. That's all you need to know. Those are your marching orders. That's your polestar. And only after you sufficiently counter his allegations of physical and mental illness, only then do you get to engage in the sexy work of impeaching his credibility with all these juicy details you're addicted to. Yes we want to bloody him up where he can't get his story straight. But not until after you cover the bases of causation and injury. And don't ever write about it in fucking iambic pentameter."

He was conflicting himself. I wanted to tell him that maybe if he hadn't spent so much time sport fucking and hockey sticking and grab-assing and handballing and mouth sputtering that maybe he'd get his fucking instructions straight and stop lining up moving targets for me to shoot upside-down and backward so that he could yet again Rough Rider in at the eleventh hour and yet again manage to pull off a win with the grip of his handshake and his self-inflated gravitas but that it wasn't stable. It wouldn't last. It couldn't last. And he was bound to fall. And he was certain to fail. And that as much as I never wanted this to happen I also did. To teach him that the same rules which applied to me and Kath and Attika and everyone else also applied to him.

He raised his eyebrows a quarter inch to enjoin my executory insubordination. My mouth sealed like a tomb. I pushed against it. It was no use. The stone wouldn't budge.

"Look, Stephen. I want you pulling this oar alongside me. You're like me. You need that extra bit of juice to keep it moving otherwise this all sucks. And I get your need to try and make these cases more interesting. But the time for that is over now. The time for that has passed. You need to evolve. You need to show me you can do this on your own without me babysitting you. We're engaged in a money war here and the battle is all about momentum and alliances. Who is your go-to guy. I want you to be my that guy. Otherwise you're out the door shucking cases like Nelson for a mediocre paycheck, an apartment in Union City, wheat beer, and potato skins. Is that going to work for you?"

He was going into my future, armed with objective evidence. I retracted into my shell.

"Stephen, here's the truth. You want the truth? Here it is. The partners around here are beginning to talk. Your billable hours are terrible. Again. You're not bringing in any work. You have no clients. You have no files of your own except for the pro bono case with the Chinese seafarer and even that you can't get done. And don't forget I went to bat for you for that. You're coming up now on your eighth year and decisions have to be made and right now for a lot of these guys around here you're a giant question mark. That's what they see when they see you. A big fucking giant question mark. But I get you. You work hard. You care. But it's important for your own personal growth that you start pushing back against all the Harker doubters by delivering above and beyond what you've come to expect from yourself. Any associate can drive a car to Pennsyltucky and dig some dirt out of a backwater courthouse. But you have to up your game, man, and I know you can. Christ, do you really think I want to spend the rest of my career working with Whitey? No. I want you here. And Attika as well. I love you both. But these guys also know what they're doing and how to spot talent and they need to see that from you.

"Are you even listening to me?"

I told him yes.

"What did I just say?"

"That I'm a giant question mark."

I didn't want to stand here anymore. He stood and approached me. A tic commenced beneath the soft flesh of my right eye, where the ocular muscle attached to the cheek.

"Look, we have a big night tonight. Some clients who send me a lot of work are coming into town for this Risk Rewards thing and it wouldn't be a bad idea if they got to know you a bit. Rick Hemmings will be there tonight. Really good guy. I'll give you him. You know why? Because I have enough work and because I care about your professional development. Get him to like you and I'm sure he'll send you some cases. Christ, I'll tell him to send you some cases. But you have to earn it. I can't keep re-drafting your shit forever, Stephen. I don't have enough time for that. At some point you have to fly."

He opened his mouth and flapped his wings as if he was a baby pterodactyl. Attika entered his office holding a folder and a winter coat. Tiny bandages fastened to where her heels had worn through the skin of her ankles.

"Am I interrupting something?" she asked.

"Not at all, Attika," Fleeger said. He accepted the folder and thanked her. Told her good job. He gripped my tricep.

"You lifting weights, Steve-O? Getting firm there, buddy."

I shrugged away from him. Attika discerned I was pouty. That this little meeting with Fleeger had been rough. She asked if we could all head uptown together to Risk Rewards. A town car was en route and she was meeting Tucker in the lobby. We'd all fit. Fleeger declined, said we still had some things to discuss, that we would see her there. She exited his office.

"Rework this and give me something we can use," he said. "I know you can do this. You have an hour."

14

FLEEGER'S CRITICISM WAS LEGITIMATE. My analysis was hazy, my recommendations regarding strategy and future handling flaccid, with too much emphasis on the conflicting facts and not enough on the tactics of refuting specific allegations. The reality was that World-Score would have to pay Thomas something. It was our job to ensure it was something very little.

"Ready?" Fleeger asked, standing in my doorway and wearing a freshly dry-cleaned suit jacket. We exited the building, both of us nodding good night to the security guard donning saggy pants and an empty holster. I hadn't thought to call a town car beforehand, neither had Fleeger, and so we stood on Maiden Lane struggling to hail a cab in the cold wind. It was the switching hour, all lights on, medallion and off-duty, as the taxi drivers raced north on Water Street to hand over the keys to the nightshifts.

Fleeger nodded toward the uptown 2/3 and we walked to the subway. My phone double vibrated with a new message. The vibration made me feel whole, like a whole note, with the spaces filled. It was a new message from Kath. I read it inside my jacket pocket as Fleeger walked a few steps ahead of me.

"I want to taste you."

Followed by a photograph of red lips eating a banana. My tuning fork hummed. I looked ahead at Fleeger, also lost in his phone. We pushed through carousel doors and entered a fake oasis of plastic palms and old black men playing chess and mirrored ceiling tiles and descended into the subway station. The turnstile blocked me when I swiped my MetroCard. A homeless man yelled into the empty tunnel. Tyndall effected by carbon dust and strong dirty yellow lights.

"Fuck," I said.

"Give me a swipe," Fleeger commanded.

"I'm out."

"Come on, man, we're going to be late."

"Don't you have one?"

Robert watched me, mouth agape. Yet another example of me once again failing. Some sticky goo coated the kiosk's touchscreen. My credit card was unreadable; contact your bank. A quick blast of the subway horn announced the train's impending arrival. The machine dropped a new yellow card into the lit chamber and I swiped us in.

"I can see what you all trying to hide in there," a brown kid yelled on the platform, muscles flexed as he gripped the handlebars of his fixed-gear bicycle. "Don't think I'm unsuccessful because I'm a nigger. Ha ha. Ha ha."

He laughed like a barking madman, hopped-up on synthetic marijuana—K2, Scooby Snax, Mr. Nice Guy—and slurping from a bottle of cherry-red cough syrup to control the anarchy of the vicious high. The long train entered the station, silver corrugated sheds, small blue lightning, red and green signals, a procession of unfathomable American flags. Fleeger and I boarded the crowded subway. Japanese tourists clutched their expensive handbags as the black kid jammed his bicycle onboard. An African woman with medusa-like curls wept. "You know when you cry and fall asleep that be the best sleep ev-ah," her friend consoled her, clutching her arm. Bandages and Betadine. Velcro sneakers. Hand sanitizer tubelettes dangling from parachute packs. Sixty-four ounces of Cola Icee. Candylicious. Oh we can handle that jelly. Then the ominous opening of metal latches, the echoing tunnel as the train raced north, the closing of internal subway doors as we entered the stretch between Union Square and Forty-Second Street, prime turf for begging.

"Ladies and gentlemen," a homeless man began. His jaw scissored and missing dentures. "We are out here tonight because we're homeless. And we need food, and donations. Because we're homeless."

The brown kid holding the bicycle stumbled into Fleeger.

"My niggers, I want to let you know," the kid menaced his captive audience, competing with the homeless man. "They got gold glitter in all your sidewalks."

Fleeger pivoted away. The kid watched Fleeger, rested his bike against a pole, and moved through the subway car, slowly, as if he owned the space. "Don't want to look at a black man?"

Fleeger ignored him.

"The real racists are upstate. The real white racists are upstate. They kill a motherfucking nigger. Go up there and tear up and eat the motherfucking sidewalk. Tear it up and eat."

He was boiling, on the threshold of berserking while having a conversation with himself. Fleeger continued his pivot away from him.

"Conventional man residual racisms. Ha ha. Ha ha. Damn, did I say all that? Goddamn. Where is my respect? Where does my respect come from? Telling people what's going on that's where from. Nah nah nah nah nah nah. I ain't disrespecting myself. I help the cause. You don't help the cause, bro."

He was almost in Fleeger's face.

"You don't help the cause bro. Because you think I'm one of those niggers on the train going nowhere?"

My intestines stiffened. The kid's shoulders bigger than Fleeger's and his face cascading sweat. I felt responsible for some reason. Fleeger gripped the subway pole and turned away from him.

"Pay attention to me you white racist. I'm going to work."

"Why don't you stop disrespecting yourself, young man," the homeless man exhorted him, breaking the kid's grip on Fleeger.

"You old fool, you smell like piss."

The doors opened at Forty-Second Street and the subway disgorged its contents, the urgency of public discomfort compelling the riders' quick exit. I shuttled Fleeger out the door. The black kid and the homeless man now almost alone in the subway car and yelling at each other behind shatterproof glass as the train proceeded north.

"Thanks, man," Fleeger said. Puffing his cheeks to communicate that could have been bad. He removed a tiny bottle of hand sanitizer from his jacket pocket and rubbed the contents into his hands.

"You OK?" I asked.

He nodded yes without looking at me. The sound of the subway cars entering and exiting the station augmented the silence between us, cars clacking against cars clacking along the tracks. The cracked prerecording in the speakers above announcing delayed service due to a medical emergency at Columbus Circle a scintilla more intelligible than the sound of the sun's electromagnetic radiation recorded by NASA. I wanted to drape my arm across Fleeger's shoulders and talk about what happened and tell him it was OK, the kid was a freak, the kid was high as shit, but didn't know how he would take it and so I didn't. Regaining his composure was a solo act and I let him let his process unfold. Once that happened it would be my fault for not having ordered a town car. He would mock me for it in front of others. Yet another indignity he suffered in the city. No wonder he lived in Hoboken. Still not speaking, we entered the hotel and departed the lobby in elevators shaped like gel capsules and approached the dining hall, where Attika and Tucker Nelson stood pointing at their table assignments.

"You took the subway, Fleegs?" Tucker said.

Fleeger didn't want to discuss it. His reboot was still in process and his operating system hadn't yet reached the point of being able to joke about anything.

"Not everyone gets the town car treatment, Tucker," Attika informed him. "You're special."

Tucker and I shook hands. I told him he looked marvelous as always and Attika struck his arm.

"See, I told you Stephen liked you," she said.

Together they strolled the reception area pointing at koi fish swimming in a plaster pond as Fleeger sought his guests, still, I feared, somewhat frazzled. I followed him. He located Rick Hemmings, leaning against the cash bar and positioning his pudding-bowl hair-cut with small hands.

"Man of the hour," Hemmings cheersed Fleeger.

Fleeger embraced Hemmings with a two-handed handshake and then gripped his arm, thanked him for flying up from Dallas. He agreed that tonight was indeed an honor but it couldn't happen without his team. I shook Hemmings's small hand, then stood aft of Fleeger. He was almost back to normal. The two men looked around, taking it all in. I did so as well. Across the room, Lazlis dunked a maraschino cherry into a cocktail glass. Celeste's confident English laughter rose above the crowd, a substance lighter than air, as Judge McKenzie whispered in her ear. My phone double vibrated. Another message from Kath I prayed. It was. Telling me she needed to see me tonight. Meow. Give me two hours, I replied. Despite the fact that I risked being gibbeted above the cash bar for my crimes against the crown.

"You've all been so generous inviting me here tonight to dine with you. Let me get the round," Hemmings said.

Fleeger wouldn't hear it. They grappled and shoved each other. Hemmings escaped Fleeger's grip and handed a platinum credit card to a slender Caribbean bartender with a French name and ordered a round of highballs while tightening his forearm around Fleeger's neck. The bartender poured three drinks. He moved like a man found in the woods as a child raised by parakeets. We gulped from the glasses and Hemmings out of nowhere commenced denouncing his daughter's liberal politics, which we in the city must be inundated with, good God. As Fleeger finished his drink he faux-nodded in agreement, yes it's true that's the way it is, and a seersuckered Louisianan, as if detecting this topic of conversation via some strange political olfactory cluster of nerves, approached us, looking to gab and network. Nelsonesque but more porkneck. He congratulated Fleeger on the honor of tonight's Risk Rewards recognition and asked the Kilgore crowd to please consider him whenever we needed Louisiana counsel. He was, he explained, defense minded.

"Because there's just too much judicial emphasis on compensation and not enough on defense," he said.

I thought he would spit on the carpet.

"How do you know that?" I asked.

"Come on now, son."

Hemmings consumed handfuls of nuts from the hurricane glass positioned above the barman's icebox. Pecans and peanuts and walnuts and shells dusted with salt and monosodium glutamate spilling from his hand and mouth. I had stood here before and this was its breeding ground. The primordial ooze of tastelessness. It had been so ordained. The Louisianan's instincts were keen. So be it. He asked if we wouldn't mind if he told a slightly off-color joke. Fleeger and Hemmings presented him the floor. I looked to ensure Attika was still pointing at koi fish with Nelson. There she was. Thankfully beyond earshot.

"So this teacher says to her student, now Billy, can you spell what your father does for a living? And he says his father is a doctor and he spells that on the blackboard and the teacher says very good. And then she asks Felipe to spell what his daddy does for a living and he spells mechanic. And then she asks Jamal to spell what his daddy does and Jamal is silent and he doesn't say anything and the teacher asks him to spell again and he says he can't because his daddy ain't got no job."

There is a thing white men do when they switch off a part of themselves to laugh at something that is awkward and offensive. It causes them to laugh harder. Hemmings did that now. So too did Fleeger. A loud, confirming, careless laugh, to establish for the Louisianan that his offensiveness was no big deal. That he was among his tribe of peers. That he too was judgment proof.

"Hey, now see if you can figure this one out," Hemmings joked. "Why do aspirins work?"

Hemmings matted his pudding-bowl hair while entering a football stance and in doing so knocked backward the hurricane glass of walnuts and peanuts and pecans and cashews and flakes and shells and nut oil and MSG into the cash bar's icebox. The barman twitched in silent disbelief at the mess we just made for him to clean as a silver bell summoned us to dinner. There was no apology. Because none of these men were capable of speaking to the barman other than to order something, as if the neural passageway from the part of the brain that forms speech to the part of the throat that makes sound had been clogged for life in these circumstances. Fleeger left an extra five dollars on the bar and I topped it with a twenty as the barman shoveled his bin of ruined ice into a trash can only to have to refill it again with fresh ice extracted from some industrial machine located in the service bowels of the hotel. I entered the bathroom and Fleeger followed me.

"Hemmings is a great guy," Fleeger said. "Loves Kilgore."

Now it was my turn. As if we were bouncing up and down on some seesaw. I leaned into the urinal and pissed a puddle of frog spawn as Fleeger fixed himself in the mirror.

"How can you stand these guys?" I asked him.

A square device near the bathroom ceiling discharged an atomized cascade of citrus deodorizer that dissolved in midair around his shoulders.

"Put it in a box and forget it."

We entered the convention hall dining room. Tabletops stocked with multiple wine bottles and a rectangular block of ice sculpted into a model of the Manhattan skyline. It was already melting. Fleeger shook hands with well-wishers en route to his seat at the banquet table on the stage at the front of the room, a dining hallful of Hemmings and Nelsons and porkneck Southern lawyers and the occasional but still rarer Celeste. One of whom now walked my way. Longer black dress, silver rope chain, hair slightly frizzed, shiny black heels punching holes in golden carpet.

"Charlie Parker," she said. She kissed my cheek and sipped her wine. "I don't know how much more of Judge McKenzie I can take. He won't keep his hands off me. Says it won't hurt a bit. Promise that you'll shoot me if I give you the sign."

"OK."

"OK what?"

"I'll put you out of your misery," I played.

"I didn't say kill me, Stephen. I said shoot me. Maybe in the foot. Just to get me out of here. But don't cause any permanent tissue damage, OK? Is that a deal?"

She winked. It was a warm, friendly wink. Fleeger stepped between us, still shaking hands. He kissed Celeste's cheek.

"I was just telling Stephen I could always count on you guys. Even for the dirty jobs." She nodded at Hemmings and the Louisianan. "How's the company?"

"Typical," I said.

"It could be worse, dude," Fleeger said. "You could be working for Lazlis."

He had a point.

"Don't you owe me a report, Mr. Harker?" she asked.

"It's almost done," Fleeger said. "You'll have it tomorrow."

"You better. Otherwise I'll take away your Risk Reward. And I know how long you've been gunning for it, Robert."

"One hand giveth," I added, pantomining.

"And the other taketh away," she replied.

Celeste kissed us on our cheeks and sauntered to her table, punching a trail of holes behind her. I told Fleeger to make us proud.

"You want my advice?" I asked him.

"What's that?"

"Don't fuck up."

He gave me the finger, the second of the day. It was a friendly finger, and he walked off toward his spot center stage.

Hemmings orbited the round dining table holding a cocktail glass and debating where to sit, displaying no affect in the grip of another awkward moment. A synchronized team of hotel workers donning white gloves filled our water glasses and set small plates of salad before us atop the table. I asked one of the servers how she was doing tonight.

"All right," she replied.

I thanked her.

"Protein is actually the next big commodity," Hemmings explained to Nelson as he capitulated to the reality that his only remaining viable option was the empty seat next to me. "What they do is they fish farm out in the Gulf in these big cages, tilapia mostly, and then process the fish into protein bricks at sea, which they then sell to the UN for feeding refugees. They're making a killing."

"Really," Tucker said, with pure interest. "You know the biggest money maker in the London insurance market has been the refugee crisis? You know how much it costs to insure the logistics for shipping food to Syria?"

Hemmings, more interested in tilapia than refugees, let Nelson's efforts to engage in polite professional conversation dangle while watching Celeste pivot between the tables.

"You know her?" I asked.

"You should have seen her twenty years ago."

"I didn't peg you as someone into foreign women."

"She's not foreign, son. She's English." He forked salad into his small, lipless mouth. "Ever since my wife died I have this insatiable desire for dark-haired women. South Asian. Middle Eastern. Latina. English. I don't care where they're from, so long as their hair is black and they're in their early forties. You can just pluck them off the vine." He popped his fingers. "It's a beautiful thing. You know where I can find some of them?"

I lacked all empathy for the man, even if he was a widower. His frat boy performance at the cash bar had incinerated the already-miniscule possibility I was capable of such.

"I don't," I said. But delighted myself with the thought of giving him Soncha's number. Just to see how that would play out.

We sat around the table eating and drinking almost in silence. Red-veined chard speckled with dried cranberries and almonds. Phyllo dough—wrapped chicken and butter-soaked baby carrots and string beans. Pastries constructed around balls of vanilla ice cream. Hemmings tried again to speak with Nelson. Nelson tried again to speak with Attika. Attika tried again to speak with a thin man seated next to her who specialized in legal seminars. I tried again to speak with Hemmings. It was impossible. I couldn't fathom why he would agree to send me cases per Fleeger's instructions when we lacked a common anatomy necessary to communicate over dinner.

The lights above the dining room dimmed and the white gloves cleared the plates before us and topped off the wine glasses, red or white. A projector screen descended from the ceiling above the banquet table at the front of the room. It was followed by that voice of long and short risk and cowbells and bulls over bears, greeting us tonight via satellite from Palm Springs, like a banker playing God in a Hamptons production of The Ten Commandments.

"Of course I wish I could be there with you fine folks tonight as we celebrate one of the great unsung heroes of this economy." Money Man paused. "Lawyers."

The crowd laughed.

"In particular, tonight we celebrate the important work of frontline insurance defense lawyers. Whereas once there were masters of the universe, now there are masters of risk. For instance, we know there will be car accidents. We know some of our fellow Americans returning home from working in war zones will file spurious insurance claims for injuries with no discernible pathology. We know that electronics will occasionally start fires and burn down houses and medicine will occasionally be tainted and cause illness, sometimes severe. Such are the risks inherent to our mechanized, industrial, consumerist society. And we know that stocks will rise and fall based on events beyond anyone's control. But what we don't know is the financial value of those occurrences. How much those occurrences will cost us as individuals, the company, and ultimately the shareholders. That's the rub. And that's where insurance steps in. To close that gap. And who does the actual work closing that gap? Frontline attorneys. Lawyers. Trusted counsel. That is why we are here tonight. To celebrate those at the vanguard of ensuring this vital industry's maximum efficacy."

A picture of Fleeger appeared above the crowd, looking over his shoulder and smiling for the camera, like a photograph his mother would hang from her living room wall in homage to her successful, adorable son.

"Over the past four years, one New York law firm has really stood out when it comes to representing the interests of the insurance industry. Whether it's keeping a tight rein on PTSD claims, or defeating plaintiffs' efforts to develop new injuries with no detectable pathology, one law firm has routinely been voted above the rest. And that firm, which we recognize tonight, is Kilgore. Particularly the team led by Robert Fleeger. Robert, you and your team have been . . ."

"First Class" the crowd chimed in upon the prompt of Money Man's upturned thumb.

"And Robert, in recognition of your achievements, we would like to present you tonight with a special award. In honor of your contributions to the insurance industry, the effectiveness of your insurance defense practice, and ultimately your steadfast commitment to the rule of law."

The crowd clapped, looking around itself, nodding in agreement, to the sound of a thousand upturned rainsticks cascading little shells and manmade thunder. Another moment belonging to Fleeger. Another speech, another res to place on his Kilgore bookshelf alongside the trophy sprites and Tiffany's crystal apples and alma mater beer steins and all-Ivy commendations. Two women in black pantsuits and red lipstick escorted Fleeger from the banquet table to the podium, to where his honor awaited him, draped and hidden behind a small curtain of red silk. The presenter on Fleeger's left untied a gold tassel and the slip dropped, and there it was. The awe-inspiring zenith of Fleeger's superlawyerness.

"Here's to sticking it to plaintiffs for the past ten years, Robert," Money Man said.

Laughter arose from the front of the hall, growing louder now, forced backward through the room by identical fungible laughter, as people squinted, realized what it was, no, it can't be, succumbed to the awkward communal pressure, well she's doing it too, more guffaws and cackles, both upward and backward, sines and cosines of laughter moving through the room at the speed of Fleeger's humiliation. Drunk female shrieks punctuated by fine fellow huzzahs! and hey-nows!

"And here's to sticking it to plaintiffs for twenty more," Money Man yelled. "Job well done, Robert F. Fleeger."

Fleeger spun his thing on its pedestal to take a look. And there it was. A bronzed, King-Kong–sized tube of KY personal lubricant. Superimposed, embossed, possessing texture and heft and impaled on a pedestal by its anal fin. Money Man now summoning cloudbursts of audience laughter—you know you want to—and whistles and jeers from the tables of dark suits and almost empty dessert plates.

"USA, USA," the crowd chanted.

Celeste turned and gave Judge McKenzie a high five. Everyone in the cavernous dining room laughing now, the girls with white gloves clearing the plates, the French parakeet bartender chuckling "you guys" as he continued dumping ice with a large silver scoop, the innumerable Tuckers and Celestes and Lazli and Hemmingses. The laughter's pressure inflated the room, pressing against the banquet hall's padded moveable walls and smothering the room with collective laughter, everyone except Fleeger, as the trophy presenters presented him his present, smirking "Oh, too bad—you don't like it?" and synchronized-air-kissing his cheeks. Depositing him at the podium, alone in the hot white Kleig lights, where he now fumbled for something to say.

"Come on, Robert. You can't think on your feet?"

It was Lazlis, dining tonight with the enemy to generate good-will. He chuckled in his seat and leaned into the ear of someone sitting next to him. Both of them now pointed at Robert on the podium, taking full joy in the unexpected comeuppance.

"Just a second," Fleeger said into the microphone.

The audience began to turn, from almost still good-natured to undoubtedly primal, like time-lapse photography, but reversed, as the men and women in the dining hall devolved in shape and form. Their skins toughened into sandpaper. As they held their grimaces, their skulls narrowed into snouts, their mouths expanded into pink orifices ringed with rows of serrated, triangle teeth. Beneath the hems of their skirts and through the flies of their pants they popped dorsal and caudal fins, swinging atop their seats with jerky movements at the looming frenzy of Fleeger's public humiliation.

One drop of his pure Ivy League blood squirted from a shaving nick into the sea of sparkling wine glasses, the audience's eyes now rolling behind nictitating membranes as they circled to take a chomp. Fleeger gripped the podium with fear as his shark cage dived into the perilous sea, cut loose from the deck above. The chair felt light in my grip as I stood and walked backward from the table.

"Jesus, Robert, you're fired," Nelson yelled. Except it wasn't Nelson, it was a hammerhead shark, wearing a suit, with Nelson's slurring man tongue licking the insides of his slurry pink mouth.

I moved along the wall, up the metal stairs, confident in my kinesiology. Thinking that by thinking about tripping on the multiple cables traversing the stage I was bound to do so but by thinking about thinking about tripping I had protected myself from a stumble. I removed a folded pamphlet from my suit jacket pocket. *The Arc of the Universe Bends Toward Justice.* I handed the pamphlet to Fleeger. His pupils spun like yo-yos.

"This room is full of people who want to destroy you," I said.

He stared at me. His eyes glistened. His pupils stilled and tightened. He got it. He was free from the fall. Whatever it was. I squeezed his shoulder and he squeezed mine.

"Thanks, man," he said.

I nodded a silent it was nothing and exited the stage down the opposite stairs, working my way along the opposite wall and around the distant opposite corners of the dining hall. The diners perplexed but ultimately relieved as they reverted into quotidian form, again aware of themselves, examined their suits and dresses, at where the fins protruded from and disappeared to, as I worked my way back to the table.

"First, I would like to thank my associate Stephen Harker, who just handed me the notes for tonight's speech, which I apparently left on my desk."

I nodded to the polite applause, almost invisible in the back of the room.

"And Attika Roberts. Where are you? Over there with the Kilgore crowd. Attika stand up for me please."

Another gracious round.

"And second. I just want to go on the record as saying, Lazlis. Where are you? There you are. I just want to say, once and for all—I hate you."

Torrents of laughter. Buckets of the stuff. Steak choke worthy in napkins and baritone hey-nows and the tinkling of glasses with dessert forks and coffee spoons.

"No, really, I do. I'm sure there are some good qualities there somewhere. But I have no idea what they are. Maybe I should ask Mrs. Lazlis?"

Lazlis sat behind an empty dessert plate. Now silent like a Moai.

"I mean, come on, has anyone ever had a better adversary than Lazlis? He makes everyone look good. Jesus. Talk about a lack of personality. Come on now, Jim. We all hate this job. But at least we try to hide it."

The diners laughed without care, clapping their hands between their legs and coughing up old cigarettes while letting Lazlis have it from all sides.

"I don't know who invited you tonight," Fleeger continued, now hushing the testosterone-foam-supplemented roar, "but I hope to God they poison you. Garçon, fix Mr. Jim a round of drinks. Put it on Kilgore's tab."

More laughter as Hemmings pushed back my chair and motioned for me to sit next to him despite the fact it was my seat, and Celeste watched me from across her dessert plate. I pretended to tie my shoe.

"No, seriously," Fleeger said. "It's always an honor to dine with your competitors." The crowd subsided. "Now Jim I hope you choke on your steak." The laughter rose again and crashed over the rocks. Fleeger hoisted his bronze award like an Oscar, thanked the Risk Rewards panel and his team for making it happen, and returned to the banquet table, collecting handshakes and back pats as he worked himself behind his dinner plate and the next speaker took to the podium.

"Talk about grace under pressure," he informed the crowd. "I'm going to give Robert Fleeger every file I have."

15

THE CEREMONY ENDED. FLEEGER and Hemmings walked toward the hotel elevators, arms gripped around each other's lower backs, playing hot potato with the award. Celeste approached me, listing forward in heels.

"Well played tonight, counselor," she said.

"I don't know what you're talking about."

She smiled. A dusting of foundation around her eyes shattered into a thousand barren tributaries.

"Don't be so coy, Stephen. I like a man who takes the initiative in a tight spot. How about I buy you a drink at the hotel bar? I could use some smart company. The only thing anyone talked about over dinner was their vitamin intake and what gluten does to their digestive tract. My God, do they not realize the implications of speaking about one's intestines?"

"It's a classy crowd."

"Indeed. So? You'll come have a drink with me."

I demurred. She looked disappointed.

"Why are you always disobeying me, Stephen?"

Attika and Tucker exited the dining hall and walked along a distant wall, again near the koi fish, returning to where the previous magic may have almost happened. He whispered in her ear, her long coat draped over his forearm, and she whispered into his and he dropped two steps behind her.

"I can't," I said.

"Stephen, nothing you have to do is more important than having a drink with us tonight. We're your team. Now come on. Don't make me force you. We're celebrating."

This woman pulverized my intentions. I capitulated. Told her just one drink at the hotel bar. She winked.

"Good boy," she said.

Lazlis approached us, pride more than intact, as if empowered by the attention Fleeger had showered on him.

"Can I speak with you, Stephen?"

I told him sure.

"You're not going to discuss the Major now here, are you Jim?" Celeste asked. "After you practically crashed the dinner?"

"We got something important we need to discuss," Lazlis replied.

"Is it absolutely necessary?" Celeste asked again.

This was up to me. Otherwise we were trapped in a logjam of conflicting obligations. I told Celeste to give us a few minutes and I would meet her downstairs at the bar. To my surprise she capitulated, departed with a slightly intoxicated dismissive wave, and joined Hemmings and Fleeger as they entered a downward elevator capsule.

Lazlis leaned into me. Breathing meat and wine.

"I got a call today from my client," he said.

"Which one?"

"Who do you think?"

"Just messing with you, Jim."

He wasn't having it.

"Listen. He said he woke up the other day and discovered a yard full of footprints in the snow. You wouldn't happen to be stupid enough to send Honda down there to film him while he's in his house, would you? Filming him in public I can't really do anything about, but in his house? Young man, that's a gross violation of the rules of professional conduct. Subjecting you and Fleeger to sanctions under Rule 11."

I told him no, we would not be so stupid as to send Honda to film him in his house. The ease with which I lied surprised me.

"I'm not so sure I believe you."

A smirk was all I could muster. There were no good answers.

"Let's talk about it Monday."

"I like you guys, Stephen. I know it may not seem like it, but I do. Even with Fleeger busting my balls. Because for the most part you guys are straight shooters. I get that you have WorldScore as your client and that you need to look and play tough, but at the end of the day I also know we're both just trying to make a decent living within the four corners of the system. You bill the client. I chase your client. Pitch and catch. Now you're on the mound and you can make this go away easy. Just recommend to Celeste that this case is getting too hot, with too big of an exposure, we do the dance back and forth, I start high, you start low, and we end up somewhere around the sweet spot of $250,000, and then it's done. All gone. And then I don't have to get into whether your investigator is illegally breaching my client's right to privacy."

He had me. He knew it. My silence conveyed as much. My ability to lie and duck and weave still amateur. His eyes trained on me, from both sides of his blue-black nose.

"We got a deposition next week," Lazlis continued. "You want to play with the big boys? Then get this settled and I won't have to bring any of this up before the judge. The last thing you want on your tender record are judicially prescribed sanctions for unethical conduct. We all have an obligation to police the profession. Don't make me play bad cop, young man."

He walked away, taking with him all that remained of the fleeting buzz of my surprising act of pro-Fleeger heroism.

A tear descended Hemmings's cheek as he stomped the ground, cradling Fleeger's award in his forearm like it was a swaddled newborn. Demanding to know when Fleeger became the voice of reason. Fleeger ignored him for a moment, looked at my empty hands.

"Dude, where's your drink?" he said.

"We need to talk," I said.

"Of course we need to talk. We always need to talk. Communication is the key to every good relationship. What's wrong?"

"Lazlis threatened me upstairs with sanctions."

"When?"

"Right now."

"Da-da-da-da-da-da-da," he shushed me. "Have another drink."

He summoned the bartender to pour me a second scotch. Two drinks at the hotel bar.

"I think—"

"Drink. Come on now. Drink."

I followed his prescription. The second scotch lacked the burn and twang of the first.

"Come on, man. You can't handle a couple of threats from Lazlis? Do I need to change your diaper? Jesus, if I had a dollar for every threat some plaintiff's lawyer made against me for apparently acting contrary to the rules of professional conduct. What's Lazlis gonna do? Tell me. Move to sanction you? If he does it's career suicide for him and he knows it. We'll never settle another case with him. So relax."

He possessed a convincing answer for every twist and turn involving the ethics of the profession.

"He's a good man," Hemmings said, raising a small glass of beer to me. The award now like another person between us perched atop its own barstool, caped with the red silk sash.

"He's a great man," Fleeger corrected him. "He just doesn't know it."

"You're in a sweet spot right now," Hemmings said, pointing at me. "What are you, thirty-five? This is the age, man. You're not a kid anymore but you're not old either. All you have to do is start realizing you're an adult."

He was drunk and on a roll.

"Now what you don't want to do is follow where Fleeger here is heading with all this Internet dating. At some point he's going to contract a venereal disease and then he's going to want to get married and have kids but at that point he'll be the forty-five-year-old guy with the twenty-five-year-old wife and a dormant case of warts and you don't want that either. Because then none of your friends' wives will talk to her at the cocktail parties. Not because of the warts but because of the age difference. So she'll be standing there by herself all night staring at the floor while you're trying to talk with your buddies and where is the fun in that? Huh? But then you also don't want to be the fifty-five-year-old guy with the fifty-five-year-old wife either because by then you'll be relying too much on lithium ion batteries and pharmaceuticals and where is the fun in that? Huh? You'll be lying in bed with your old wife on top of you and a remote control vibrating dildo up her ass and you hitting the pulse button and the next thing you know the batteries go cold and well there's no fun in that either. Huh? Fleeger's in the same boat as you. Except he doesn't have your problem."

"Which is what?" I asked.

"Your problem is that you think too much."

"Bingo," Fleeger said.

"You can't be a great lawyer if you think too much all the time," Hemmings continued. "You'll fry the hardware."

He tapped his skull with his finger as Tucker leaned against the baby grand piano and wrapped an arm around Attika's waist.

"Can you handle all this attention?" Celeste asked me, swinging around my starboard bow.

"I'm working on it."

"So what was all that about with Jim?"

I followed Fleeger's advice and buried any thought of actual repercussions.

"He's pissed off we won't settle."

"Of course he is. That's the point. Tell him to make a reasonable settlement demand and we'll entertain it. But there is no way Major Thomas is getting anywhere near what he's demanding."

"He wants two-fifty."

"He's a fool."

I looked in my drink and she swung to my opposite side. It would be fatal for me to tell her I needed this case to settle. That I needed it off my back. That it was becoming a drag.

"We'll discuss it more after I receive your full report. Because I don't want to talk about work now. I'm drunk. And I hate talking about work when I'm drunk because I don't have full control. So instead I want to talk about you. Most men in your position, Mr. Harker, would be thrilled to find themselves in my good graces, because I could easily send you enough cases to move you through the ranks into partnership."

"I know."

"Really? Then be honest with me, Stephen. Are you having second thoughts about your choice of profession? If so I want to know before I invest any more time in our relationship. Is this not for you?"

"It's not for anybody," I replied, reckless.

"I disagree. Clearly it's for Robert. I'm not sure he would choose to do anything different. But you?"

"But me what?"

"Don't get so defensive. My God, it gives you away."

I ordered a beer from the bartender and he wrapped the bottle with a red paper ascot. Nelson's hands continued to rub Attika's lower back. She didn't order him to stop.

"Don't try to substitute disdain for dissatisfaction, Stephen. It can't hold forever. And nothing good ever comes from it."

I shut my mouth. Tucker belted a round of lyrics, breaking the grip of Celeste's attention.

"Oh dear," Celeste said.

"He means well."

"That's worth something, right?" she said.

"Most certainly is."

I had to go, couldn't lock on anymore. My conviction held fast. I said my goodbyes and kissed Celeste on both cheeks. Fleeger picked me up, set me down, and they let me leave with minimal protest but collectively disappointed I insisted on doing so. I looked back at the bar. Fleeger and Hemmings hunched over and conspiring. Tucker and

Celeste scrolling their phones. Attika, eyes moist with drink, waved goodbye.

The subway buckled and bumped and deposited me at Canal Street. I avoided the groping palm of a shirtless man doubled over in pain, smeared with carbon, shaking a cell phone vajazzled with the rhinestones of the Puerto Rican flag. Unsure which way to walk, I texted Kath. Asked if I could come over. My phone vibrated a series of messages released from some digital holding pen. Stephen where are you? Stephen come over. Stephen come find me I'm out with friends. Stephen now is too late. Stephen I made us lunch reservations later this week at Shoemacher's. It's close to your office. Your treat.

I didn't reply. Because I wanted Kath to be disappointed as well. Because I wanted her to await my reply. To have to wait for me too. I admonished myself for being annoyed and disappointed. The neon light above the noodle shop sizzled red and gold sequins. I turned the doorknob and entered my apartment.

"Stephen?" Gregg said. He and a guest sat perched on a bench in the courtyard below, before a fire burning inside a terracotta saucer, both holding French horns that glowed with the reflection of the significant flames. "Are you home?"

I opened the window.

"Want to join us?"

"Thanks man, but I'm beat."

"OK."

I switched off the lights and rolled an all-natural cigarette and looked around the apartment. I felt supersaturated. At the point of dissolving into a cloudy mass of swirling broken particles. In the great white light of the open refrigerator I poured myself a long vodka and sat by the window. Kath's avocado pit had sprouted one tender root, stretching microscopic increments with each passing moment as Gregg and his guest commenced tuning their horns.

16

WITH HASTE, I REACHED for the phone in the dark, vibrating across the coffee table. Caller Unknown.

"Hello."

The digital disintegration of a human voice, as if trapped between the satellites and telephony, likely corrupted by another cloudburst of solar radiation. I told myself it must be Kath, the call blocked by celestial forces. I hung up the phone. Caller Unknown vibrated the phone again, now in my hand. The voice on the other end yelled in a language I couldn't comprehend, crackled and distant. As if calling from another country. I hung up. It vibrated again. Caller Unknown was trying to get through to me. I let it vibrate.

"This is Stephen," I said, as if answering my office phone. The line now clear but Caller Unknown remained silent. "This is Stephen. Who is this?" A few seconds passed and they hung up. I sat there staring at the phone. Hating the device for its constant presence, my incessant accessibility, its constant impact. I convinced myself that after breaking through the digital obstructions Caller Unknown finally realized they had the wrong number. It vibrated yet again. Caller Unknown. That was enough. I refused to answer and the vibrating ceased.

I closed my eyes and struggled to fall back asleep. Stimulated by the phone's blue light and the paranoia induced by the multiple calls, I lay on the couch, fighting myself, menaced and agitated by

Caller Unknown. I didn't want to be inside, couldn't continue fighting against the couch and the pillow. It was only eleven. I dressed and exited the apartment building and walked outside into a cold, hard rain, its individual drops striking the earth like jacks. Through a kaleidoscope of yellow and white and green and red lights, above, speeding past, suspended over intersections, aglow in tavern and restaurant windows, I walked toward the Village, smoking a soggy, hand-rolled cigarette, in search of a bar where I could regain myself.

A black man shuffled toward me, sheltered against the rain inside a long, tan raglan, wheeling behind him a torn carry-on suitcase. A thick keloid scar bulged the length of his left cheek and his hands were splotchy and pink with vitiligo. His upright thumb communicated that he needed a light and asked if I had one. My disposable Bic failed to ignite the soggy butt of his half-smoked Newport.

"Hold on," I said.

He followed me and we stood beneath the awning of an East Village junk store, across the street from a papal bust weeping in the rain, a Bud Light tallboy impaled on the Polish church's wrought-iron fence. I removed my tobacco pouch and rolled him a straight, dry cigarette. My hands clear and steady in the warmthless neon lights glowing in the junk store's window.

The man cupped his pink and black hands around the blue-orange flame I maintained with my thumb. We held it together, protected from the elements. If I was an artist this is the energy I would strive to capture on canvas or film. This reflection of light we held, our flesh glowing incandescent with light and water and red blood cells. Hunched over the flame, I could see the thick roll of the haphazardly stitched scar running the length of his mandible, tiny dots where doctors had sewn him shut with gaping sutures. One strong punch would knock free a piece of his face.

"Thank you, my man," he said.

I liked doing this. I needed the conversation.

"You have someplace to go?"

"What kind of question is that?" he snapped, but he wasn't angry. "You think I'm homeless? Wandering around in the rain? And if I am, what are you going to do about it? Offer me your couch? Serve me a hot, home-cooked meal?"

He paused and we smoked.

"Probably not," I replied.

"Probably not. But that's not the question you should be asking right now. The question you need to ask yourself is, do *you* have someplace to go?"

"I'm working on it."

"Well, you better figure it out soon."

I asked why.

"Because by my calculations there's just a few more weeks before that sun disgorges a billion-ton glob of plasma straight toward planet Earth that wipes out the North American power grid with a runaway, hemispheric electric current."

"You think so?"

"I know so. Those black dots on the sun are in flux, expanding and moving, going berserk. I've been watching and measuring them. And when they merge, you better have someplace to go."

"I'll keep that in mind."

"Do or don't, but it'd be better for you if you did."

I felt damp and chilled, craved warmth and a drink, would worry about the sun over beer. We finished smoking and flicked the butts into the rushing gutter, where they coursed toward a storm drain, like miniature whitewater rafts, en route to the East River and out to sea.

He thanked me again for the cigarette and walked east on the narrowing numbered street, trawling his tattered suitcase. Beneath the shaking trees, he disappeared in the rising squall of the late-winter storm.

I walked in squares. East on Fourth. North on Second. South on First. Thinking about the man and his busted face and his fading hands. About what he said about the sun and his brutal scar and whether the scar augmented or diminished the veracity of the warning. It did the former. But whereas tragedy worked against Thomas, there was credibility in this man's conviction, despite how farfetched. Perhaps because he attached no blame and claimed no entitlement. Perhaps because he was black I believed him more, loathed him less. If so, then so be it.

Now past the white-tiled Halal chicken restaurants and the mosque beseeching respect for all God's prophets, outside of which Arab men in denim jackets argued in Arabic over a compact disc. I entered a bar decorated like a souk and ordered an Efes. Radio Istanbul in the exposed-brick corner strumming an oud and slapping a drum and smoking grass and drinking beer. Someone winked, face hidden by the fug, and toasted the crowd. We raised our drinks and I downed another Efes.

I departed in search of another bar, for something I knew I wouldn't find. The new bartender excited about the craft selections she had on tap. NYU kids blowing spent cocaine into mangled Kleenex and arguing about baseball and declaiming that the New York teams don't have a chance, man. Because no one wants to play baseball in the snow and rain, man. Because baseball is as much about rhythm and chemistry as individual talent as well as the weather, man.

"But it's the Latins. You can't deny the Latins are the best ball-players in the world. And they just refuse to play here."

I couldn't comprehend what they were talking about.

"Latins. Man," another kid said. "They fucking hate the cold."

The girl sitting next to me wore a Seahawks jersey. I inquired whether she was a Seahawks fan.

"You staring at my tits?" she asked and walked away laughing.

I exited and wandered, entered, drank and exited, the bartenders blending into one common denominator of mistaken tattoos and gaping ear lobes. I spent money on drinks as if both were sworn enemies. Hipster kids at the bar, dispensing hipster wisdom to justify their viewpoint that Donald Trump was all right. Explaining the difference between a five-pane and a six-pane baseball hat. That intelligence was the new rock and roll. That intellect jacked up prices of obscure pharmaceutical drugs. "Ain't nobody bringing new drugs to deez streets widout ya boy getting a taste." Now drunk, I read a Reuters article about drug-makers' patchy investment in tropical disease vaccines due to uncertain commercial prospects. Fantasized about Zika breaking out across the South. Whole colonies of microcephalic children abandoned and left to fend for themselves in the Everglades. Reverting to primitive life. Waging war on the bigheads with clubs and poleaxes pillaged from rednecks' living rooms and tossing bigheads' remains into the swamplands. To appease the angry gator god.

As I scrolled the news on my phone a woman endeavored to make a new connection with me. She adjusted her bra in the mirror above the bar. If Magritte lived here in this time he wouldn't paint apples and men wearing bowlers falling from the sky. He would paint multiethnic cocks with puffy white wings, flying like geese, forming a V, in search of willing cunts . . . with Groucho Marx eyebrows cracking open décolletage in the angled mirrors above the liquor bottles illuminated by rows of votive candles.

"That looks interesting," she said, nodding at the article on my screen.

She was pink and broad-nosed with frizzy brown hair, racially unidentifiable.

"I find the whole situation with what's going on in the Middle East these days fascinating," she said. "My family has always been into war. I had a grandfather who fought against the English brigades at Aleppo. He taught me everything I know."

With one eye, I peered into the bottom of my pint glass as a man grabbed her almost by the back of her neck. His designer T-shirt adorned with crumbling skulls and shattered mandibles. The distinct, combative, upright gait of the tattooed and gel-spiked white man uncomfortable in his surroundings. I wanted to comment on that fine-looking razorblade dog tag hanging around his neck but didn't. He was already enraged, and I was in no state to take or throw a punch.

"No, Bob," she told him. "I am staying right where I am. Talking with?"

"Jackson," I said.

"Very nice."

Bob walked away.

"Can you believe how rude that bloke was?" she asked, reclaiming her seat, pretending she didn't know him.

"Not at all."

I slipped into the doldrums of drink. Ignored the woman still talking as I paid my tab and finished my beer, freed myself from another encounter, exited the bar, and walked east through the New York projects. Past cars propped on milkcrates and up the red-gated spine of the Williamsburg Bridge, where I peered down at the fires and tents and cardboard bedding of the protestors' camp. Alone, I reached the bridge's apogee, prayed a meteor would strike Brooklyn, turned around, vertigo rising, like walking across the roof of a steel cathedral. It's the imagination that gets you.

Now north along the East River, across a patchwork of halogen lights and freezing puddles. I reached the end of an abandoned pier fashioned from springy greenheart planks and stood before a row of silent, bulbous capstans, half expecting them to turn and greet me with cartoon faces. The river smelled of tar and motor lubricant. A small bulk carrier approached the long expanse of an open Brooklyn berth. Now came her wash, rippling against the hourglass pilings. I walked home beneath the Big Dipper, spinning above New York City like the errant hand of some malfunctioning galaxy clock.

The cold wind resumed and my legs stiffened. I hailed a taxi, rested my head against the frigid window, paid the fare, and exited the car a few blocks from home to avoid paying for wending through one-way streets.

"Go with God, young man," the driver said.

Night had passed into the purple-blue sky that appears just before dawn. The hour of the crows, now amassed in the wet trees and circling overhead. A penumbra standing two floors above the street watched me pass, pivoting on its spot. I stared back. It pulled curtains closed. The moment before you think something momentous will happen but it doesn't. I reminded myself it was a ruse. That I was no Nostradamus.

I turned onto my street. Failing to discern the threat because I wasn't paying attention. GOTTA GO. Too wrapped in thought to react as Thomas's burnt sienna GMC Avalanche sped at me, lights off, dumping fuel into the roaring valves of pistons and chambers of steel. GOTTA GO. The vehicle swerved, all wheels pulling my direction as I quickened to the curve, where I tripped and twisted over knotty tree roots that buckled beneath the sidewalk and landed on outstretched palms, now indented with minute pain inflicted by pebbles and glass. The vehicle slowed for a moment, that moment in slow motion, as Thomas turned to face me, the breathing mask covering his face, tiny filters pulsing, before the motor revved and the Avalanche churned around the street corner. Red testicles swinging from beneath his angry, patriotic bumper.

I struggled to solidify my guts. Commanded myself to solidify. My brain and body were sheared. I couldn't remember the last time I fell. Didn't remember the ground being this hard. My hands shook. The key refused to enter the lock. The substance in my veins and muscles turned to putty. I shouldered open the front door shaking and breathing. Fumbling with the apartment key. Tiny glass fibers of the shattered phone inside my pocket, inside my skin, between my fingers. I entered the apartment and ran to the bathroom.

17

I RUBBED MY PALMS through the remains of my hair, rolled and smoked a cigarette, rolled and smoked another. Sat on the couch, stood, paced, searched the apartment for Thomas despite knowing he couldn't be there, under the couch pillows, behind the shower curtain, inside the closet. I looked out the window, expecting to discover Thomas had gone infrared, squatting inside Gregg's copse of plastic trees, calling in the coordinates for the drone strike.

The radiators banged and hissed, smelling of steel and steam. I couldn't take the noise. The pressure increased and the radiator spit foul boiling water. I found the radiator key in a cluttered drawer next to the Leatherman. I slid the Leatherman in my pocket, for offense or defense, I wasn't sure which, my only weapon a tool, and tightened the radiator valve with the key. The hissing ceased. I looked out the window again. Checked the flat roofs and fire escapes above the courtyard for Thomas the sniper. Thomas the Avenger. I looked at my watch. There was no one to call. Composure solidified around the edges. My fear began to clot. It was almost dawn.

Again I checked the window. Enough time passed and again I checked it. I stood. Opened the fridge. Grabbed a beer. Tossed the cap in the sink. Raised the bottle to my mouth and set it down empty. I laced on my boots and exited the apartment.

The rental car bounced atop the New Jersey Turnpike, as if there was extra air in its tires. The highway beneath me howled in slices. Military flags hanging from the overpasses, fastened to the protective cyclone fencing. I drove faster, straddling the yellow dash lines, pushing the car's limits, the RPM pin into the red zone, draining the fuel tank. The steering wheel shook. The roar of American trucks, sounding capable of space travel, but just for a second, as I passed their spinning tires and spiked hubcaps. Cars cleared my path, their drivers assuming I was a state trooper behind the wheel of a speeding American sedan.

I raced a landing plane, myself and the pilot, both of us operating comets. The sound of our engines throttling forward and backward as the plane descended from the sky, his pistons reversed but mine still churning. The phone vibrated atop the dashboard, its touchscreen shattered into shards and splinters, cobwebs of busted glass. A new message from Fleeger, on a Saturday morning, because we needed to talk about my billable hours. Again and soon. I tossed the shattered phone to the back seat and rolled down the window and breathed in cold benzene and ether. Again through the skyline of smokestacks, miniature city of energy, cracking open carbon compounds. Now parallel to a silver westbound train. Through the woods of central New Jersey. Union excavations. Business parks. Wetlands. Beached ferries in the marshes. Silver trucks bulging with tanks and spigots. Up and over the Oz-like bridges and deep into the granite hills of Pennsylvania as the sun rose higher in the rearview mirror.

Whipsawed, I exited the interstate. Past the strip malls and the Pentecostal churches and the flapping bendy car showroom Gumbies and into the open fields of winter wheat. The snow thinner now and the thaw almost upon us and the trip shorter than last time. I drove past Thomas's split-level house and deer stand buttonwood and pressed the brake. A yellow Gadsden flag now flew from the house's front porch. DON'T TREAD ON ME. The eastern rattler. I parked the car down Mill House Road and my broken phone vibrated again in the back seat. More messages from Fleeger. Saying we needed to talk ASAP. What did you tell Lazlis? Celeste concerned your heart is not in it? What did you tell her? I sat in the front seat and sipped cold coffee. Listened to the engine cool, the upholstery settle, my stomach churn. I rolled and smoked a cigarette, tapping random words against the backs of my two front teeth.

I walked up the driveway, crouched behind the Avalanche, approached the two-car garage, stood on my toes, and peered through the garage door windows. Something massive hung from the ceiling, my eyes adjusted to the darkness, a full-sized deer, gutted and skinned down to suet and bone and spinning in small quarter turns by a thick chain bolted through its small mouth. A murder of crows alighted from the woods in unison and circled above the house.

The soft, soggy ground soaked the hem of my pants as I entered the woods that surrounded Thomas's house. A small, steep ridge collapsed into a clear, turbid creek that coursed beneath melting, bubbled ice. I walked atop the flat, slippery rocks. Stepping from one to another to another, teetering but not falling. I hoisted myself up the bank by the crooked trunk of a fallen dogwood and approached the small encampment and hillock of dirt filmed by Honda.

Thomas had since half-cyclone-fenced the encampment, a warren of huts and passageways constructed with two-by-fours and plywood and polypropylene tarps. Thick electrical wires linked the encampment to the transformers. The single-prop airplane that before lay in pieces had been cleaned of moss and partially reassembled, its engine hauled from the fuselage and hanging from a hoist sheltered beneath a tarp, undergoing repair via the tools and parts stored in the shipping container, whose doors were now propped open, a single lightbulb hanging above the interior workbench. I listened before I moved. Only the looping crows.

My thoughts moved faster and I reappeared to myself. Neon-orange NO TRESPASSING signs now tacked to the trunk of every tree. I circled the pile of dirt, maintaining a long radius, then I ascended the ridge and peered inside. Thomas's gut pile. Mounds of offal and intestines and meat-stripped deer carcasses caked with lye, grimacing at death, and swarming with the buzz of black, green-headed flies summoned to the stench. Of bucks and does, even a few fawns, butchered for their tender meat. I felt nothing. Thought of only what this meant for the case while circling the gut pile and photographing the dead deer with my cracked phone from multiple angles.

The questions formed themselves. Explain for us, Major, how you can claim total and complete physical disability due to multiple orthopedic injuries on account of your employment with FreedomQuest when you also regularly hunt ample-sized deer. That you then dispose of in the gut pile behind your house, after butchering the animals hung from a chain bolted to the ceiling of your garage. Doesn't sound like something a man with your extensive disabilities should be capable of doing, does it? Just off the top of your head, how many deer do you think that is? I count about twenty. You? And how about that airplane engine? How many pounds does that weigh? Did you hoist that by yourself from the fuselage? And, by the way, do you have a license to hunt that many deer? Out of season? I didn't think so. Because a license to hunt this many deer out of season doesn't exist.

Someone moved through the woods, lumbering like bigfoot in Mossy Oak 3D camouflage, clearing a path before him through the bare vines and bramble. Almost hidden against the pattern of the leafless woods but for his movements. It was Thomas. It looked like Thomas. There was no debate. There was no thought. Gotta go. I sledded down the embankment on the side of my leg, still bruised from last night's fall. Over rocks and sticks. Splashing now through the creek, mud sealing each footfall, stumbling forward. I reached the edge of the woods and crossed into the open lawn and sprinted toward the road. Past the side of the house and now past the garage. I hurried alongside the Avalanche, crouched behind the rear bumper, removed the Leatherman from my back pocket, snipped the Avalanche of its red bull balls, heavy and round. They weren't plastic. They were rubber. I chucked them as high and deep into the woods as I could muster. The American art of long distance throwing. *Gotta Go!* They landed without a sound. I located the fob in my pocket and unlocked the car door and started the ignition.

18

MONDAY MORNING. THE BUILDING'S hand scanner denied me access to the elevator bank. I bumped against the turnstile, bumped again, bumped once more. It wouldn't budge. I assumed Kilgore had finally fired me. The ex-cop security guard swiped me in, nodded, walked away. I was wrong.

Money Man again on the tiny elevator television, now sharing his entrepreneurial recipe, his foolproof method to make a fortune. "Early to bed, early to rise, work like hell and advertise." He grabbed the television camera and zoomed it on his face. *"If you want to walk like a duck and talk like a duck then be a duck."* He's going to bite the camera, I thought. But instead he advised that it's never a bad time to invest in petrochemicals.

I sat down behind my desk and attempted to work. Money Man would fire me. I would fire myself. My interest in billing law had reached a new low. I played Jenga with the Department of Labor regulations governing WorldScore's obligation to pay Thomas compensation pending resolution of the underlying dispute. IIs and As and iiis. The pieces fell. The tower tumbled. I billed two and three-tenths hours for researching a question I couldn't answer. My inbox pinged with a fresh email from Fleeger's secretary warning about the inherent risk of leaving your GPS in the car.

"Not only gives robbers a map to your home. The very fact you are where you are means you are not there. Think about it."

"What if more than one person lives at home?" I replied.

No response.

Here it was now.

"Good point."

"Come see me now," Fleeger emailed.

I entered Fleeger's office. He sat behind his desk, hunched behind his flat screens. He was dressed like a candyman. Fruit Stripe shirt. Candy Dot tie. Violet suit. Probably matching Fruit Stripe or Candy Dot socks. His rainbow of fruit flavors spreadsheet of women displayed in the glass window behind him.

"I'm Robert Fleeger," he explained into the speakerphone. "No. I'm Robert Fleeger."

The female robotic voice asked him to please repeat his name.

"Rob. Ert. Fleeg. Er."

"I'm sorry I didn't understand that."

He ended the call with a fuck.

"You're late," he said, maneuvering his mouse between the flat screens. Snipping data from one woman and pasting it to another. He didn't look at me. He watched me from the narrowing space between his hairline and his eyebrows. As he aged his hairline advanced rather than receded. I wanted to ask him what shampoo he used. I told him I had a stomach thing. He asked if I was OK. He sounded sincere. I told him yes. He leaned back in his chair and flipped open a stapled invoice dashed and crossed with red ink, pressed the soles of his burgundy strapped loafers against his battered desk, and looked up at the popcorn ceiling tile. He was in a good mood. Or rather, he wasn't in a bad mood.

"Did you really spend only three hours studying product liability cases when researching the summary judgment motion in Wuxi?"

"Is that what the bill says?"

"It does."

"Then it must be true."

He looked at me. There was no miasma like before. He was all detail, high definition. The plate tectonics of his face had ruptured a nose between the broad plains of his cheeks. Stains beneath his eyes

175

from lack of sleep, where a skin tag had begun to sprout. Ears slightly asymmetrical. Strands of dark black hair—thicker than the hair on his head—sprouted from the ridgelines of his ears, which glimmered in the bright morning sunlight entering is corner office windows.

"I think I know what the problem is. You're underbilling."

"I don't think so."

"Maybe not but I know so. We cited like fifty cases in the motion for summary judgment. And yet you only spent three hours reading them? Impossible. And even if not impossible then we're going to add to it. Because it warrants more."

He placed his feet on the floor and leaned back in his seat.

"This is something else we're going to work on. Your time notes need to possess an air of billability." He said billability like he was conducting Mozart with his hands. "Billing is like making hamburgers. You need to add a little fat in there to make it sizzle. And we need to start making your time sizzle. Because in addition to Whitey now I got the accounting department on my ass about you. You're almost at the point of starting to cost the firm money."

"Can you handle it?"

"Of course I can handle it. But what will I get from you in return?"

"My undying commitment."

"Is that a promise?"

I saluted him. He saluted back.

"Lazlis has been on me and Celeste all weekend threatening sanctions for harassing his client. Me and Celeste decided that we're going to throw him a bone and approve paying for Thomas's bladder surgery to get Lazlis off our back a bit."

"Since when did his bladder become an issue?"

"I don't know. Apparently he's incontinent and it's making his life hell. We've also agreed to a monthly stipend if we can't settle after the deposition and this thing ends up going to trial. But that will depend on the economist's report, which I assume you've already ordered."

"Yup," I lied.

176

"Good. And I'm not sure how we play the family court angle. I don't know the ethical and legal boundaries. I'm not a family law lawyer and I don't know the rules. I purposefully avoided practicing any area of the law that is messy and emotional. And now thanks to your zealous advocacy I got Lazlis claiming we should be sanctioned, so you may want to research the case law on that as well. Just to make sure we're not completely putting our foot in it. What else do you think we should do?"

He had never asked me this before. I stood on the cusp of telling him about my encounter with Thomas and my weekend expedition and the pile of deer carcasses but I refrained from doing so. Because I wasn't sure how he would react.

"Don't give him anything."

"Really, Stephen. It's like a roller coaster with you. Up and down. Hot and cold. Tell me why."

"Let Lazlis make his threats. All this does is drag out the case. Time is our friend and Thomas's enemy. We need to make him heel. And the more months he waits for his disability checks and the longer this goes on the more likely he is to heel on our terms and not his."

Fleeger stared at me.

"There is something about him that I can't put my finger on and I can't quite process and it's bothering the hell out of me. He's so weak but he was once strong. I think our ability to tolerate pain was once much higher."

His phone rang unanswered.

"What do you mean?" He was interested in what I had to say. We had crossed a new threshold.

"People were once drawn and quartered. It was nothing to take a punch in the face, let alone twist your ankle."

"What are you getting at?"

"The guy was a soldier. And then he was practically a soldier for hire, a mercenary, some kind of corporate Hessian. He voluntarily put himself in harm's way for significant compensation. And now he's wasting all this time and money and effort and energy because he's addicted to pain meds, can't find a job, and can't take care of his family. He has everything he needs. House, truck, wife, tools, food, a roof over his head. I don't get it. The only thing that makes sense is that he can't take some pain. Or, worse, he's a total liar."

"I guess I was wrong when I said he was your hero."

"Elements of him were once heroic but now he's pathetic."

His phone rang again and this time he answered it, told them to hold on, covered the receiver.

"Let's talk later. I want your opinion about how we should proceed with next week's deposition. But we still need to talk about this," he said, holding up the invoice. "And start making the time on the bills sizzle. Add some more fat." With the backs of his swinging fingers he motioned for me to leave his office.

The mailroom clerk had deposited a fresh batch of Thomas's medical records on my chair. I was tired of reading about his night sweats and back pain. About his increased anxiety and dysuria and snoring and dry mouth and ulcers. The man was fine. We all knew he was fine. I knew he was fine. Wacked-out on pain meds and marooned on the other side of fortress America, but fine. I stood from my chair, tossed the records in their box, wanted to toss the box out the window, and felt the pleasure of standing, of blood moving through my legs. My phone buzzed.

"Lunch time," Kath texted.

"Mos def," I replied.

The Mexican host, donning a white Eisenhower jacket pinned with a red carnation that looked shot by a flower gun, greeted me as I entered the restaurant. I followed him to a tan leather booth, back to the wall, with a view of the bar and the large, clear windows that looked out onto Lower Broadway.

"Please," he said, handing me a menu.

I ordered a pilsner and watched the crowd of big-faced women who spent their mornings cardio-kickboxing and power-yogaing followed by low-carb, high-protein, and lightly boozy lunches donning

Lululemon pants and tight, zippered sweatshirts. I finished the pilsner and ordered another and dismissed the possibility of Fleeger discovering his cuckoldry around the corner from the office and pondered whether this even still applied postseparation. I knew it did. And I knew what would happen. Fleeger suited as a colonial paleontologist while Attika dusted my prehistoric spine, fossilized inside the earth's stratum and discovered beneath Thomas's gut pile.

"You can see here, Robert, where Kath got fed," Attika says. "And Harker got slaughtered."

I finished the second pilsner and arrived at the threshold of two-beer equilibrium and watched Kath one block north on Broadway liberate her hair from a black-and-white keffiyeh while sipping from a Starbucks cup rimmed with waxy red lipstick. Bouncing curls, bumble and bumble, she rounded the bar and approached the table with her confident, jaunty stride. She gave a little wave to the side, rolled her eyes, annoyed with something, the city perhaps. She looked hungry for fame and fashionably pro-Palestinian. I stood, kissed her cheeks, probed her mood with my invisible instruments as I tucked her against the table. She ordered a glass of chardonnay and she studied the menu.

"It's all beef," she said.

"It's Shoemacher's."

"So. How is your day?" she asked.

"Typical."

"Oh boo, that's no good, Stephen. I don't want to hear about typical. Do you want to hear about mine so far?"

I told her I did.

"I spent the morning editing these up-close portraits I shot of the grungy kids living in the protest camp. They're so real and so amazing."

She sipped her wine and peered inside the glass and fingernail-extracted a bit piece of cork, stared at it cross-eyed, and flicked it away.

"OK," she said. "And then there's Soncha's upcoming presentation where I'm going to display some of the work. I'm so busy you wouldn't think I'd be so broke all the time."

This was a lie. But trust funds set up by Main Line orthopedic surgeon fathers aren't an open topic of discussion when you're a struggling artist. Nor are the alimony payments you are entitled to receive from your well-off soon-to-be ex-husband, whenever you decide to make the raw decisions regarding distribution of property and finances. They were still in the boiling/denial stage, too wrapped up in their own anger to do anything other than fuck other people. But the time for judicial intervention would come. And then there would be that to not talk about as well. But until then you discussed the symbiosis between your art and your poverty.

"So you're coming to Philly with me next weekend, right?" she said, texting a reply to someone. She was a skilled phone user, which was obvious by the way she held it. "Remember, you promised. And I already told Benjamin we're going to his fortieth birthday party and he's really excited to see you."

"I doubt that."

"Don't be negative."

I asked where we would stay.

"He bought this ginormous Victorian in the ghetto. Said all the kids there smoke wet and it makes them fucking cray-cray."

"Wet?" I asked.

"Angel dust."

"Oh," I replied.

"He's been my rock."

"Who, Anhel Dust?"

"What?"

"*Me llamo* Dust," I said, attempting to soothe the raw expectations between us with some corny levity. "Senor Anhel Dust."

"Don't be an asshole," she said.

I sipped my beer and hid my displeasure. She had no right to scold me.

"How're your parents?" I asked.

"My family still doesn't understand the breakup with Robert. My dad doesn't. Benjamin doesn't either. My mom does but that's only because I tell her things I don't tell my dad and certainly don't tell

Benjamin. Even though they were so different my dad and Benjamin loved Robert. But it's my life, not theirs."

This was the first time I detected a microscopic crack in the confidence of her post-Fleeger existence.

"How's that working out?" I asked.

"What do you mean?"

"Your life."

"What kind of question is that? You know how my life is working out. It's fucking awesome. I'm doing what I want to do and being with who I want to be with. After suffering Robert for so long what else is there to do but be happy?"

She looked at the tablecloth. We ordered another round of drinks and I ordered the filet mignon and Kath ordered the wild salmon. I laid my open hand across the table for her to hold. She rubbed the soft meat of my palm twice with her index finger before her hand retreated to her lap.

Lunch began to feel forced. I felt pinned behind the table, behind the salt and pepper shakers, the sugar caddy. Kath's safari boot touched my wingtip and hurried to her side of the leg stand. It was an accident and not a purposeful erotic act and this augmented the distance between our expectations. Together we drifted, silent, in our respective currents, conscious of submerged hazards, of the things we couldn't talk about. I needed something to happen. Something for us to discuss other than ourselves.

Near our table an affair bloomed at the bar, heavy with tannins and scent. The woman's blonde hair slicked like she just swam laps in a pool, rubbing her man's hand, both sides, against her curves. I hadn't felt cotton like that for a long time. She laughed and threw back her head and exposed her veiny neck to his curled lips and bonded teeth. The bartender winked at them while refilling their glasses.

"Cherry and leather," the man said, as he aerated the wine with a swirling wrist.

"Chocolate and tobacco," she replied.

Kath watched them too and they cheersed, rubbing each other inside the shadows beneath the bar.

"That's quite an engagement ring," I said.

"Maybe. But it's not from him."

"How do you know?"

"Because no woman touches her husband like that in public."

The waiter placed the entrées on the table and removed the saucer lids to reveal our selections of protein. Kath flaked her salmon with a fork and I touched my meat with the steak knife. I sliced off a chunk and blood pooled inside a lagoon of au gratin potatoes.

Outside, to the south, the protesters resumed their constant marching. A centipede working its way around and over and through the squares and blocks of Lower Manhattan. The cacophony of their plastic bucket drums echoed through the canyons of granite and brick. The sound now omnipresent and somehow patriotic and defiant as the protestors marched past the restaurant windows, petit nosegays of carnations and baby's breath, swinging arms, pewter and glass, plastic whistles, porcelain and ice, that upside-down American flag still hanging from a pole once used to clean swimming pools. A phalanx of police mopeds corralled the protesters inside the southbound Metro bus lane as a tall black man donning a sparkled motorcycle helmet riled the crowd with his banged-up bullhorn. It was the man with whom I smoked a cigarette in the rain, surrounded by white Kokopellis blowing their ocarinas of no justice, no peace. He turned his head and there was the vexatious keloid. Kath pointed with her knife.

"That's Jupiter," she said, spearing my steak with her fork.

I refrained from telling her that I had already met him.

"That's a cool name," I replied

"It's a slave name. He gave it to himself."

"Think I can call myself Mars?"

She looked at her plate.

"Come on. You don't think I'm worthy of a slave name too? After all, I work for Robert."

"Yes, but he's a prophet."

"Who is? Robert?"

"No, idiot. Jupiter is."

This stung.

"And I'm not?"

"Stephen, you are many things but you are not a prophet."

We were five thousand miles from the initial promise of lunch. The maintenance of a constant topic of conversation collapsed. Editing and then reediting myself before I spoke became exhausting. Kath, I could tell, didn't want to be here either. We had both been to enough restaurants and this one wasn't very good. I wanted to walk out the door.

"I think it's farmed," she said, forking the salmon.

She extracted a slice of tomato from the salad and slipped it past her now nude lips.

"How's the salad?" I asked.

"Good."

Like a herd of foraging herbivores looking up one after another from their plates, ears twitching on account of the presence of a stalking predator, we all sensed the change as the straggling remains of the protestors' peaceful march trotted past the windows, followed in the shadows and on the sidelines by a crew of moody anarchists passing things to one another from fist to fist as they crossed Broadway and approached the steakhouse's big windows that now felt exposed. The anarchists amassed outside the restaurant on the sidewalk and then stood calm, watching us watching them.

"Have a bite of my French dip," cackled a tall, thin woman wearing middle-aged, conservative Manhattan finery, waving her soggy sandwich at the crusty anarchists, her wrist adorned with silver and amber-tipped bangles.

Their response was immediate. A protestor chucked a hard pellet against the window, where it burst into a splotch of purple dye. The gang screeched in delight, headbanging and cheering in a crusty form of pidgin English, as the instigating diner uncoiled herself from behind her table, flicking ashes from a one-hundred light cigarette into a crystal ashtray that she held in her long, thin hand.

"Eat," she commanded the rest of us. "Don't give these beasts the satisfaction of spoiling your meal."

The protestors yelled at her: full throated, mouths opened, black cavities, lips pierced, gums tattooed blue. Now chucking ever more dye against the glass and sending the white Iked Latino waiters in a tizzy as the bartender moved through the crowd, agreeing with the diners, "Yes, where are the cops," as she placated the more senior and wealthy among them with the contents of the bottles chilled in their individual wine buckets.

Kath extracted her digital camera from her bag and pushed back from the table and began her shoot, tossing her hair and her keffiyeh over her shoulder as she shot the bartender, the French dipper, the lovers. Working the room, she switched in and out lenses and quickened to the soiled windows and threw her legs over a booth, camera now mounted at the ends of her outstretched arms.

"Find something more interesting to do with that thing, young lady," said the bartender.

"What could be more interesting than this?" Kath smiled.

"All you're accomplishing is riling them up more," the tall, thin woman chastised Kath.

"Really? Pretty sure you already did that on your own."

Outside on the sidewalk, a young woman, still half a girl, head shaved, frayed mustard shorts, tank top of slapjack paps, stepped through the crowd of boys, a protest unto herself against popular notions of femininity. Her eyes widened as her cohort whispered in her ear. She grinned, and with quick work dropped her pants and dingy sailor-striped panties and pressed her pimpled butt cheeks against the window, opening up herself for Kath's camera as the diners collapsed, revolted, taken down by the rifle of her Aegean stables. Kath gripped the table to remain in place as two waiters tugged her boots and the diners counter-rioted against the anarchists, shaking clubbed fists, Maytag blue cheese, Russian dressing, jus de boeuf, while outside the girl danced a happy impish jig, warmly ensconced within her coterie of misfit lepperchauns, all of them now yelling fuck, fuck you, fuck, what the fuck as they crumbled beneath the swinging, swatting billy clubs of New York's finest. Kath still shooting but with one hand while sliding backward atop a tablecloth pulled by two Guatemalan busboys at the bartender's command, as outside the cops grappled the mass of anarchists into plastic straps, hog-tied and deposited them on the sidewalk in a pile. All of it, them, the commotion, over but a few minutes after it began.

The diners stood and applauded their appreciation and the cops ignored them at first but then nodded in recognition of the recognition. Off to the side of the pile and looking over her shoulder, the crusty girl gasped on a torrent of thick red blood discharged from her nose and crawled from beneath the hog-tied pile and sprinted, straight backed and arms pumping and fast and chubby toward the river. The cops let her run for it, some of them laughing at her lack of natural athletic capability. I rested my finger against my temple and felt a blood vessel swell and pump. The bartender shoved Kath out the door and I grabbed her bag and flagged a waiter to pay as Kath stood outside laughing and taking pictures of the restaurant staff. The cops. The bloodstains on the sidewalk.

I hurried after her. She was flush. Technicolor. A swirl of green eyes and red-black hair but electric. Once again one of those magic boardwalk lollipops. The neon sign for the magic lollipop store. With her thumbs, she shuffled through a digital zoopraxiscope of the images she captured. Some periscope of hers now up, scanning south and east, now north and west, searching for her proper direction. Her tongue clicked in the back of her mouth.

"I think there's a fish bone in there," she said, pointing in her mouth.

She tilted back her head and I placed my hands on her face. Gentle and firm. I peered inside. Her pink mouth filaturing gossamers of saliva. The caves between her gums and teeth clear of plaque, tartar, food and her uvula dangled swollen and pink and wet. I spotted no bone. I wished I did. If I did I would have extracted that fishbone without buzzing her alarm.

With a life all its own, the silken tendrils of her thick hair wrapped around my fingers and pulled me against her as she stuffed her hands into the back pockets beneath my coat. Her jeans against my pants. I coursed with her current, her warm tongue against the back of my lips. We launched. I held back. Something wasn't free. I stiffened and she reversed. A red hair extended from my lower lip across our mutual canyon and her breath ceased for a minute particle of a second. Smaller than the particles revealed after physicists smash seconds into seconds within the confines of a deep underground particle collider. She squeezed my hand. I broke the link.

"Come on, let's go," she said.

"Where?" I asked.

"To the protest camp."

"Why?"

"I want more. Come with me, I need you."

She extracted from her bag an orange hard pack of American Spirits. Cracked open the fresh box and reversed her lucky smoke. She inserted one in my mouth and one in hers and lit our matching cigarettes. Smoke blew from her mouth in the same direction the wind blew her hair. She squeezed my hand.

"You OK with that?" she asked.

I told her yes. Very much. Let's go.

19

MISCHIEVOUS VANDALS HAD TWEAKED the don't walk street crossing lights with black electrical tape, turning the halting red hands into devil horns and middle fingers. Yellow boxes bolted to the traffic poles bending in the strong, low winds of almost early spring. Bobbing beneath the weight of CCTV cameras and police radio antennae. Here, where the city pressed against the converging rivers and the rivers pressed back, the city felt like an island. The brackish water of New York Harbor smashed against the staunch rectangle hull of a scow laden with gravel, a white tug made up to its starboard bow, flying an American flag from her upper wheelhouse.

"Stephen, let go," Kath said, and I released her hand.

The camp appeared before us. Tented and intricate and governed by posted rules about respect and property and privacy, but also broken down, by the wind and entropy and perhaps a looming apathy borne of the nascent realization that a proper revolution depended on a convergence of conditions that here, in this time, didn't exist. At least not yet. After months of protest, the dominant paradigm had proven more fixed to this earth than the protestors presumed, and some had begun to dismantle their tents and pack their things, in search of somewhere else to belong.

Strings of lights glittered in the almost-warm sun. Clothes swung from clotheslines. Boys wrestled and kicked one another while fist-smoking cigarettes, as a girl hid from them, changing beneath the shadows of the elevated highway scorched black with the pitch-black runic: IXXI IXXI IXXI IXXI. She removed a torn GWAR T-shirt, revealing a bare back tattooed with an outline of the state of Montana. Back to where you come from, I thought. Anarchy flags still fluttered atop the roofs of the hurricane-flooded maritime bars and sugar shacks, hoisted atop scavenged plumbing and sticks and torn by the incessant wind. But it felt like the final innings. Subjected to its own energy, the protest was burning out.

Donning a soiled white kufi, Jupiter reclined on a vinyl restaurant booth, his encampment nestled behind a former taco stand. In his small, designated space there was a library of books and bottles of wine stacked in milk crates, and a simple red telescope mounted on a flimsy tripod pointed at the sky. He bit into an apple, the chewing of which revealed the depths and the brutality of the scarring to his face, as if he had been chomped by the pinchers of a giant ant that poisoned its prey to prevent the skin from properly healing. Death via sepsis that he had barely managed to survive. He was holding court with a gang of fidgety anarchy boys.

"Of course the cops are going to beat you. Why wouldn't they?" he asked. "Your responsibility to yourself is to accept the consequences of your decisions and then move on. But wiser from experience. We were raised to be exceptional. Taught the importance of being exceptional. But there's not enough around for everyone to be exceptional. The word by its very definition denotes that those who are exceptional are different. So to be exceptional you will have to take it."

He removed an old dictionary from a milk crate and held it with his vitiligo-bleached hands.

"You know how many niggers out here are happy to take a doorman job for fifteen dollars per hour? You're fucking expendable, man. But it's your responsibility to fight against that." Jupiter spotted Kath approaching his encampment and dismissed the class, to be resumed tomorrow.

"Your hair looks redder," he told her, matter-of-fact, sitting up with straight forearms. He looked almost pained, as if he too had taken a billy club to the back and shoulders. "Redder or more red? Which is it, dear?"

"Redder is fine," she said and kissed his non-scarred cheek. "Stephen likes it this way."

She introduced us and Jupiter continued staring at Kath despite the fact he and I were now shaking hands. His pink, melaninless hand was strong and dry. The word Koolstar tattooed on his neck was something I hadn't noticed before. Affixed there long before whatever happened that led him here.

"We already met," Jupiter told her.

"It's true," I said.

She asked where and how. I explained that we crossed paths in the rain. She was incredulous at the odds. Jupiter confirmed that the odds were indeed small but not infinitesimally so. As we spoke, police boats escorted a massive cruise ship through the harbor and out to sea, a shiny Norwegian flag painted to her funnel a mile above the water.

"Let me show you both something I've discovered," Jupiter said. He led us over to the telescope. "Remember what I told you about the sun, young man?"

I confirmed that I did.

"Well, look at this."

He squinted into the telescope's eyepiece and positioned the telescope toward the sun, but still careful not to stare at it directly. The optical tube now aligned with the sun, he positioned a dull, ceramic plate on the ground, marked with a series of parallel concentric circles and numbers for taking measurements and degrees. The light from the sun reflected through the telescope onto the ceramic plate, where it shined with a painful brightness. In the middle of the shining plate, a collection of black dots converged, of various degrees and at various positions.

"See here," he said, pointing at the plate with a pen. "These are the sun spots. But if you watch these as I've been watching them, you'll notice that they're moving a little bit closer to one another every couple days. They're starting to dance a little. They're not static. I've been tracking them. And I think it's only a matter of time before they overlap, and when they do—"

"Then what will happen?" Kath asked.

"Nothing less than a full meltdown of the entire North American power grid."

"Really, Jupiter?" Kath asked. She lit a cigarette and offered him one. I was almost hurt she didn't offer me one as well. "I don't buy it. Doesn't that seem a little dramatic?"

"Maybe it is. But imagine the possibilities if it happens." He exhaled smoke. "We could be on the cusp of complete and utter cosmic futility. And they know it. Yes they do. Why else do you think they're putting everything in the cloud? To keep it off the ground.

"Given that the end of the world is nigh, how about a drink," he asked us. He removed a bottle from an orange milk crate stored at his feet and handed both me and Kath a mug of wine. As he did so, I noticed that he possessed the small, hard eyes of a wine addict. His entire biological systems—nervous, endocrine, muscular—replaced over the years of drinking with new organs and glands that properly functioned only when steeped in wine. Withdraw would possibly kill him.

"What do you know about Pommards, dear?" he asked her.

My purpose for being here in the protest camp turned questionable. I thought of the work on my desk, that I had been out of the office now for hours. My only reason for being here was to accompany Kath as she initiated some kind of ceremony. To request access and information from Jupiter. For her, it was all self-serving, but rolled into something she believed was honest and fair. He cared for her, that was evident. And though she needed Jupiter more than she needed me at this moment, she also assumed I wouldn't leave her, because she knew I needed something from her as well. And I knew that if I stayed beside her she would give it to me.

Jupiter toasted us with his mug. The wine tasted like vinegar and I removed a cigarette from Kath's bag. She didn't notice and it was the first time I had done something like this with her. Jupiter extracted another bottle from beneath his booth and set it on the table.

"What does that say?" he said, squinting to read the bottle's small print, scrunching his nose and opening his mouth. My desire to leave and return to work swelled and filled me with lead. The only thing keeping me here was her. Kath slipped on her cheetah-print-framed reading glasses.

"Borgyne," she said, nodding.

"I can see that," he said. He sipped and paused. "Yes, it will be a real shame when civilization ends. But maybe it's for the better."

"Jupiter," Kath chided him. "Don't be so negative."

He turned away from the wind, coaxing a tear that was now trapped in his eyelashes. One small fiery particle of that golden incandescent empathy wafted upward from within the darkness. Lighter than air and hotter than fire. Jupiter looked at me. He nodded. He smiled. Kath touched Jupiter's knee.

"Can I ask you a favor, Jupiter?"

He agreed, and she proceeded to tell him about our lunch and the photographs, removed her camera from her bag and showed him the subjects, the angles, the composition. She wanted to find the girl with the bloody nose and she also wanted to know her name. I watched the stalking anarchists to ensure they didn't rush Kath's camera. Jupiter listened, he looked at the ground, finger-steepled his pink-and-black folded hands. He explained that the girl lived in a tent near the Bowling Green subway entrance and Jupiter agreed to take Kath there but on one express condition.

"Name it," she said.

"Don't poverty pimp us, Kath."

She consented and followed Jupiter and I followed too, wondering what Jupiter meant by poverty pimping. What poverty pimping entailed. Trekking across cobblestones, we approached the old subway station, its entrance surrounded by short-haired mongrels and dozing-off children nursing their billy club bruises with cans of Four Loko. Jupiter kick-started a sleeping boy with fishhooks tattooed around his chin.

"Where's Dutch?" he asked the kid.

Eyes closed, the kid pointed toward a yellow tent and Kath put her hand in my back pocket and I felt ridiculous standing here like this but she wanted me close to her.

"Dutch," Jupiter said inside the tent, motioning for Kath to follow. Kath detached from my pocket and crouched, almost on all fours, the large camera lanyarded around her neck. Jupiter pressed down on the lens to communicate to Kath that this was a bad idea but Kath persisted, pushing forward behind the lens. From inside the tent came the low growl of an angry canine as Kath pressed forward, the servo inside the camera shooting more images. She crossed the tent's threshold, triggering an impulse, spacious white mongrel teeth followed by muddy work boots. Kath backed away, bent over, still shooting her subject, as the girl exited the tent, face bloodied and bruised like something from the wasteland north, from the other side of the tar pits, smeared like a lesbian leatherneck with a busted nose stuffed with red-brown tissue.

Kath stumbled. I quickened between Kath and the girl's barking dog and it snapped at me, scraped my hand with its canines, the soft fleshy chunk around my trapezium. The girl's hobnailed boot descended in a swift motion toward Kath's face and the camera, about to smash them both, but Jupiter was there to protect her. He kicked away the dog while catching the girl's wound-up foot midflight.

"That's enough, young lady," he said. "She's a friend."

"The fuck she is."

Dutch shook herself free from Jupiter's grasp and stomped toward the flags and joined a gang of anarchy boys, who attempted to console the irate girl, all of them now yelling and pointing at me and Kath.

"Maybe you two should go," Jupiter said.

He looked at my hand. There was a faint trickle of blood, as if bit by a baby vampire.

"Make sure you wash that," he said.

"Thank you, Jupiter," Kath said, and again kissed his nonscarred cheek. We said our goodbyes and Kath handed me a satin scarf adorned with little Roman crests. The one she used to clean her glasses. We walked north on Water Street. Catching our breath. Replaying events. Adrenaline dissipating into mild dizziness followed by euphoria.

"You should have been a war photographer," I told her.

She wrapped an arm around my waist, thanked me, and kissed my cheek.

"For what?" I asked.

"For being awesome."

I looked at the watch. Too much time had passed to return to the office. And if I did I wouldn't accomplish anything. The day was wasted for anything other than her.

"What are you doing now?" she asked.

"I don't really feel like going back to work."

"Good answer."

She took my hand and squirted colloidal antiseptic goo onto the scratch and rubbed it in with her warm hands. The alcohol burned but only for a moment.

"Then let's go to your place," she said. "So I can give you your treat."

20

FLEEGER LEANED FORWARD IN a leather swivel chair at the head of the conference table, hands knitted behind his head, elbows on the table, his pose for dealing with thorny legal issues. Leaning into the Bluetooth speaker, he poked the air with his long finger. I entered my office and unspooled the confidential envelope the mailroom clerk had deposited on my office chair. It contained a cover letter from Honda asking me to call him as soon as possible. The disc's contents downloaded to the computer's hard drive.

Video 1. 1 minute, 03 seconds: Thomas in his garage, gripping an acetylene torch with elbow-length gloves, protective goggles, leather vest. He laughs at the fire in his hand with pure joy, like a deranged metal butcher, slicing chunks of steel into strips and shards.

Video 2. 1 minute, 45 seconds: Surrounded by boxes of Depends, Thomas at his basement workbench planes a wooden edge. He lifts and fits the lid atop the side panels, dips a rag into a small yellow can, and commences staining a wooden coffin. His fingers dig into his scalp, violently scratching. A bald spot appears on the side of his head. He's now scratching himself bald.

Video 3. 32 seconds: Thomas berates his daughter on the pressure-treated deck. Multiple bald patches across the back of his head.

Video 4. 18 seconds: Thomas, atop his deer stand, pivots, pulls, launches a steel-tipped arrow from a compound bow that strikes a multipointed buck tiptoeing through his rhododendrons. The arrow pierces the deer's neck. The deer collapses.

I called Honda. He answered on the first ring.

"Honda, it's Stephen. You got him using the deer stand. Fantastic. This is some pretty good fucking surveillance work man. Refutes a whole bunch of the orthopedic injuries, especially the archery. And what's up with that coffin? Weird, right?"

There was a pause.

"Look, Stephen. He made me. I'm done. He came after me with a baseball bat and I'm done."

"OK, understandable man. Besides, you've done yeoman's work on this already and I think we're in good shape for the deposition. Perhaps it was inevitable. We've been pushing the limits on this one. But it's true what they all say. Honda Tadakatsu always gets his man."

He was in no mood to banter. I almost told him to lighten up, we were in good shape.

"Look, one more thing, Stephen. And I'm going to let you decide how you want to handle it, OK. I got another look inside his house. I couldn't photograph it because of the light and the glare in the windows. But you should know that he's got pictures of you and Robert taped to his dining room wall."

A bubble of fear rose within me, down and to the side.

"What kind of pictures?"

"The portraits posted on Kilgore's website."

I should have been more alarmed. Perhaps I was numb. I wanted to go straight for him. The gas bubble dissipated. "Thanks, man. I'll discuss it with Robert and we'll take it from here. And Honda."

"Yeah, Stephen."

"Good work."

We said goodbye. I sat behind the desk pondering what to do next and entered a time note in the billing software. 444/15 RF/SH: In re telecon with investigator in re new surveillance: .4 hrs. My inbox pinged with an email from Lazlis.

"Stephen: My client informs me there was an Asian man filming him the other day in a grocery store. I can only assume it was Honda. As such, I'm requesting WorldScore's production of all surveillance footage taken of my client prior to his deposition. Your obligation to produce the footage is well established by recent jurisprudence."

A couple more weeks of this and we would be well positioned to shrink their settlement demand into something WorldScore could live with, pack up these boxes, place them in storage for five or six years, whatever the rules required, and move on. And I could start focusing on what Kath referred to as my "empowerment."

"Jim: I'm confused. Are you asking for all surveillance taken prior to the deposition? Or are you requesting production before the deposition? Your request is ambiguous."

"Stephen: Both."

"Jim: First, I'm in in no way, shape, or form even admitting that surveillance footage exists. But, without prejudice to all of WorldScore's rights, if my recollection serves me correctly, the rules don't require us to produce the footage until before trial, not before the deposition. Production, as you know, dilutes their impeachment value."

"Disagree completely, Stephen. Will bring it up before the judge. One more thing—now that I have your attention. We need WorldScore's approval for a cervical spine fusion at C4/C5 as well as debridement of the spondylosis at L4/L5."

"Why?"

"He's got a procedure scheduled for after the deposition but it can't be scheduled until we have written approval that WorldScore will pay for it."

"Will run it up the flagpole," I replied. Knowing full well I wouldn't.

"Thxs."

"Anytime. Best. SH."

I typed up and entered another time note in the billing system. 444/15 RF/SH: Review/reply to email correspondence with opposing counsel re production of surveillance footage and request for approval re spine procedures: 1.5 hrs.

I entered Fleeger's corner office. He wasn't there. Above the city, to the south and west, the clouds parted, converting lower Gotham into temporary Stonehenge as the sun traversed the asphalt, cleared the tip of a verdigris volcano, and struck the mirrored glass facade of a Jersey City office tower. Radiating the canyons between the buildings with the light you would expect to find above the Ganges, bobbing with garlands of marigolds, like molten magma. I closed my eyes and felt the orange-blue light, now glowing inside Fleeger's crystal apples and beer steins and bronzing his jelly gong, illuminating the trophy sprites of his insurance industry golf tournament prowess, warming their wings. Reawakened by solar radiation, the sprites detached from their wooden podiums and twinkle-belled in the office's dusty, golden light.

I stepped behind Fleeger's desk hungry to pry. To open the drawers and look under his desk. Beneath the pile of old *Wall Street Journals*. The carpet protector eroded by years behind the machine. His essence resided here. In the leather chair cracked open by his massive legs and back. In the groove of the hard, plastic mouse. I scrolled the cursor across his trinity of screens. Some of Tara's squares still required filling but a fuller picture had emerged. Accountant. Searching for a position with a nonprofit organization (preferably housing or women's rights). Avid flosser. Insecure about her gums (thinks they're too big). Loves Spain. Loves tapas and paella. Loves her parents. O'Malley. Perez. Petra. No O'Shaughnessy.

I looked up from behind the screens at Fleeger standing in the doorway of his office. Both of us now bathed in the city's golden, radioactive sunlight.

"Find what you're looking for?" Fleeger asked.

Some tropism of blame cracked through its eggshell. Uncoiled its slimy body, also reaching for the sunlight. I crushed it with my heel as outside the protestors' plastic bucket drums resumed their beat. There were fewer now.

"There's one thing maybe you can explain for me, Stephen," Fleeger said. "If your hours are consistently low, then what are you doing all day?"

"What do you mean?"

"What are you doing here? Every day? In your office? Behind your desk?"

"Working," I said. "What else would I be doing?"

Outside the corner office window, a skyscraper released a plume of steam that curled in and around itself like a Möbius strip.

"You tell me," he replied.

None of this would hold for much longer, I thought. I squeezed his shoulder and stepped past him and exited his office.

21

KATH WAS EN ROUTE. Estimated time of arrival: two hours. She wanted to continue discussing my empowerment and her upcoming exhibition of the protest photos at Soncha's quarterly gathering in the Village. She also needed my help to protect her intellectual property. I suggested that we meet here in my apartment over dinner to discuss and she agreed. Together we had coined a new mantra: Live free of Fleeger or die.

The toilet and the shower were scrubbed. On the bathroom windowsill, I arranged the trail of products she had left here, for lips, for hair, for skin, contact lens solution. Sniffed her now-indelible scent on the pillows while changing my sheets. Extracted anchor-hitches of her red hair from the shower drain. I arranged the candles to coax her to spend the night. Because she loved candles, she said. What the Danes called *hygge*, she explained. The way they glowed in the dark, the promise of light. Bequeathing us time to get it done right. I wanted a long night and a good long morning with her.

I lay on the couch and opened a binder of Thomas's medical records. For continuous review and study before next week's deposition. Pages of notes and charts for cross-referencing reports and records that contained no reference to the incidents that allegedly caused the man's injuries. I opened the folder of photographs. Of Thomas the deer hunter, the slaughtered deer, the family law pleadings, Thomas on his tractor, Thomas hauling beer. A narrative was evolving, the pieces fusing. We were winning. I napped on the couch with the binder splayed across my chest. Confident that after this case I would start looking for another job. That I owed it to myself to be happy.

The nap ended. I awoke in a panic but realized I hadn't slept too long. Kath would arrive soon. I prepped the food so we could cook together. Removed a cookbook from the bookshelf, *Gourmet in 60 Minutes*, by a celebrated Scandinavian Somali chef. Leaning against a butcher block stacked with organic bounty, I felt the anxious glow of Kath's impending arrival. Would keep it high protein and low carb. Every woman I'd ever loved gained weight once we were together. Because they became too comfortable, thus becoming less desirable, commencing the downward spiral. I would prevent that from happening with us. The clove of garlic resisted the knife, required extra pressure. There we go. Another and another. I crushed the flavors into a rub. Poured grapeseed oil into the steel pan and set the blue gas flame on high. Billions of metric tons of the stuff brought to you by American Pipe. The stove lit the round, blue flame with a quiet roar and I stirred the shallots with a wooden spoon. The shallots cooled in pepper and salt as the steak absorbed the garlic marinade. I wanted a beer.

Gregg again stood on my fire escape. He was overdoing it with the glowing bumblebees and dragonflies, I wanted to tell him. The gaps between the lights as important as the lights themselves. He would test that theory. Wearing fingerless gloves, the bees and dragonflies fell from his hands and glowed in a swarm, dangling from the wrought iron fire escape. Electric faeries glowing in the wineglasses. Kath's spindly floating avocado pit had cracked another vertical shoot.

"Why are you always in my window?" I asked.

"So I can keep an eye on you," he said. He tugged at the lights. "There was a man here earlier today looking for you."

"Who was it?" I asked.

"Some delivery guy. He said he had a package for you. I told him I would sign for it but he said he needed to give it to you personally."

The fear formed again, about to release a bubble.

"What did he look like?"

"I don't know. Like a delivery guy. FedEx uniform. White, kind of gaunt, clean shaved."

The fear of Thomas dissipated.

"He said he would come back later."

Gregg continued tugging at his lights.

"You're having a guest over?" he asked. I waved around the knife to point out the obvious and Gregg nodded down and to the side.

"That crazy woman on the bike?"

Below the fire escape, Gregg's friends—a white man and an Asian woman—entered the courtyard.

"What are you doing up there, Gregg?" she said. "You're going to get yourself killed."

"Gregg come down here and say hello, tell us what you plan to do with all these goodies," the man said.

"I've never seen so many pine trees," said the woman. "You know they're going to die in these pots. There's not enough room for the root balls. It's too crowded."

"Looks like you need to entertain your friends," I said.

"They're very demanding," he replied, and climbed down to greet them.

There was still time to buy beer. Outside, the cold had resumed and women tucked their arms into the folds of their men's coats. I flipped my jacket collar and rolled and lit a cigarette and walked to the bodega. My cracked phone buzzed the Reuters newsfeed. Sign of the Times: Major US Insurers/Reinsurers to Underwrite Cyber, Political Insta-bility, Solar Radiation Policies. Yet still nothing from Kath. I hauled home a twelve-pack of Budweiser bottles. Still no message from Kath. I cracked open a beer and lay on the couch. Entertained prying open Thomas again but couldn't penetrate the binder's force field. The beer went down in four gulps and I twisted open another and ignited the broiler. It was time to cook. I snugged the flank steak beneath the flame and set the pot to boiling, to blanch the kale. Thereby willing Kath's impending arrival.

I repacked Thomas in his box and fluffed the couch pillows and dunked the boiled kale in ice water to stop its internal cooking. Shredded the warm greens with the German knife and sprinkled in fried shallots and shook them together in a wooden bowl. The steak now cooked, I slid it in the warm oven to absorb its own juices. Kath now forty-five minutes late. Her customary arrival time. I set the table. Lit two candles. Texted her to ensure her okayness. That she wasn't hit by a bus. I opened another beer. It went down easy. Outside, Gregg's friend explained the impact of *Silent Spring* and how this was emblematic of the influence one determined person can have on the world. And not just influence. Real, positive change.

I switched on Mingus. Switched him off. This was bad. Bad for me to do to myself. I told myself to remain calm. She wouldn't not come for no reason. Yes, there had to be a reason. My cracked phone vibrated a new message. I fumbled with the lock. It was an email from Fleeger's secretary about unfathomable amounts of crude oil pooled beneath the Rockies. I didn't care. I cared about Kath and why she wasn't here. I cared about the Nazca lines of past patterns scorched into the mantle of my almost-barren earth. I opened another beer and waited for a signal. At a certain point if the message is not forthcoming, it will never arrive. This was the stage we entered. A premature denouement. I rolled another cigarette. There was no way I could stay here in the apartment. If I did I would asphyxiate.

I opened the closet and extracted a jacket.

"Stephen, come down here and join us for some cheer before your guest arrives," Gregg said.

I told Gregg I would join them later, closed the window, and exited the apartment. Capitulated to myself and sent Kath another message: just wanted to make sure you were OK.

Cash flitted from the ATM and I gathered twenties from a puddle. I walked to the Village. Around the back of the Bowery Hotel. Past windows stacked with restaurant kitchen machinery, Hello Kitty dolls, sous-vide vacuumizers, soft ice cream machines. Past bars and restaurants and galleries specializing in cocktails and cuisine and culture. Deep fat fryers, rubber kitchen mats, Hobart food processors and small Chinatown apartments packed with Mexicans. Emotional affibrilation revved inside my chest. I needed to see her. Wanted to see her. To determine if she was alone and if not bury my loss in the bars. I picked up the pace. Alone again among the tenements. I looked over my shoulder, uncertain why, but there was no one there. Perhaps I was worried Thomas had snatched her. Neon church crosses and slick pavement. My phone vibrated a message from Kath. Thank God.

"Stephen, where are you?"

As if she was outside my door. My thumbs fumbled with the proper response. With whether the proper response was no response. You're repeating past mistakes, I told myself. Comporting with hardwired patterns of thought and behavior. I succumbed. Capitulated. Responded that I was walking. That I didn't understand why she didn't come over. Don't write that, I told myself. I hurried to shut down the phone to abort the message's transmission but the quick little bar told me this was futile, that the message was already sent. Ellipses of Kath's response now in production.

"Come over."

I refrained from answering.

"I want you to come over."

"How much?"

"Very much."

Levity returned to my thighs. There was clarity in the streetlights between here and her door. I saw the path before me and asked her what I should bring.

"Just you."

Newspapers strung across a newsstand. Gucci Mane or Lil' Wayne hanging from a wire. Alongside baggies of candies and nuts. Why anyone would tattoo an ice cream cone to his cheek was beyond me, despite whatever subliminal message this may convey on the street. The Pakistani newspaper vendor nodded as I stepped to Kath's building, as if he recognized me. I shouldered open the battered door and ascended the fifth-floor walk-up, climbing a trail of apple-flavored shisha through the warm, dry stairwell, like a cartoon dog following the trail to a cartoon ham baking in a cartoon kitchen.

22

A CROWD GATHERED ON the landing outside the apartment, all of them with saffron markings to their foreheads, parallel lines connected by a golden swirl evidencing the omniscient third eye of consciousness. The Frenchman was among them.

"Our deepest regards to Swami Vishnu Vishnu," he said to Soncha, standing beside her open door. I barely recognized her. Thick mascara had narrowed her eyes, like some optical illusion that induced desire. I said hello to the Frenchman. He nodded toward me and descended the building's cubist stairwell. Soncha gave me a deep, silent hug and I felt the ribs of her chest, the heavy collective swish of the red ribbons tied to the ends of her forty braids. Per her instructions, I removed my shoes.

"Yes, be comfortable, Stephen," she said.

It felt like entering an apartment in a foreign country. Orientalistic. Beiruti. Tehrani. Purposefully designed to evoke something far away and cherished. Black crystal chandelier set to low, checkered inlaid wooden frames, photos of Soncha's parents and siblings taken before the revolutions and the wars forced the family into exile. A grandfather surrounded by boughs of blooming jasmine. Mothers in dark round sunglasses and silk scarves posing with mustached husbands on the road to the Chouf. To Chambal. Chased brass plates hanging from the walls.

Kath reclined on the red divan, barefoot, legs wrapped in a white blanket. Two vertical saffron lines and a gold swirl in the middle of her forehead as well. Amid all this rich, undulating texture she looked ochre, earth-toned, almost bland. There was no kiss. There was no embrace. She motioned for me to sit on a floor pillow, beside a man gurgling a shisha pipe constructed from a forty-ounce bottle of Crazy Horse. I introduced myself to him.

"Ali," he replied. His hand was small and strong. "Absolute pleasure to meet you, Stephen." He too had received the parallel saffron lines, which intersected with his long black eyebrow, thereby forming multiple right angles in the middle of his forehead. "We were just discussing Kath's newest photos of the protests. Such energy, yes?"

He offered me the knitted shisha pipe. I inhaled deeply and filled my lungs with molasses and apple vapor, the water gurgling and the charcoal brightening, its heavy presence detectable only upon exhale. Soncha reclined on a chaise lounge next to the divan, fingering Kath's hair as Kath flipped through a copy of *Artforum*.

A serious undertaking had occurred among the women and Ali and the guests who departed and I didn't know the rules and I didn't know its objective and my attendance at the gathering was never under consideration. I felt that. I was a plot twist. An unexpected visitor stepping in from the night, bearing unmet expectations and questions, here to impose my presence before they retired for the night.

Soncha answered her phone, told someone to just bring him.

"Why do you want the date? What if it just happens again?"

She listened to the phone and lit a white cigarette.

"Don't fixate on so much control. He wants to come, he comes. If they have something else they would rather do, they do that instead."

She ended the call with a dramatic press of a button.

"Why are American women so obsessed with planning?" she asked. "No wonder their men are always acting like women."

I took no offense to this, because I knew what she was talking about.

"Allah," Ali said. "She should find an Arab man." He repositioned himself atop his floor pillow, as if he possessed the chest of all Arab men. "He will tell you what he wants."

"He will rape you," Kath said.

Her candor inflicted a wound. Secreted a hot oil through the chambers of my loculated chest. I should leave, I thought. To preserve and protect myself from their exclusive hospitality.

As they lounged, Ali explained to Kath the Arab word for when music makes you high, and how this word doesn't exist in English, and how this is yet another serious defect in the Western paradigm, the Western mentality. Because we don't feel music. Ali dialed up on a laptop a video of tribal music, soldiers in long shirttails and carrying heavy weapons across their shoulders and scaling a bare, granite valley. They took their positions near a road, crouched behind boulders. They're going to detonate an IED, I thought. A urial appeared above the men, with its alien candelabra of antlers, sniffing the air. They rose from behind the rock spraying bullets at the animal as it galloped higher into the monotone valley, abandoning its ewes in flight.

"Do you feel that?" Ali asked. "Do you feel the passion and the soul of this music?"

"I do, Ali," Kath said.

He closed the laptop and no one spoke. We sat there in the near dark, with no expectation of a transcendent experience via conversation, no emphasis on being clever or lighting laugh bombs. Kath too was silent. She had invited me here not to discuss her absence from dinner but to try and put me at ease. Her efforts failed. I felt claustrophobic, incapable of eating their lotus leaves. Ali offered me a fleshy chunk of bitter pomegranate and leaned against the divan rubbing his hands through his thick black hair, crossing and recrossing his legs. I stared at the carpet as they discussed upcoming projects and Kath opined that it all sounded very interesting.

"Is that how you say it, Stephen?" Ali asked. "Play my cards right?"

I confirmed that it was indeed as Kath flipped through the pages of a magazine written in a language she couldn't read. In the chandelier's shadowy light, I noticed she had dusted her skin with something that gave her a sandy complexion, the source of that ochre-toned skin.

"Kath?"

"Yes Ali?"

"I'm really happy that you're here with us," he said.

"Thank you," she replied.

I followed her along a Persian runner into the empty kitchen.

"Where were you tonight?" I asked. "I made dinner."

My confronting her surprised us both.

"Stephen, don't make things more complicated than they already are. I don't need the morality on top of it."

"What are you talking about?"

"Must we run through all the reasons right now?"

"Yes we do."

"But you won't like what I have to say, baby."

"I'll be fine with it."

"But it doesn't matter how you interpret what I feel?"

I told her it matters.

"I think I'm done with you, baby," she said. She hid behind her hair, like bolts of yarn, marshaling her honesty. "You're taking this all too seriously."

"And you're taking this all too casually," I retorted.

Something solid and heavy dropped a number of floors inside me.

"I'm done doing things I don't want to do anymore, Stephen. You won't understand. Because you're a Gemini, Stephen. And I'm a Taurus. I don't do well with Gemini. Christ, you even have me changing my hair color."

"You stood me up because of a horoscope?"

"That was just the sign, Stephen. There's more to it than that. Then Swami Vishnu Vishnu was here tonight and he told me to follow my heart. I have to live by my feelings now and I didn't want to come over and so I didn't. You can't understand. We're so different."

"I thought you liked that about us."

"No, Stephen. There is different by degree and different by species. We are different by species. I want different by degree."

I was annoying her. But I didn't care.

"Did Swami Vishnu Vishnu tell you that?"

This lodged a stinger. She sighed.

"It's because you're not a creator, Stephen. You're a consumer. There are three types of people in this world. There are critics. There are creators. And there are consumers. Stephen, you are a consumer. You drink too much. You eat too much. You don't want to be empowered and that's OK with you but it's not OK with me if I'm with you. Look, Stephen, I have a gift. I know it may not be easy for you to understand, but I do. And the challenge of that gift is that relationships and people come secondary to the gift itself. And that's my struggle. To follow my spiritual calling. Even if it means hurting others. Which I don't mean to do, baby, but I must."

She was chasing a phantom. Her misadventure sponsored by a trust fund. I refrained from being mean.

"But, Stephen, I have learned it is a beautiful curse."

She sounded ridiculous. I looked ridiculous, hands on my hips, leaning into her, awash in the irrational concerns of a spoiled woman suffering from delusions of grandeur surrounded by a coterie of sycophants. Opiating themselves with pastiche orientalism.

"Even if you did understand, Stephen, this will always be taboo to you."

"What will?"

"Pleasure, Stephen. Pleasure is taboo for you. You don't enjoy it. You hurry to the point where you think we're done and the moment you feel it's good enough for you, you leave me barely satisfied, wanting more. And I'm left wondering where you're off to. We have different tachometers, Stephen. I need more than what you can offer me."

"I'll give it to you," I said.

"But you can't."

"Why not?"

"Because you will always feel guilty about us. Because I will always be your boss-slash-best-friend's ex-wife."

209

"He's not my best friend."

"Once he was."

"But not anymore. And besides, when this case is done I'm leaving the firm."

"Really?"

"Really."

"Because you know it's killing you, right?"

"Because of you I do."

"I don't know, Stephen. Even if you do leave Kilgore there are still too many slashes to deal with. Too many conditions and too much history. You were there when I really needed something and I couldn't stand being alone. But I was weak. I was a sheep. It was snowing. I was drunk. I needed company and I used you for that. And now you're cooking me dinner and I'm changing my appearance and leaving shampoo at your house. What do you want, Stephen? You don't know. And even if you knew what you wanted, I probably couldn't give it to you. Because you can't give it to me in return."

"And Robert did?"

"No, he possessed something altogether different. And there was a time when I needed that too."

"And what was that?"

"I needed his ability to tell the world to get in line. To take what he wanted from it. There was a time when I would have killed for him if he told me to. But we don't have that connection, Stephen. Because you can't tell the world to go fuck itself."

I placed my hands on the sides of her head and choked down the globular sob forming at the base of my esophagus. As if there was nothing more catastrophic in the world at this moment than shedding a tear.

"I need you," I said.

My words warbled.

"You're lying."

"I need you."

"Is this what you want, Stephen?" she said, waving her hand around her body and her apartment. "You don't hate this?"

"No, I don't. I love this."

I needed to play this right. The bottom had yet to fall out. Soggy, yes, but intact. The hard lump of her positions began to thaw beneath the neon kitchen ceiling lights.

"Do you really want to be with me, baby?" she asked.

"I do."

"Do you know this for certain?"

"More than anything. I'm falling in love with you."

"Really?"

"I swear."

"Oh, Stephen, I love you too."

She kissed me and hugged me and I leaned backward into relief, ebullient with her approval. Ignoring the fact that despite the long five minutes something between us still failed to click. Something important, but difficult to reach, yet vital. I followed her to the living room. She offered me a clementine. I was too lazy to peel it. Soncha peeled it for me. She apologized for it being mealy. I said no problem. Kath shoved a clementine slice in my mouth. We still sat in silence. Kath ran her fingers through my hair and passed her hands across my shoulders and kissed me on the back of my neck and said she was exhausted and that it was time to sleep. She entered the peach and yellow light of her open bedroom door. I remained sitting on the floor, unsure whether Kath and I needed to make love to banish the avoided catastrophe. Soncha entered Kath's room and closed the door behind her and Ali and I sat in silence until he dozed off, still leaning against the divan. Standing in the doorway on one foot, I pulled on my shoes and headed home. Telling myself it was best this way.

My phone vibrated the coffee table. It was from Robert.

"Lucky number twenty-three," he said, "is very lucky indeed."

"Good work," I replied.

"We ready for the Major Asshole's deposition?"

"On it."

"Good. We're all counting on you."

23

THE CASE WHITTLED DOWN to a sole binder of questions and exhibits for the taking of Thomas's deposition. I felt tall, straight backed, anxiety shielded by preparation and the fact that the other side was near. That I'd both done and had enough. Thomas's boxes of discovery production lined the conference room windowsill. Like a python swallowing a deer, I had consumed their contents, the tiny colored flags and Post-it notes, the mimeographed fonts of decades passed. I climbed atop the conference table and trained the track lighting to where Thomas would be seated, then crawled beneath the table and removed the glides from the chair's front legs, thereby cantilevering Thomas's chair a few degrees forward. No reason to make the man too comfortable. Across the street, a prewar building disgorged a black ball of carbon and it sat there, still, in the hard, warmthless sun.

The hum of the vending machines, the buzz of the tube lights, the exhale of the building's ventilation system. Fleeger sat in silent study behind his desk. Fresh. Deodorized. Shaven. The starch pressed into his white shirt and the crinkle of his laundered cotton. Licking his fingers as he turned the pages of my deposition outline. Marking salient points with an index finger.

"I think we're good," I said.

"OK."

"Did that thing with the chair and the lights."

"Good."

"You think we're good?" I asked.

"If you say so."

"We're all set up."

"Mmm."

That noise which communicated he heard what I said but felt no need to reply. Once it gave rise to the paranoia that he no longer liked me. That my days were numbered. Or perhaps I didn't do a good enough job. But the days of caring had passed. The window had closed on the crucial verve of focus. I had seen the other side. Soon I would be back at Kath's side for tonight's presentation of her protest photographs at Soncha's quarterly intellectual gathering in the Village. According to Kath, they were all excited to meet me.

Live free of Fleeger or die.

Across the hall, Attika entered her office, listening to headphones and removing her jacket. She closed the door behind her. I knocked. She told me to enter as she sat behind her machine. She looked tiny behind the paper stacked on her desk, and hollow eyed. As if the partners had kept her awake all night to test her commitment to the firm's trials of partnership initiation.

"How's Tucker?"

"Don't bother me right now with trifles, Stephen."

"Why not?"

"Because I got this thing to do and it needs to be filed with the court in a couple hours and that's all I have to say."

Silver hairs coursed through her avocado-relaxed bob. In the span of weeks she had become an older woman.

"Really, Stephen, I have to work. It's not that I don't like you and I don't want you to get all sensitive about it, but I'm buried here." She reinserted her headphones and leaned over a notepad. The veins in her forearm bulged as she gripped a pen. "Don't take it personally," she almost yelled, on account of the music playing in her ears.

"Hey Attika."

She removed the headphones. I pointed at her arm.

"Who's Jamal?"

She reinserted her headphones and continued working. I stood there in her doorway. She steadfastly ignored me. So much for that, I thought.

I reentered the conference room. Salved myself with thoughts of none of this mattering anymore. I had something new. Fresh. Exciting. That lived outside these carpeted walls. And it gave me a new perspective. The stenographer extended her tripod and bolted her machine to its base. Her big teeth had imprinted vertical lines in the skin above her lip. She fluffed a lavender bow tied to the front of her blouse. We said hello, exchanged business cards, and she resumed her preparations for transcribing Thomas's deposition.

The receptionist paged me, announcing my guest had arrived. I entered the small Kilgore foyer between the conference room and the elevators. Lazlis stood there alone.

"Where's your client?" I asked, shaking his hand.

"Downstairs smoking. He's a nervous wreck."

"Really?"

"You'd be too if you were in his position."

We stood there with nothing to say. The elevator bell rang. Here now was Thomas. He had changed. He was gaunt but also meth looking, as if he subsisted on pop and Twinkies, with deep circles beneath his eyes. His once hedgehog-thick hair now patchy and thin, skull grooved with purple scratch marks where he had scored himself with his fingernails. But the handlebar mustache remained. As did the fresh soft pack of Marlboros with the little blue tobacco leaf stuffed inside his front jacket pocket, the consumption of which had stained the hard, curled tips of his mustache yellow-tobacco mustard. His face had collapsed in various places. It looked possible he had lost a few teeth. He moved like a tired robot, faux-dependent on his four-corner cane and a plastic orthopedic brace strapped around his thorax, a prop that appeared to steady his debilitated lumbar sacrum. In a Warner Brothers' jean jacket. Marvin the Martian pointing his ray gun. What was it that Martian said?

"Stephen, you remember Mr. Thomas," Lazlis said.

"Yes, sir," Thomas answered. I nodded my acknowledgment. There was no reason for us to shake hands. We weren't friends and I wasn't his lawyer. Fleeger had taught me that.

Lazlis and Thomas followed me to the conference room. Swinging his four-cornered cane and wincing with each step, I showed Thomas to his designated seat. He paused behind the chair. I looked him up and down. No tactical folder tucked in his pocket, no visibly concealed firearm bulging in his jeans. A WWJD purple rubber band bangle dangled from his wrist.

"Sir, in the event of an emergency we need to know our exit strategy," Thomas informed Lazlis.

"Major," Lazlis said, folding his fingers around themselves, as if they were his source of attorney power. "Let's not say anything until we're spoken to, OK? The key to these exercises is to say nothing of any consequence that the other side may later use against us. Right, Mr. Harker?" Lazlis said, winking at me, as if he and I were now friends.

Thomas grimaced as he lowered himself into his chair. He was hard on the eyes. The lights illuminated his oily face and patchy, scratched scalp and soon he would feel the seat's forward pitch adding some extra stress to that pretend broken back of his. I offered them a plastic tray of bagels and Danishes. Lazlis declined and pressed his shirt against his round belly.

"Need to maintain this figure," he said.

Thomas accepted a cheese Danish and bit into it with a not-quite full set of stained teeth and I poured them both coffee from a cardboard box.

"How was your trip, Mr. Thomas?" I asked.

"Jesus saw me here," he said, wincing in his seat.

He surveyed the boxes of records aligned the length of the conference room windows.

"Those all mine?" Thomas asked.

"Yes," I said.

"How long is this going to take?"

"A couple days," I said.

"I don't think I can sit for more than two hours at a time."

"Because of the pain?" I asked.

"Yes, sir."

"Please, Major," Lazlis repeated. "Let's try not to talk so much."

Thomas picked at a hand callus as Fleeger entered the conference room and took his seat with one motion. He stared at Thomas, took in his appearance, and looked at me. To confirm that we both noticed the man had changed. RFF monogrammed to Fleeger's white shirt cuffs and cherry throat lozenge cufflinks. Ignoring Lazlis, Fleeger introduced himself to Thomas and positioned his pen next to his legal pad. He explained for Thomas the rules governing the deposition and that Thomas was to audibly answer questions yes and no because the stenographer was incapable of reporting shakes of the head, grimaces, and nods. It felt as if we were about to sit for an examination.

"So, let's begin," Fleeger said.

"You sure this building is sound?" Thomas asked Robert.

"What?" Fleeger replied.

"What is the probability of this building falling down?"

"That won't happen," Fleeger added.

"How can you be so certain?"

"Because I'm certain, Mr. Thomas," Fleeger said. "Now we're here today to talk about you. Not the structural integrity of this building. And your claims for compensation that you filed against WorldScore."

"What do they call it? The world is not enough?" Thomas said.

"It's actually Risk in Profit," I replied.

Fleeger stared at me with disapproval. I wasn't to speak unless spoken to. Thomas surveyed the walls, the ceiling, the floor. Squinting in the lights. He dug his index fingernail into his bare scalp with such force it cracked a knuckle. He shook his head, as if he couldn't dig deep enough. Lazlis and Robert and I looked at one another. It was a rare moment of mutual concern or confusion; for how long would this continue. Thomas composed himself, rubbed the scar above his eyebrow, where according to the military records he'd been struck by a spent .50 millimeter shell during live-fire rounds in '82. Thomas pleaded to see the building's exit plan. His hands shook.

"Counselor?" Fleeger asked Lazlis, holding up both hands.

"Now Major," Lazlis said, almost mimicking Fleeger, the blood coursing through the veins within the circumference of his magnetic copper bangle extracted of impurities. As marketed on TV. "Try not to forget what Dr. Spectrum taught you. That the key to overcoming your phobias is to destroy your imagination."

Thomas quieted and bit his Danish. Fleeger explained to Thomas that he wanted to begin with some background information.

"Sir, I believe you have all my background information," Thomas replied. "I've been sending it up here to my attorney for weeks to answer to you."

"That's true, Mr. Thomas, but we need to hear it from you as well. To corroborate the records."

"But I'm not going to know it any better than what's in those records." He pointed at the boxes. "Those are military records. I don't want to say something that contradicts whatever is in all those boxes and then you accuse me again of not being truthful."

Lazlis lost his patience.

"We can't get you properly compensated, Major, if you won't play baseball," he said. "Come on now, you love baseball. Remember we discussed that? How much you love baseball? And how these pro-ceedings are like baseball? We're tied now, four-four in the bottom of the sixth. You're at bat, with runners in position. So come on now, let's play some ball."

Thomas sipped from his cardboard cup of coffee.

"Now, before I begin with my questions, Mr. Thomas, can you tell me whether you are taking any medications today?"

Thomas nodded that indeed he was taking medications today as he did every day. He removed a clear plastic rectangular tray of pills from his jean jacket pocket, shook it like a rattle, and placed it on the table, pointed at the little chambers one by one, Sunday to Saturday.

"I take Tuberol and Xyphelene every day. That's these two. The yellow and the blue-yellow ones."

"And those you've already taken today, I assume?" Fleeger asked.

"Yes, and I will need to take another dose shortly."

"On account of the pain?" Fleeger asked him.

"Pain and anxiety, yes. I don't like to take this brown wafer-looking one unless I have to because it puts me in a coma." He pointed to a pill almost the size of the Catholic host. "But if I don't carry it on me then my wife will steal it to get high."

"God damn it, Major," Lazlis snapped. "Do not volunteer that kind of information to these men. They are not your buddies at the VFW."

"How many pills do you take per day total?" Fleeger asked, ignoring Lazlis, further conditioning Thomas's comfort zone, to induce his self-incrimination.

"About thirty."

"About thirty?"

"Yes, sir. That's what they prescribe for me at the VA and so that's what I take."

"Thirty. OK," Fleeger said. "Moving on."

"OK, moving on," Thomas repeated.

"Yes, sir, moving on. I'm going to ask you some questions about your education, where you're from. Some basic background information."

"I got a bachelor's degree in aeronautical engineering from Central Florida. I'm forty-five years old. I grew up on the Delmarva Peninsula. Rejoined the reserves after 9/11."

"Slow down, Mr. Thomas, please. I didn't ask you about all this yet."

"Blew out my patella at Camp Echo. Conducted black flag operations in the Swat Valley flying body bags out of Peshawar. Went to work for FreedomQuest. Biggest mistake I ever made. Now I got night sweats, anxiety, PTSD, and a bunch of other ailments and conditions I'm sure you're already aware of. I don't know what went wrong but something went wrong over there and that's why I'm here. Because something's wrong."

To divert attention from the fact that he was about to cry, Thomas blew his nose into a napkin.

"Can you elaborate for me, Mr. Thomas?" Fleeger asked. "What do you mean when you say that something went wrong?"

"What I mean is, something went wrong over there and it ain't ever been right since. I went over there with the reserves and then FreedomQuest one type of man and I come back another type of man. It's a feeling. It's a real feeling. Like I can't feel the ground beneath my feet and I can't tell up from down. And I don't see what else there is you need to know other than the fact that FreedomQuest caused this feeling and FreedomQuest made me feel off. I'm just off, and I don't know how to feel on again. Like myself. And still I need to take care of my family and put food on the table and pay the mortgage and I got this feeling I can't get rid of and this feeling is making it impossible for me to be myself. It's killing me."

Lazlis nodded in approval and Fleeger let Thomas run with it. To warm him up, become accustomed to sitting twenty-five floors above street level, to the conference room, the omnipresent skyline, the woman working the long-keyed stenographer machine, the track lights now blistering his scored scalp with sweat and the seat adding extra strain to that alleged bad back of his. Maybe it was a good thing he wore that brace, I thought. If his back didn't hurt before, it would after a couple days answering Fleeger's questions. Fleeger nodded for me to take notes. I hated when he did this. Because there was no need to take notes when the stenographer was transcribing Thomas's testimony. I shorthanded salient facts in the margins of the yellow legal pad. Thomas shifted in his chair. Lazlis asked him if he was OK.

"I'm sore as hell, that's all," he said. "But it ain't nothing I can't handle."

He asked Lazlis if he could take a pill.

"Of course," his attorney replied. Thomas removed a red pill from his tray and audibly swallowed it with a mouthful of black coffee.

The questions and the answers continued. Fleeger asking Thomas to tell us more about his experiences overseas with the military, Thomas pleased to comply—as if someone was finally listening to him—despite the fact we were his adversaries. Lazlis should have admonished Thomas to stay on point but he didn't. Because he too was susceptible to the pleasurable distractions of his phone: settlement demands, fantasy sports, upcoming engagements. Despite the fact that Fleeger was lancing Thomas like a picador, to fatigue his stamina. And so Thomas rambled and grumbled. About Shia shrines in Pakistan decorated with Christmas lights. The Moldovan hostess in Beirut he punched in the face. Not really a brothel. More like a closet with a sheet. The Chilean sea captain of a Liberian-flagged bulker who offered Thomas's team the use of her holds for the right price. Chipped granite stairways and broken sidewalk tiles. Hyper-vigilance in and out of interrogation rooms. A Kurd lying in the cot next to him wearing only a loincloth. The guilt of cheating on his wife with the Moldovan who laughed at him afterward. Rediscovering salvation in Jesus Christ.

"Thank you, Mr. Thomas. That was very interesting," Fleeger said. "Now I'm going to ask you some questions regarding the claims you filed with FreedomQuest. After your first alleged injury in Afghanistan, you filed an LS-208 with your employer, correct?"

"Sir, why do you keep saying alleged?"

"Because it's alleged, Mr. Thomas."

"But I'm not making this stuff up. I don't want to be this way. You think I want to be this way?"

Fleeger continued.

"You filed an LS-208, correct? And then afterward you filed an LS-203."

"A what?"

Lazlis touched his client's arm.

"That's a notice of assertion of rights, Major."

"Sir, I really can't remember if I ever did that," Thomas answered Fleeger.

"Well you can't file an LS-208 for war hazard benefits without first filing the LS-203 notice of assertion of rights?" Fleeger said. "It's a two-step process."

Thomas entered a thick, red pill–induced fog.

"A what?" he asked.

"I'm explaining it's a two-step process," Fleeger said. "First you file the LS-203. And then you file the CA-94."

"I thought you said it was an LS-208," Thomas replied.

"I did."

"You did?"

Whatever hard, sharp edges Thomas the warrior still possessed had now completely disappeared beneath his opiated, indigo surface. *This makes me very angry.* That's what Marvin the Martian said. That was the line he purred, like an alien gladiator. The Marvin patch glued to the breast pocket of Thomas' denim jacket pointed his silly raygun at Fleeger.

"OK. Let's go back, Mr. Thomas. That's just one issue I have with your claims. There are more, and, truthfully, between you and me, I have a lot of issues with your claims. But moving on, have you had a chance to review the doctors' reports, Mr. Thomas?"

"Yes, sir."

"So then you are aware that on one occasion you reported to one doctor that it was your lower back that caused you pain. But I have here a record where you reported to another physician it was your cervical spine. Which is essentially your upper back. Which is it? Lower or upper back?"

"Both, I think."

"If it was the shrapnel that struck your upper back, your cervical area," Fleeger said, reaching over his head with both hands to illustrate the location of the cervical spine, "and not your lower back, would it be true that the difficulty you allegedly experienced caused pain to your upper, and not your lower, back?"

"Maybe."

"And then wouldn't it also be true that the medication you were taking for your lower back was actually prescribed for your cervical spine, which is more akin with the previous diagnosis predating your employment with the assured."

"Negative. Maybe. Negative," Thomas said. "I don't understand the questions, sir."

"Objection. Badgering the claimant," Lazlis said. He uncrossed his fingers and sipped his coffee. Pleased that he had defended his client from Fleeger.

"Sorry about that, Jimbo."

I discovered that my comfort level depended on where I placed my feet beneath the table. Thomas indicated he had a point he wanted to make.

"I think some of these inconsistencies result from the cultural gaps between me and all these foreign doctors they sent me to at the VA," Thomas said.

"I didn't ask you about your cultural gaps," Fleeger said. "What I need to understand is how you expect me to believe, WorldScore to believe, that all of these boxes. You see all these boxes? That one man can actually really suffer all of these ailments and injuries and conditions that you allege result solely from your employment in Afghanistan with FreedomQuest, where you were employed for less than two years. Especially when there is nothing in the company's contemporaneous incident reports during the years at issue that all substantiates any aspect of your multiple claims."

"When I got home it all just cascaded, sir," Thomas said.

"It all just cascaded," Fleeger repeated.

The receptionist knocked on the conference room window. She motioned to me that she needed to speak with Fleeger. I ignored her.

"This entire exercise is about the veracity of your allegations, Mr. Thomas. And my job is to find, question, and verify objective proof that you in fact suffered the injuries that you allege," Fleeger said. "And if I can't find that proof, I have to deny your claims. Look at it from my position. You tell one doctor that five events caused your injuries. You tell another doctor it was two. And yet to another doctor you say it was a single, catastrophic event. But here's my position: that your military records are replete with references to the claimed traumatic exposures, all of which predate your employment with FreedomQuest. Which means they are not compensable by World-Score. Because they didn't happen on our watch. That is my position. Now I understand you've filed an additional claim with WorldScore for terrorism benefits. Despite the fact you live in Pennsylvania and haven't been in Afghanistan for three years. Can you explain that one for me?"

The receptionist again tapped on the window.

"Harker go take care of that?" Fleeger said.

I exited the conference room. Watched Fleeger in the glass window with an outstretched arm, pointing his ballpoint pen at Thomas, the man's scored scalp and chin now dripping with sweat.

The receptionist looked nervous.

"There is a woman here to see Mr. Fleeger," she said.

"Who?"

"She won't tell me her name. She says if she tells me her name, then Mr. Fleeger won't speak with her. She wants to make sure he's OK."

"How did she get past the security downstairs?"

"It's not Fort Knox, Mr. Harker," she said. She looked at Fleeger. "She seems determined. And."

She paused.

"And what?" I asked.

"She's very pretty."

I followed her to the reception area. Atop the oriental rug, next to the orchid in its ovular vase, rubbing one leg against the other, stood Tara. *Sarda chiliensis lineolata*. Lucky number twenty-three.

"You're not Robert," she said.

I told her no, I am not Robert, and asked her what she needed.

"I need to see Robert."

"You can't see Robert," I said. "He's busy."

"I need to see him right now."

She removed her jacket, revealing a black lace bra beneath a sheeny translucent blouse.

"He's taking a deposition."

"I don't care."

She stepped out of one tall red heel. Untucked her shirt and began to sob. The receptionist placed a hand on her shoulder. She screamed. Acrylic fingernails stopped typing. An office phone rang unanswered. I entered the conference room and closed the door behind me. Thomas stared at the table as Fleeger almost berated him. I whispered near Fleeger's shoulder.

"You have something you have to deal with."

He looked at me, confused, opened his hands, what could it possibly be? What? I pointed at Tara outside the conference room. Leaning her face against the glass and discharging rivulets of crusty mascara.

Fleeger cursed, stood up, banged his knee against the table.

"Take over, Harker," he commanded, pressing himself through the conference room door with one hand holding his knee as he led Tara down the hall toward his office.

"How about you?" Thomas asked me. "You think this building is safe?"

We were different men than on the night he drove at me on my street. He was scared, nervous, almost defeated. Because we were the bastards now and we had what he needed. And so he needed us to obtain it. Lazlis wasn't going to get it for him. Lazlis would allow us to let this drag on forever. Thomas was desperate, more desperate than before, that was obvious, and because he was desperate, we had this. And he was on the cusp of accepting almost anything in order to obtain something.

"I think we'll make it through," I said. I cleared my throat. "Mr. Thomas, let's just be open here, shall we. Let's be transparent."

He looked out the window. I pivoted him to the deposition.

"Can you take me back?" I asked.

"To where?"

"Tell me about Afghanistan."

He shifted in his chair, winced, sipped his cup of black coffee.

"This chair is killing my back. Can we take a break, sir?"

I didn't want him to. Not yet. If so I could lose him.

"In a few minutes."

He nodded. I repeated my request about Afghanistan.

"Well, for starters it's a different world."

He was dismissive of the place. Different worlds being no big deal. For him, the only thing anyone needed to know about Afghanistan was that it wasn't the world in which he wanted to live.

"And where did you reside in this different world?"

"At first I lived in the Green Village. Then in a three-story building off-site."

"Did you live alone?"

"No, there was me and two other Americans."

"What were their names?"

"I can't tell you that."

"You can't or you won't?"

"Both."

"OK. I'll just subpoena the records if we have to call them as witnesses to corroborate your version of events."

"They're dead."

"They're dead? And yet you still can't tell me their names?"

"Affirmative."

"We'll look into that."

I scribbled "dead colleagues?" on the notepad.

"OK. Moving on. What were your duties with WorldScore?"

"I was a military trainer. Training Afghan soldiers and police officers on the use of firearms."

"And how was that?"

"What do you mean?"

"Tell me about your typical day."

"Well, at any given time probably 15 percent of the class were insurgents. So you were always concerned that one of them would turn their gun on you. Blue-on-green you. That's what they called it. On account of the different colored uniforms. Which was why there were three of us at first. Two to watch the class of trainees while one performed the firearms training."

"What kind of guns did FreedomQuest provide you for the training?"

"FreedomQuest didn't give us the guns. They came from the Afghan army. Which meant they came from the US Army." He paused, itching to scratch again. He took a deep breath to control himself. His face was filled with pain and sadness.

"At first M4s but the M4s kept breaking so we arranged to get some AKs. Because the Afghans preferred the AKs."

"OK. Then what happened?"

"We started experiencing a lot of mortar fire. It was indiscriminate. Killed a lot of innocent civilians."

"How do you know that?"

"Because I saw it."

"What did you see?"

"Dead women, dead children, dead fathers holding dead children. But that was normal."

I sipped my coffee. Lazlis stared at Thomas while doodling on a Kilgore pad.

"Then what?" I asked.

"Then they cut the budget and at first there were two of us teaching the classes but then there was only one of us."

"And that was you?"

"Correct."

"Why did they pick you?"

"Because I spoke a little Dari."

"Any other reason?"

"And because I volunteered to stay."

"Was that typical of something you would do? Considering the fact you didn't want to be there?"

"No, sir. That was atypical."

He intuited my next question. I now also had him on a roll. He was opening himself to me and that was exactly what I wanted. Soon he would incriminate himself and the veracity of his allegations and we were on the road to him and Lazlis settling for a fraction of their initial demand.

"I wasn't ready to go home. My home life wasn't so good and I wasn't prepared to deal with it and so I continued working with FreedomQuest to put away some money and try to have some options when the job ended. Despite my better judgment."

"And despite the fact that you were allegedly injured?"

"Correct."

Strike one.

"And despite the fact that you were allegedly mentally traumatized?"

"Correct."

Strike two.

"And yet still you agreed to continue working for FreedomQuest? Despite being injured?"

"Yes."

"Because the injuries weren't really that debilitating?"

"I guess."

Strike three. Maybe. I commanded myself to keep it moving.

"OK. So now you're alone in Kabul. Tell me what happened."

"Honestly?"

"Of course."

"I began to experience a lot of anxiety."

"On its own?"

"What do you mean?" he asked.

"Or was there something that triggered it?"

"Yes, there was something that triggered it."

"Tell me about that."

He shifted in his chair, winced, sweating throughout the hollows of his intense, sad face.

"It was night. I was driving at night. In a soft-sided vehicle, meaning there was no armor. I had just dropped off my Afghan translator and was driving home alone. I lit a cigarette and I guess I wasn't paying attention because I struck the car in front of me. Not real hard but hard enough to make them stop. I exited the vehicle before they did because I learned in these situations you don't want to be sitting and waiting for the Afghans to approach you. Rather, you want to approach them first. Four Afghans exited the vehicle, all of them dressed in white and heading off to pray. The road was real dusty and the dust kicked up around the traffic lights of the passing busses and cars and the men walked toward me through this yellow, dusty cloud. With no expression. They just stood and stared at me. I had a 9 millimeter in my satchel and I placed my hand on the weapon, disengaged the safety. A crowd formed around us. First it was four but four became eight became twelve and then became twenty. Multiplying. Walking from roadside tea stands and exiting busses and cars to watch what would happen between us."

"And why was that?"

"Because traffic accidents are like a form of public entertainment in Afghanistan. There were now maybe two hundred Afghans around me at this point. And they all just stared at me. Kind of as a way of asking what I was doing there but also to see what I would do next. They have this way of staring at you where you can't tell what they're thinking. Whether they mean you harm or not. There's no other way to say it. I panicked. I took out the 9 millimeter and aimed it at all of them. But they didn't react. They just kept staring. This made me even more nervous because I knew a man, a good man, who was killed by a crowd in Afghanistan. Bludgeoned to death. I fired the weapon in the air to make them step back but they didn't. They moved in on me instead. Because the odds were in their favor and they knew it. I knew it too. I couldn't shoot all of them. I only had eight bullets in the clip plus one in the chamber. Then they surrounded the truck and so I shoved a few of them out of the way and entered the vehicle pointing the gun at all of them. I started to drive through the crowd. They moved out of the way, but they also started banging the truck with their flat hands and as I pulled onto the main road and hit the gas, I clipped this motorbike with a man driving his wife and his infant daughter. The bike wobbled and fell and they all spun out on the ground. Like it was nothing. Almost like it was supposed to happen. You ever been in an accident you think was supposed to happen?"

"Why do you think it was supposed to happen, Mr. Thomas?"

"Because it triggered what was there, just waiting for me, just below the surface. First a rock smashed the rear windshield. Followed by a pipe to the driver's window and now there was glass all over me. I kept driving but they kept smashing at the truck as I was driving. Coming out of their homes and shops and shadows and smashing the windshield and the hood and the headlights and the brake lights and going for the tires and trying to pick up the truck and flip it. Rocking it. Afghans are skinny. Most don't weigh too much. Unless they're a warlord. But when they come after you in a pack there's not much you can do but run them over."

"How many did you strike with your car?"

"Maybe twenty."

"And what did that do to you?"

"What can it do to you when you have no choice?"

I wrote "have no choice" on the notepad.

"And then what?" I asked.

"I drove home to the empty house."

"Did you report the incident to FreedomQuest?"

"No, sir, I did not."

"Why not?"

"Because they wouldn't care."

"You sure about that?"

"They would say I had it coming to me."

"Why?"

"Because they hated me."

"Why did they hate you?"

"Because they thought I was a pain in the ass."

"And why did they think you were a pain in the ass?"

"Because I was always telling them they were doing everything wrong."

"And why was that?"

"Because they were. Because they were getting paid millions of dollars from the Department of Defense for US military contracts and they had no idea what they were doing."

"And you did?"

"Yes, sir. I had been in the region for almost ten years with Special Forces. I knew what and what not to do when it came to working with the Afghans. But they wouldn't listen."

I scribbled "wouldn't listen" on the notepad.

"Did anyone follow you? After the accident?"

"No one. It was as if the accident never happened. Like it was all make-believe. If only the Afghans were steel and bulletproof. Then none of it would matter. But that's not the case. They're not bullet-proof and I was tired of hurting people. I couldn't do it anymore. I awoke with the morning call to prayer before dawn and called the head office in Raleigh on the sat phone and asked them to send me home. Told them that I was done."

"And what did they say?"

"They said I had a contract and I wasn't allowed to leave for another six months and if I did leave I would forfeit my bonus and half of my salary."

So that was it, I thought.

"And then what did you do?"

"I hopped a private flight to Turkey and then from Turkey home to the States and I haven't been back since. And when I asked FreedomQuest for my bonus and the rest of my salary they refused to pay me. Not even a prorated sum. On account of me leaving Afghanistan without their permission. So they punished me."

Thomas stood to stretch his legs and his back. His forehead, nose, temples, and chin glistened. He gestured that he needed to take another pill, the yellow one, and again he sipped it down with black coffee. He retook his seat as Lazlis stared out the window.

"Mr. Thomas, can you explain for me how one individual's insurance claim for work-related injuries can result in this much paperwork?" I asked, pointing at the dozen boxes. "I get that Mr. Lazlis may find it tactically advantageous to try and bury us in paper. And he's not alone in that, others do it as well. But I've been doing this type of legal work for almost eight years and I have never seen this much paper for one claim. Can you understand, objectively, why we question the veracity of your allegations?"

He took his seat, looked at his hands, which remained strong, and placed them, folded, on the table. Then he leaned a couple of inches toward me.

"You ever been in a situation, Mr. Harker, where you've been given five things but you really needed six? Because your survival depended on having two sets of three each? But because you didn't have six now you're stuck with an impossible choice between one and two? A and B? Because all you have is five? But you need six to survive? Because your survival depends on having both?"

"I don't follow, Mr. Thomas."

"What is there not to follow?" he asked.

I avoided the distraction. It was my deposition, not his.

"We'll come back to it," I said. "Now can you explain something else for me Mr. Thomas?"

"What else do you want to know, sir?"

"Are you subject to any court orders with respect to members of your family?"

"Objection," Lazlis interjected. "Irrelevant."

"I mean, are you prohibited from being alone with any members of your family. Particularly with your daughter?"

"Objection again, Mr. Harker. That is totally irrelevant."

I doubted whether to do this now to this man here in this room. I had no choice. I did have a choice. I chose to follow through.

"Who currently has custody of your daughter?"

"Objection again. Mr. Harker if you continue with this line of questioning I will call the judge and have him rule on this objection. Don't answer him, Mr. Thomas."

"It's a reasonable question, Jim. It goes to your client's current mental state and his mental state is at play here because you put it in play. But I'll rephrase the question. Mr. Thomas, are there any court orders you must comply with regarding your daughter?"

Thomas stood again and shuffled to the window and looked down.

"I have a court order here in my hand, Mr. Thomas," I said. "Reporter, I would like to enter this as an exhibit."

"Objection again, Stephen. You were obligated to produce anything you had on this prior to the deposition. You didn't. And therefore you are precluded from using it now. You can't ambush my client like this."

The reporter fastened a yellow sticker to the exhibit and returned it to me. I handed it to Lazlis, who reviewed the document and passed it to Thomas as Thomas again lowered himself into his seat.

"I'm producing it now."

"But this isn't relevant, Stephen," Lazlis objected.

"Mr. Thomas," I continued. "This is an order from a Pennsylvania court prohibiting you from being alone with your daughter. Do you see that?"

"Major, don't answer that," Lazlis continued. His blood pressure rising through the crackled capillaries of his chubby, crimsoning cheeks. "Stephen, I will move the court to strike this whole deposition if you continue with this."

Thomas scanned the exhibit.

"This was my ex-wife's fault," he said. "She filed this thing against me when I was overseas."

"But it does contain that prohibition, correct?"

"But it was blackmail."

"Have you been staying home alone with your daughter in violation of this order?"

"Negative."

"Are you sure about that?"

"Mr. Harker?"

"Remember, it's my deposition, Mr. Thomas," I said. "I ask the questions. You sure you didn't violate this order?"

He stood. I thought he was going to remove a handgun from behind his back brace. I stared at him. The warrior had returned.

"Sir, what would you do if I choked you with that fancy purple-and-blue tie of yours?"

The stenographer stopped typing.

"Keep typing," I commanded her. But my dormant fear began to trickle and pool, beyond my control, summoned by an event that I had put into motion. We could return to the order, I told myself. For now I wanted him calm.

"I smell fear on you, boy," Thomas said.

My hands began to shake. I hid them beneath the table.

"The hit on the head, the dizzy spells, the anxiety, the panic attacks, the headaches, the backaches, the torn rotator cuff, the orthopedic injuries, the tent pole, the mortar fire, the alleged PTSD, the totally irrelevant bladder surgery, the lack of any objective evidence at all to substantiate your allegations." My voice quailed. With a shaky hand I gestured toward the boxes on the windowsill. "Do you see why we have a hard time accepting the veracity of your allegations,

Mr. Thomas? Why we can't just pay you what you are demanding? Because ultimately you're fine. I know you're fine and you know you're fine and WorldScore knows you're fine. It's all in your head, man. You need to get over whatever this is and move on."

"Jim, I don't think I can answer any more of this man's questions."

He stood and exited the conference room and walked to the elevators, without a limp, leaving behind his cane.

"He's going to have to come back here and resume the deposition. You know that, Jim."

Lazlis stood and released a long breath, almost like a whistle.

"Jesus," Lazlis said, pointing at the boxes. "This case is a fucking disaster. Have you ever seen so much paper? Can't we just settle this, Stephen?"

"Not yet."

"Why not?"

"Because we can't."

I walked to Fleeger's office. The door was closed. I pressed the handle. The door was locked.

"Harker," Fleeger said through the door. "Is that you?"

"Yes."

"Are we done?"

"For now."

"Damn."

He was kidding.

"What do you want to do?" I asked.

"Call Celeste."

"And tell her what?"

"Figure it out."

I turned away from his door.

"Hey, Stephen."

"Yeah, Robert."

"You know what the problem is with beautiful women?"

He sounded happy. He was having a good time.

"No, what?"

"They're needy."

A giggle wiggled its way beneath the door.

"They're weak and they require too much attention. Ow!"

I returned to my office and phoned Celeste. She answered on one ring.

"Tell me something good," she said.

"Thomas went AWOL during the deposition."

"Stephen?"

"Yes?"

"Nothing. I just assumed Robert would be the one calling me now."

"Fleeger's busy."

"With what?"

"With something more important," I said.

"What's more important than Thomas?"

"Something came up," I said.

"This is a catastrophe."

"I think we got him. And Lazlis knows his case sucks so I don't expect we'll see any unreasonable demands anytime soon. We'll get Thomas back here for the rest of his deposition. Even if we need a court order. Then once we do we'll tie him down until we're finished."

"Stephen, please make it go away. This case is beginning to bore me."

"I think we're almost there."

"Good."

She hung up the phone.

I emailed Lazlis to paper the file, informing him we needed to resume the deposition that his client had prematurely aborted. Dictated a letter memorializing the day's events. Called Lazlis and left a message on his voice mail asking him to call me back. Certain I could accomplish nothing else for the rest of the day, I sat at my desk, counted the hours, and billed the whole day to WorldScore. 444/15 RF/SH: In re deposition of claimant Major Mike "Bud" Thomas: 8.5 hrs.

24

I ARRIVED EARLY TO Kath's presentation. After Thomas's aborted deposition, I felt the pull of a strong drink, which meant ten. The Village bistro's management prepared to host your private parts, read the marquis. Which was why I was here tonight, for Kath's private parts. I entered the dry ice–motif cocktail lounge and ordered a Beefeater and tonic from a bartender who resembled Achilles, dipped at birth in a vat of Dolce & Gabbana. We would have to kill him by his ankles.

You see there is a system, I should have chided Thomas. Except here it didn't matter. Here there was a system different than the one in which I operated. What mattered here was knowing people who did things, disruptors and aggregators, who worked the interstices between concept and code, venture capital and launch. People who specialized in connecting talent to talent, and attaching talent to themselves, in pursuit of which they licensed themselves to walk away from you midconversation in search of the delicious gooey duck burrowed inside another's wet sand hole.

A clutch of Soncha's forty braids, sans cute little red bows, swept my face as she kissed my cheeks, her eyes once again open, brown and white without the smoky, illusionary eyeliner. It was easier to communicate this way. Her eyes narrowed for a second, inquiring why was my hand still placed on her lower back. I caught myself.

"I'm happy you could make it," she said.

"Me too."

I commanded myself not to talk about work. Work didn't matter. Company mattered. Kath's protest photographs mattered. I admonished myself to stop thinking so much. Because these people could sit for hours in a room without talking. Follow their example and don't say anything stupid. Soncha extracted her phone from her square leather bag.

"I'm sorry," she said.

I offered to buy her a drink. She would take a whiskey and honey on the rocks with a lime. The bartender polished a large ice cube into a sphere and placed the drink before me on a bed of napkins.

"Does that do something?" I asked.

"Like what?" the bartender replied.

"Does it do something to the drink when you do that to the ice?"

"It gives it flavor and style."

Kath stepped through the crowd, her and Soncha now holding each other's elbows and whispering into each other's ears. Kath kissed my cheek and hooked her arm across my lumbar sacrum. Rubbed my cervical spine. After Thomas I had become part chiropractor. We felt like old friends.

"Looking forward to tonight?" I asked.

"I'm so nervous."

She laughed, waved at a well-wisher, cheeks scrunched like a filet of skate.

"You'll be great," I said.

More women crowded around Soncha, removing overcoats and scarves. They were slender, with straight backs, and wore blue-soled heels and black lace. Two tall Arab men wearing suits without ties escorted them, golden Arabic alphabet necklaces draped around their hairless chests. The Komodo dragon of jealousy, of Kath's past lovers, appeared at my feet. Scratching my ankles with coarse claws and hissing for attention. One if not both of the men had been with her during the interregnum between me and Robert. I could just tell. Ali looked at me and smiled.

"And how are you, Stephen? Everything is good?"

"Everything is fine," I said.

"Still saving your clients from the great unwashed masses?"

"Is that a dig, Ali?" I asked.

Soncha looked up from her phone and Kath raised her eyebrows.

"Not at all, Stephen," he said. "I am very happy to see you. You are our brother."

Ali rubbed my shoulder. Good to see him as well, I said. I tolerated the social discomfort because of Kath, asked Ali as well if I could buy him a drink.

"Club soda with a lime," he said.

"Come on man have a drink," I said. "It ain't Ramadan."

He pointed at my glass.

"May I?" he asked.

He took a long sip.

"I would like one of those. What kind of gin is that?"

"Beefeater. If it was good enough for the viceroy of Mumbai it's good enough for me."

Ali smiled.

"Tell that to the inhabitants of Kharg Island. They may disagree with your atavistic affinity for the glory days of English colonialism."   —

I smirked. Because I had no idea what he was talking about. Kath wanted a Diet Coke and bourbon and another honey drink for Soncha. I ordered the round. Two bronzed hands simultaneously deposited four cocktails on the bar. Form of a cube. I drank mine with angst, to hurry along their consumption. It was like offering Native Americans their first taste of whiskey. This wasn't something they did. Except for maybe Kath. I would get them all drunk. Pick up the tab. They would love me for it. I ordered another round.

"Really unnecessary, Stephen," Ali said. He placed his half-finished drink on the bar and informed us that he wanted to check on the room's preparations. Off he popped. I leaned into Kath and draped my arm around her shoulders. We were in neutral. The space between our stomachs vibrated. Like a small warming coil. I wanted to shield it from the elements. Man discover fire bush. Man carry fire home in small thing made from tree. Man protect fire from rain and wind. She touched my arm and walked away and the tall Arabs detached from their crowd and moved on her. Shoes polished like honed bones aglow in the almost darkness of the bistro. Laughing at what they simultaneously whispered in her ears, she pulled back her hair to hear all of what the men had to say.

"How you doing, I'm Stephen," I said. A traveler from another galaxy.

Soncha introduced me to Hussein and Hassan. They nodded at me. I told myself to control the juniper berries; don't let them control you. The DJ spun dirty southern rap and Hussein bent at the knees while Hassan moved in behind Kath. A big smile took over her face. Soncha touched my shoulder.

"Be careful what you pine for, Stephen," she said.

I looked at her. She knew what I was feeling and acknowledged its legitimacy, thereby half-enabling me to do the same.

"You want to help me get ready?" she asked.

I told her no I would stay here spying on Kath but thank you. She nodded her head toward the back room to let me know she would be there if I wanted to join her. I ordered another gin and tonic, quinine an ineffective prophylaxis for Kath sandwiched between two Armani Arabs. To protect us all from me pressing the detonator. I walked away from their apparent position in the bottom of my glass.

A horde of boys, Generation Axe, approached the dance floor and descended on the girls in black lace.

"You're from Egypt? Cool. Where shall I go in Egypt? I hear they have an awesome mall there."

"That's Dubai."

"I hear you can ski in it."

"I hear the architecture is amazing."

"Like the world's tallest building."

The girls walked away.

"Hey Kath, it looks like we're boring your friends."

Kath ignored the boys, lost in the pleasure of the dance of Hussein and Hassan. I stepped outside but lurked near the bar's open window doors. It was the first warm night in months. Together Hussein and Hassan and Kath walked toward the back room and Kath nodded for me to follow them.

25

ALI CROSSED NAMES FROM a printed list and Soncha assigned guests to their places at the U-shaped table. Attractive men donning too much designer clothing, the black lace girls, sisters and cousins in shearling tunics and leather boots suitable for playing polo.

"Stephen, you're over there," Soncha said.

She pointed to the back of the room and I took my seat as the table filled around me. A short man with curly hair opened his jacket to reveal a Mondale/Ferraro shirt. Salvaged, he explained, from a thrift store while covering the Iowa caucuses.

"Always hand wash in cold water," he explained to an admirer of his vintage shirt, "in order to keep the color."

I felt like I was sitting in the kids' corner, pirouetted through the crowd to the open bar, ordered another gin and tonic, the Knicks four points behind on the bartender's radio, didn't know where else to be or what else to do, returned to my seat, pinched the lime into the boozy effervescence, and hooked the spent rind to the glass. I wondered if a rectangle cube is cubical or something else. Rectanglical. The rind hatched into a hungry green caterpillar as a gay man with a funny accent complimented my choice of beverages. He was full of statements and act.

"I only drink organic mixers," he said.

He offered me a sip. We were all sipping one another's drinks tonight. It tasted like tonic water.

"You have to be exclusive," he explained. "It's the only way to truly set yourself apart."

He introduced himself as Alfredo. From Arhentina. Navy sport coat with gold buttons and a canary pocket square. He explained that he was both a tastemaker and a proud fiscal conservative.

"I'm all for trickle-down economics." He looked around the room. "Can I tell you a little secret?"

I motioned the floor was his.

"You know poor people are impossible to market to. But if you pull it off they are golden. Golden! They will buy anything you convince them to buy. Within reason, of course. You can't convince a poor woman to buy an Aston Martin, of course. But you can get her to buy your chicken nuggets. "

He wanted to show me something on his phone. Feigning interest, I switched to the autopilot of yes while unclasping my listening device to determine Kath's precise location. The device telescoped over the table and around the corner, detected her via a series of sonar pings standing against the wall and speaking with Hussein. Or Hassan. I would soon be drunk enough not to care, I told myself. I had crossed the Waterloo between jealousy and dread and now paddled my way across the Rubicon from dread to disaffected. Oars wrapped with cotton, undetected, not making a sound, I changed perspectives.

"Am I boring you?" Alfredo asked.

"No, not at all."

"Don't worry about the dinner. It will be fine."

My ability to follow him was destroyed, drunk on the floor in pieces, each eye converted into a lowercase x.

"Do you remember everything I told you?" Alfredo asked.

"Everything," I told him.

"Good. It's important."

"I doubt it."

He laughed at my joke and then shifted his gaze to a young, fit man who looked like a Duke lacrosse player.

"Maybe if it wasn't for that saggy jaw old man," he rebuffed Alfredo, and Alfredo whimpered away, like a cat sprayed with water to stop chewing on the houseplant.

Soncha spotted me watching the door and held up a finger. Either another drink or another minute, I couldn't tell which. Her I could fall in love with, I told myself. Her I could get over myself for. Someone behind me was thankful they suffered their bikini wax yesterday, because of the possible late-night festivities. I didn't belong here. Other than to follow around Kath, I had no reason to be here tonight. If I had accepted the obvious long ago I wouldn't be here now. I would be home with my appropriate wife, adorning her neck and the space between her amply jeweled earlobes with kisses, entering time notes into the laptop at the suburban kitchen table after she fell asleep reading light contemporary fiction, our two children asleep in their different but similar rooms, rotating nightlights casting silhouettes of trains and stars on their bedroom walls stenciled with baseball bats and basketballs.

Kath entered the back room, completing the troika, she and Soncha and Ali touching one another's elbows and shoulders and conspiring. Soncha and Kath quasi-glowered at me. Summers ago, when Kath and Robert were still married, we all day-tripped to Jacob Riis beach. Robert drank too much beer as Soncha capoeiraed on the beach with an American boy and Robert wanted to know what was the point. Badgering the boy to explain to him why he possessed a Brazilian-flag towel and wore tiny Brazilian-flag shorts. He demanded to know just what was so fucking cool about Brazil. I took Robert for a walk to calm him down and when we returned to the girls sunbathing and the boy scared off that was the same look they both gave me. Holding me joint and severally liable for the awkward moment on account of my proximity to Fleeger.

I scanned the evening's agenda of presentations. A bestselling author would explain our collective need for new vocabularies. An activist would discuss her efforts to provide safe abortions in Bangladesh. Followed by Kath, who would explain her new photo series, Faces of the Ciudad (a.k.a. The Miserables).

Ducking beneath the doorframe, the author entered the room and bent forward to kiss Soncha on the cheek. Even if down on one knee he would still be just as tall as her. He possessed the confident air of a very tall man who had slept with a great number of women and perhaps a few men. The Argentine watched the author take his seat next to Kath and kiss her cheek too while asking the waiter if the salad was gluten free.

"Don't be such a baby," the Duke lacrosse player scolded him.

The juniper berries bit and my fork couldn't strike the Parmesan slice atop the cranberry and spinach salad. Soncha thanked everyone for attending tonight's Qommentary, an exclusive forum for discussing the planet's changing cultural and political landscape. I ate with drunk, hungry relish. Soncha announced how pleased she was to introduce tonight's first speaker, author Christopher Fitzgerald.

"Excuse me if I sound lethargic," he said, smiling, but almost hoarse. "I just returned from the Falklands last night and appear to have caught something of a cold during my travels."

"Please," Alfredo said.

"Why were you in the Falklands?" asked a large-boned blonde woman wearing black, cat-tipped glasses, her fleshy arms tattooed vintage Village rockabilly.

"I can't tell you."

"Why can't you tell us?" asked the lacrosse player.

"Perhaps, Chris, it has something to do with your next book?" Soncha asked.

"No, nothing like that, Soncha. I just woke up last week and had an overpowering urge to go to the Falklands." He faced the audience. "Because as creators, we must follow our urges, the sources of creativity, our empowerment. We must listen to our muse. If she says, 'Chris, go to the Falkland Islands,' I must go. I can't question her. Otherwise she'll leave me for someone else."

"Is it absolutely necessary that muses be female?" asked one of the black lace sisters. "Why can't my muse be a male?"

"Now that's an interesting point," the author said. "What's your name?"

"Mona."

"That's a really interesting point, Mona. It's true. Some nouns do take the feminine pronoun."

"They don't *take* Chris," Mona replied. "They're *imposed* by the hierarchy."

This back and forth pleased Soncha, who possessed a front-row seat to her own private, intellectual Wimbledon.

"Must the feminine pronoun always be associated with fickle inspiration?" Mona asked. "With whimsical ephemera?"

"Oil tankers," I retorted, surprising myself.

"Speak up, Stephen, please," Soncha said, enthused.

"Oil tankers. Ships. Vessels."

"What about them?" Mona asked.

"They take the feminine pronoun," I said.

"Not ours. Not our hospital ship," Mona said. "He was our *Hercules*."

"And why do you think that is, Stephen?" Soncha asked. "That ships are given the feminine pronoun?"

"Because they're possessed by men," Kath injected.

"Not sure I agree with your choice of the verb 'take' either," said Mona. "More like branded."

"Did you just say branded?" Alfredo asked. "What does branding have to do with his muse?"

We returned our attention to Fitzgerald, standing patiently behind the podium. He pressed the projector button and the image of a skinny runner with a blond ponytail appeared on the wall behind him. Staring at the camera in horrific surprise.

"Chiva Blanca, ladies and gentlemen," Fitzgerald said.

"And he never stops running?" asked Hassan or Hussein.

"He never stops."

"Must be great for his core strength," Alfredo confirmed.

"What about footwear?" asked the lacrosse player.

"He runs barefoot," Fitzgerald explained.

"No," the Argentine said. "Who would run barefoot? No way."

Fitzgerald again pressed a button and displayed a picture of Chiva Blanca's feet, bloody and calloused and bruised almost beyond recognition.

"He runs for the pain," Fitzgerald explained. "Pain is his fuel."

The diners gasped in awe, both in denial and intrigued, interest piqued to maximum capacity, where one's consciousness expands. The point where true Qommentary can commence.

"You see, we don't possess the vocabulary, the consciousness, to comprehend the reality of Chiva Blanca's pain," Fitzgerald explained. "It requires photographs for me to convey this man's uniqueness. My challenge to you is, how do I do this with written words?"

"I understand what you are saying," Kath said. "I can see the problem."

Fitzgerland thanked Kath for her qomments and continued.

"Chiva Blanca is a runner, that's evident. But he is also a vessel. To how we communicate. Which raises the very subject of how we formulate language. If language is our source code, akin to our source code, as I have posited in my last eighteen books, then we can program the words and acquire the image in our imaginations. But if language is more primordial, derives from our collective conscience, evolves from our experiences, the memories of collective humanity, then how can we even begin to comprehend Chiva Blanca as anything other than a pure masochist?"

"Either a guide for the future," Soncha said.

"Or a mirror to our past," Ali added.

"Our primitive, collective, unconscious past," Fitzgerald replied. "Which brings us to the next logical question. What then is a typo?"

I finished my drink, trying to discern their logical connection, as the green caterpillar commenced chewing the white tablecloth with its sharp, tiny teeth.

"If writing is what I like to call accessing our personal containers of metadata, then there is no such thing as a typo."

"Please explain yourself more, Chris," Soncha said. "I don't think I get that."

"Let me give an example. If I write the words 'fattened calf' on a piece of paper. If my intent is to write the words 'fattened calf.' But I instead write the words 'flattened calf,' is that a typo? Or is it something else?"

"It still evokes the image," Soncha said. "But of both a fattened and flattened calf. Or two calves. One fattened and one flattened."

I zoned out. Wanted to ask the bartender the score of the game. Whether there were any Latins on the court at Madison Square Garden. Fitzgerald finished his strange speech and the crowd applauded and the man took his seat, knees up around his ears, raised his glass to the audience, thanked Soncha, and offered to continue the conversation after dinner, if anyone was interested, which he didn't want to presume, though he knew this was the case.

The waiter set before me a square plate of fish in red sauce and Mona took the lectern, standing on her toes.

"So, hi, everyone. I spent the last six months at sea," she said. The image of a hospital vessel appeared on the screen behind her. Along with a map of the ship's voyage from Singapore around the Straits of Malacca to the fingers of Bangladesh's mangrove deltas.

"Now, it's never easy to provide safe, effective abortion services in South Asia," she explained. "There are all sorts of nasties you have to deal with. Mullahs, husbands, fathers, brothers. Acid attacks. Customs officials."

Something raucous, sudden and unexpected, on the other side of the room's entrance and back toward the Village bistro's bar, halted Mona's talk. There must be a fatwa against her, I thought, sitting up in my seat. To be served and executed at once. Soncha bolted from her seat with her thin outstretched arms to halt what could not not be a suicide bomber from detonating her Qommentary to bits. Behind her, Hussein and Hassan wielded chairs like human plows to repel this mess of dirty boots and scabby skin, lice and ringworm, forcing its way into our realm of pure Qommentary. Wherein Jupiter now entered, crawling beneath the jostle, supine, de-supining, upright, mouths agape, Jupiter's too, all of us more surprised by the sight of the other than the other.

"Who is this funny black man?" Alfredo asked.

Jupiter prowled back and forth in the projector lights. Big eyes bright like Koh-i-Noors, like a nocturnal photograph of a leopard, scarred in battle with a thrashing wildebeest. The underlying event and Qommentary no longer symbiotic but synchronized. In real time. I half-expected Chiva Blanca to run into the room and join the fracas. Jupiter came strapped, with an old bullhorn and a cardboard sign around his neck that commanded: YELL AT ME FOR A DOLLAR! Kath rushed at him. Some inner servo of hers no doubt wanting just as much to film him as to make him disappear.

"Jupiter" *click* "please" *click* "don't" *click click click* "do this," she pleaded.

"Where's my dollar? Where. Is. My. Dollar? Read the sign, Kath. Don't yell at me without paying the price."

He blew invisible fuzz from the mouthpiece of the beat-in bullhorn. It's a slave name. He gave it to himself. The smooth keloid the length of his mandible shined in the lights of the projector.

"Whose streets? Our streets," Jupiter chanted into the bullhorn, as the crusty kids overpowered Soncha's and Hussein's and Hassan's defenses and now plundered and pillaged bread and breadsticks and cocktails and fish from the U-shaped table, none of them concerned with gluten or peanuts or thirty-day cleanses, scarfing down food and drink without swallowing, in true paleo fashion, before the seated, dumbstruck crowd: Mona and her black-laced and blue-soled and polo-booted crew; Generation Axe; the Argentine; the Duke; men wearing too much fashion; women donning too much jewelry. Geraldine motherfucking Ferraro and Walter fucking Mondale. Brazilianed—and not the people. Too proud and confident in their constant search for exclusivity, originality, creativity, fame, recognition, disruption, stickiness, *empowerment* to realize that for Kath and Soncha and Ali—their friends—this was a catastrophe. Now taking in the destruction almost like it was performance art.

"Send in the mariachis," the lacrosse player yelled, laughing. "I'll pay."

Jupiter & Co. present to you tonight the arrival of a risky, unanticipated thrill. Something more than a little unexpected. Traversing the distant realms of true Qommentary.

I couldn't resist—I dipped a sugar packet into a glass of water and lobbed it at Alfredo. A direct strike to his canary pocket square. Who did this to him? he demanded to know. Ali grabbed the microphone and struggled to assume the podium, jostled by homeless anarchist youth, way out beyond his zone of efficacy.

"Please don't do this," he implored Jupiter and the protestors. "We empathize with your cause. We are all subject to the dominant paradigm. There is plenty for everyone."

I tossed a soggy sugar packet at the Duke lacrosse player, emptied the caddy on the table, and lined up additional projectiles to salvo. Kath ran back and forth, between Jupiter and Soncha, Soncha and Ali, back to Jupiter, struggling to discern what to do. Her soft propeller now whirling in the opposite direction of where she believed the evening was destined. Bow straight ahead, stern in reverse. The pressure cracked apart her hull, her propeller quickly losing thrust as Jupiter scolded her with a long pink finger.

"I warned you, Kath."

"Warned me about what?"

"Not to poverty pimp us," he said, shaking his head.

I finally kind of understood what he meant.

"What does that even mean?" she pleaded.

"I shouldn't have to explain."

A body in motion must stay in motion. No one in this room possessed enough force equal in strength and magnitude to contain Jupiter and his miscreant gang of youth as they leapt atop the table, the girls in black lace now scattering from their chairs beneath the tablecloth, pulling their sisters and cousins to safety, covering their faces with forearms. On cue, more motor-greased youth in raunchy salivating death punk finery entered the room, strumming banjos and plucking Jew's harps and wrestling amongst themselves and knocking over chairs and tables, tablecloths and drinks and food and flower arrangements whole hock. Crashing sounds and shrieks, grunts and screams.

"Whose streets? Our streets," Jupiter yelled, goose-stepping through the empty core of the once-U-shaped table. Fitzgerald stood tall and telegraphed a punch in Jupiter's direction, but he too succumbed to the mass of crusty kids and down good Fitzy went, beneath a pile of sweat and dirt, until he broke free from the rumble and crawled toward the fire exit. His hands agleam with a generous application of hand sanitizer that filled the room with the toxic effluvium of jellied isopropyl alcohol.

"Over here," Fitzgerald said, signaling to the sisters cowering beneath the table.

Dutch climbed atop the table behind Jupiter, donning a golden paper crown, kicking over mushroom soup, tearing meat with her blackened, pointy teeth. Soiling the vintage fabric of Mondale/Ferraro '84 as a quorum of diners escaped through the fire exit, dusting off their clothes. Even those unscathed did the same. I ducked a Frisbee of a dining plate and followed the crowd through the open fire door. Someone said tonight was clearly a success. Someone else that they loved coming to these things.

"Always something unexpected."

The narrow Village street now the staging ground for a throng of police officers snapping on white helmets, plastic hog-ties dangling from their belt loops, pulling on latex gloves, reinforced by the mounted brigade polishing their billy clubs in unison and preparation. I spotted Kath yelling at Jupiter.

"I tried to find you," she said. "To tell you about tonight."

This was a lie.

"You failed."

"But I couldn't find you."

"Well, doesn't that make everything all white."

The police marched in lockstep, phalanxed behind plastic shields. For no discernible reason a bomb-disposing robot joined them, robot arms raised in some type of rejoice. I pulled Kath by the sleeve as she berated Jupiter for ruining her evening, stretching the blend of her Lycra-cashmere, until she capitulated, now dangling one long sleeve as she looked back at him over her shoulder. Jupiter couldn't have cared less, and he pointed at me as if I would get mine too, someday. We exited the alley and regrouped on the sidewalk with Ali and Soncha. Now down now to twenty-eight braids.

The riot rumbled onto the street. With the force of a tsunami moving through a coastal village. Through the window doors of the bistro. Past the marquis of private parts. Onto the sidewalk. More police officers and more dirty American kids stomping the ground, ready for a fight. Smoking broken cigarettes as the tall, thin women drinking at the bar leapt from the open windows. Little colorful triangles of thongs visible between their waxy bean legs. Ali picked from his hair what looked like cheesecake as Jupiter galloped away atop a commandeered horse, chased by a team of cop jockeys donning midnight-blue pennies.

"Stephen?" Kath asked.

"Kath?"

"Why didn't you protect me tonight, baby?"

"What are you talking about?"

"Why didn't you protect me from Jupiter? Every time I looked up you were nowhere. You should have been by my side."

"That was between you and Jupiter."

"I need you by my side, Stephen."

I told her I would keep it in mind.

"You can't keep disappointing me, Stephen. It's not nice."

Biting my tongue, I walked her home. Ali and Hassan and Hussein and Soncha walked crestfallen a half block ahead of us. Like a girl-fronted indie band. Kath hooked her arm inside mine and rested her head on my shoulder. She kissed my cheek while I looked at the ground and told me she wanted to be alone with her friends, that she thought Soncha needed her. I told her I understood.

"You're still coming with me to Benjamin's birthday party?"

I had forgotten about this as well, the last thing I wanted after tonight. I hedged.

"You promised," she said.

"I did?"

"You did."

"Can I think about it?"

"No," she replied. "I'll text you in the morning."

I entered my apartment and turned on the light and poured myself a double vodka and lay on the couch. The lit cigarette and the household electronics communicated their positions to each other. Modem. Stereo. Cable box. Cigarette. Bluetooth. Cable box. Stereo. Modem. I felt spent. My phone double vibrated a message from Kath, telling me she caught the late train to Philadelphia. That she needed to get out of her apartment. That she and Soncha argued and that Soncha blamed her for ruining the night. And after all that Soncha had done for her and after Soncha had put so much work into it.

"She said it was my fault."

"Baby, it wasn't your fault."

"I feel like it was."

"Soncha's not being fair. Why didn't you come over here?"

"I'm trying to give you some space."

"You could have come over. I'm here."

"I really need you to come to Benjamin's tomorrow. We'll have a good time. Don't be scared."

"I'm not scared."

"Come."

"OK."

26

I DESCENDED INTO PENN Station and bought a seventy-five-dollar ticket from another goo-coated computer kiosk for the one-hour-and-ten-minute ride to Philadelphia. A banner strung across the retro architectural warren of escalators and stairways thanked the terrorists. I read it again. Thank you, tourists. Some kind of Freudian American slip there. If they could read my mind I'd be sent to Guantanamo, permanently bivouacked in an open pen under twenty-four-hour guard. Chained to the wall of a black site prison in Slovakia, strapped down with a towel draped over my face and a pitcher of water coursing down my throat, forcing open my epiglottis. Don Henley's "Boys of Summer" piped through the staticky foam speakers above. A peon to a much simpler time. When there was only Russia and AIDS to worry about.

The buttery pretzels and donuts and bagels and tubs of cold beer and shiny pizza offered no defense against the physical discomfort of Penn Station. Pretty black girls looked me in the eye, reciprocated my gaze. We are all little monsters of desire. I queued to board the train.

"Don't tell me there's nothing in your pocket," an Amtrak cop scolded a jaundiced African, the cop's big-tongued New York accent like hot pastrami on rye. "I can feel it right here."

The train cop waived me around the African and I descended the steps into the electric-diesel labyrinth, freshly scrubbed with bittersweet disinfectant. I stared out the train window lost in a labyrinth of meaningless, meandering thought.

The train slowed and entered the warehouse flatlands of North Philadelphia. Every city has its colors, and here the city was brick red with aquamarine elevated trestles, neon graffiti airbrushed color guards, bare lightbulbs and broken windows and corrugated tin. Abandoned egg factories and pediatric hospitals. I expected a rock to shatter the train window as it curled through Frankford. Kath texted me the address of her brother's house and I exited the train at 30th Street Station. Pushed through the heavy, brass, and broken automated doors. The city smelled of automobile air freshener, relaxer, weed. I hailed a taxi.

The driver swung his wheel behind the art museum ringed with massive buttonwoods, past the straight backs and ribbed gills of athletic women in all-weather running gear. A buttonwood trapped inside the manmade falls that dammed the Schuylkill River. We spun off the boulevard, up a hill, through a park, heavy and dark with shadows. The driver spoke but I couldn't hear him above the angry alto tenor playing in the speakers behind my headrest.

Here the city was old and white, with recently painted brick facades and Spirit of '76 flags and Union Jacks and the occasional French tricolor. Fresh copper domes and verdigris gutters and gargoyles atop the dormers. We passed a Belgian café with a padlocked door and a vandal's tag etched into its glass with a stick of hydrofluoric acid. Demarcating the northern boundary of the city's gentrification. The driver headed north ten more blocks, pressed the brakes, pulled to the curb, and pointed to the green street signs to confirm this was indeed where I told him to bring me.

Spanish kids watched me from the sidewalk. They wore puffa jackets and long white shirts that looked like hospital gowns and jeans belted across their hamstrings. I paid the driver through the slit in the plexiglass barrier and exited the car and pulled my bag tight against my shoulder and walked north on Seventeenth Street. The

Spanish kids communicated up and down the street with clicks and whistles. To communicate I was either a customer or not interested and not a cop. Bushy ponytails and fitted baseball caps and plastic diamond ear studs. I wanted to ask who among them was Senor Anhel Dust. Up the street, one of the Spanish kids cupped his hand to his face and made a wolf-bird sound and the kids standing on the corner kicked over a milk crate and a basketball appeared. The basketball bounced. A police car rolled through the intersection.

I stood before the high concrete steps of Benjamin's four-story brick Victorian flaking gray paint, a panopticon of red-iris security cameras trained on his stoop, up the street, on his vehicle garaged behind his gate, a yellow International Harvester. I pressed the doorbell and the lock buzzed and I pushed my way into Benjamin's old, big house.

The floor was uneven and sloped toward the back of the house. At some point he would have to jack up the foundation and joists. The hallway's brittle lathe was snapped into erratic cubbyholes. Behind spackled drywall, dogs wrestled and growled, yanking one another's chains. The lock shook inside the strike bolt as Benjamin opened the door, cigarette crushed between his stained teeth, wearing black jeans and a torn flannel shirt and BluBlockers. Since I'd last seen him, he'd grown thick blond burnsides. They looked both ridiculous and imposing. I thought better not to comment on them. Because the last thing you need or want from a newly arrived guest is a pithy comment about your changed appearance. He shook my hand.

"Yeah, man," he said. "I remember you. Good to see you again."

He kicked away the dogs and I shielded my crotch from their roving snouts. Innumerable tattoos of indecipherable designs and patterns covered his large, calloused hands. Also ripe for Qommentary, I thought, and I suspected he had either gotten his strange hands around Soncha before or would do so one day. Because they were similar beasts she would choose to have him. He noticed me staring at his hands as he tossed me a beer but there was nothing for us to say. They were noticed, they were noticeable, that was all. I caught the beer in the basket of my hands, told him the trip was fine. Kath entered the kitchen from the basement stairs, her denim thighs and semi-wide hips covered with sawdust.

"You made it," she said.

She kissed me on the cheek and hugged me. If Benjamin wasn't standing there she would have called me baby. The empty word floated there for an invisible moment.

"I did."

"Why wouldn't he?" Benjamin asked.

"I almost didn't make it," Kath said. "We were almost killed last night."

"No one almost gets killed in New York anymore," he said. "They almost get killed here."

This seemed a strange thing to get cocky about, but Philadelphians, I had learned, were preternaturally inclined to boast about strange things. Like crime rates. She punched Benjamin's arm, to defend her urban pride, and her knuckles rapped his bicep. As they grunted and wrestled, with an outstretched finger perpendicular to my beer can I inquired whether I could explore the house and Benjamin nodded his consent. Kath jumped on his back and applied a headlock to her brother and Benjamin tossed her over his shoulder, now gripping her hamstrings. I struggled to avoid the hyperactive dogs as they banged around beneath a glass table and stepped outside into the hollowed-out core of a square block that Benjamin had demolished, expanding his freehold with a backhoe. Mounds of honeycomb plaster, cracked porcelain, lead pipes, a haycock of rotten joists and ancient lumber impregnated by termites. Their wrestling match done, Benjamin stepped outside and rocked and pivoted two large speakers onto the patio. He waved me over to help him and we picked up the speakers and set them atop tripods. He nodded his thanks and returned inside and I sat on a broken beach chair missing half its vinyl straps and rolled a cigarette and stared at the pinkish-blue sunset of impending spring.

A tribe of urban homesteaders arrived. They congregated in the kitchen and the backyard, couples and dogs, the men in canvas workpants with slits for slide rulers and hammers and marijuana cigarettes and the women in blue jeans and work boots. Rehabilitationistas of vintage bars and coffee shops with dropped tin ceilings and bronze light fixtures scavenged from abandoned, crack-destroyed row homes. They were sentries of gentrification. Unique. Original. Capable of doing things with their hands, like replacing boilers and wiring fuse boxes. They stood in the corners of Benjamin's kitchen discussing the process of infusing homemade liquor with homegrown herbs and how to access the city's water mains. I stood among them, alone, leaning against the sink, nothing much to add and no one interested in what I could. Kath had disappeared.

Benjamin entered the kitchen, freshly showered, tying his wet hair into a ponytail. He removed a bottle of Wild Turkey from the dusty liquor cabinet and smiling at the women and slapping the backs of the men he poured everyone shots of bourbon in red plastic cups.

"Here you go, Stephen," he said, handing me a cup but not looking at me. He looked around the room. "Everyone meet Stephen?"

The guests grumbled that they did or they would and someone said not yet and I downed the bourbon and fought to keep it there. It struggled against me.

"Refreshing." Benjamin smiled.

Together the men stepped outside, following Benjamin to survey the houses he had demolished and to discuss renting a backhoe for big jobs as I stood alone in the kitchen with the women in jeans preparing the food they had brought with them in reusable grocery bags.

"So you're just down for tonight?" one of them asked while cutting carrots into slices, pulling her hair behind her head, revealing armpits of superfine grit. She wore a tight Stones T-shirt that accented her ample, strong curves. All tongue and lips. I offered my hand and introduced myself and she wiped her hands on her thick, soccer thighs.

"Rebecca," she said.

Finished with the carrots, she commenced slicing bumpy cucumbers and then dried salty meats and a loaf of rustic bread, and arranged the presentation on a wooden cutting board. I nodded to one of the other women that she too could toss me a beer and again it landed in the basket of my hands. They didn't know why I was here or who I was, and Kath, it seemed, had done little to segue my welcome by this unfamiliar tribe. Just some dude who happened to be here. I thought of the pleasures of the train ride home.

"And you?" I asked.

"Me and my husband live a couple blocks north of here."

She pointed with her knife and emphasized the word husband.

"We just bought an old factory that we're converting into live-work space."

"Sounds cool," I said.

"It is."

"Rebecca, stop boasting," another woman said while slicing limes. She too wore tight jeans and a tight shirt, along with a pair of heavy, brown climbing boots with red laces. They were the strong women of the strong men. "Stephen," I introduced myself.

"Sam," she said, nodding. The tiny papillon tattoo on her right breast fluttered as she pestled avocado, onions, and tomatoes inside a stone molcajete. Her husband, she explained, was Benjamin's business partner.

Introductions made, we were a bit more comfortable with one another now. Under certain circumstances I gravitated toward the women in a group and this was one of those occasions. At least it felt that way. I instructed myself not to ask too many questions and sipped my beer in silence as the women set the food on the counters and the men walked the property with Benjamin, all of them with their hands behind their backs.

Kath entered the kitchen from the basement, bright in the white dress that wrapped around the cello of her almost flat hips. An orchid amongst the scrubby, resilient *Pachysandra*. She looked at me as she entered the kitchen and detected that I needed her to touch me. She rested the tips of her fingertips on my shoulder, for a moment soothing my hum, and offered her hands to the strong, tough women, who spun her as she explained that she picked it up in SoHo.

"How pretty," Rebecca said.

Failing to mention I had bought it for her. I worried some hidden splotch of epoxy would stain the dress and cracked open another beer. Done talking business, the men entered the kitchen and commented on Kath's appearance, made loud, guttural noises and emphatic sounds of naughty pleasure and mock serendipity. Everyone enthralled by Kath except Benjamin. He brushed past her and opened the fridge and drank a can of Budweiser and tossed the empty can into a cardboard box and opened another can and walked outside, dogs circling his feet.

The music became louder and more guests arrived. They were less carpenter and more carnal, the candy men who brought the candy. A tall man donning an LBJ entered the sawdust-covered living room and the women danced around him, ribbons between their teeth. Something primal, important, was now underway, which I could not dismiss because I didn't know its source but knew enough to know that it mattered because it made me nervous. The women now feting and long-touching Kath, disrobing sides of her I had never before seen. Sides that were wholly unconcerned with anything I needed. The sweat from my fingers soaked through the thin rice paper as I struggled to roll a cigarette. It turned crooked and twisted, almost too tight to pull.

Benjamin amped the music's volume and speed. Without him noticing, I followed him outside to speak with him about how cool this all was and also to thank him for inviting me. He removed a Zippo from the pocket of his jeans and lit gasoline-soaked rags hanging inside the haycock of scavenged lathe. The thin, dry wood, cracked and brittle, quickly took to flame. As he worked the fire he ignored the crowd of guests gathering around him. A bearded carpenter removed a spliff from the pocket of his overalls and handed it to me. I pulled on it and the marijuana fishbowl descended over my head.

"No more for me," I said, handing it back to him.

I sat next to the slat fence that circled the property, stoned, drunk, and alone.

"You remember that young buck who used to come over here and sit with her all day long?" someone said on the other side of the fence. I didn't see them and they didn't see me.

"Yeah."

"He got twenty-five to life."

"He did?"

"Now that light-skinned nigger is coming to see her."

"Who, Webb?"

"Yeah. That's him."

"Let's get some juice and kill this bottle."

"You know Nat?"

"Of course I know Nat."

"Who the fuck is that? Right there?"

"Some dude on the other side of the fence."

"Fuck him."

I crawfished in my chair away from the fence.

"Crocodile Dundee motherfucker," one of them said and then spit over the fence. The glob arced and landed somewhere in the hard dirt lawn of Benjamin's expansive property.

I returned to the carpenter and his spliff. He was friendly and open and his ample cheeks glowed red. The flames reflected inside the black lochs of his big, round eyes. He handed me the joint.

"What do you do?" he asked.

"I'm a lawyer," I said, exhaling.

"In Center City?"

"New York."

This elicited no response.

"And you?" I asked.

"I'm a steeplejack."

I wanted to tell him of course he was a steeplejack. Why wouldn't he be a steeplejack.

"How long have you known Kath and Benjamin?" I asked.

"Feels like forever."

A woman approached and cuddled the steeplejack. She told him he was so sweet for doing what he did and he nodded in my direction as they walked away from me. I worried they were pitying me, but pity wasn't something to which they were accustomed, because they were unaccustomed to spending time with people they didn't know. Their pity therefore risked descending rapidly into disgust. As that worry grew—that I was being pitied—I wanted more and more to leave. I reentered the kitchen and sat on a busted wicker chair as Benjamin tapped white powder from a small, glass vial onto an octagon-shaped glass table. Rebecca chopped and snorted a tiny line with a rolled-up five-dollar bill.

"What is that?" she asked as if holding her breath.

"Special K," Benjamin said. "It's for the animals."

"How appropriate," she replied. She handed him the rolled-up bill. "Happy birthday, my man."

Benjamin leaned over the table and snorted a birthday line. The crowd gathered around him and sang happy birthday and he sat there with a silly smile on his face as the ketamine traveled through the open capillaries of his sinuses into his bloodstream. He snorted three more lines, each progressively longer and thicker, he would snort up almost the whole gift. Now leaning back, eyes wide open, eyebrows arced.

"Wow," he yelled. And with that he launched into middle age.

Within the core of the party, something had changed, its metamorphosis contingent upon my absence as I sulked and smoked outside. Only then did it have the right combination of elements and personalities to practice its magic. The girls squeezed and grabbed and stroked one another's denim, all of them now covered with sawdust, as they lapped up the remnants of the Special K from the glass table. Outside it had started to rain and the rain was black and the girls dancing around the fire wrapped their arms around one another to keep warm and also for something extra. The cowboy beckoned them to get back inside and he led the girls to the couch by the hand and there were now four, five girls making out, struggling to unbutton and remove shirts over arms and heads. Multicolored everyday bras and unbuckled jeans and penumbras of nipples and the firm, steady breasts of women who hadn't yet birthed children but were now the prime age to do so. Beckoning Kath to join them; their mascara water soluble, cheeks streaked with blackened water. Kath now short of breath as the cowboy led her too by the hand. Her hands now down around the hem of the dress, she too just about to, half off it comes. Until, as if commanded by their master to go forth and wreak havoc, Benjamin's dogs snarled into the living room and leapt atop the couch.

"Damn it, Benjamin," the girls lamented. "You and your fucking dogs."

Only exciting the dogs more. Now rolling atop one another in the pile of wet women.

"Damn this life. It was just getting good," cursed the cowboy as the girls snapped and covered themselves.

"Rebecca, stop always trying to fuck my sister," Benjamin yelled.

He was high and serious and angry and his voice filled the ceiling and the dogs stilled. Rebecca and Sam retreated into a corner as they pulled on their shirts and Kath brushed dog hair from the white dress. Benjamin ripped the stereo chord from the wall and some portal door closed and the revelers had no choice but to leave the party because the man-god Benjamin was angry. They exited the living room and kitchen through the holes in the walls and out the long, thin windows.

I walked outside to the bonfire. The structure had collapsed onto itself and the ground was now a bed of charred joists and a blanket of glowing hexagons. I looked through the fence erected to demarcate the boundaries of Benjamin's compound. A man, neither white nor black nor Spanish, pressed his face against the fence while smoking a blunt and blew smoke into Benjamin's yard, watching me.

"Stephen," Kath said. As if she had been looking for me for an hour and I was hiding under the laundry inside the wicker hamper, all of us now back to a more innocent time.

She stepped through the door and I could see only her silhouette in the yellow halogen security lights that ringed Benjamin's house. I was relieved she wanted to speak with me.

"Come on, we're going out."

27

THE KITCHEN LAY IN chaos. Tables covered with beer cans and crushed soft packs of cigarettes. A half-eaten honey-baked ham and a tray of burnt tater tots removed from a dented toaster oven. Benjamin and Kath spoke in low voices, discarding plastic plates heavy with half-consumed slices of carrot cake. Benjamin tossed a plate in the nylon bag to protest the task's futility. I realized there was nowhere here for me to sleep and slung the swish messenger bag stuffed with a change of clothes and toiletries over my shoulder, in order to spend the night in a hotel. It was late but I would try to find one. There was nothing for me here. I needed to communicate this to Kath.

"Leave it," Benjamin told Kath. "We'll clean it tomorrow."

He wanted to go to the bar and Kath and I followed him out the front door to the street, deserted but for the bushy-tailed Puerto Rican kid in his slackened jeans and a girl sitting between his legs on a stoop across the street. Kath fumbled with her camera phone as Benjamin deadbolted the house's front doors and pulled on his padlock behind us.

"Don't look at them," Benjamin said.

"Why not?" Kath asked.

"Because they're pieces of shit."

"They're just kids, Benjamin."

"They're fucking criminals."

He started the yellow Harvester and it rumbled from its parking space like one of his pets. Like a bigger pet fed bigger chunks of meat and walked only on special occasions. He gripped the hard, plastic steering wheel with knuckles bearing those strange patterns. Celtic-Scandinavian. Runestones. We rode without music or headlights, past blocks of cyclone fencing and black men gesturing toward one another, crossed a wide, empty avenue and beneath a skywalk that echoed the heavy engine and over a stretch of railroad tracks. Benjamin spun the hard steering wheel down a boulevard and I bounced across the back seat. Gray alleyways. Yellow streetlights. Shackled storefronts and dumpsters crawling with people.

"Stop," Kath said. "Back up."

She struggled to extract her camera from her bag and now it was in her hand. Benjamin reversed the car and Kath began again with the photos. Of figures surrounding a man on the ground, kicking him in turn. Nine on one, ten on one. This wasn't the reckless flailing of a drunken brawl, I thought. This was premeditated. An arm raised a crowbar in retribution.

"Shouldn't we help him?" I asked.

"There are like twenty guys beating him, Benjamin," Kath said. "Do something."

"None of my business," Benjamin replied. He shifted the car into drive and pressed down on the gas.

"They're beating that guy," I said.

He stared at me in the rearview mirror. I let it go. Maybe he was right. Maybe it was none of his business. None of our business. Kath said something beneath the sound of the wind and the engine.

Benjamin parked the car and you could tell it was a bar because there was a television visible through the blackened windows. A beefy Turkish bouncer shook hands with Benjamin and kissed Kath on the cheek and she introduced me as her friend. He nodded at me. I nodded back. We walked to the bar and ordered three big, cheap mugs of porter and lit our own cigarettes and leaned forward on our elbows. Like we were leaning against the inside of a dugout. The cash register locked on the bartender and he smashed it with a rubber mallet and it opened with an antique copper ring. Benjamin handed him a fifty-dollar bill and the bartender set three shot glasses on the bar before us turned upside down and then propped open a floor hatch that led to the taproom.

"Benny, come with me," he said and together they descended the staircase into the taproom. I moved closer to Kath, to speak with her for the first time in hours. I wasn't ready to tell her I needed to find a hotel for the night. But I would do so once we had reconnected.

"How are you?" I asked.

"I'm so tired."

"That was quite a scene at your brother's house."

"I know. I don't know what came over me. I hope that didn't hurt you."

"A little. But I'll get over it. Besides, I don't own you."

I didn't believe a word I said. Yet I was incapable of telling her what I truly felt. If I was capable of telling her what I felt I wouldn't be here now. I would have been back in New York hours ago. I never would have left.

"Benjamin wants me to move back here and stay with him. He said he'd give me a floor of the house."

"What do you think?"

"I don't know. There's a lot of room to work and I could have my own studio. But I don't know. It's not New York."

"Did you hear from Soncha?"

"She still doesn't want to talk to me."

At least she's honest, I wanted to say, but didn't.

Kath looked at her beer. I put my arm around her waist but the distance between us pushed us apart. As if we were two positive magnets. I placed my hand on her hip. The gap between us yawning. We had approached the beginning of the end, I thought. What would I do without her? How would that be? But this too passed. I would be fine. And so too would she. On the television above the bar, security ushered a fat kid from the hockey stadium. Replaying his offensive act of sticking his finger down his throat and puking on a younger fan.

There was a row of photographs on the wall. Photographs taken inside the bar, inside another era, when Kath was in art school, a wall of mounted frames. Kath pointed at a row of half-miniature portraits.

"See the second one from the left? That's Robert. We had just started dating then."

I walked over to the wall and stared at the portrait. Here was Fleeger as I had never seen him before. Young and handsome. Idle but almost furious. Kath stood behind me and we stood before the portrait and she belted her arms around my waist and stood on her toes to rest her chin on my shoulder. Why hadn't she done this hours ago? Her lightest touch reinforced my decision to be with her. I would stay with her tonight. Even if it meant sleeping on Benjamin's floor.

The bartender popped his head from the taproom. With her touch, levity returned to my thighs and I felt air again in my lungs as the invisible monolith rolled across smooth, sandy ground, unsealing the tomb in which I had locked myself the moment I entered Benjamin's house.

"I still don't know how I managed to convince Robert to pose for that photo," she said. "But he has such a face. His face is like art."

Small red votive candles flickered on the bar tables, along the walls. Like those lit in the alcoves of cathedrals for prostration before Ave Maria. Candlelight blessings in consideration for change. For Fleeger as art. Kath said she needed some fresh air. That she would be back in five minutes. I let her go. I was good like that, I told myself. I could always give a woman her space. Benjamin and the bartender ascended the subterranean ladder, the bartender smacking Benjamin's steel-toed foot as they climbed the rungs, trying to trip him. Both of them marked with small Führer mustaches of ketamine or coke or both. Benjamin blew his nose in a red cocktail napkin, bunched it in his hand, and left it on the bar. I thanked him for inviting me to the party, for his hospitality, to try and backfill his unspoken enmity toward me. He drank from his mug of black beer and I faulted myself for sharing the honest sentiment.

"Hey, I want to ask you a question," he said. He rested one foot on the shelf beneath the bar. I told him go ahead.

"Why are you here?"

"Kath asked me to come."

"Yeah. But why? What do you expect will happen?"

"I think we're just seeing where it goes."

His jaw clenched, pinching the Camel Light between his teeth. I placed both feet on the ground and stood before him and he stood up straight and did the same above me. I had no more words. I was blank. I felt nothing. Had nothing to say. Anything I said would lack the velocity of an honest response and without that honesty he would swat it away. All I could do was stand my ground. He curled and gripped his strange hands around an invisible ball and shook it.

"She doesn't need you, man. You have nothing to offer her. You think because you got a good job, up in your office, smooth sailing, that you can do this to her?"

This was the ketamine talking. There was a freshly minted nickel on the bar. In the red and yellow lights hanging from the ceiling Thomas Jefferson looked like an ape. Benjamin stood there, waiting for my response. I wanted to say more. That Kath told me she needed me. That she told me she loved me. That I loved her too. Benjamin watched me trying to ignore him. I fidgeted. He wouldn't budge. I was an obstacle between him and what he needed to know and what he needed to know was inside me and he would come right through me for it if he had to. The bartender again struck open the cash register with a rubber mallet and he smiled at Benny with long, pointed teeth.

"You work for Robert. She tells me tomorrow you're going to have dinner with my parents. When she and Robert aren't even divorced. You follow her here. What are we supposed to think? That you guys are going to build a life together? While still working with Robert?"

"She asked me to come."

Something in his system refused to be assuaged by this.

"But don't you see? That doesn't make a difference. Right is right. And that doesn't depend on what she says or asks you to do. She's vulnerable right now. She's got no stability in New York, no husband, no job, it sounds like she may be kicked out of her apartment, she's borrowing money from our parents to pay her rent, and now she has this crew of artists she hangs out with and the next thing you know she's obsessed with Hinduism and taking pictures of homeless kids. She's completely lost. And then you come around, and all it does is add a whole other layer of complication for her. You seem like a smart guy. I don't understand how you don't know this."

He leaned backward against the bar with his elbows.

"Just don't deny it, man," he said over his shoulder.

"Deny what?"

"That you're fucking up my sister."

"What?"

"No, not what. Why? Why are you doing it? And more importantly, why are you lying about it? Because you're not really that into her? Because you know she's not really as great as you tell yourself she is? Because you don't want Robert to know? Because you don't want to lose your job? Because you don't know how Robert will react? I'll tell you how Robert will react. He'll fucking crucify you. Do you even know why they separated?"

I was done with him. The bartender called me an asshole as I picked up my bag and exited the bar at the same moment he cracked open a roll of quarters on the drawer of the brass register. Outside, Kath stood on the sidewalk chewing on a finger. She tore off a hang-nail. I put my hand on her waist. Removed my hand from her waist and realized this was all a mistake. It was a mistake for me to come. It was a mistake for me to be here.

"Lucky cigarette," she said, removing the upside-down fag from the orange hard pack.

"Harker."

I heard someone yell my name and I heard it again.

"Harker."

I looked around and there across the street stood Fleeger. Heat and vinegar bloomed through the nerves and arteries that ran the length of my neck and down my back. He paced the sidewalk, waiting for traffic to pass, back and forth, now down the curb and across 15th Street, wearing bulky cargo pants and beyond all fathomability those orange Vibram FiveFingers. Slapping the ground with ten gloved finger toes as he crossed the asphalt, vengeful in the high-watt glow of the electric marquis for Buca di Beppo, Italian American bistro.

He said my name again. Babbling so this was it. This was why. Now it all made sense. Between each accusation an electric sizzle. Buca. About taking his wife. Buca. Because mine left me. Buca. That I didn't make enough money to support her. Buca. Something inside me fell three stories and landed on a cool, dry floor. Bounced a bit. My intestines stiffened. I was ready for him.

"Oh dear, we need to perform open-heart surgery on you too, Robert," Kath said. "You're like an open wound."

Kath looked tired. Exhausted by the evening so far and this drama on alcohol now a further cause of yet more exhaustion. She didn't fear Fleeger in general and she didn't fear Fleeger now and she didn't fear Fleeger for me. Her teeth tore off another hangnail.

I couldn't see Fleeger's face, failed to discern the whole. There were the hard eyes. The rampart chin. The jackfruit lips. But the pieces didn't connect. The sharp edges blurred the closer he approached. His face now almost a cloud as he huffed up the curb, fingertoes smacking the concrete sidewalk. Now he was upon me. I can take him. With outstretched arms, he grabbed me with his hairy hands and shook me.

"Please, Robert," Kath said. "Don't be so gauche."

"What are you doing with her?" he asked me. "Are you insane?"

I pressed my hands against Robert's broad chest as he huffed his way through my defenses.

He released me. I brushed off something that wasn't there.

"Please, Robert," Kath said.

He turned on her.

"And you? You said he was pitiful?"

"Robert I was weak. I needed someone."

"You hate him."

"I don't hate him, Robert."

"Hey," I said. "Easy."

Robert shoved me.

"Easy?"

I shoved him back. He moved less than I did when he shoved me. He shoved me again.

"Robert," Kath said. "Don't be ridiculous. Besides, it's not like we're still married. Well, technically we are, but we're separated. We're not even friends. If I'm with Stephen then you just go ahead and consider yourself the winner."

"Hey," I protested.

He shoved me again. He was angry, but I could calm him down. He shoved me again. Now up against the bar's black windows, he tripped up my hands and gripped my arms. I remembered something from the one martial arts class I took in college. I landed the tip of my shoe beneath the curve of his left patella, triggering a deep-tendon reflex. Fleeger buckled and punched me in the gut, knocking the wind out of me.

"Man, you are fucking my wife."

I struggled to breathe. It was almost like drowning. I needed to lie down. I lay on the ground. I was dying. My lungs lacked the oxygen to speak.

"Robert," Kath said. Still insufficiently concerned for my well-being. "Look, you hurt him. Go easy. He's much smaller than you. And besides, we're separated. Remember? Please. You're scaring him."

They sounded like they were playing a game with me.

"I'm not scared," I wheezed and coughed as the cement moved beneath me and I rolled on the ground, gripping my solar plexus in a vain effort to make it all stop. Fleeger scooped up the metal ashtray by the door to impale it through the window or my chest. I moved at the last moment and it struck the mass of my arm, inflicting soft tissue damage. No objective evidence of permanent injury. I stood up. He rammed me again with the base of the ashtray and knocked me to the ground again.

"Take a shot, Harker," Robert commanded, now above me. "Come on. I'll give you a shot."

"Robert, don't," Kath said as Fleeger pulled back the ashtray to harpoon me with its base. The halogen streetlights above him formed three large yellow crosses. A celebratory spotlight danced across the dense, low cloud cover that separated the city from the sky. Fleeger cursed me again. "You're a fucking asshole, you know that, Stephen?" Then he paused and looked at me, his expression changed, from anger to curiosity, and he pointed in another direction. He wanted me to see too. The grainy sidewalk scraped against my cheek as I turned my head, to face the direction of Fleeger's finger, north on Fifteenth Street. Where, in a tricorne hat, stood Thomas, gaunt and patchy beneath the electric red lights of an Applebee's Grill & Bar. Costumed like a minuteman in breaches and buckled boots, leather jacket, full-length navy great coat, russet wide belt.

I knew that rifle. It was a Kentucky rifle. My father once possessed one. There were tricks to making it right and Thomas knew what he was doing. The long rifle cradled horizontal across his body, tamping the black powder from a leather and brass flask, tapping the flint. Now he was done. Thomas dropped to one knee and pulled the trigger. An electric cloud of urea and sulfur enveloped him in gray smoke. I could see the iron musket ball, traveling at six hundred feet per second, like Sputnik, circling the planet with whiskers of antennae, broadcasting Cold War messages from the ionosphere, four hundred foot-pounds of pressure per inch. Plenty enough to penetrate Fleeger's skull. An infinite number of choices over an unknown number of lifetimes necessary for that consummation to occur. Consequences of decisions rippling ever outward. The force of the impact popped something inside him. I didn't hear it. I felt it through the ground. Followed by a silent internal ringing alarm. Like the noise employed by an audiologist to test your hearing. Deafening me to Kath on her knees yelling and picking up Fleeger's head. His beautiful head. Now something inanimate. Almost like a melon. Its operating system failing as it struggled to reboot and deaf to Thomas's whistling as he removed another musket ball from his leather pouch, detached the ramrod from the rifle's barrel, folded a sabot around the musket ball to maximize velocity, and punched the musket ball into the nether regions of the rifle's barrel. Preparations complete to fire another shot as Fleeger lay next to me gurgling. Shiny metal parts oiled and clean. Perhaps this one for me. Perhaps I deserved it. A brain for a brain. A pop for a pop.

As if performing microscopic experiments in a laboratory, Thomas closed one eye and peered down the barrel. He presented his arms for inspection, spun the rifle on its butt, placed the musket beneath his chin, and fired the thing with the toe of his buckled boot. No electric cloud of black smoke this time as together the energy and the matter followed the path of least resistance. Tossing what was once part of Thomas's brain up against the window of the Applebee's. City kids in the window with a natural look of wonder on their faces. Eating onion rings dipped in ketchup. Whoa.

Kath hyperventilated and beat Robert's chest. Here now was Benjamin. His work boots standing in the blood flowing from Fleeger's scalped head. Benjamin picked up Kath with his strange tattooed hands as Fleeger mouthed something he never said before and would never say again. I sat on the sidewalk cross-legged and listened to his final breaths. To his tongue lolling inside his mouth. Consciousness flickering across the still intact sections of his brain, as he turned tallow on the street, surrounded by gawkers, the man revealed himself to me. And it was then, at that moment, that I realized how much I loved him.

28

I LAY IN BED playing memory roulette. Riding alongside the Quiché in the back of a runaway pickup. Dragoning heroin with Moroccans in Málaga. Dancing in Haidian with a Chinese woman tattooed with eyeliner. Kath handing Mei the red box of silver ornaments and Fleeger wishing me Merry Christmas as he handed me the bonus check.

"Don't thank me, Stephen. Thank yourself. Really. You've done a great job this year."

All of it lost. Yet still I couldn't comprehend it. Because as a concept loss was not something I could feel. Despite the fact it had now piled up around me. Like icebergs on the shore of a frozen sea. The distant land to where things disappear. Instead, I felt intact, whole, solid, certain that not one chunk of myself had been displaced. Despite all that had occurred.

I dressed in the dark and slapped the doorframe as I exited the apartment, feeling capable of something new, as if overnight I had grown giant, skilled hands. Gregg sat on the stoop, drinking cappuccino from a bowl-sized mug.

"What are you, a longshoreman today?" he asked.

I shrugged. Kath's bicycle still bolted to the building. Tires ripped on purpose by something serrated that required force. It didn't matter. We would never speak again.

"Can you tell your friend to move this?" he said, pointing to the bicycle. "It's becoming an eyesore."

"Sure, Gregg." I paused. "Can I ask you something?"

He said of course I could ask him something.

"Remember that delivery man you said was looking for me?"

"Kind of. But that seems so long ago."

"You said he was clean shaven. You sure about that?"

"Oh, heavens. I don't know, Stephen," Gregg replied. "I'm really very bad with details."

I told him I thought so and then walked to the subway. A dusty haze hovered above the gray asphalt. Of ozone in spring. Its billion particles reflected and energized by the white morning sun. I entered the subway and stepped through the car's sliding doors and took a hard orange seat beneath a ribbons of adverts. The science of extralong lashes. Dr. Zog will beautify your dog. You too can own your own home for just under $325,000. I wanted to date the women in the period-proof underwear ads, digitally peeled into garnish while yogaing in tank tops.

The imagined stories of those around us. Eyes closed in silent prayer to arrive safely. A bookmark fashioned from a 9/11 mass card beneath a face etched by sixteen-plus years of grief. Mouthing hail Mary, full of grace, the Lord is with thee, behind lipstick. Leather-bound Judaica exhorting the faithful to atone. A Pakistani man pushing the button on a small device attached to his finger, counting his pulse. A blue-eyed Slav, face hidden by a black balaclava, glaring at me as he grooved a line into the plastic subway seat with a carpentry nail. A teenage girl, face hidden beneath a floppy cap pinned with a velvet tulip, rubbing the palm of her hennaed hand while her father, some poet emeritus, with a brass scarab fastened tight around his neck, rested his chin on the handle of his goose-headed cane. This day out and about with his daughter. This day of new experiences. I nodded at him. He nodded back. The train scattered rainbow-colored lights through the prism of the rear window, behind us, swirling in an optical illusion of carbon and speed.

I exited the subway at Chambers Street and walked south toward the stolid almost-Presbyterian Catholic church and climbed the steep concrete steps and entered tight, consecutive glass doors. Dipped my fingers in the marble basin of cool holy water and genuflected. Said a prayer for Fleeger and touched the Jesus foot of the pietà. I was the first to arrive. I sat in the transept and waited for the service to begin.

"Does anyone have a few words they would like to say about Robert?" the priest asked the congregants.

I raised my hand. He ignored me. Someone must have pointed me out beforehand. Instructed him anyone but me. That guy. Hiding in the shadows behind the columns. The reason we're all gathered here today. The reason Robert Fleeger is dead.

My hands needed something to do. I wouldn't check the news-wires or email anymore. I rolled a cigarette instead. My fingers shook at a high frequency. I heard them. They sounded like an orchestra of mosquito wings. I snapped the crooked cigarette in two. Looked over my shoulder at Our Lady of Copacabana preserved inside her glass box. Doll tiny and fierce and wrapped in wax and peach chiffon and lace, staring at me with her timeless black doll eyes.

Now if the priest would just give me the chance. Show some com-passion. If so, I was prepared. I had notes. A scroll of notes tucked here inside my jacket. Typed and edited and torn by the awl of my ballpoint pen. The complete record of what went wrong. From then to now. Here to there. And though perhaps there were too many facts and details, there was a lesson to be learned and it boils down to this.

Distraction was the root of all evil.

"A few words about Robert?" the priest asked again.

Round white beard. White stole. White hair. His spotless yolk-yellow robe swayed an inch above his soft black shoes, his Vel-cro almost-sneakers. He marked the gilded page with a wooden reed ordained for such a task and closed the purple catechism.

I stood and approached the lectern. Not just a consumer anymore but also a critic. They looked at me like I was slithering on my belly, snapping the air with rows of jagged teeth. Writhing across the dunes of yellow sand in a torn, coarse robe, weepy with conjunctivitis, in search of salt water and fish. Some things were doomed to fail and die,

I thought. Even relish it. Take it easy, I told myself. Calm down, calm down. This is not about you. It's about Robert.

The priest looks at me. His chinstrap beard jutted almost an inch from his chin. I felt as if I were standing before God's own lieutenant. I removed my black watch cap. Apply nothing to anything I told myself as I extracted the notes. Enter the gateless gate. All you need to do is read.

To my surprise, the priest raised the microphone and motioned for me to take his place. I stood there at the lectern, in the scent of the church. The meter-high candles flickered before me. Subtle notes of advent and paraffin. Candles dipped by cloistered Bolivian nuns that would require one hundred years to burn. Thurible smoking Catholic incense. One tall candle burned at each corner of Fleeger's granite urn.

Cross sections of his life occupied the pews before me. An isocephaly of saints and demons. Color-coded women in heels and miniskirts. I expected them to do a number, like the Rockettes. Oh, what a Fleeger! Something along those lines. The Kilgore partners and Attika pewed together, checking their phones, muffling displeasure at my audacity to speak at Robert Fleeger's funeral. Fleeger's family up front, massive blue-blooded American Hapsburgs. The women of the clan strong-jawed sentries of where fetuses gestate into Fleegers. Celeste Powers in black, sponged with foundation, weeping into a cocktail napkin, examining its contents, platinum quatrefoil still spinning at her wrist. Tucker Nelson wearing a seersucker suit before Memorial Day to a Manhattan funeral mass. Perhaps he was off to Belmont later that afternoon, on another firm's dime. And Kath O'Shaugnessy, sitting alone in the back by the heavy glass doors. Angry and hiding and ashamed behind sunglasses and grips and knots of her once-again black hair. Benjamin was here before as well; he exited the moment the priest handed me the microphone.

All of them now before us. Before me and Fleeger. Together again for one last time. The death of a man was the death of a friendship. I removed the notes from my pocket and flattened the pages against the lectern and set to the task of clearing my conscience. The one last thing I had to do before Fleeger's entombment. To prevent some part of me being buried with him.

"At the time of his untimely death, that honest Yankeeness that Robert Fleeger once possessed was not completely spent. Becoming partner at Kilgore had consumed about half of it. And another couple tons were incinerated by his separation from Kath O'Shaughnessy. And, true, before he was shot in the head by a mentally disturbed claimant, he was engaging in an unseemly amount of online dating. But some core of who he was always remained intact. And like all my friendships that survived the transition to adulthood, I loved him. Very dearly . . ."

The exodus had already ended. Even Fleeger was gone. Like Benjamin, his family exited the church the moment I began to speak, cradling his granite box. Probably through the Holland Tunnel by now. Heading north in a fleet of black German sedans. Silent on leather cushions. The lead car bearing Robert's ashes. Only the priest remained. To bear witness and then to bolt the glass doors behind me.

The last of the congregants rounded street corners and descended subway steps as I exited the church and walked to the office. The palm scanner denied me access to the building's elevator banks. I squeezed past the turnstile and rode the elevator to Kilgore. Money Man pushing big gains in aluminum futures. Advising his audience that it might be time again to take another look at freight derivatives, folks.

During my absence from the office the work piled atop my desk. Bills of particular. Responses to discovery demands. Requests for production. Notices to admit. Summonses. Complaints. Subpoenas. I sat behind the papers, holding a fax from Lazlis's office advising Judge McKenzie he would amend his complaint to include claims for wrongful death on behalf of Thomas's estate. Another from the Fleegers' family lawyer demanding preservation of the entire Thomas file. Through binoculars I studied the prewar apartment building across the street, now undergoing demolition and renovation. Floors torn up and walls knocked down. Spaces opened and the sockets stripped, with pipes and wires dangling from the ceiling and overhead hazards marked by strips of yellow tape.

I entered the conference room and glided my hand along the wall of Thomas's boxes and discovered an unopened padded envelope from Honda Investigations addressed to Fleeger. The disc downloaded its contents to the hard drive and the videotaped footage bounced around the flatscreen. Kath's boots up a flight of subway stairs. Safari jeans jaywalking across Broadway. Me, pensive, behind the table at Shoemacher's, as Kath applies lipstick in the mirror of her phone. I stand behind the table and welcome her with kisses. Now at night as I walk the sidewalks. Surprised by my height, by my nocturnal, upright posture. In and out of bars and halfway up the Williamsburg Bridge. Up Kath's stairs. Down Kath's stairs. Boarding the Amtrak. Fingering the tears to Kath's shredded bicycle tires.

I looked up from my computer screen and there stood Fleeger in the doorframe. Not holding his Kilgore tote, not scrolling through his phone, but staring at me with dead black eyes and his iron brow furrowed with betrayal.

"You still owe me for that sign you smashed," I said.

"I do?"

"Yes. You do."

"I don't know, Stephen. I think we're even."

"Maybe you're right."

"Beer later?"

"Sounds good."

He vanished.

29

I READ THE WORDS on the pages around me. Scooped up the minutes and words like fungible dice. I shook them in my hand and then shot them across the desk. An order from the court arrived in my inbox, regarding a different file. Words that meant nothing. Because there were too many of them. They spilled from the pages. Floated around the paper and buzzed on the screen. "And a plague of words shall go upon thee, Pharaoh." I felt guilty of a new felony. The abuse of words.

Goldman entered my office. Bespoke suit. Hair gelled with a product whose sale is limited to millionaires. His forehead and scalp flaky and inflamed where a dermatologist applied a chemical peel to remove suspicious basal cells.

"Stephen, the partners have made a decision," he said. "We want a full report by tomorrow morning latest as to just what this Thomas file entails. His psychological condition. His physical condition. His medications. And most importantly, who knew what and when about this man's mental instability. Including you, including Robert, including Celeste. We need a full, detailed report. You think you can manage that?"

I grinned.

"Maybe we should assign this to Attika instead. Give you a little break."

For hours I sat there. The buildings outside were LEGO pieces. Erector set joints. Plastic Ts with serpent eyes. Fallen bricks. Worldscore One now spiked with a brand-new pickelhaube.

I opened the door to the janitor's closet. Calcium-crusted custodial sink and industrial gallons of pink liquid. I extracted the Virgin Mary night cart, rolled it to the conference room, and stacked it high with Thomas's boxes. Six high by six deep times two. For the protection of the attorney-claimant privilege. Per the dictates of military confidentiality. To extinguish the liens on the compensation. Collateralized. Assigned to paper. Securitized. Insured. Obligated. Sold. Brokered. The brewing battle over who bore responsibility. I had an answer for that. We all bore responsibility. For what we did to them and what they did to others and what we did to ourselves.

Top-heavy and wobbly, the cart steadied as I pushed it into the building's freight elevator. Together, Thomas and I exited the building though the parking garage, unmolested by the valets praying in the corner facing east beneath the pipes. I pressed the cart north on Water Street. Past skyscrapers rising at narrow angles. I pushed on toward the bridges. Again remembered the old, lost friend who climbed them to overcome his fear of heights. The cart's plastic casters rolled over cobblestones. The boxes teetered but would not fall. I lifted the cart over a curb.

Together, Thomas and I entered the protestor's camp. Past an unfathomable linga yoni bathed in fresh milk and ringed with marigolds. Rows of girls sipping tea before the night's work, the names of their pimps tattooed to their exposed coccyges. I offloaded a box from the cart and set it next to a young protestor stoking a cooking fire with a radio antennae. He looked at me. Opened the box. Removed a handful of Thomas's military records and placed it on the charcoals. He smiled at me with big gaps between his teeth. The papers burned bright and quick, sizzling his small filet roasting atop a scavenged grate.

An African woman wrapped in kente cloth and hair braided with cowrie shells gestured to ask if she too could take one of the boxes.

"Of course, of course," I said. "Take."

I dumped the contents of the bottomless boxes. A cascade of paper and words. I stacked them atop the protestors' carts and hand trucks. More protestors stepping forward now from the shadows to ask if they too may take a box.

"Yes, yes," I said. "But burn it. Make sure you burn it."

The paper poured forth from the boxes and bushelsworth covered the ground. To be burned. Incinerated. For food and warmth and light. The earth now and finally forever devoid of Thomas, I left behind the cart and entered the shadows of the overpass.

I walk north along the river. Up and over and down the Williamsburg Bridge. Imagining the light show, the borealis, of the impending solar storm. Ribbons of red and green solar radiation draping the sky, cascading toward earth, then touching the electrical grid, setting the city to sparks. There won't be anything sublime about it. Now toward the port. The sweet smell of coal tar epoxy. The surprising speed of machinery and tonnage transported on water. An arriving vessel summons winds from the south. Up ahead there is a lightship, *The Ambrose*, anchored and red atop the black river, with retrofitted diesel stacks and radio wires strung between its twin, illuminated masts. Ready to assist in the event solar radiation renders mankind technologically helpless. From sea level the city looks small. Exposed on all sides. A buoy rings its hidden maritime bell and rotates atop its chain. Above the highway there is a billboard, graffitied by a gallant vandal.

TERESA, the sign commands, FREE YOUR MIND AND SOUL WITH XAVIER.

Acknowledgments

Maxim Brown at Skyhorse; Keir Politz for early support and continuous friendship; Ensieh Esfandiari for early morning assistance getting out the door to finish the manuscript; Erika Lunkenheimer, Michelle Vitale, Haleh Atabeigi, Liz Keenan, Conor Politz, and David Jacovini for encouragement; Brendan McBride and Miriam Ackerman for time and space on the Mullica River; Louis Prieur and Flore-Anne Bourgeois for time and space in Nernier; Payam Zarbakht and Nadia Esfandiari for time and space in England; Joel Zighelboim of Jones Street, Andre and Brenda (Duza) Wilkinson, Emad Kiyaei, Anne O'Callaghan, Tom Griffin, Aleksandr Ilchuk, Peter Dee and Susan Lee, Charles Hoffmann, Eric Matheson, Andy and Valerie Loy, Alessandra Lacavaro, Maurice Al-Haddad, Nick Kratz, Paul Ryan, and Juen Romanoff for friendship and support; and the family for having my back.